ROAMING THE WASTELANDS

ROAMING THE WASTELANDS

H. Millard

Writers Club Press
San Jose New York Lincoln Shanghai

Roaming the Wastelands

Writers Club Press
an imprint of iUniverse, Inc.

For information address:
iUniverse, Inc.
5220 S. 16th St., Suite 200
Lincoln, NE 68512
www.iuniverse.com

Any resemblance to actual people and events is purely coincidental.
This is a work of fiction.

ISBN: 0-595-22811-9

Printed in the United States of America

BOSTON

CHAPTER 1

❀

"Can I give you this flyer?" asked the dark-haired girl, as I walked past her where she was standing on the sidewalk in the Boston Common.

"Sure," I said, as I reached out my hand and took one of the light-green, eight and a half by eleven inch sheets of paper that had an artsy drawing of a bridge over the Charles River at the top and a bunch of copy below. As I walked on, I started reading the flyer in my hand. It was an ad for an avant garde art gallery across the Charles River over in Cambridge.

"There are some among us who can't help but listen to a different drummer. The drumming they hear is from their DNA. Some try to block it out, but it is heard in the blood which has no ears that can be covered to stop the sound that is not a sound. It is a call of the wild from centuries past to the wild in some humans. Those who try to deny the drummer are doomed to live unhappy lives, for they are denying what they were born to be. Some of those who listen to the drummer become explorers. Others become artists of all types. Some are the homeless. Some are inventors. Others are just crazy. They are born to be bohemians and different. The straight life isn't for them. They have always existed in our societies both under-ground and in plain sight. These genetic nonconformists, when at their best, produce our art and explore new worlds, for they are forever outgoing and wandering in order to satisfy their inner urges for novelty and to find stimulation. Meanwhile, those not born with these different drummer genes become the straights in our society and they remain as the shopkeepers and bookkeepers and all the other stationary and normal things. And in these and other genetic determinants, we find free will to be somewhat less than it has been made out to be. We find genetic specialization among humans much as we find it among honey bees and ants.

Break away from your hive and come to the grand opening of the Different Drummer Art Gallery this Saturday."

And then the flyer went on to give the address. I tossed the flyer in the first trash can I came to, and continued on to where there was a little crowd composed of a couple of white people but mostly of black, brown and yellow people listening to an old white guy with a beard and sad, kind eyes, who was standing on a park bench and talking to them. I looked at him and he seemed to look into me. Maybe it was my imagination, but when he looked directly at me, the sadness didn't look like personal sadness. It looked like some sort of ancient, wise sadness mixed with resignation. I was curious, so I joined the crowd, just as a light snow started to fall. He looked at me again and said, "Another one of the old ones joins our little crowd of mourners as we stand here in the ruins of post-American America, waiting to die off and be replaced by those who are unlike us. They will use our buildings, drive our cars, mind our stores, play in our parks, and do all the things that we did before we died off. And a thousand years from now, when the forests cover all, scientists will wonder what happened to the builders. 'Were they defeated in war?" they may ask. How did the genocide happen?

"Let me tell you this my friends. John Wayne's America is gone. It's been replaced with post-American America. No more straight shooting and plain talking. Now, we have a Mexican way of doing things. The ten-gallon hat has been replaced by the sombrero.

Checking the daily papers for a job has been replaced with standing on street corners soliciting work. See a problem? Look the other way. Have a form to fill out? Cheat a little. Taxes? Don't pay them. Just work under the table. The Fourth of July has been replaced by Cinco de Mayo.

"You're a racist," said one of the black men in the crowd. The white guy on the bench ignored him and continued on without missing a beat.

"Need a special favor from government? Give a bribe in the form of cash or votes. Laws mean little. You don't call the police, because they're now a social service agency, and most of the officers are in class to learn to speak Spanish. You don't complain to government officials, because they're often corrupt. Discuss your concerns with politicians and they'll wag their manicured fingers at you and tell you that diversity is great as they whistle past the grave and hope against hope that this type of talk will help keep them in office when someone with a Mexican surname decides to run against them. If you're white, you just try to live small, and not make waves. You try to act like a guest in your own home. You're one of the outcastes of this post-American America, forever marked by your white skin that says you're not part of the new America that is assimilating the America that your ancestors started. Gone are the days of self-assurance and bold visions. Gone are the blond surfers. The United States has now institutionalized an anti-American culture at all levels of government and society.

"You should be arrested, you old racist," said the same black man who had heckled the speaker before.

"Let him speak," I yelled, "we have free speech in this country." This seemed to shut the heckler up and it seemed to keep others from joining in. The old man looked at me again, and gave a slight, wry smile and continued speaking.

"This is an America that would not be recognized by previous generations. It is America as the Third World. It is a knock-off

America made in a Tijuana maquiladora by tequila guzzling laborers who may have seen too many repeats of scenes of Rick's Café in Casablanca and who then imported the whole mess to the U.S. on their wet backs across the smelly sewer filled Tijuana River. It is America as shifty eyed little brown people, all on the make and take, who eye others for signs of weakness and opportunity. 'Pssst, wanna buy some (fill in the blank) drugs, porno, hot watches, stolen cars? No problem, Amigo.'

"Need medical insurance? Don't be silly, that's for the old people. 'Old people?' that's a euphemism for white people, of any age. It's as though the white people are like the last remnants of the Druids in Europe a thousand years ago, except these modern day last of the Druids are not only the last of their religion and culture, they are the last of their race.

"Sick? Don't worry, just go to any hospital and the old people will pay for your visit.

Need food? Go to the charities. Need clothes. The charities will help. Auto insurance?

'That's for the gringos, Senor.' Tiny rips in the fabric that is the American society that were first seen in California have now turned into major tears throughout the nation. What started as a little "compassionate" wink and nod to illegal aliens has now grown into a major rotting of the soul of

America. A Third World mentality has now become institutionalized in the U.S. as bonafide citizens are made into second class citizens to non-citizens by their own public officials who vote favors for non-citizens.

"And as this lawless world encroaches further and further into the formerly nice towns and cities of post-American America, we see the Father Knows Best and the Leave it to Beaver families of pre-post-American America—the wide eyed and apple cheeked European-Americans who still try to live the old myths and who because of this, deny the new reality—move further and further away into new suburban communities. "Oh, we're not moving because we don't like the people moving into our old neighborhoods," they beam, with pasted on idiot's smiles. "We just found this really nice home with the extra room we needed." And, sadly, many of those who are moving, have even deluded themselves into thinking that's why they're moving. Their conscious minds have often blocked out the real reasons why they're moving, because they can't stand the thought that they will, themselves, then evidence "racism" and "xenophobia" which they so often preach against, without even knowing why, other than it is the latest PTA rage. So, they move out of their browning old neighborhoods and into all white (except for a token this and that) brand new planned communities. Then, from those insulated locations behind the gates, and next to the golf courses, they often continue to rail against people who are just like them except these others have decided to fight the problems head on and try to reverse the downward spiral and destruction of this nation.

"So, the Father Knows Best and the Leave it to Beaver families now live in a shrinking land of manicured lawns; and the blue bird of happiness sings to them each morning and they are self-contented. In their old neighborhoods, the birds that sing to them would now be roosters. They hardly notice the newspaper reports of murders, burglaries and other problems in their old neighborhoods. And, if they do notice, they are emotionally disconnected from these problems and the human misery that has happened to other humans just like them. Meanwhile, the Third World spreads ever closer to them, and then it becomes time to move again. And, they say, once again, "Oh, we're not moving because we don't like the people moving into our old neighborhoods. We just found this really nice home with the extra room we needed."

"They believe this, even in the face of statistics that show that while they are still trying to uphold 1950's Americanism, the world has changed. Songs of innocent teen love have been replaced on the music charts with rap songs about killing whitey. Maternity wards have been replaced with abortion clinics. People sleeping on sidewalks in the cities of post-American America are now as common as they once only were in Calcutta. Murders are now so common, that murder mysteries no longer intrigue. This is America in decline.

"And if you're intelligent and not brainwashed, you ask: What went wrong? After all, you paid your taxes. You mowed your lawn. You tried to do the right thing. You scanned the skies for foreign enemies. Still, this wasn't enough. Evil crept into America and ate it alive from the inside out. Before you were aware of this, you tried to block out such thoughts when others said such things. You dismissed them as alarmists, or racists, or bigots, and the evil grew and grew. Still, why didn't you notice the steel bars going up on houses in your neighborhood? Why didn't you notice the rising crime statistics? Why couldn't you put two and two together to understand that America—the America of legend—was essentially a European nation on a foreign shore? Why couldn't you understand that you were being manipulated to your destruction with hoary childish stories saying that "America is a nation of immigrants" and that "we all bleed red blood"? Weren't you bright enough to know that EVERY nation is a nation of immigrants and that humans have always moved from one place to another except when the people who had previously moved to that place, simply said, "You can't come in. We're here now, and we plan to make of this chunk of dirt what we want to make of it. Go someplace else"? Weren't you smart enough to know that millions of different animals bleed red blood, and that it doesn't mean a thing?

"Maybe you didn't notice the destruction because it was an incremental slide to oblivion. The flesh and bones of America were being picked a tiny piece at a time by vultures who knew they would be seen if they moved too fast, and they were unwilling to take on a healthy nation, so they waited until its soul was sick, introspective, dispirited, and mewling, and then they came in for the carrion.

"And, like a cancer, this evil that is growing is metastasizing and it's spreading all across this land. So this then is how America shall end; not by the actions of an external enemy, but from the enemy within.

"Out in the gated new communities where the Father Knows Best and the Leave it to Beaver families live, there is hardly a notice that the evil is getting closer. 'Did you finish your paper route, Billy? Dress for dinner, dear, before father gets home from work.' There will be others who will hate you and there will be those who will love you. The ones who love you are more dangerous than the ones who hate you. Seek to be hated, and you may survive as a people. Seek to be loved and you will be bred out of existence. Look around you, look around the country. If you any sort of higher than average consciousness you'll see the decline. And, if you see the decline, you can sit around in despair or you can try to save the old people before we become extinct. Wasteland! Friends, the wasteland isn't your TV and it isn't in a book. It's all around you. Pray that a savior comes my friends or we truly are doomed."

"Yeah," I said. And as I looked up at the old man, he looked back again and held up his left hand and pointed at me with three fingers extended, which looked a little odd. He then smiled that wry smile again, and produced a little burlap bag about the size of a very large tea bag. It looked vaguely familiar to me, but I couldn't remember why, so I turned and walked out on to the crazy dirty street located in the wasteland that is this falling apart before our eyes post-American America. This is a land where the old people are white people even if they are white children. It's sort of a reverse on the way "boy" once meant Negroes of any age. Behind me, the guy with the beard was still talking to the small crowd and to the bums wandering by. I walked over homeless people sleeping on the sidewalks. I walked past cheap hookers. I walked past stores with signs all written in Spanish. I stepped over trash. Once, this had been a great city. Now it was a big dump. It was a place for the damned and the depraved. It was one city among many similar desolate cities built by a dying people, who were so arrogant that they thought they could defy the laws of nature and assimilate millions of people unlike themselves and not be assimilated themselves. They forgot that it takes effort to keep a light burning, and that without effort the light goes out and everything decays back to the dark.

I figured that it was time for me to ramble. There was no reason really, other than that I was bored with this city and my itchy feet wanted to move. So, I got on the interstate bus and left the dregs of this crumbling city. I moved on to another place of social misfits, malcontents, the maladjusted, homeless people, artists, actors, poseurs, the petty and major criminals. I moved on to another place of ever fewer white people. This was Earth, after all, and what could I expect on this brown planet? But, I had no escape. I was born here and we hadn't yet developed ways to move to other planets. With the devolution of humankind, maybe we never would. It wasn't the stars that I could see in the future, but a return to the caves. All evolution is change, but not all change is evolution. Much change is devolution. Most cities in America are homogenized and mostly the same, except for a diminishing number of minor differences, just as is the case with the identical fast food restaurants all across this increasingly blended and center of the Bell Curve nation. It didn't matter though. I needed the traveling to stimulate me in the decaying America of the twenty-first century. This was America as the wastelands and I was part of the outcaste underground of American society that existed as if in another dimension right in the midst of the larger society. And, the wasteland was spreading, the way cancer spreads.

D.C.

CHAPTER 1

They call Washington, D.C., Chocolate City. This is because most of the people who live there are black. That also accounts for its horrendously high crime rate, but everyone wants to pretend that race and crime have no correlation in post-American America where whites are afraid to speak out and tell common sense truths lest they be thought to be racists. During the day, white government workers commute in from the Virginia and Maryland suburbs, put in their eight hours, and then get out of the place before the sun sets.

I got off the bus in downtown D.C. and asked a black guy who was leaning against a wall where the nearest homeless shelter was located. He gave me directions and I headed over there and was able to get a free meal and a bed for the night.

"You new in town?" said the black guy in the bed next to mine.

"Yeah." I replied.

"Where you from?"

"No place special. Here and there," I said.

"What you doin' in Chocolate City?"

"Sight seeing."

"Ain't nothin' to see here. Just slums behind the shiny government buildings. This place is like a Hollywood movie set. You see it on TV and all you see is white people in suits in front of fancy buildings.

You come here in person and all you see is black folks in rags in welfare lines. This here's an African colony."

In the morning, I left the shelter and went over to Georgetown and walked around a little. There were white people there, and if you only came to Georgetown, you'd think the whole city was a college town. You'd be very wrong. I didn't care for D.C. Maybe if you're a politician or a high government employee and can afford to live in the suburbs on the backs of the American tax payers, the place would be okay, but for me it just didn't feel right. This was the place where America had been driven low. This where the rot started and where it was kept going. I headed back to the bus station, as a cold wind started to blow, and the sky looked like it might open up and drop some white snow all over Chocolate City.

NEW YORK

CHAPTER 1

$\mathcal{E}$ ven in the middle of hot and humid summers, New York City is a wicked cold, and hard place. And this sure the hell wasn't summer. Smiles in New York are as rare as tans on the diminishing number of white people who live there, and both are immediately suspect by the non-white hordes who have come to remake the place into a third world city in the image of the places they fled.

In winter, the coldness of the people is made worse by the glaring, harsh, blue winter sun, long stripped of any warm orange rays. Winter makes the whole city look as though it is being lit with a glaring 200 watt unfrosted light bulb. In such light, the living look dead, and the dead look even worse. Cold, gusty spiraling winds blow and pick up speed as they round the buildings as they mindlessly order and reorder piles of trash in a natural organization of chaos. Up and down the grimy streets, the walking cadavers try to retain body head by hunching their shoulders inward and by bending forward as though they are sickly pale pill bugs rolling themselves into balls to protect themselves from the world outside in the false safety of their too soft shells. There is no protection. Even in the best weather in New York, people avert their eyes from others. In winter, they drill the sidewalks with their eyes as though they're trying to find a lost penny. Steam rises from man holes and from grates on the sidewalks. Crazy homeless people huddle around trash can fires and sleep where they can find the steam, hoping that they'll get through another night without freezing to death, so they can spend yet another meaningless day on the Earth doing nothing more than the living and the experiencing that all living things are born to do, as the sensory organs of a God that sees, smells, feels, and experiences through each living thing.

Free will, my ass, we're all just thermometers, cameras and microphones for a God who doesn't give a damn about any of us, because He is just a force of nature who spins order from chaos only to destroy it and spin again. A homeless guy standing by a fire is sending a message of the smell and the warmth of the fire to God. And maybe that's the only value this guy or any of us who have ever lived or who ever will live, really have in the big picture. We are the walking, talking, fertilizer of the Earth, and we are sent to make it ready for the growth of something new.

The cold in New York is tough to take, especially if you have no money to buy the comfort and warmth that only comes to those flush with cash. I had a lousy five dollar bill in my pocket. I had come into the city on a diesel smelly interstate bus in the dead of night just as the snow flurries were starting to fall and were dusting week old snow on the ground. There is no beginning and there is no end when one drifts. It's just a circle. I seem to have been on one bus or ersatz bus all my life, always moving aimlessly about in some sort of orbit, I imagine, but it is an orbit whose track is difficult to measure while one still lives, and is only recounted in obituaries, and then only rarely. Mine will read, "Alex Lavoie, born such and such date, died such and such date. He didn't do much. He didn't amount to much. Tough shit."

That's the way it is with all that lives. You're born to be fertilizer to make the Earth bloom for those who come after."

Anyway, the trip up from D.C. was uneventful, and I wasn't from there, so I didn't miss the place and I wasn't from here, so I didn't have any great hopes for this place. Of course, who the hell is really from anywhere and who the hell is ever really going anyplace? We are not plants who are from a particular piece of land, and who may then be uprooted and transplanted to another piece of land. We are from particular flesh. Our homes are in the flesh. Where I was from was a place carried in the blood of those who were in my line before me.

Why then the wandering over land from this place to this other place, when home will never be found in land? I'll tell you why. It is a search for comfort; for a place where this flesh feels comfortable, and where this mind is at rest and feels that this place is the place that embodies that genetically determined sense of comfort more than some other places. But, we don't talk that way. We just say, "I like it here."

"You got a match, baby?" said the late-twenties make-believe floozy. She didn't really need a match, but was just using the age-old street way to size up a John and start the ball rolling. This one was a poor imitation of a street hooker. Her hookerness was right out of the movies. She looked like an undercover cop who had gone to an Ivy League school and who had been given this assignment by the guys back at the station, in a sort of casting against type thing, or a joke on a rookie. She was white and had short brown hair. She was wearing high heels and fishnet stockings under a short skirt and a bright red coat with cleft showing at the top, but her boobs weren't even that big. This outfit, at this time and place and with this weather, was absurd. No self-respecting hooker would dress like this.

"Nah. I don't smoke," I replied, while thinking, Okay baby, the ball's back in your court. Your move.

"You looking for a date?" came the inevitable and predictable next question from her over lipsticked lips.

"Golly, ain't this a great city though," I said with just a hint of a false country boy accent. "I just get off the bus and already I'm popular with the girls. Geez, where do you want to go on a date? Maybe a movie or something?"

"Are you putting me on?" she asked.

"Yeah, just a little," I said, already tiring of the game. "Look, thanks for the offer, but I'm broke," I lied. Actually, I had the $5 bucks and that was probably the going price for a date in this neighborhood, had this babe actually been a hooker, which I just instinctively knew she wasn't. Anyway, I wasn't interested in playing along any more, so I decided to call her bluff.

"I think you're a cop."

"Oh yeah, what makes you think that?"

"You're carrying a purse for one thing, and you're too obvious, and you're also the only girl out here. I think you cops did a sweep, picked up all the working girls and put you out here as a decoy."

"Hey, I ain't no cop."

"I don't really care, and I'm not interested. Can you point me in the direction of Greenwich Village, officer?"

"Yeah. Just keep heading south. It's about 20 blocks or so," she said.

That's the way it was in New York. Never miles, always blocks. I set out walking through the dirty slush. It was like walking through a very big shaved ice drink from your local convenience market, only the coloring and flavoring agents weren't cola or blueberry, but exhaust residue and dirt. I was freezing my balls off with each step, and then I saw a rat scurry out of a sewer grate and run to a trash can. Man, speak of freezing your balls off. Rats drag their balls on the ground as they walk, that's also a little of how I felt. Here I was in the middle of New York City in the middle of winter. No money to speak of. Not knowing a single solitary soul. It was like I was just born here but already grown up. All was future. All was potential. I had no past that I had to claim. It was glorious. I felt great. Except for the cold. Still, everything was new. Every step an adventure. So I schlepped down Broadway. "Schlepped?" Oi Vay, my first day in New York and I'm Jewish already? So, here I am an Irish, French Canadian, Scot,

English, German, mix, from a marginally Catholic family, suddenly being Jewish.

I trudged south, block after cold grey block with the snow blowing in my face. I pulled my watch cap down over my ears to keep them from freezing.

Finally, I hung a left on 14th Street for no particular reason and headed on over to Third Avenue. Man, it was frigid like an icebox but then it started to snow even harder and that warmed things up a little or at least made things seem sort of fuzzy cold like a refrigerator instead of sharp cold like a freezer. That lasted for a few minutes. Then the wind suddenly kicked in even more and picked up into a regular blizzard blowing on my side. I wanted to feel the full force of the blizzard so I turned down the next street, whose street sign I couldn't see in the white blowing wall of individual snow flakes that were now shooting like icy sharp snow bullets into my face. I took off my watch cap and put it in my pocket so I could experience the storm. I was alive. I could feel the wind blowing my hair and I liked the feel of the tug on the roots of my hair. The wind got so hard that it almost blew me over with some gusts. It didn't take long before I was the only one on the streets. Even the cars and taxis were all gone as the storm raged. Every once in a while I could see people in the apartments all around me, using their hands to clear little port holes in the steam on their windows and look out at the mad man walking in the storm. I wondered if they were looking at me the way regulars in temperate beach communities look at people from colder places who visit their communities in winter, and who hang out in bathing suits while the regulars save their bathing suits for the suitable season.

The stares of these others made me even wonder for a brief moment whether or not I really was a madman or maybe I was just too stupid to know that the weather was bad. Then I came to my senses and realized that such thinking was what let societal pressures affect people and made them artificial. I determined that I would follow my senses. If it feels good, do it. But as I thought about it, I realized that there was more to it than that for me. I sought purity of individual action as free from the constraints of others as possible. I sought freedom. Damn it! I liked the blizzard. In fact, I loved it. I felt alive as the snow and wind snapped into my face. Had I been inside a building at that time, I would have found some way to get outside and into the storm. That's the way it always was with me. If there was a storm, I would no more think of going inside for cover than I would of jumping off a building. I suddenly shivered as I got that delicious warm-cold that comes sometimes when the wind is moist either with rain or snow and blows hard in your face. And, this had now turned into a wet snow. That dry crinkly stuff that seems like small shards of plastic or glass was gone. This was snow that was like little tiny melting soft pillows thrown underhand at my face by the wind. "What a wonderful and glorious night to be alive," I thought. And it was. A picture of stubby legged Gene Kelly flashed into my mind as he swung around a lamp post enjoying the rain—except, the point was that the rain was just made tolerable by love. In my case, the rain or snow was, itself, the source of the joy. It was a great time to be free of the convention of having a house to go into. Maybe New York wasn't such a miserable place after all, I thought. Hell, at least it had great weather.

In my twists and turns to keep walking directly into the wind, along with getting blinded by the snow, I had somehow ended up traveling across Manhattan instead of down toward the Village. I realized that, when the storm broke for a minute and I saw a sign that said 2nd Avenue. No problem. I knew that if I turned left again, I'd soon be down by the Village. As I walked, I suddenly became aware of a high pitched sound, and I looked all around to make sure I wasn't about to be run over by some strange sounding motor vehicle; maybe a snowplow of some kind. But, I didn't see anything. Then, I looked up, and just a couple of feet above my head but out above the middle of the street was a red laser beam shooting north up 2nd Avenue. I followed the beam for about a block where the beam hit a mirror, kind of like one of those big rig mirrors, but this one was duct taped to a light pole about ten feet up from the sidewalk. The beam was then reflected across the street where it hit another mirror which was pointed upward at an angle. This sent the red beam to the top of an industrial building on the far side of the street where there was another mirror hanging off the eaves of another industrial building. The beam hit this mirror which reflected it back across the street where it finally hit a couple of other mirrors and went up the street and around the block. Curious, I followed the beam. Around the corner about half way up the block, the beam hit a mirror in front of one of those old six story brick factories that have been around forever. It then shot across the street through the large glass window of what looked like a bar or restaurant that was on the ground floor of another old factory building. I crossed the street and looked at the front of the place. There was no name. I wondered what it was and thought that it might be some sort of private club. I looked through the windows and saw that the place was full of people. The laser beam was above their heads and shot around the place off various other mirrors that kept the beam inside.

I decided to go in and see what the place was. I had always lived my life with the sure knowledge that every step I took had the potential of bringing me to a whole new part of my life—almost a whole new existence or world. The bar was mostly full of men. I wondered if this was a gay bar. I looked around. Maybe not. Most of the customers didn't have that clean preppie look that many gays affected. It was a bohemian looking crowd, mostly. There were beards, long hair, short hair, dirty clothes, a few suits. People were sitting all along the bar and in the booths around the wall. Others were clustered in little groups at small round high tables in the center of the floor.

"Hey, what is this place," I asked a guy standing by the door who did look gay, but who was the first person I saw who wasn't in the midst of a conversation with others.

"Jack's," came his short and nonchalant reply without a hint of swish in his voice. So, maybe he wasn't gay after all.

"Is this a private club or bar or what? I'm new around here and I just followed the laser here."

"It's kind of a hangout for artsy types and wannabes and art groupies."

"You an artist?" I asked. I figured he looked like an artist, and if he wasn't, he probably wouldn't be insulted in being thought to be one, after the intro he had just given me to the place.

"Yeah. Well, sort of. I'm a photographer."

"You make money doing that?"

"Sometimes," he seemed amused at the directness of the question. "How about you? What do you do?"

"Oh, not much, really. I kinda travel around a lot. Sort of drift." Then, because I didn't have much to say, I figured I'd reinvent myself, so I lied, "I write a little. And, I've done some acting," I lied again. "I mostly take odd jobs when I can find 'em," I told the truth. "Right now, I'm trying to get a place to stay, and a job," and that was the truth also.

"Why don't you talk to Jack," said the guy. "I think he's looking for a dishwasher, and he'd probably let you stay in the empty loft upstairs. It's mostly full of junk. That's Jack over there talking to the TV." I turned around and saw a 35ish guy with a beard and long dark hair talking to a drag queen who towered over him and must have been at least 6'7" in bare feet."Can I tell Jack, you mentioned the job?"

"Yeah, Jack knows me. Tell him Dan sent you over. Mention the writing. It'll help."

I went over to where Jack and the drag queen were talking and said, "Hi, excuse me, I don't mean to interrupt; my name is Alex. Dan over there said you might have a job washing dishes. I can use a job. I also don't have any place to stay, and Dan said you might have a spare storeroom or loft or something. Can I work for you?" He sized me up, and excused himself from the drag queen, and took me back to the kitchen. The place was full of smoke and the smell of butter, garlic and cooking steaks. When we got to a quiet corner near the dishwashing sink, that was piled high with dishes, he asked "Where you from?"

"No place special. I've just been drifting around the country for a while." Then, because I knew of the artsy nature of the place and remembering what Dan had said, I threw in the business about writing a little and of acting sometimes. As I was about to find out, Dan was right that the writing lie was the right thing to say.

"The law after you?"

"No. Not that I know of."

"Well, I hope not, because we get a few off duty cops coming in here. Some of them are undercover and some are detectives just looking to detect something and get promoted. Mostly, they don't mess with the regulars and are pretty loose and cool, but if you're on the lam for murder or something big, this isn't the place for you." I figured that he was lying about the cops, and was just trying to make sure than he wasn't taking some kind of psychopathic killer into his joint.

"You say you write a little?" asked Jack.

"Yeah. Mostly short stories and stuff. I've had some published in some magazines," I lied, "but nothing big. I've got an idea for a novel, that I'd like to write though, if I can ever stay in one place long enough to do it."

"Itchy feet, huh? I know how that is, I think most of my customers and I have that disease. Here's what I'll do. I can't pay very much, but I will throw in an old bed up in the loft. There's a bathroom with an old working tub up there. It's not much, but its warm and that's a hell of a lot more than those guys sleeping out on the streets have. You can sleep there and you can eat with the kitchen staff for free. No breakfasts, but we open the kitchen for lunch so you can get two meals a day, and maybe clean leftovers if they don't gross you out.

I've even got an old typewriter up there that you can use if you want. I got the thing years ago when I thought I was a writer. You buy the paper and ribbons. If it breaks, you pay to fix it. It's not as convenient as a computer, but it'll do the job. What I need you to do is wash dishes and keep the kitchen and the bar area clean, and do whatever else is needed to fill in. Here's the deal on this place, though; everyone minds their own business and no one gets anyone in trouble. This is a see no evil, hear no evil, speak no evil joint, if you know what I mean."

I knew. I accepted the job. That's how I got set up in New York. The loft up above the bar wasn't that bad, especially to a guy who often slept in boxcars and under bridges. It was mostly a store room for the bar and restaurant, and had boxes full of napkins, toilet paper, and large bottles of olives and maraschino cherries. The rest of the place was full of all sorts of junk. There was an old broken stove, a grease hood, some broken bicycles and similar things. There was an old faded poster of Che Guevara on one wall near the bed, and some books and magazines probably left behind by a prior dishwasher or someone else who Jack had let flop there. Sitting all by itself in the middle of the floor was an old metal typing table with a dust covered IBM Selectric typewriter sitting on it, with an extension cord leading up to a light fixture on the ceiling. I hit the on button, and it took a few minutes for the motor to start, but then it kicked in. I picked up an empty piece of white typing paper that was on the typing table and put it in and started typing.

"We are born and we die, and in between we live either as others want us to live or as we ourselves want to live. If we live as we want, then we must free ourselves of as many peer group pressures as possible and we must do what we want; constrained only by our own internal sense of right and wrong.

"How do we know what is right for us as individuals? By asking ourselves if we like this or that whatever it is that we're thinking about. We then try to do as many of the things we like and try to do as few of the things we don't like.

"There are rules, laws, mores and customs all around us to hem us in and we can't be totally free of them, yet if we are to be free, we must avoid as many of them as possible and be happy and complete within ourselves and with kindred spirits.

"Let lesser souls conform to the norms of others."

I left the paper in the typewriter and went about making the place a little more habitable, by cleaning a little. The place was musty, so one of the first things I did was open a window and push the bed over in front of it where I could feel the wind.

The work downstairs wasn't hard, but the hours were long because the place opened at six in the morning for the professional drunks and closed at two the following morning. I was the only dishwasher and helper. I didn't actually have to work at six in the morning, unless there was an emergency, but I was usually up until three, in order to clean up after closing. My busy time was from about seven at night until closing.

When I wasn't working, I found time to bang away at the novel that I told Jack I wanted to write. In fact, since I got the job and the loft based on saying I was trying to write something, I figured I better actually try to do that. Jack was pretty understanding, since he was a frustrated writer himself. I think he lived his writing desires through me. Even though I was supposed to buy paper, I never had to, because reams of paper would mysteriously appear next to the typewriter whenever I was getting low. It was like that with the typewriter ribbons too, because someone, probably Jack, kept putting new ones in the typewriter. This also let me know that someone was reading what I was writing, and this kept me focused on writing. It was a focus that I had always lacked before in life, because of my itchy feet that forced me to keep moving. I once wondered if I had ADD or something, because it was always torture for me to have to sit still.

As I hung around the place more, I came to realize that Jack was sort of a blue collar patron of the arts, and his bar was full of some genuinely famous people from the art world. Oh, there were poseurs too, but I started recognizing people who I had seen on the covers of magazines. They mingled with a bunch of other artsy people who I don't think I had ever seen, but who must have been important because of the company they kept. There were some underground film makers, poets, writers, playwrights and painters who were regulars, and also a couple of porn stars. There were various trans-gender types from exotic female impersonators with glittery short skirts, to dykes who looked like lumberjacks. There were also rock musicians, and drug dealers and other unsavory types as well. And, there were also the weak minded groupies and hangers on who just made themselves into whatever happened to be hot at the minute.

Although the word eclectic comes to mind, it doesn't really seem to fit, because these people were all so odd compared to what one thinks of as middle-America and they were all so non-conformist, that their non-conformity was a sort of conformity. It was like a circus sideshow in real life. Maybe the conformity was to be found in a particular turn of mind or world view. There was an underlying sameness to all the freakishness. It was a subculture, but I couldn't name this subculture. It had elements of Gypsies, bikers, starving artists, and more. I could sense a subtle group pressure to toe the line, even though the line was wavy.

I guess it was at Jack's that I developed an obsession for trying to find a name for people like me and I guess like the people at Jack's. Where they, we,…Beats?…Hippies?…Bohemians?…Genuine non-conformists? Somehow none of the standard words seemed to fit exactly. All these words had been colored by other people in other years. To be any of these things would have been to put on an act and would have made these people all phonies, because each of these terms defined earlier non-conformists in particular ways that have been wedded to certain times and places. This was something new.

These people; at least the ones who I thought were genuine, were a little of all that had gone before, but they were different. I tried to think of a word that I could use to identify them and which made it easier to write about them, and yes to even encourage more people to join in this…movement? This, whatever it was, this culture of pulsing protoplasm in flux, this freedom, made me feel comfortable. I was becoming preoccupied with thinking up a name to describe them and me. I felt at home among these people. What the hell were we? What could we call ourselves to make we who don't belong any-place else, belong now? We were like that Hindu concept of not this, not that. We were nihilists. We were intellectuals and pseudo-intel-lectuals. We had angst. We had art. We had writing. We had acting. We had poetry. We had politics. We had nothing, yet we had every-thing. We lived through the senses. We didn't fit in to straight soci-ety. We were a little like the expatriate writers who left the U.S. for Paris in the 30's, except we hadn't left the U.S.; it had left us. We weren't comfortable with the work-a-day world, yet we weren't exactly bums either. Why weren't we bums? Because we seemed to have a variety of purposes to our existence that involved some sort of art or expression other than just hopping a train and eating a can of beans. But, like bums, we moved around a lot, and we lived in non-materialistic surroundings. Also like bums, we weren't concerned with clothes, cars, fancy houses, or careers.

"Hell," I thought, who is 'we'?" What did I really know about any of these people? I just blew into town a couple of weeks before, and I was living in a storeroom and washing dishes, and I was defining others? I figured it was kind of arrogant of me to include me in the we that I experienced. It was really just me, as it always had been since I could remember. Still, I found some comfort in being a we for a change. As the days passed, I got more into my writing, and would sneak up stairs even when I was working, to pound away on the typewriter. Finally, it dawned on me that if I was going to think in terms of "we" that I had better overcome my natural shyness and force myself to talk to people who came into the bar who I thought looked interesting. Of course, interesting to me mostly meant skinny girls who looked like they might like me. This meant they couldn't be too good looking, if my past experiences with women was any clue.

CHAPTER 2

❀

One night about nine, a tall, thin, beautiful blond came into the bar while I was sweeping up the floor. I swear, her face was so smooth that it looked like porcelain. I wondered if she even had pores. Maybe she was a freak of nature and was born without pores, I thought. I wondered if she would have beads of sweat on her face if the place were hot. It wasn't too crowded, so I struck up a conversation with her. I really liked her looks. She had tiny slim hands with delicate long fingers, and her face was narrow with a thin, slightly long nose, and close set large blue eyes—not like one of those pug pooch face looking girls with the bobbed noses and Jackie Kennedy wide set toad eyes that you see sometimes. Her hair was wispy fine white blond and she had it pulled back into a pony tail. "Hi, I'm Alex," I said. "I wash dishes here and I've never seen you in here before, what do you do?"

"I'm Nadine," she replied with a flicker of her lips that I took as a smile. "I paint."

"Do you make a living at it?" I asked, with my usual directness, and immediately realized this was a bad question after she gave me a dirty look. She didn't say anything.

"Look, I'm sorry. I didn't mean to insult you. It's just that I ask everyone that question to see if they're hobbyists or really committed and making their art work for them. I do some writing, and, no, I don't make a living at it. I think there must be a lot of people in here like that, you know, artists or things like that who don't make a living at it, but whose souls are turned that way permanently no matter what happens. I've been trying to come up with a word to define what we all are. I mean, please don't think that I mean you and I are alike, but I mean the larger "we" of all the people who hang around in here. And, there must be many other places like this around the city and country. I mean, the people in here don't look like business people and they don't look like yuppies or bums. I don't see too many real druggies. What the hell are all these people?

"They're lonely," she finally said, and in doing so, probably revealed more about herself than she wanted to reveal, but then again, maybe she wanted to reveal it.

"Lonely?" I asked, as if I didn't know what the word meant, in order to draw her out some more.

"Yes. They're all looking for something to make them unlonely. They don't know what it is and it may be different with each one, but that's what's going on. I think some of them will say that they're just looking for a good time, but even if they believe that, that's just the surface thing they're looking for, because having a good time, no matter how they define it, just leaves them lonely and empty again once the immediate good time is over. So they bridge their loneliness with a series of good times. It's kind of like we're all looking for a way to find that sense of home we had when we were about two years old and our mothers loved us just because we were. We felt loved, just because we were alive."

"Hmm. Maybe. I'm not sure that's it, but it may be a part of it," I said.

"Do you live around here?" she asked, changing the subject.

"Yeah. I sleep upstairs.

"Do you want to come to a film screening with me tomorrow night?" she asked.

You could have knocked me over with a feather when she said that, but I finally managed to answer. "Yeah. Ah, I guess I can get a night off. I mean I've worked every night for two weeks straight. Where do you want me to pick you up?'

"Do you know where SOHO is?"

"Yeah. Down by the Bowery, right?"

"Yes. Here's the address. I'll meet you out front at 8:00 sharp. I'll introduce you to some of my friends."

I went to sleep that night with dreams of Nadine in my mind. I wondered if she was just lonely as she sounded and if I was a fill in for someone who might have just left her. Shit. Who the hell would leave someone like that? Maybe she wanted to make someone jealous by showing up with me at some event. Well, whatever she wanted, it was no sweat off my brow. I was going to go through with the date, if you could call it that, and see where this road led. I knew that guys in bars often had an in with girls because the guys were considered safe, being that they worked in public in the place where they met the girls, and I figured Nadine felt that way about me. I didn't care. I'd take any opening that I could get.

I spoke to Jack in the morning and we arranged to have one of the busboys wash the dishes so I could take the night off.

At about six, I left the loft and started walking down to the SOHO, taking my time and taking some long ways around. It was cold, and there was some snow still on the ground. I got there about seven thirty. I already knew about SOHO, from my short time in New York. It was an area South of Houston Street just below the Village and just over from the Bowery. It had once been an industrial and warehouse district but had morphed into a yuppie hip area over the years, while still keeping the factory funk. The place where I was supposed to meet Nadine turned out to be a dirty old five story factory building with lots of broken windows and an old rusty fire escape on the side. It was actually just outside of what was probably the official

SOHO. I paced up and down with nervous energy as I waited for Nadine to arrive.

I was starting to wonder if I had the wrong address. Every so often someone would show up and yell "Hey, Ralph throw down the key," or something similar. Then a head and arm would appear from near the top of the building and a piece of wood with a key attached would be dropped to the sidewalk. "Maybe, she wrote the address down wrong," I thought. I walked up the block and went around the corner only to find more of the same kind of old, mostly deserted, buildings. I went back down to the first building and paced some more. Suddenly, a cab drove up and Nadine and a guy with a shaved head and a tatoo of a star on the very top of his head, got out.

"Hi, Alex. Any problems finding the place?"

"Nope."

"Alex, this is Adam. He's an old friend. He's a writer too."

I shook hands with Adam. "Hi, nice to meet you."

"Same here. Nadine says you work down at Jack's. I think I saw you in there. Where you from?"

"Originally, from Maine." I replied.

"Man, you don't have much accent."

"No. I've been traveling for a while. It guess it just rubbed off someplace down in North Carolina or Virginia. Maybe the southern accent canceled out the New England and led to a Midwestern non-accent or something." Nadine figured that we should be going in for the screening, so she asked Adam to get the key. Adam looked up towards the top of the buildings and yelled, "Hey, Ralph, throw us the key will you?" At this, a head poked out of a window on the fifth floor. The head then disappeared but a hand and arm could be seen sticking out the window, and from the hand a key attached to a small board was dropped near us.

"Lock the door behind you, and come up to the fourth floor," yelled the key thrower. We went in, and immediately came to a used looking freight elevator. It was one of those things with a wood gate on the front that lifted up. Nadine lifted up the gate and we stepped in on to the rough wood floor. She closed the gate and hit the button for the fourth floor. The elevator made a grinding noise and jerked up a little. Then it moved slowly up the elevator shaft making all sorts of strange noises as though it might fall down to the basement at any minute. When we got to four, Nadine opened the gate and we emerged directly into the loft that took up that whole floor. The place was full of paintings and blank canvases and junk. The odd thing about the place, though, was that there was no ceiling for about twenty feet of the loft, so this loft opened up through its missing ceiling to the loft above. It wasn't a clean professional job of ceiling removal as might be the case if someone wanted to give this lower loft a more open and airy feel with a high ceiling. It looked as though someone had made the modification with an old ax. Parts of the floor beams of the loft on the floor above poked out all mangled at their ends as though there had been an explosion. Near the far end of this hole in the ceiling there was a rope dangling down from the loft above and someone was climbing down the rope to our floor.

"Hi, Nadine. Hi, Adam," said the skinny guy on the rope. He was the guy I had seen throwing down the key earlier.

"Hi, Ralph. Are we early?" asked Nadine.

"No, no. Everybody's already up on tar paper beach. I had most people come early so I could get them a little drunk and more likely to open their wallets. Come on, let's take the elevator." So, the four of us jumped back on to the rickety freight elevator and started up to the top floor of the building. As we rode, Nadine introduced me to Ralph. She told him that I did some writing and some acting. He nodded and made a little wave like greeting to me with his hand. When we arrived at the fifth floor, we all got out and went over to a narrow black metal ladder that went up through a hatch on to the roof. Ralph motioned for Nadine to go first, but she told him to go first. Then Adam offered to let her go, and she waved him ahead of her. Finally, I figured she'd probably want me to go before her, but she smiled and told me to follow her.

"Alex, the ladder is a little spooky, so don't look down, okay?" she said.

"Okay," I said.

Nadine got on the ladder and started up, and immediately turned around and said "Come on, Alex."

I started up the ladder just a couple of rungs below her, and got a surprise. I did as she told me and didn't look down, so I looked up. This was when I learned that Nadine liked me, because as I looked up, I could look right up her skirt and she wasn't wearing any panties. I just kept climbing and looking up, wishing the ladder were much longer than it really was. For a brief moment I wondered if I really should keep gawking, or if I should be a gentleman, and look away. Almost as quickly, I realized that she couldn't possibly not know that she wasn't wearing any underwear, and that she had also intended to flash me by asking me to follow her. Now I wondered if that meant that she thought I was harmless, or if she was trying to entice me. I liked the thought that she was trying to entice me, because there hadn't been too many women in my life that had, and the few that had, had never been as pretty as Nadine. No one was a pretty as Nadine. So I climbed, and I looked. The ladder really was much too short, I decided. All too soon, we arrived at the roof. The tar paper roof was full of people all standing around as though they were at some fancy cocktail party. Some had glasses with booze in their hands, others were smoking joints. Some were wearing tuxedos, but most were wearing jeans or work pants. There were a lot of beards, pierced ears, pierced noses, pierced lips, pierced cheeks. I recognized a few famous people I had seen on TV or in newspapers. There were a few famous politicians in the crowd also.

I whispered to Nadine, "I don't get it. I see some big shots here. How come they're up here on a cold, dirty, factory roof with people like me?"

"What do you mean people like you?" she asked.

"I mean, I'm just a dishwasher."

"No you're not. You're a writer. And, what's wrong with washing dishes?" She moved on to talk to some other people, who were standing near one of the several 55 gallon drums that were full of burning wood to supply some heat. Pretty soon, Ralph moved to a kind of parapet at the back of the roof and turned on a movie projector. On the screen at the other side of the roof, his movie started. It was a black and white film called "Flailing Flyers." It was a weird, but interesting, vampire movie, I think. I couldn't follow the story, because maybe there wasn't much of a story. Mostly there were a bunch of transvestites all running around some old house. While the movie was being shown, a hat was being passed through the crowd, and everyone was dropping money in. I guess everyone up here but me knew that Ralph was a really famous artist and underground film maker and he had bought this whole building a couple of years ago. Whenever he needed to make a mortgage payment and was otherwise low on money, he'd throw one of these film parties on the roof and invite the New York art-world set, and others who were afraid not to come, lest they no longer be considered important or relevant.

As I was watching the movie, a swishy little guy with bleached blond hair and purple eye makeup came up and started talking to me.

"Ralph is such a genius, don't you think?"

"Yes," I replied, since that seemed to be the polite thing to say.

"Nadine said that you're an actor?"

"Actor? Well, I'm really a dishwasher. I do a little writing. Yeah, I can act. Why?"

"Well Ralph said you might be right for his next film and he wants to talk to you."

"Me? I'm not sure I'm right for Ralph's films."

"Why?"

"Well, I'm just kind of a regular guy," I said, trying to be polite.

"That's why Ralph wants you in his movie. You look like an American, and there aren't very many American looking people around anymore. That's why many Hollywood movie companies now shoot small town America in Canada. Ralph noticed you when he threw the key down, and says you're perfect."

"Well, I don't know."

"Don't be coy, sweetie, Ralph is big time. Guys would kill to be in one of his films."

"Well, I don't wear dresses, for one thing," I blurted out.

"Oh, you thought because of Flailing Flyers that all Ralph does is transvestite movies? Honey, Ralph does all kinds of movies."

"Does it pay anything?"

"Of course not. This isn't Hollywood you know, but you can put it on your resume, and that counts for a lot."

"Will Ralph make any money from the movie?"

"Maybe. Why?"

"Well, how come he makes money but I don't?"

"Because he's the famous guy and you're not. That's why," said blond swish, suddenly sounding very peevish, like maybe he was on the rag. "I have to go tell Ralph your answer. Do you want to do it or not?"

"Well, look, I'll agree to talk to Ralph about it."

"Okay, can you come by here tomorrow at about 10:00 am?"

"Sure." With my answer, blond swish swished away. Soon, Flailing Flyers was over and everyone was leaving. I caught up to Nadine in the elevator figuring that we might spend the night together. She was with another girl who I think was a famous model, at least she looked like a famous model, or should have been a famous model. She was almost as pretty as Nadine, but had raven black hair, probably not her real color, but it looked good.

"Hi, Nadine, can I help you get home?" I asked.

"Thanks, another time. Francine and I will get there alright."

After we climbed down the ladder, the three of us got on the elevator and rode down to the ground floor in silence. Nadine and Francine got off the elevator and, holding hands, walked out of the building. So, I guess Nadine was just teasing me and maybe that's how she got her rocks off. The way she and Francine were looking at each other was a pretty good indication that she didn't like guys very much. Anyway, as I was leaving the building, Nadine and Francine were leaning against the building groping each other. Damn. I guessed that Nadine was too pretty for me. I guess she was too pretty for most men. But she wasn't too pretty for Francine. That started me thinking about natural selection. No kidding. I mean, the way different species have evolved in this regard. In some species, the male is much larger than the female and in others the female is larger than the male. In humans, males and females are pretty close to each other in size, but maybe females are just much prettier than males. Maybe it's like butterflies with Nadine and Francine. Maybe they're both just too delicate, sweet, and beautiful for the male of the species. Well, anyway, I wasn't mad or disgusted or anything like that. I was just disappointed that I wasn't kissing and groping Nadine, or Francine, or Nadine and Francine, or, hell, maybe even the bag lady who just passed by as I was walking down the street.

I went back to Jack's. Since I wasn't tired, I just went in to the kitchen and washed a whole bunch of dishes that had piled up while I was gone. Eventually, as I had hoped, I got tired and went upstairs and flopped into my bed. I was now too tired to think too much of Nadine, and what might have been.

CHAPTER 3

❀

I arrived at Ralph's loft at about 10:15 the next morning. Following what I had seen others do, I yelled up to the windows. Ralph's head popped out, and a key was dropped. "Lock the door behind you and come up to four." I repeated the procedure of the previous night. When I got out of the elevator, Ralph was busy swinging back and forth on his rope.

"Hi, Alex, thanks for coming. Would you like to be in my new movie?"

"Can I see the script first?"

"Sure. Actually, the movie is a little down the road, because I need to raise some more bucks to buy the film, so I'm going to do it as a play, again, first." With that, Ralph swung down and went over to a small table. He then came over to me with a single white page in his hand.

"Take a look," he said.

At the top of the page it said, "The Crabman and Marilyn Monroe." The page was a standard page of typewriter paper, typed single space front and back. I looked it over quickly, not really reading, just taking it in, in one gulp.

"Where's the rest of it?" I asked.

"That's it."

"This is the whole thing? How long a play or movie is this going to be?"

"Well, the first time I put it on as a play, it lasted forty-eight hours, but I didn't have the hole in the floor or the rope then, so it might actually go much longer this time."

"Ralph, are you putting me on? Are you saying that this single page is your whole play and that it'll take more than forty-eight hours to put it on?"

"Uh huh."

"I guess you do some improvising, or maybe the staging is a little different. Can you kind of tell me what it's about so I can get the sense of it from you in your own words independently of the script?"

"Well, you see those marijuana plants over there by the window? Those are going to be palm trees in the movie version. You'll be the Crabman and you have to save Marilyn Monroe's panties after Atlantis sinks. That's the basic story. It's sort of a romantic adventure on the surface, but underneath it's about man's lack of genuine free will. Do you know what I mean?"

"No," I said.

"Well, look, humans think they have free will, but they don't. It's kind of like we're cars on roads. We can change lanes and we can take different roads. We can even speed up or slow down. We think that's free will, but it's not, because we can't leave the road or the car will get bogged down. You see? Free will is strictly limited."

"And, the story of Crabman and Marilyn Monroe's panties has that as a subplot?"

"Right! I knew you'd get it," said Ralph. "The audience has to follow you around during the play, and we'll be using this whole building as our stage. How are you at climbing ropes? You're not afraid of heights are you? My last actor was afraid of heights, and the guy was a professional stuntman. I asked him what kind of stuntman he was since he was afraid of heights and he said that all he did was horse stunts. Can you imagine? A horse stuntman in New York City?"

"Well, look Ralph. Let me think it over will you," I said. With that, I left. Actually, I kind of liked the idea, but I wasn't too wild about swinging around on ropes, so I put off making a decision and that was my decision. I don't know if Ralph ever found another actor, because I suddenly got busy with another play being done in a basement theater under a coffee shop in the Village. I was cast for five parts: A cowboy, a cop, a soldier, a killer and a Senator. Besides me, there were two other male actors and three transvestites. I was starting to question why I seemed to be running into all these weird people. Maybe I was some sort of weird-magnet, or maybe most of New York was like this. I liked women, yet I kept falling in either with transvestites or lesbians. I finally figured that Blond Swish must have been right, about me looking like an ordinary white American. In New York, there were fewer and fewer people who looked like ordinary white Americans. I was becoming the white American to go to when a play wanted someone who looked like what America used to look like. Still, I was wondering if I was just rationalizing. Maybe I had entered some really strange world, or someone had given me an LSD patch that kept everything weird, and which helped me give up the habit I had for reality. Where had all the white Americans gone? Actually, I guess there really wasn't any exotic reason for my surroundings and the strange people who would wander in and out of my life. Sure, there were fewer white people around, but I was an open minded person and I needed the stimulation of things that were a little different, and non-conformist. As a result, I attracted it. I was never much for the suburbs and the white picket fence, even if that's the kind of person I looked like, but, still, if I was so non-conformist in outlook, how come I didn't look that way? Don't people often look like what they think? Aren't we all sort of living versions of the Picture of Dorian Gray? So, I finally decided that I might be just a little peculiar, but not out of my mind as we normally think of those things. I was told by a girl once, who had been seeing a psychiatrist for some reason or another, that he told her she should move to

Greenwich Village where she would fit in. Maybe, that's the answer for all the Bohemians, if that's what we are. Just up and move out of your small towns with the small town things and the small town minds and the small town mores and move to the Greenwich Villages of this world, where differences are not only normal, but are appreciated and expected. Anyway, I went back and forth on this and finally went to sleep. But I had nightmares all night. My subconscious must have worked overtime, because when I woke up in the morning, I suddenly decided I was going to pursue a straight life. I went out and picked up a newspaper and turned to the want ads. I found some interesting looking jobs and I made some calls and then showed up for some interviews. I was offered a job, and I took it.

CHAPTER 4

On the first day of my new job, I arrived wearing a pair of cheap brown plastic faux leather shoes, and a suit, shirt, and tie all of which I had picked up at a second hand store. It was the same outfit that I had worn to the interview. It was the only dress outfit I owned. The suit was a grey pinstripe and the only problem was one sleeve was about two inches shorter than the other, but I just hunched my shoulders over a little and the sleeve wasn't noticeable. My job was to help out in the back office of an advertising and PR firm. I think I got the job because I told them I was a writer, and they had me write some on the spot advertising copy for a couple of fictional clients. Even though my job wasn't actually involved in writing ad copy, they must have liked what they read, and probably figured that I was at least of the correct mind set for their type of operation, and that I might eventually be able to help out with creative things. The job didn't pay much, but it gave me the feeling that I wasn't completely nuts. I told Jack I would be leaving, but that I would help with the dishes after I got off work from the other job until he found someone else. He appreciated this and let me stay in the loft during the transition. It took about a week, but Jack came up with another guy who needed a place to stay, and a job. We both stayed in the loft together for about another week, but because of the difference in hours, we didn't see each other much.

I then got lucky and found a rent controlled seventh floor walk-up, just off Second Avenue. It was tiny, but it wasn't a storeroom like at Jack's and it gave me some sense of normalcy. If you consider walking up and down seven flights of stairs to get home, normal. The shower was in the kitchen right next to the stove, and was resting on cinder blocks so that it was about two feet higher than the floor. It worked out that I could cook and take a shower at the same time. I got used to the place pretty fast. When my trash accumulated, I just dropped it out the window into the alley. Sometimes I got it in the trash cans down below and sometimes I didn't. I figured that drop-ping the trash out the window proved that I was sane, because only a crazy person; maybe some sort of anal retentive, obsessive, compul-sive prig would run up and down seven flights for trash. There was a homeless guy who hung out by the trash cans, so I'd usually yell before I dropped my trash. Hell, I didn't want to wipe the guy out.

I really fell in love with my little apartment when I realized that during thunder storms I could stay awake all night and watch from my bedroom window as the Empire State Building got hit with thou-sands of lightning strikes. It was beautiful.

I met this girl at work named Roxie, who was half white and half-Puerto Rican. She was nice and seemed to like me. Roxie lived with her parents up in the Bronx and commuted in to Manhattan every day. She was skinny to the point of looking as though she were a pris-oner in a World War II concentration camp, and had dark brown short hair and bug eyes. Probably some kind of medical condition. Pretty soon, Roxie was walking down to my place with me after work each night. We'd get off work, then just start slowly walking the blocks from 58th Street where we worked, down to 25th Street, where I lived. Then, Roxie would come up and sit on my bed and talk for a few hours, while I was usually working on my novel on the type-writer that I had bought from a guy named Tony Greenblatt, who worked in the mail room where we worked. Tony had a side business as a booster. He'd come to work with a small shirt pocket notebook of the kind that reporters would often carry. He'd then write down orders for TV's, stereos, computers, or whatever anyone wanted that could be carried by one thief. Then he'd try to fill the orders from his notebook. He seemed pretty fair to his customers and set his prices, depending on the item, and its condition, from ten to twenty percent of what the item would cost new. It was pretty professional.

"I'm good at what I do," said Tony. "That's because I'm mafia on my mother's side and kike on my father's side. I got criminal genes and good business genes in one handsome package."

Anyway, after typing away for several hours, I'd fall asleep, and Roxie would let herself out and presumably go back to the Bronx. That's just the way it went. We never had sex. She was nice, and she did appeal to me a little, but there was just something missing. This went on for months. I never made any demands on her, and never promised anything, and she never made any on me or promised me anything. I've never had a relationship—if you can call that a relationship—like that with a girl either before or after Roxie. I kept thinking back to what Nadine had said about everyone being lonely and trying to not be lonely. Maybe that's the way it was with me and with Roxie, and all the other millions and millions of humans. Maybe my traveling around the country was my way to find someplace that would make me unlonely. It's as though I was always looking for something, but could never find it.

It's not that I traveled as a hobo would travel. I only tried to ride the rails a few times and I'd slept in box cars, but mostly the damn trains were always going too fast so I couldn't hop them. It sounded sort of romantic to say I rode the rails, though. I figure my traveling always had some logical reason behind it rather than just aimless wandering. Hell, when I had been up in New England and going to certain bars mostly around colleges, I had heard all that wandering kind of music, but I don't think it got into my soul or made me envy the lifestyle. Something just seemed to kick in when I was about seventeen years old. That's when I left home. I wasn't running away from anything particularly, except a sense of ennui, which was a word I didn't know until years later, and I wasn't running toward anything except some unknown future where I might feel at home. Maybe Nadine was right about this. There seemed to be something inside of me that kept me from being, say, a shopkeeper or staying in one place for too long. I just couldn't stay still for long, and the thought of having to be cooped inside a small shop all day to help customers, sounded like torture to me. Maybe, I was hyperactive. Maybe I just needed stimulation and change. I was kind of like the face you might see on a bus as it whistles by you on a country road in the mist. You see ghostly shapes of people through the windows in the bus, but you may see one face staring directly out at you and into your soul; a face so cosmically lonely and lost in this universe that you shiver inside and pull your jacket just a little closer and you quickly head for home lest the face in the bus window show up at your doorstep and turn out to be Mr. Death, himself.

And once you've seen that lonely face on that lonely road, you are forever changed as though you have been touched by a trapped soul who has received enlightenment but has been told that he must remain on the Earth to travel the back roads on a bus until Gabriel blows his horn. Yeah. It gets all mixed up, and thoughts from various traditions and religions just seem to cascade at times like this. And what exactly are times like this? Why, they are times like all other times. People are born. People live. People die. The big Spirit in the Sky keeps on wheeling across the universe thinking His thoughts, and His thoughts then become what is real. A lonely God. So alone. No home. No mother. No sense of anything being completed. A God of loneliness who creates creatures of equal but smaller loneliness to share his cosmic loneliness; but they can't share, and they give him no comfort, so he snuffs them out by the billions and starts over. Instead of looking out from spinning, whirling galaxies, as God must do, we, some of us, peer out through the windows of busses, and we see standing by the road a lonely man looking at us as we whizz on by and we sink back in our seats and we dare not turn away, for the lonely man looking in at us has us transfixed, and we wonder why he looks so lonely. He's only there for a moment looking all blue and white in the pale light. Why is he standing all alone out on this lonely country road. Where does he live? Why is he out here? In a minute, he is gone, but his image is forever seared into our consciousness as our image is seared into his, and then we realize that the lonely man we saw, was us, and he realizes that we are him. It is loneliness looking at loneliness.

Where is that warm and comfortable little place of the soul that we see in children's books when we're kids? Where is that little home built into a tree stump in the side of a hill where we pad around on little fuzzy feet and twitch our noses and sit in overstuffed chairs in front of a tiny fireplace while drinking Catnip tea? Is that the home our soul seeks? What do we find, instead? A world of blue light and skinny shadows. A world full of people made bone thin by meaningless lives as they try to eke out a living in the post-American America that we have been born into.

We find a world with too many people and too little meaning. We find a world where we struggle just to survive so that we can struggle again the next day so that we can birth our children so that they can struggle as we have struggled. There is no meaning, because we do not know what meaning is. We do not think the big thoughts, the soaring things. No. We think about food on the table. We are like ants and we don't know it, and even as ants we're not very good, because we are ants without purpose, and without a colony. We are the lone army ant, each one of us, and we march around as though we are the whole army until we are squashed by the years as they creep up on us, and like some giant thumb, they crush us. And as we look around, we realize that there are fewer ants who look like us each day, and that there are other ants, different ants, who are taking over our ant hill and replacing us. And, we, the ever fewer albino ants who see what's going on are sad for we see our own extinction and we try to scream out against our march to oblivion, but we can't, because we are only ants and that is not the way we are.

And as we live, we read many things and we see many things and we hear many things and we come to realize, if we have insight, that the world is full of very ordinary people who have little originality, and maybe it's not really everyone who has this cosmic loneliness at all, but just those who have, for whatever reason, reached a certain level of consciousness. Maybe the rest are just ignorant and happy. If this is so, then why are some of us the lonely travelers that we are? What is it that we've seen, and what is it that we seek? And why are we the only ones? and how many of us are there? And when we look at each other, do we know in our souls that we are the same and does this then increase our loneliness rather than lessen it? Would the lonely soul looking out from the interstate bus window have been made more comfortable if the man beside the road had not been another lonely soul, but, instead, a dim witted smiling and happy country boy? Who knows. We hurtle on through the night never seeing a golden dawn nor a warm sunset. Instead, we see a cold hard dawn and a blue sunset—a world illuminated by flashing neon signs. A world that is always on the other side of the railroad tracks. A world where one hears the plaintive wail of both the late night train and the lonely sound of the fog horns on the ocean at the same time and all the time.

So, I was once again caught up in what seemed to be my eternal introspection. I was living life in my head instead of in the real world. Man, I figured that maybe New York was getting to me. I figured I'd better make a plan to move on. But where to go? How about the West Coast? I'd been up and down the East Coast a dozen times, and the middle of the country had no ocean, so I wasn't even interested in that piece of geography. Alright then, it was going to be the West Coast. I was going to break my pattern. I was going to go West. Forget the bus. This time I was going to fly over the great dry middle of this country that had no ocean, because I couldn't stand being away from the ocean for the length of time it would take to cross the land by bus. That meant I needed to make some money. I took a second job in an office where all I did was open envelopes, take out checks, stamp them received, and pile them up. Simple. After a couple of months of this, and my other job, I was ready to leave.

The night before my flight, I went down to Jack's and told everybody that I would be out of my apartment by noon of the following day, and that I was leaving most of my stuff behind. I told them that the door would be unlocked, so whoever wanted my TV and bed and other stuff was welcome to it all. I then went home, packed my back pack with the essential things and got some sleep.

SAN FRANCISCO

CHAPTER 1

It was foggy when I arrived in San Francisco. It was the thickest fog I had ever seen. I had no idea that fog could be that thick. It was like a snowbank that you could walk through as though you had some magic power to walk through solid objects. It was sort of like ghosts in reverse. The ghosts were solid and everything else was ghostlike. I couldn't see more than three feet in front of me, if that. I wondered how it was even possible for such a fog to exist and hang there without falling. It was like a white darkness. Now, why didn't anyone bother to tell me that San Francisco was foggy about six months out of the year? I guess people probably mention that San Francisco has fog, but with this kind of fog, they should do more than just mention it and they should tell you that this is the original pea soup fog that makes you lose your orientation and become fog blind. This was none of that wispy fog that I had experienced on the East Coast from time to time that would usually quickly burn off. This was like a white night, or like sticking your face in a snow bank. And the damn stuff lasted all night and all day, and it went on day after day after day. Shit. Is this why the PR types called San Francisco the air conditioned city? They should have called it the gloomy-can't-see-your-stupid-damn-hand-in-front-of-your-stupid-damn-face city. What the hell, and people are supposed to like this city?

Geez. And, to think that I thought the friggin' place was going to be sort of tropical. How in the hell did I get the idea that the tall palm trees in Southern California that I had seen in movies were also up here in this gloom? This place was like New England without snow. And, I actually thought this place was going to be full of blonde girls in string bikinis running around all over the place. I guess I hadn't given much thought to the fact that San Francisco was in Northern California and wasn't where all those beach bunny movies had been made. Christ, Northern California should be it's own damn state. Ah, what the hell. It was just another adventure. Another lonely new city. San Francisco was before me. A city where I didn't know a soul and where no one knew me. All was new. I quickly found a cheap hotel room in the Tenderloin near some all night porn theaters. Hooker heaven, again. I was always running into hookers. I figured that maybe I'm just low class and that I gravitate to the seamy side of every town I hit. But, on my travels I came to the realization that the seamy sides of town are growing and are taking over the good parts of town, so maybe it was just getting harder to hit the nice places. It didn't much bother me. I was just passing through. But, what about the people who had to live in these places all their lives? In truth, I realized that even if the crappy parts of these towns weren't growing, I'd probably still have sought them out. There was more life in these areas than in the manicured parts of town, there always is more life in rot than in things that aren't rotting. Maybe I liked these areas because the people have fewer pretenses and are more open. Maybe it's because I just genuinely like people who have checked out of the straight life, and who don't try to impress others. Man, there I went again. What are we, we lonely ones? We are the Neobohemiananarchisttravellerintellectualmisfits. Hmm. I figured that wasn't too catchy. Maybe that's what I'm looking for—to be the one who names a movement that isn't really a movement at all, but which become one as a result of the naming. Then again, maybe what I wanted to do is fit in someplace instead of being the eternal round peg in a world of square holes. But, this was becoming increasingly hard to do, in what had become post-American America. There weren't many Americans like me where I rambled.

I knew that there must be some others out there like me, because I had run into a few of them, but mostly they were scattered. Besides, even with some who are like me in some ways, the differences often overpower the sameness, so there isn't much of a feeling of kinship. This is because we don't know that we're alike, and because we have no name to rally 'round. Maybe we're revolutionaries without a portfolio or rebels against everything. Maybe, that's it. We're rebels rebelling because that's what we do. We rebel. Maybe it's not a cause we're looking for at all, but a rebellion. Eternal rebellion. I kind of liked that. Maybe that's what God is. The Cosmic Rebel. The One who rebels against all that is, to Become. Naturally, we need to hang our rebellion or revolution on some cause, otherwise we would just seem vapid. Change. Turmoil. Chaos. Isn't that what storms and the ocean are all about? Everything in flux. Isn't that what a far away spinning galaxy is all about? It's just a big shuffling and reshuffling of the deck.

So, first I had been introspective in New York. Now, I was introspective in San Francisco. I wasn't finding what I wanted, because I didn't know what I wanted. I decided to try to get a job and make some money, so I answered an ad at one of the local newspapers and got hired to correct classified ads in the newspaper. This gave me the money to buy an old rat-bike motorcycle that ran pretty good most of the time. I got a good price on it because the last guy had been killed on it and the frame was a little bent. Anyway, the dead guy's girlfriend just wanted to get rid of it. It was painted a flat black with a lot of drips in the paint. The dead guy had done the paint job with spray cans on his living room carpet. I could see the outline of the bike on the carpet laid out like a corpse, when I went inside to pay for it. Because of the bent frame, the back wheel was always a little to the left as I rode it, but that didn't bother me. The main problem was that it leaked a lot of oil all over the place, including on my pant legs, so I mostly always had oily pants.

When I wasn't working, I was usually riding up to the Haight or North Beach. In the Haight, I hung around at the old Hippie Hill with a bunch of crazy old hippies who seemed to be locked into the late '60's in their minds. They'd just sit there on that little sloping hill smoking weed as though it were still 1965. Sometimes they'd throw one of those plastic discs around as though they were still eighteen years old. I half expected some of these guys to have heart attacks over this, but none did while I was there. Maybe that was because they were all so vegetarian-walk everyplace-and-smoke-weed skinny. In North Beach, I spent a lot of time in bookstores and coffee shops. One day in one of the coffee shops I met a girl named Carla who was a sales manager for a computer company. I hit it off with her, and not long after that I moved into her place. She was a spoiled rich girl and I figured she was rebelling by going out with me. I didn't really care about the psychology of it, it was a relationship that gave me some comfort. The fact that she had to travel a lot on her job, pretty much kept me from feeling trapped.

Pretty soon I found an acting agent and got some bit parts in some films that were being made in the city. It was no big deal, but I liked it. I also pulled out my manuscript that I had hauled across country from New York, and began working on it again. Since I no longer had a typewriter, I did it in long hand at first, and hoped that some day I would be able to read what I had written so I could type it. I decided that I'd have to find another old typewriter, or maybe a PC. I needed to find another Tony Greenblatt.

My agent called and said I could get more acting work if I had better pictures. So, I found this loopy guy who lived in the Haight who would take a roll of pictures of me on the cheap. Actually, I think he wanted to take nude pictures of Carla. Anyway, the guy took the pictures and he then said I could have this comic book publisher he knew print them for me cheap. So, I took my photos to these whacked out guys at this old tiny warehouse who put out these underground comics, and they agreed to print up a composite for me. Unfortunately, when I got the composites, these guys had printed my name upside down on the front. What the hell. I got them to knock off some of the bill and I took them. I figured they were good enough for the small acting stuff I was likely to get. I gave the composites to my agent. She wasn't pleased with the upside down name, but she took them anyway.

CHAPTER 2

One foggy day, Carla and I were out riding the hog, and as we were going up one of those hills that are all over San Francisco, we got lost and made a lot of wrong turns, until finally we came to a weird area not far from some docks, but still on a hill. The neighborhood was definitely blue collar white and turning all Mexican. It was was full of run down industrial buildings with dumpy houses in between them. It was hard to tell if the houses were out of place or whether it was the industrial buildings that were out of place. It reminded me of a neighborhood I had once seen in a New England mill town, except in the New England mill town, most of the people were white, not Mexican. We drove down the street and came to a place that maybe was what fate had determined I was going to find, even though I didn't know it at first.

It sat there squat and fat and red and all blurry through the moist fog. It was three stories tall with wooden clapboards and a flat roof. It was more a square than a rectangle. There was a small sign above the door. The sign was one of those vertical metal boxes with neon, except the neon on this one had long ago been busted out. So, instead of neon, the metal box had been painted black and the word "POOP" was painted vertically on the sign box, in faded white letters.

I stopped the Harley across the street from the place and asked Carla if she knew what the place was.

"No," she replied.

"Do you think it's a club or something?" I asked.

"It looks like it. Why? Do you want to go in?"

"Are you game?"

"Sure."

So we pulled the Harley up front and I backed it to the curb. The front door was actually two halves that swung open in the middle. Each half was clad with a stainless steel jacket stamped in a diamond pattern and had two nautical looking round windows about the size of basketballs at eye level so you could look in or out to see if someone was about to push the door from the other side. We pushed the two halves of the door in and entered the place. Immediately, we found ourselves in a big barroom with a dull, but clean wooden floor and a dark wood bar about twenty feet long over to one side and about t fifteen feet from the door that we had just come in through. The bar room reminded me of some of the old bars in New York used by skinny old Irish drunks who looked like they lived in the place, and who would always turn to look through blood shot eyes with half closed lids at whoever had just entered. There was a small raised stage at the far end of the room. There were some tables and chairs scattered around the place and a couple of wooden booths with wooden bench seats. There was an obviously drunk old guy sitting down at one end of the bar, but other than him and the bartender, the place looked empty. Carla and I went up to the bar and sat down. The bartender was an attractive woman about thirty years old, with long black hair. She was dressed in a black T-shirt and jeans. She came over and asked what we wanted.

"A couple of beers, please," I said.

"What brand?"

"Whatever you have on tap," I said. When she brought the mugs over, I struck up a conversation. "What kind of place is this?"

"Just what you see," she said. "It's a bar and restaurant. Upstairs is a hotel."

"Unusual name for a restaurant," I said.

"Yeah. It used to be Poop Deck, seeing that we're near the bay and the docks and all, but the Deck part fell off. Now it stands for People and Objects Out of Place."

I liked the place. It felt a little like Jack's but it didn't have all the people. Carla and I stayed there for hours that night and soon a bunch of hip people came in who were apparently regulars, as Carla and I were soon to be also.

While we were there that first night and starting to feel really comfortable with the place and its people, a couple of motorcycle gang members came in wearing their colors and rockers. One guy was about 6'3 and 300 pounds and had a full beard. His partner was bigger and hairier. The small one looked around and said "Who's got Shorty's ride." Suddenly the bar fell silent. No one answered. I didn't say anything, because I didn't know what the hell he was talking about. The guy suddenly looked real angry and bellowed "I just passed Shorty's scoot out there at the curb. Who rode that here?" Shit. I suddenly realized that he was talking about my Harley.

"That's my bike," I said. "I don't know anything about Shorty. I bought it from a girl who lives on Potrero Hill."

The biker cracked a grin. "Okay, bro, no problem. Shorty was a pal. We buried him a couple of weeks back. You better take good care of his bike, or we're going to come looking for you."

"Sure," I said. Then as a sign of friendship, I asked, "Can we buy you guys a beer?"

"Yeah."

So that's how I started meeting a bunch of outlaw bikers. They were pretty good guys so long as you didn't cross them. Many of them were making and selling speed and other drugs and working as muscle for some local Mafia types.

As Carla and I kept going into Poop, we learned more about the people and the place and became part of the family, so to speak. The guy who owned the place was called Talkin' Bob, because he never talked to anyone. He apparently could talk, but he chose not to in the interest of world peace or something like that. He was friendly though, and just smiled when spoken to. The residents of the two floor hotel upstairs were an odd lot. There were four rooms to a floor with a hall bathroom on each floor. All the rooms were occupied with permanent tenants. On the second floor there was Percy, who was in his forties and who sometimes ran around Poop with whips and chains and those evil looking S&M black rubber masks on his face, so he looked a little like a medieval executioner. Next to his room there was a forties something hard looking hooker named Gladys who had mammoth boobs as a result of a couple of boob jobs, that really made you think she was going to fall over as she walked. All the rest of her was starting to look saggy, but her boobs were like two artillery rounds sticking straight out. Cookin' John, the guy who rented and ran Poop's restaurant also had a room on the second floor. Apparently, descriptive nicknames ending in "in" had caught on in Poop, at least for Talkin' Bob and Cookin' John. Some of the other regulars were sometimes called similar things, but not as consistently. The last room on the second floor was Talkin' Bobs. Up on the third floor there was a portly guy named Jason Lang, sometimes called Filmin' Guy, who falsely, we thought, claimed to be a descendant of Fritz Lang. No one really believed him and figured he just took the name because he was a porno film maker and thought the name gave him class and an entre to the film world. The girl who tended the bar and who we had talked to on the first day, had a room on three also. She went by the name of Joan three nipples. If the reason for her name wasn't clear, she'd be glad to show you her third nipple—if you gave her a couple of bucks. One of the other rooms belonged to a dead serious biker, with hair down to his waist and a full beard, who pretty much stayed to himself and who everyone figured was probably some sort of hit man or who was making meth in his room or something. He was a friend of the two bikers we had met the first night. We all knew the guy was never late with his rent, but no one knew what the guy really did for a living. He also didn't seem to work any sort of regular hours and he was mean looking. The last room was occupied by a guy who played guitar in a rock and roll band. He had ear rings, a nose ring, an eyebrow ring and an upper lip ring.

One day, Cookin' John, heard on the radio that someone had abandoned hundreds of baby chicks out at SfO, and that anyone who wanted them need only come out and pick them up. I guess Cookin' John figured that this would be profitable for the restaurant, so he borrowed a truck and drove out to the airport. When he came back, he had more baby chicks than I had ever seen. The only problem was that he had no place to put them where it would be warm enough so they wouldn't all die. Being an innovative guy, he hit upon the idea of simply dumping them all in his room. And that's what he did. He moved out into the hall and slept in a sleeping bag next to his door. A couple of times a day he'd throw chicken feed over the transom. He'd then lower water in a gallon sized plastic milk bottle over the transom with a rope. The water filled milk bottle had some holes cut in the sides so the chicks could drink it. Well, it didn't take long before the board of health got wind of this, and gave Talkin' John, as the owner of Poop, an ultimatum: get rid of the chicks or get closed down. Anyway, Talkin' John and Cookin' Bob had a sit down about the problem. Talkin' John wrote his words and Cookin'Bob answered by talking. After about a half hour of this, they hit upon the solution.

Soon, Poop became well known for its hot Pygmy Chickens on a stick. The chicks were mostly all bones, but when they were broiled just right, and then baked in a hot sauce, people bought them. There wasn't much meat, and many people who bought them didn't actually eat them. I suspect they bought them just so they could say they had. After a time, there were no more chicks, and the item was removed from the menu. The other big item on the menu was fried rabbit and rabbit burgers, and their was no shortage of rabbits. Cookin' John raised the rabbits out back in cages that sat on 2 x 4 legs about three feet off the ground. Below the cages, he had his worm farm. When he butchered the rabbits, he saved the pelts, which he sun cured, and sold to a woman who used them to make all sorts of tourist things that she sold down at Fisherman's Wharf. He also kept the feet and sold them for good luck charms at the bar. What Cookin' John was trying to do was have a self-perpetuating symbiotic business. He even grew some potatoes out back that he used for french fries. He was very ingenious and obsessive about being self contained. He considered it a personal failing if he had to buy anything from the supermarket for the restaurant. One of the crack heads who was something of a regular, gave Cookin' John an almost new garbage disposal unit one day in exchange for a meal, and Cookin' John rigged it up in a spare sink in the kitchen and had the pipe lead outside so that it drained on the worm farm. All the kitchen garbage went into this special disposal and to the worms. At first, all the garbage would just sit there in a great big pile that Cookin' John had to go out and shovel. But then he attached a big plastic hose to the end of the pipe and could adjust where the chopped up garbage would fall on the worm farm. He put the garbage out in rows and put little date signs on the piles so he'd have an idea of when the garbage had been processed and the worms had moved on. He'd then take the worm castings from the oldest former garbage pile and put it in bags and sell it as potting soil to the gay guys down on Castro Street. The logo on the bags was supposed to be a worm, but it looked like a penis. That's probably because Joan Three Nipples drew it and maybe she was a little cockeyed. Anyway, the stuff sold big to the gays. He'd also sell some of his worms to fishermen who would pass by on their way to one of the old piers that were nearby. Cookin' John wasn't getting rich, but he was paying the bills and he was doing what he wanted to do.

CHAPTER 3

A couple of months after Carla and I had been hanging around at Poop, a guy we quickly dubbed Actin' Al asked Talkin' Bob if he'd mind if Actin' Al built a theater in the basement of Poop. Talkin' Bob immediately agreed, and also indicated that Actin' Al could use the small stage in the bar if he wanted. The deal was that Actin' Al would put on plays and pass a hat. Actin' Al would keep all the money and distribute it to the actors. Talkin' Bob would make his profit from any increased business he got as a result of people coming to see the plays.

The play Actin' Al wanted to put on was an avant garde horror thing that had been written by Percy, the guy with the chains from the second floor of Poop. It seemed to make sense to put on something like that in the creepy basement of Poop. Actin' Al got some chicken wire; he didn't have to go too far because Cookin' John had gotten some of that when he got the chicks. Actin' Al took the wire down to the basement and started building the single set which was supposed to be a cave wall. The idea was to cover the wire with papier mache. He was also building a ten foot long, four foot high papier mache tunnel that the audience would have to duck down to go through in order to enter the theater. He planned to hang strings in the tunnel to feel like spider webs. On the one hand, the whole thing was sort of Halloweenish, but given the fact that the play was for adults and it was in the basement of a bar, Actin' Al figured it wasn't too juvenile and that no one would think of Halloween. The major problem Actin' Al was having was with large rats that would come up from the wharfs and eat the papier mache at night. Plus, rat poop had a foul and unmistakable smell, and then there was that thing I remembered from New York about rats dragging their balls all over the place. Well, anyway, Actin' Al got just about all the residents and regular customers of Poop interested in the theater, so they all pitched in and helped build the set. It was pretty elaborate and very cave looking. In the center of the cave where the audience would have their eyes focused, was a cut out section where Actin' Al was going to have an oracle. The oracle was going to appear to be a severed head with wires and tubes connected to it. When the customers got into the theater itself, they were to be given free bowls of cooked long grain rice and they were to be purposely kept waiting until they started eating the rice. At that point, the lights would be dimmed and a short film made by Jason Lang would begin running against the face of the cave wall in front of the audience. In the film were bowls that were identical to the ones given to the audience, but the ones in the film were full of maggots crawling all around and out of the bowls. Well, the whole thing didn't make much sense to me on one level, but on another level I could see that Actin' Al was trying to get the audience to viscerally feel what they were seeing, and not just be passive spectators. I figured the wannabes who came down to see this would just figure Actin' Al was some sort of mad genius and then they'd be too afraid of being thought to be unhip to ask what the play was supposed to be about.

While they were getting everything ready for that play, Actin' Al and the group of actors he put together decided to do something more traditional, so they put on that hoary old thing called The Drunkard. They did this one upstairs in the bar itself. It was well received by the winos who would have appreciated anything. It was something different to look at while drinking cheap wine at the bar and coughing your guts out and dying by the minute.

Then tragedy struck, because while that play was running, Carla happened to get a good look at Cookin' John and, man, the guy was yellow like a banana. His skin was yellow and his eyes were yellow and he was complaining of a stomach ache. Carla told him that he looked as though he had hepatitis, which she had once had, and she said that he looked like that, but worse. Carla insisted that he go to a hospital, so a couple of us got him into the back seat of someone's old Ford and got him to S.F. General. He was unconscious by the time we got to the hospital, but we manhandled him inside. The doctors took one look at him and rushed him onto a gurney and then pushed him through some doors and down the hall out of our sight. The doctors came out and wanted next of kin information, and no one knew any relatives. Someone said that they had heard Cookin' John say that he had originally came from Ohio, but no one was sure. Anyway, the hospital was able to come up with the name of Cookin' John's sister who lived up in Marin County. She came to the hospital and told the doctors that she was his only living relative that she knew about. They told her that he was in a coma and on a life support machine and that he was brain dead. Without a moment's hesitation or even a look of concern, she told them they could pull the plug, just like she might have been saying "Turn off the TV." They did so, and that was the end of Cookin' John.

The restaurant just closed down for a while after that because no one wanted to run it. Then finally, Gladys, the hooker from upstairs said she'd run the damn place. And she quickly got into the swing of things. She even had a cross dresser come in to be a waitress. Man, it was something to see. The cross dresser had a beard, but wore a tiny black and white upstairs French maid looking waitress dress. Now, that was class. Anyway, after Cookin' John kicked the bucket, no one wanted to put the play on in the basement so they just let the rats have it all. Real late at night, we could hear them chewing up the set in the basement down below.

After that, but not just because Cookin' John was gone, Carla and I drifted away from the place, but it still figured in my life and it was always a place to go to when there was nothing else to do.

One day about a month after Cookin' John was gone, I was up on Ashbury Street outside Carla's apartment building fixing my Harley and an old friend from Boston came sauntering down the street past me. "Hey, Gil. Man, is that you?" I yelled as he walked past. He stopped and turned around and got a big grin on his face.

"Alex?"

"Yeah. Hey, Gil I didn't know you were in San Francisco. How long you been here?"

"Oh, a couple of weeks. I haven't been here in years, so I thought I'd take a look. Man, it's gotten real gay, since I was here last." Gil was kind of a deep thinker and liked to talk about religion and philosophy. I don't know where he got his money, but he always seemed to have a few bucks—never enough to help out anyone else, but always enough so that he always paid his own way. And, that was good. There were too many moochers around. Anyway, Gil and I did some talking and right there on the sidewalk we decided, by damn, to do a little traveling together. He said he had an old beat up VW bus down the street that already had his stuff in it. Anyway, I wheeled the Harley into the garage under Carla's building and put it flat against the wall in her stall, so she could still get her car in. Then I went upstairs and threw some stuff in my backpack and wrote a note to Carla telling her to take care of the Harley and that I'd give her a call pretty soon. She was at a meeting in Atlanta, and she'd be back the next day. I called my boss at the newspaper and left a message on his machine that I had to go into the hospital, and I'd be out of work for a while. As we went to the bus, I took a pretty good look at it. It wasn't one of those ancient ones with the split windows like the hippies used to drive around in, but it had a few miles and years on it. It had one of those permanent raised fiberglass roofs on the top, so you 'could stand up inside. There was also a home made sunroof made out of plastic.. The exterior was all painted in a kind of weird copper penny color and it had no shine to it. I touched the paint, and it was all bumpy like very rough sandpaper. There were also several short spiral antennas on the roof. "You paint, this Gil?" I asked. "No, that's the way it was when I bought it. So, we got in the bus and headed out. There was a half seat in the back right behind the two front seats, and behind that was a big slab of plywood with some blankets on it. There was also a plastic toilet back there, but that was about it. It looked like a poor man's home made camper.

As we drove, I noticed a peculiar low pitch humming sound just within the hearing threshold. "What's that sound?" I asked.

"Don't worry about it. I think it's just the tires. You get used to it after a while."

"How about the radio, can we turn it on?" I asked.

"Sure," said Gil. So we continued on, listening to music on the radio.

We were about half way across the Golden Gate Bridge, when wind caught the plastic sheet covering the sunroof just right and ripped it from the bus and sent it flying over the side of the bridge.

"Shit," said Gil.

"Damn," said I. Then we both started laughing so hard that it's a wonder we didn't run the bus off the side of the bridge. Pretty soon it started raining but it wasn't any problem, because so long as Gil kept the speed up, the rain would just blow over the hole in the roof. It was a little cold, though, and Gil pulled his sleeping bag all around him to keep warm. We headed up through Sausalito and just kept going north, along Pacific Coast Highway, or California State Highway 1, which pretty much hugged the coast. It wasn't long before we got to Bodega Bay, and there was a guy standing there hitchhiking. He was about twenty-five years old with long blond hair and a blond beard. He had a backpack with him and was wearing a pair of sturdy hiking shoes. We figured he looked okay, so we pulled over.

"Where you headed?" asked Gil as he spoke across me to the guy outside my window.

"As far north as I can get. Maybe Alaska. You going that far?"

"Maybe. That is if we can keep finding money for gas. You got any gas money?"

"I got some, but not much. What do you think is fair?"

"Hell, I don't know." said Gil, "What do you think, Alex?"

"Well, we've got the wheels, so if he puts gas in, maybe that'll be fair." I looked out the window, and asked the guy what he thought about that.

"That might be okay, but I really don't have too much money."

"Tell you what," I said, "what if we just keep driving north until we need gas. Then you fill the tank, and we'll keep heading north until we need more gas and you fill it again, and we'll just keep doing this until you run out of money or we reach Alaska, or you decide you don't want to go any further? What do you think Gil?"

"That's okay with me." said Gil. "Oh, he might need to buy oil too, this burns some oil."

"Sounds good to me," said the guy. My name's Zack, by the way." Gil and I introduced ourselves, and Zack climbed in the back. As soon as Zack got in, the radio went on the fritz and all we got was static. We turned it down low so we could hear when the static went away, but it stuck with us. So, the three of us drove off, heading north. As we drove, the three of us talked to get to know each other, but mainly to see if we really wanted to continue past the next tank of gas.

"Where you coming from?" asked Gil

"San Francisco," said Zack. "I used to live under some bushes up in Golden Gate Park until the cops rousted everyone. So, I figure I'll see what's up north. There's too many people in California for me anyway, and it's turning into a new Mexico. I was comfortable in the park, but I was kind of like an object at rest that remains at rest until pushed. I've been pushed, so now I'm moving. How about you guys? Where you from?"

"Maine, New York, Virginia, North Carolina, San Francisco, Boston. You name it and one of us has probably been there for more than just a pass through," I said.

"New York, Boston, Chicago, Toronto, Dallas, New Orleans, Los Angeles, San Francisco, and a bunch of other places," said Gil.

"You guys running from the law or something?" said Zack. "I mean I don't really care…."

"Nah. I guess we're running to find something and we never find it because we don't know what or where it is," I said. "You know, I think it's sort of like an onion. I mean if you set out to find the essence of an onion—that which is the soul of the onion, and you peel off layer after layer of the onion—all you'll ever find is more onion. The onion is the essence of the onion. It is just more and more of the same."

"Wow, man," said Zack, that's the truth, though."

"I think everything in the universe is simple," said Gil. "I think it's just the explanation that is complex."

"Yeah. I think I hear what you're saying. I thought about things like that while I was living under the bushes," replied Zack.

But, I wasn't finished with this little philosophical trip that we three had embarked on. "You know the binary code?" Just a couple of numbers repeated over and over and over again? It's like DNA. Man, all living things are composed of just four chemicals. I mean their DNA is composed of just these four chemicals. Shuffle the chemicals one way and you've got mold. Shuffle them another way, and you've got a whale or a man or a mouse or a tree."

"Maybe God is the shuffler," said Gil.

"Yeah, but how does he do the shuffle?" said Zack.

"I figure it's gotta be something very simple and primitive in order for it to work forever," I said. Then it occurred to me what God, or maybe nature is a better word, does to shuffle. "I'm not boring you guys with this, am I?"

"No," said Gil

"No," said Zack.

"Okay. Here's how I figure God does the shuffle...no, wait a minute. Pull into this restaurant over here, Gil. Come on, follow me, I gotta take a leak anyway." I took Gil and Zack into the restroom. "Watch this," I said. I flushed the toilet. "Look. Do you see it? There, that's how God does the shuffle. See how the water spins as it goes down? Look at this. I turned the water on in the sink. Watch. See, the water is going down the same way as the toilet water. I think that's the secret of all existence. The spiraling, spinning action is what does it all, and everything is constantly spinning. Everything is turning."

Gil and Zack were looking at me like I was mad. We quickly left the restaurant without buying anything and got back in the VW where we continued the conversation.

"So, it's like God flushes, and that's how everything came into existence?" said Zack.

"If that were the case, then how did the big toilet in the sky come into existence to flush in the first place?" said Gil. "What is behind the spiraling? Maybe it's just something simple like heat and cold, but then what's behind those?"

"No. I'm serious," I said. "Forget the toilet. Think about it. A strand of DNA spirals. Tornados, hurricanes, water in your sink, far away galaxies, the way trees grow, even the wind that tore off the plastic on the bus all spiral like that. Do you see what I'm saying?"

"You're saying that God uses a swastika to create?" asked Zack, out of the blue.

"Swastika? Ahhh, I hadn't thought of it in that term, but I guess you can say that if you look at a far away galaxy that it looks sort of like a swastika spinning in the heavens."

"Say, do you think that's why the Nazis used the swastika as a symbol?" asked Gil.

"Man, I don't think so," I said. "I don't know. I never thought about it." We were silent for several minutes as each of us, individually, thought about it, as though we were some sort of cosmic scholars all thrown together to work out the problems of the universe.

"WOW!" said Zack. "Man, see if you can dig this. Do you remember in the Wizard of Oz—you know the old movie with what's her name who had some kind of booze or drug problem or something who the gay guys all like?

"Judy Garland," said Gil.

"Yeah," said Zack. Remember how Dorothy was picked up by a tornado and transported to Oz? Man, there's one of those spirals, again. And, remember how Dorothy set out on the yellow brick road to go to the Emerald City?"

"Yeah," said Gil.

"The yellow brick road started as a spiral. But, also look at us!" exclaimed Zack. "You two guys come along and pick me up and we're heading down the road to some sort Oz to find the wizard behind everything who can help us find our way back home. Man, it's just like the movie."

"Except," I said, I don't think we can get back home. I think our home is gone. America is gone. We're strangers in this land, now. We are the pale riders of the wasteland.

"So, do we each lack something that we think will be obtained when we get to the end of the road?" asked Gil.

"I don't know," said Zack. "Maybe."

"So, it's sort of like we're living in a metaphor," I said. "Too much, man."

"Yeah," I don't think we should carry the thing too far, but the thought just popped into my head," said Zack.

"Which way does the swastika turn?" asked Zack.

"You mean the Nazi swastika?" I said.

"What other kind is there?" asked Gil.

"I think there's a whole bunch of different kinds. I know Buddhists have a swastika and the American Indians sometimes used the symbol.

"I think the Nazi thing has the arms spinning clockwise," said Gil.

"Do you mean they point clockwise?" asked Zack. "If that's the case, then the spin is counterclockwise because if we're thinking that the swastika is an image of a far away galaxy, then the arms on a galaxy—the millions and millions of stars that make up the arms of a galaxy—trail. It's like the hub of the galaxy is like the wheel on a car, that has picked up a bunch of rope or something, so that the ropes are like the arms of a galaxy."

"So, the whole thing is actually spinning counterclockwise, but the arms are pointed clockwise," I replied.

"Okay," said Zack. "Then whatever way it spins, you're saying that God or nature uses that to create?"

"Yeah, maybe," I said. "Create and destroy and shuffle and reshuffle and do it forever. You know how it's said: so above, so below, or something like that?"

"I've heard that," said Gil.

"Well, it means that everything is the same," I said. "What's out there in space happens right here on Earth. I think it means that the principles are all the same. If this is the way I think it is, then we don't have to invent a God with any brains or any God at all. And if there is a God, then he could even be an idiot and still create everything. Just think of Him sitting there mindlessly shuffling cards, and with every shuffle, entire star systems come into being or disappear."

"But, wait a minute." said Gil, "If God is an idiot sitting there shuffling, who created the things he's shuffling? Is there another God, above God?"

"Maybe God just willed himself into being…no, wait a minute. Let me think about this like it's a movie. Let me pretend I'm making a movie for everyone to watch. Okay, you walk into the theater and sit down. You know, I'm sort of thinking of this crazy theater a guy was putting into the basement of a joint called Poop in San Francisco...."

"You know Poop? interrupted Zack.

"Yeah, I used to hang out there. You know the place?"

"I used to go out with a girl who tended bar there," said Zack.

"Joan three nipples?" I asked.

"Yeah. Great chick, man, really sweet, but she put a possessive trip on me that I couldn't stand, so it didn't work out."

"Man, talk about a small world," I said. "Anyway, let me get this thought out, before I forget it. So you walk into the theater and you sit down. The place is completely dark. The curtain goes up. You see a totally black screen—not a screen with nothing on it, but a screen with something...a blackness, that is complete nothing, but which is still something. It is the dung heap of the...not universe, exactly, because that's not a big enough concept, just the dung heap of all. Well, it's not really a dung heap, but just what is, when there is no light. Yeah, that's it. Look, light requires energy to exist. Darkness is the absence of light. Darkness requires nothing to be. Okay. All is dark. All of a sudden we see a tiny point of light in the middle of the screen. As we watch, it gets bigger and bigger, or maybe we're just zooming in on the light and it only appears to be getting bigger as we close on it. Anyway, we now notice that the point of light is spinning on its axis; around and around it goes. As it spins faster and faster, part of its material is forced out into arms and at the same time, other hidden material is pulled towards the spinning center—God—sitting there in the center like a spider at the center of a web. Or, maybe this isn't God, maybe this is what God has sent to represent God. I don't know."

"Wow, man, you're really going there," said Zack. "Hell, that makes about as much sense about creation as anything I've ever heard, but what about the big bang?"

"The Big Bang may be overrated. Maybe that small pinpoint of light was the Big Bang. Maybe light is matter coming into existence out of non-existence and maybe light is also consciousness coming into being from out of non-consciousness. You know, we keep saying God, but maybe it's all just a natural unfolding and doesn't have anything to do with any sort of God at all."

Gil had been silent for most of this, but now he joined in, "Well, I guess it's how you define God. I mean if we say that God is whatever caused everything to come into existence, and if this talk about the swastika is right, then maybe we worship a swastika. Man, that would be a kick for Jews, wouldn't it?" I had to jump in after Gil said this, because the ideas and thoughts were just tumbling out of us as we drove along the highway.

"I'll bet we're closer to the ultimate answers than most philosophers and religious types. I mean, why the hell not? You know, what the hell do they know that we don't know? They only study what other people have said and add some of that to their beliefs and try to make sense of everything, just as we're doing, and their brains are no different than our brains. Maybe God can only be known by this intuitive type of free-association thinking and not by scientific study. Maybe everything that really matters must be intuited first and only then can it be demonstrated by mathematical models and words. What was it that Gil said about everything being simple and it's only the explanation that is complex? Maybe that's the way it is. If that's the case, then our intuition is as good as anyone else's and we're as much experts on God as anyone else. You know, if there is a God, I bet that He must be more than just the first cause. Suppose, for instance, that there really was a Big Bang? Maybe that was like a bomb set off by God to get things moving. If this is true, then God is the one behind the Big Bang. God must mean intelligence, but not just intelligence, cosmic intelligence—consciousness. Now, if God is intelligence, how does he manage it without a brain? Is he more like a computer? Maybe the intelligence that is God is like a Will O' the Wisp, first here, then there, with no time passing in between. You know, if you make a hologram and smash it, every little bit of the hologram will have the complete picture—not just a part of the picture, but the whole damn thing?"

"Is that true?" asked Gil.

"Damn right," I said.

"It does? asked Zack. "Man, that doesn't make any sense to me at all. How can that be?"

"Look," I said. "I read about this someplace. It's true. Each part of the hologram will have the whole picture. Anyway, maybe God is like that. He's complete in every tiny or large piece in the Universe. Maybe God exploded and was the Big Bang and maybe he's been expanding outwards complete in every fragment and in touch with every other fragment no matter how large or how small. Maybe that was His plan: To puff himself up like some gigantic balloon, and then explode so that He would be in every molecule that exists. And, not just a part of Him, but ALL of him. Imagine, God complete and whole in every grain of sand, and in every bit of everything that exists. Maybe He then wanted to pull these molecules together so that He could evolve. Maybe God is trapped inside various things that…or pieces of the Big Bang, and can't get out until He evolves a creature with enough consciousness to free Him."

"Pull over, will you Gil, I gotta take a leak," said Zack. Gil quickly pulled over to the shoulder, and Gil went behind some bushes.

"Hey," yelled Gil, "see if it spirals. Maybe God is in you. Set Him free, will you?" So Zack took a leak. Then I did. Then Gil did. We decided to let Zack drive for a while. I rode shotgun as I had when Gil was driving, and Gil quickly went to sleep in the back seat. I didn't know where we were. We just kept driving north. None of us had been paying much attention to the road, because we were so caught up in the conversation. It kind of reminded me of when I was a kid up in Maine and my family lived right on the border with Quebec, for a time, and I used to hang out with my friends in the town square, talking late into the night.

CHAPTER 4

*W*ith Gil asleep, Zack and I just drove on in silence. I thought of New England. To me, it wasn't the place of white steeple churches that you sometimes see on Christmas cards. My New England was a strange, witchy, gritty sort of place of old deserted leather tanneries and mills and factories that were hard by the many streams and small rivers which had been used for many years as places to dump the chemicals used in the various manufacturing processes. The river beds had absorbed so many of these chemicals—mostly tannic acid—that they had a permanent stink to them. It was an unmistakable smell, that was slightly acrid and sharp. It wasn't pleasant, but it wasn't anything that would make you hold your nose. Many of these streams were close to and were fed by the Atlantic ocean so that they would periodically fill and then drain with the tides as the fresh water mixed with the salty ocean water. There, life adapted, and filled the niche. It was different from the ocean and it was different from the river. Life of one type or another flourished like life seemed to flourish in all other niches. Life adapted and used whatever was at hand, and the life that grew in this niche was similar to, but different from the life of once identical life forms, that had not adapted. When the tide was high, the smell wasn't so bad, but when it went out and exposed the oozing muck, the stink was there again. Actually, I've smelled far worse. This smell was of chemicals; artificial things, and perhaps that's why they weren't so bad. It's kind of like the way one almost likes the smell of gasoline and even some diesel fuel fumes. There was something clean in these smells, unlike the natural smell of skunk cabbage or of rotting bodies—and I've smelled a few of each in my day. I've smelled death, and it has a sweet sickly smell that stays with you forever, so once you smell it, if you ever smell it again, you know that death is nearby. And even in the corpses that have the smell, there is new life teeming. So, in a way, the unnatural man made smells are often better than the natural smells of living things decaying. But, I said it was a witchy sort of place and maybe that needs a little explaining. You see, the place had a feel of something old and basic that had lived there for millions of years. Perhaps, it lived in the granite that was underneath the dirt. I know that sounds weird, but there was something about the rocks of that place. It was only after I left that I realized these feelings about the rocks. I hadn't thought about this for years. Maybe the talk of the Wizard of Oz earlier, had jarred my subconscious. Now, I was starting to feel a little eerie as I did when I was a kid and walked through a little wood on the way to school. I can distinctly remember feeling that something or someone was watching me. I know that many people have had the same sensation but, somehow, I think this was different. It was like there was something really there, but always just a step out of sight. No matter where I would look, this thing would just be gone. It was kind of like a quantum ghost. My very act of looking made whatever was there, not be there. Maybe that was where I got this idea of God as some sort of Will O' the Wisp.

There was more to that place than met the eye. Things that now seem odd, but which were just part of everyday life and seemingly normal, now seem abnormal. Take the cats. There were cats everyplace. It seemed that no house could be without cats. And, the cats were all big and well fed and they sat on old ladies laps all the time as the old ladies would sit on their porches and watch people go back and forth. Always watching. Old ladies and their cats. Then there was the green. There was green life growing out of every crack in every building when spring came. One could imagine why the other England, the real England, had myths of a Green Man who came in the spring when the snows melted, who made everything green, because that's the way it had been in my New England. Smelly rivers. Deserted factories. Cats. Greenery. I then remembered the Cat Nip Man. Every year, the town would be visited by this old guy who looked like a homeless skinny Santa Claus who was moonlighting in the off season. Anyway, this dirty old guy with a full white beard and all dressed in burlap rags with a rope around his waist, would come into town and go door to door selling little burlap bags of catnip, which he would take out of his great big dirty brown burlap Santa bag that was slung over his shoulder. With all the cats around the place, you can bet he sold a lot of the stuff. So, the town would have streets full of stoned cats for a while, and then the catnip would lose its strength and the cats would end up back on the laps of the old ladies, and the old ladies would be sitting on their porches watching. Always watching. There was something about the Cat Nip Man in my memory that seemed familiar to me, but I couldn't remember what it was. Maybe I had to think of these old things in the back of my mind in order to know where I was going and what I was really looking for. Maybe I'd already found what I was looking for and passed it by. Man, wouldn't that be a kicker? Maybe what I wanted all along was way back there in New England. Nah. That's just too simple, and that's the stuff of movies. It's like that story of the guy who went around the world looking for diamonds and then when he returned home he found the world's biggest diamond in his backyard. That's just a little too cutesy for reality. You expect to be told that story by some guy who's your new best friend who has gleaming eyes, a too big smile, and slicked back oily hair, just before he shouts "Hallelujah, Brother, Praise the Lord."

No, whatever it was that I was searching for wasn't that easy to find.

CHAPTER 5

*W*e hurtled on down the road in silence, and then Gil woke up in the back seat and we started talking about all sorts of things again. After a while, I took the back seat to get a little sleep and Gil took my seat. Man, with the sunroof permanently open, there was a cold breeze and it was interesting to look up at the stars.

"Do you guys think, there's life out there?" I asked.

"Maybe," said Zack.

"I don't know. What do you think, Alex?" asked Gil. Now, Gil should know by now to never ask me what I thought about anything, because it just pushed my non-stop talking button and I'd go off down a new mental track with bits and pieces of things I'd learned or read or heard about over the years and kind of string them all together in different ways and sometimes I'd even sound half-smart to those who were either uncritical or who hadn't this gadfly's knowledge of odds and ends that I had. So, I told them that I thought that there was life in outer space and that we had been visited here on Earth many times. I told them that I thought religion was mixed up with space aliens. Just then, we passed a cow pasture. "You know," I said, "I've got this theory that we came to this planet from another one. It was colder and the sun wasn't as bright."

"Who's we?" asked Zack.

"I mean white people," I replied.

"Why white people?" piped in Gil.

"Because that's just the way it is. Look, I know you're thinking that just because I tell you this that you think I don't like other people. Well, forget it. Just listen to this and see if it makes any sense to you. It could be that Earth really is the planet of the apes. Now, you know that many scientists say there is a missing link; that evolution took a jump or a giant step. They can't explain it. Suppose the aliens came here and mated with the apes. Further suppose that for some reason, this produced viable offspring. The children of these matings were in between the aliens and the apes. They were us.

"Us? I know I've read stuff like this," said Gil, "maybe we all think thoughts like this but unlike you, most of us just know that everyone else thinks these things so we don't have to trot them out as though we've just thought of something brilliant."

"Wait a minute, Gil, I haven't finished," I said. "Here's where my theory gets different from anything you've probably heard or read before. Suppose that the aliens had to leave their world, or were dying, and wanted to preserve their genes on this backward planet, even if they had to preserve them in a watered down state, in the hope that someday there might be throwbacks who would possess more of their genetic material, or maybe in the hope that someday, the alien genes would be able to be extracted from their human hosts and the aliens could recreate themselves as they themselves truly are? See, humans may be the walking incubators and repositories of aliens. We may harbor aliens hidden away in our genetic material in a dormant state, just waiting to be reborn.

Suppose the aliens also took their mixed children away from the lands of the apes, lest further mating might cause the offspring in succeeding generations to devolve back to ape hood. So, they moved away from the warm lands to the cold lands of Northern Europe, where there was still plenty of ice. Now, how would they have their children achieve the population numbers needed to survive? Maybe, they could implant the embryos in cattle. The cattle would be natural incubators and had the added advantage of being able to be driven to different places all the while carrying the children of the aliens. When the children were born, they had milk from the cattle to sustain them, and when they got older, they could eat the cattle, and use the skin and other parts of the cattle for clothes and other things.

"Where did you get this idea?" asked Gil

"Well, it just kind of popped into my head, almost full blown. You know, in India cattle are allowed to wander free into and out of homes. The people won't eat them, because they're considered to be sacred. There's also the ancient Norse myth that the first man was licked out of the ice by a cow.

"Wait a minute," said Gil. "You just talked about India. People from India aren't white, and they don't live in Northern Europe."

"Right. However, what happened was that India was conquered by the Aryans back in pre-history. These Aryans are thought to have come to India from Iran. Did you know that "Iran" means the land of the Aryans? Anyway, before they came to Iran they came from further north.

"Hold on," said Gil. "Those are Arabs in Iran, I've seen them wearing towels on their heads."

"Nope. Sorry, Gil. Iranians aren't Arabs. They're Aryans. You may have it confused because most Iranians are Muslims and wear clothing that you also see on Arabs, but they're a different people. Look, let me finish this thought. White skin is an evolutionary adaptation to places with little sunlight. The white skin allows in more sun than does darker skin, and this is needed for the body to produce the necessary amounts of Vitamin D. Did you ever see a really pale white person? You can see their blood vessels beneath the skin. That helps with the production of Vitamin D. It also makes them prone to bleeding easier than people with dark skin, and also causes them to blush, which is just the blood vessels opening up and putting more blood in the face. That means that white people are adapted to places with little sunlight. Also, I bet you don't know that white people are really a very small percentage of humans on Earth. More than 90% of all humans aren't white. Now, if we had been here since the start of humanity, you'd think we might be a larger percentage of the population, wouldn't you?

"Here's something else. You know how in the Bible it says that some of the earliest descendants of Adam and Eve lived to be a thousand years old or something like that? Well, I think white people are devolving, and the Bible is sort of a log of that, among other things. I think white people were once closer to the space aliens. But because of original sin—mating with the ape creatures—they fell from grace and were sent out of the Garden of Eden. Do you follow? No? Well, look, if there is life on some other planets, it probably isn't in our solar system. It could be…wait a minute…let me correct myself. I actually think that we'll find life of some sort on almost every planet we visit. It may be bacteria or single celled or worms or something like that, but I think we'll find life. What I'm talking about is humanoid life—life that is similar to us. Some sort of bipedal creature. Now, if I'm right, and these space aliens live outside our solar system, it would probably take them a long time to get here. This might indicate that they live a lot longer than we do. Say they live to fifteen hundred years before they kick the bucket. So, if it takes them six hundred years to get here, so what? They've still got 900 years left to live.

Zack, looked at me and said, "What about time travel? Maybe they just used time travel to get here, or something like that?"

"I don't think so, man," I said. "Maybe we'll keep driving long enough to get into that, but I think time travel is impossible. I think it's easier to just posit the notion, you know, a theory, that the space aliens, if they exist, just live very long lives, by our standards.

"You know Alex, I don't mean to be harsh," said Zack, "but you sound a little pompous with all this. It's almost as though you're saying that you're going to honor us with your thoughts on time travel.

Golly, gee, Alex, we can hardly wait as we sit at the feet of the great master."

"You're right, Zack," I said. "I apologize. I didn't mean to sound that way. I think I was really just talking to myself, but out loud. It's like the ideas flow easier when they're out there floating."

"Look," said Gil, "I didn't take what Alex said like that at all. I'm really enjoying this. Zack you don't know Alex that well, or you'd understand that he just babbles on like that. He wasn't preaching to us. Sometimes, he even manages to say something that is original, or at least something I haven't heard before."

"Yeah. It's like monkeys in a room with typewriters and no time limit," I said.

So we kept driving north, always staying as close to the ocean as possible. So long as the ocean was to our left, we figured we were going in the right direction. We were sort of going to Alaska, if the gas money supplied by Zack, held out, but we weren't really going anyplace and we didn't have to be where we weren't really going at any particular time. Ours was just a fuzzy destination.

But, isn't that the way it is with all living things? Anyway, we could as easily be sitting back in a coffee shop in San Francisco and having this conversation. Well, then again, maybe not. Maybe it was the old VW bus and the purposeless, purposeful driving that held this together for us. Maybe this was like motorcycles for motorcycle gangs. The rationale for being together was the bikes and it was those that held it together but, in truth, the bikes were just an excuse for the camaraderie. I guess the same thing could be said of golf. So, maybe this trip was that sort of thing. I felt good about this. Before, I had almost always traveled alone from this to that place, and I always thought that having someone else along would screw things up, but this was different. Perhaps we were kindred spirits or perhaps we shared the same mental problems. Who knows? All I know is that it was fun talking to these guys. Something about them helped me open up. I hadn't even realized I had so many opinions on so many different subjects or that I could actually contribute something different to a conversation about things for which I certainly was no expert.

Maybe people who have said that we never really forget anything; we just can't retrieve it from our brains, are right. Maybe there was something about this time, this place, this trip, these companions that caused me to spontaneously retrieve things I didn't know that I knew. I suddenly panicked as I realized that I might actually be thinking some things that should be in a book, and that if we suddenly stopped the trip, I'd forget everything, and it would be lost.

"Gil, do you have a pen," I asked. He gave me one and I started writing on scraps of paper, maps, anything I could find. Now, I was getting obsessive about this so I told Gil to pull over at a drug store we were passing, and I went in and bought 6 spiral bound notebooks, college ruled on both sides of each page, with 70 pages in each one. I figured that even with my constant writing, that this would give me 852 pages, if I included the inside front and back covers of the notebooks, and that this would be adequate for our trip. As I got back to the bus, I could hear the radio playing some song or other.

"Hey, the radio cleared up," said Gil, "as I approached the passenger door." I opened the door and got in and suddenly the static started again.

"What the hell's the matter with this stupid radio?" asked Gil.

Although we weren't exactly oohing and aaaahing about the ocean to our left, it was subliminally pleasant as we drove along. Then someplace up in Mendocino, U.S. 1 turned inland and merged with U.S. Highway 101, which was a hell of a lot less scenic, but much straighter than U.S. 1.

We were someplace north of Eureka, I think, when we decided to pull off the road in some scrub and get some sleep. The area was covered with dry, fine dirt and small bushes. We drove the bus behind some of the bushes where it couldn't be seen from the street. Gil got out to take a leak, and as soon as he was out of the bus, the radio started playing music again. "Hey, I said, have you guys noticed the radio seems to work only when there are two of us in the bus? When there are three, all we get is static." So, we fooled around with that concept for a while. First all three of us would get in, and we got static. Then one of us would get out, and we had music. Then we'd change seats and try the whole thing over again. It didn't matter which of us was out or where he had been sitting before getting out, any time there were three of us inside, we got static. Finally, we just decided that's the way it had to be and we each jumped into our sleeping bags and immediately went to sleep.

CHAPTER 6

$\mathcal{M}$orning came with a drizzle and the not unpleasant smell of farms and fields. We got back in the bus and headed up the road to a fast food restaurant where we went in and cleaned up in the men's room. Then we had a couple of their breakfast sandwiches, some cups of coffee and hit the road again. I guess we were about 200 miles out of Frisco, maybe more, before we let our hair down and called San Francisco by that name that is so hated in San Francisco.

"You know," said Zack, we're not making very good time, but I think we're starting to get closer to Oregon than we are to Frisco."

"Yeah," said Gil. "Screw you Frisco." He seemed to savor calling it that.

"Yeah, to hell with Frisco," I said. Then there was a silence that suddenly came over us. It's like we didn't really want to keep on going, but none of us wanted to say that. Somehow, the trip wasn't as much fun since we ran out of PCH, and got on the freeway. I finally brought up the subject after a few miles of silence. I was actually missing Carla and started getting an aching feeling about it. "You know, I don't think I want to keep going north. How about you guys? Do you really want to go to Alaska? The place is cold, man. Maybe we should just go back down to Frisco. What do you think? I mean, if you guys want to keep going on, I'll just get out and hitch my way back to Frisco."

"Yeah," said Gil. "I kind of miss the city."

"You know what," said Zack, "I don't think I really want to go to Alaska after all. Do you guys mind if I just tail along with you. I mean, I know you gave me this ride with the idea that I'd be getting out when you decided to go in a different direction, but I don't really have anyone or anything in Alaska, or anyplace else either." Gil and I just glanced a question at each other. Zack seemed to be a pretty good guy, and when it was just Gil and me, there seemed to be something missing. With Zack, there was a roundness or completeness. Naturally, this got me to thinking about personalities and the like. Could it be that Gil and Zack and I were all what the psychologists might call inadequate personalities, and by that they meant that the person was lacking something. Maybe that's what we were, something that had been broken into thirds and which was incomplete except when all three pieces were together. I don't know, but I know that my mind was racing at a million miles a second, and the thoughts were just cascading over me. I was almost wondering if I was getting some kind of contact high from some drugs that Zack might have taken. It was weird. It's not as though I was hallucinating. It's just that I seemed creative or something. So, I kept furiously scribbling in the note books I had bought.

"You ever sell any of your writing?" asked Zack

"What, and ruin my amateur status?" I asked. "Hell, if you set out to write for money, then you're not really writing from your soul. You're just a draftsman, putting lines on the paper. Have you seen the number of books that are published all the time now? I mean, it's not like the old days where everything was so expensive and slow that what went into print. was often pretty good. Now, people are churning out the most incredible trash. Now, you're probably thinking to yourself, 'What does he mean by trash?'" Well, I'll tell you. To me, trash is stuff that offers no insights. Trash gives no new ideas or opinions. Trash is writing that just rolls around like water that can't go down the drain…hey, there's that swastika stuff again. It's just throat clearing drivel.

I knew this woman who had taken an expensive writing course from some big time mucky muck New York writer who had published a bunch of crap, and who used his published status to sell himself as a writing coach. She gave me five or six pages she had written and, man, I couldn't read it. I mean literally. It was ponderous. It was trite. It was mannered. It was all constipated stuff that just didn't flow. I tried to read it, but every word seemed to have been so carefully chosen that it had no rhythm, or spontaneity…I like writing that rushes forward like a speeding train. Then, even when it does some cliche thing like stop to smell the roses, it does so full speed ahead. But, maybe this woman liked her own writing, and maybe that's the way it is with all writers. I just write what I want to write, even if it's not commercial. I guess I really write for myself, and I try to put down my ideas of the big questions. You know, the philosophers are always talking about finding answers to the big questions. Things like, why are we here? What is the purpose of existence if there is a purpose? What happens when we die? Is there a God? those sorts of things."

"So, in other words," you've never sold anything?

"Yeah," I said.

"You know, said Gil. When I talk to straights I know, they wonder where I went wrong. They're going off to fancy office buildings every day, and they're wearing three piece suits and making good money. They have the American Dream. I don't scorn them or laugh at them, but I do feel pity for them. It's as though they haven't really seen the way it all is. One is born, one lives, one dies. These people I know, and they're good people, don't get me wrong, are just living ant like lives. They don't get it. I think we have more purpose in what we're doing and how we're living than they do. Now, I think if these people had a chance to get incredible wealth so that they could do what they really want to do, then maybe that would be okay. The problem is that they don't have such a chance. They'll make their living at 9 to 5 jobs, but they'll never get out of the rut."

"Yeah. You've got that right, Gil," I said.

"I'll tell you what I think is sad," said Gil. "All the white people working at these 9 to 5 jobs are just building things that are going to be inherited by people unlike them."

"What do you mean?" asked Zack.

"Well," said Gil, "take those things that Alex said earlier about white people being a small minority on this planet, and look at inter-marriage rates, migration patterns, low white birthrates and you start to see that there may be no future for white people on this planet. In fact, it's a desolate future that leads to extinction. They are like lab rats running around on one of those little wheels thinking they're getting someplace, but they're not. It's kind of like in my mind I can see a white guy leaving an office over here or over there or a white woman leaving her house or her car, and as these white people do so, they hand their keys over to a brown person who then takes over for them, and then the white person just evaporates and is gone."

We were all silent for a few minutes.

Then, apparently to break the silence, Zack said, "You know, you might not know it to look at me, but I have a law degree."

"You're a lawyer?" asked Gil.

"Yeah. But, I never practiced much, though. It was just one of those things. I was working in a car lot to make some extra money and I heard someone say that in California, you could study law part time. So, I checked it out and it was true. There were a few colleges like that in the state that offered law degrees that qualified you to be a lawyer. So, I signed up for one, figuring I'd try it for a year and then quit it. You see, in these kind of schools, the state requires that you take the Baby Bar at the end of the first year to see if you have any possibility of ever actually practicing law. So, I took the Baby bar and son-of-a-gun, I passed the damn thing. Anyway, after I got over my shock, I just kept studying and finally got a degree. When it was time to take the regular Bar exam a guy told me that he thought there was something going on to allow more blacks and Mexicans to pass the exam. He said he figured that's why there was a written portion of the test that almost always had problems that blacks and Mexicans might answer one way and whites another way, and that this would tip off those grading the exam who was who. When I took the exam, there were these two long parts that had enough points between them to help one make up for being deficient in other areas. One of them was about a tenant being bounced out of his apartment because he was a minority, and the other was about a minority community wanting to stop redevelopment. I pretended I was black and poor and that those who were on the other side of the issue were rich white guys and I wrote from that perspective. Anyway, whether the guy was right or not, I passed. I often joke now that I'm trying to find a part time medical school so I can become a brain surgeon. I know a guy who couldn't get into any medical schools up here, so he went to one down in Mexico. That's where he still is. He's delivering babies and getting paid in chickens."

"Mexico," said Gil, "I wonder if he's seen any babies that were born to those girls who do those donkey shows. You know, the ones where they have sex with donkeys? Do you think they can get pregnant that way?'

"Get serious, Gil. You know that won't work," replied Zack.

"I'm not so sure," I said. "I think it's possible for different species to mate and bear offspring. No, really. I mean isn't a mule the offspring of a donkey and a horse? Those are different species."

"Yeah, but aren't the offspring always sterile," asked Zack.

"Most of the time they are, but not always," I said. Anyway, that misses the point which was that different species can successfully mate. The point I'm making is that I bet cross species mating and birthing is not as rare as we're led to believe. There are certain monkeys of different species that can mate and have offspring with monkeys of other species. It also happens with cats and rabbits and various other species."

"So, you're saying that donkeys and taco belles can have children together?" said Zack, laughing.

"Maybe, if all the conditions are just right. Maybe that's how we got all the strange creatures in mythology. Here's something that you may not know. Did you know that Chimpanzees are closer genetically to humans than they are to the Great Apes? Maybe it's possible for chimps and humans to have babies. Chimps are about 98.7 per cent the same as humans in their genes."

"I'll bet there are certain blood types that are more accepting of other species' sperm. Sort of a universal egg or sperm or something. Maybe it's rare, but even now they don't really know everything about blood," said Gil.

"Yeah, I said. It wasn't too many years ago that they discovered the Rh factor in blood. And what about the Duffy Factor—that most white people have and most non-white people don't have? Besides, remember we were talking about my idea that we came here from another planet and that we were carried around in cattle? Well, how come it's mostly blacks who are allergic to milk? Maybe that means that they really were natives of this planet. You know, cattle weren't even in America when it was discovered. They were imported. Maybe cattle were brought here from off-world too." I was starting to get on a roll again, when Zack interrupted me, "Yeah, and Duck Billed Platypuses and this and that and the other. Look, you can play this what if game forever, and you can find facts to fit any theory you come up with. You know, the best way to eliminate possibilities is still Occam's Razor. It goes something like this: the explanation that fits all the known facts and is the simplest explanation, is the one you accept. Or, something like that. It means that if that car up in front of us suddenly disappears, we can imagine that it was swallowed up by the earth; eaten by a dinosaur, beamed up to a space ship, or maybe it just went around a corner and out of our line of sight. It may be fun to speculate endlessly on this, but, ultimately, we have to come up with answers that make sense. So it is, with all this talk about babies in cows and donkeys and women having babies together. I mean, it's alright to talk among ourselves about these things, because we're friends and we're just jamming, but it's important that we don't fixate on these things. That way, lies madness. So, let's try to be practical. Imagination is great, but unless it has some discipline, it loses its appeal. I mean, anyone of us can imagine all sorts of things, but if we don't have a sense of discipline, then we're just throwing in everything including the kitchen sink and saying, "Look at me, I'm so clever. Why, just look at what I imagined."

"You know Zack," said Gil, "maybe you should start practicing law. No, no, I mean it in a good sense. You look like a homeless guy, but your mind seems pretty logical. Maybe that's why you're a good complement to Alex and me. This really is like the Wizard of Oz. Each of us lacks something that we're trying to find. The problem is that we don't really know what it is we lack, so we don't know what we're trying to find. It could be that all we're looking for is to be comfortable; whatever that might mean to each of us. So we drove on down the 101 heading back to San Francisco, which is what we called the city as we got closer lest we show disrespect for that foggy drag queen of a city with its ancient cable cars, aging hippies and senior citizen beatniks. We went through Ukiah, grabbed some tacos at a local joint and kept on moving. When we got down around Geyserville, we stopped at the Russian River and swam for a while. There were some nudists hanging out there and some of the nudist girls were pretty. So, we stayed a while. We even gave out our addresses, such as they were, to a couple of the girls. Actually, the girls told us that they weren't real nudists. Their parents were old hippies who had come up here from San Francisco years ago after the Haight started getting weird and street criminals started moving in to take advantage of the peaceful flower children. They finally settled up here. So, these were the progeny and remnants of the flower children, just as we three were maybe remnants of something else that we couldn't put our fingers on. I kind of envied the latter day hippies at the river, because they had an identity and they knew what they were. They had an excuse for being as they were and doing what they did. We three didn't.

This started me thinking about all the sub-cultures in this country. All little nations. There were the hippies. The bikers. The Muslims. The Black Muslims. The Latinos. The born again Christians. The laborers. The office workers. The government bureaucrats. The lawyers. It went on and on and on. All little subcultures. All with their own ways and mores, and even their own lexicons. All of these identity groups had their own ways of looking at the world and their own ways of addressing life's problems. I guess none were either right or wrong and that you couldn't really use those terms to define them.

Then you came to the three of us. I was obsessed with defining us, or at least me, and in defining me, see if anyone else rallied around and was also like me. Sometime, I guess I should take stock of what I am and what I like to do; not when I'm trying to impress others, like putting on a certain kind of music because I might want someone to think that I have the attributes of those who like that particular kind of music.

"Zack," I said, "why do you think blacks are better boxers than whites?"

"I dunno. A way out of the ghetto, I guess," he replied.

"No. It's physical. It's genetic. They have thicker bones. In the face, the jaws are bigger and thicker and the nerves in the chin are more protected. That's why it's harder to knock them out in boxing. Also, they have quicker reflexes and a longer Achilles tendon that gives them an advantage in foot speed. Also, their skin cuts less easily than white skin because whites have their blood vessels closer to the surface. It's all an evolutionary thing. Animals who evolved in hotter climates evolved differently than animals that evolved in the cold. Both climates required different survival mechanisms. It's like we were talking about before, white skin was needed in the north to let in the dim sun. Black skin was needed in the south to keep out the sun. I wouldn't mind training a good white fighter though, to test my theories on this. I bet I could train a white fighter to beat most blacks.

"How?"

"Well, you have to take advantage of the other guy's weaknesses. The white fighters often treat black fighters like white fighters, and this is their basic mistake. Call it an ignorance born of all the phony anti-racism bogus truths of our day. What would knock a white out, may not even phase a black fighter." Gil was starting to get interested in this conversation.

"How would you train a white fighter?" asked Gil.

"First, I'd tell him that the rules and training of boxing, favor blacks. This is so, because boxers are taught that the way to knock out an opponent is to hit him on the point of the chin with a right cross. As I just said before, that works against whites, but it's not such a good technique to use against blacks, unless the black has a lot of white blood. I'd tell the white fighter that he needs to fight dirty if he wants to win, and that he needs to be able to do this without the referee seeing what he's doing. Blacks are susceptible to punches to two areas of their bodies. One is a punch to the veins in the neck. A white boxer has to give rabbit punches to the side of the neck of the black boxer just below the ears. The second weak spot is the heart. A white fighter has to give hard punches to his black opponent's heart area. The problem is that these two areas are so weak on most blacks that you can kill a black by striking these areas, easier than you can kill a white. Boxing isn't supposed to be about killing. Now, as to how the blows are delivered. Remember, that blacks have quicker reactions, so if you start to throw a punch, he's already seen it coming and is moving out of the way very fast, while throwing a counter punch at you. So, here's what you do. You throw, say, a right cross aimed at the chin, then immediately, without thinking, throw a left hook to the neck below his right ear. Chances are he would have been moving to your left to avoid the right cross, and he'll move his head right into your left hook which will increase the impact of the punch. The key to this is that the second punch—the left hook—must be thrown without thinking or looking. that's how you overcome the quicker reaction time. If you simply throw the right cross and then wait to see the reaction before throwing the left hook, it won't work. It's gotta be, BOOM, BOOM.

Now, we also have to be scientific about this and look at nature and use our strengths as well as the weaknesses of the opponent. Whites usually have shorter arms and legs than blacks. Why? It's evolution again. Shorter arms and legs help white people stay warm in cold weather. Longer arms and legs help blacks stay cool in hot weather. So, whites, with shorter arms usually have to fight blacks from the inside. This is counterintuitive to kids just learning to box, because they don't want to get hit, so they stay outside. Big mistake because they get hit more out there because of the longer black arm length. A longer armed black will just pick him off. the best thing to do is get right in on the inside, then your short piston like white arms can pound away at his heart while he harmlessly flails away with his arms over your shoulders and behind your back.

Remember Rocky Marciano, the only undefeated heavyweight in modern boxing history? The guy was short and had short arms, but he'd get on the inside and he'd punch so hard with those stubby, ugly, short arms that I've heard reports that he would sometimes paralyze an opponent's arm with one punch. By all rights, you'd never believe that Rocky was any kind of boxer, let alone the world champ. Man, if I were a trainer and this little pug came in and said that he wanted to fight, I'd probably tell him to forget it before he got hurt."

"So, if you know so much about boxing, how come you haven't trained anyone?" asked Zack.

"I never had the opportunity. And, besides who would believe me? I'm not a professional at boxing. But, if I ever get a chance to be close to some good white boxers, I'm going to tell them what I've just told you."

"How do you know about this heart and neck stuff?" asked Gil.

"I just put two and to together from things I've read and heard about over the years. Look, why do you think most police departments outlawed the sleeper hold?"

"I dunno."

"Because blacks were dying from it. Cops would tackle a criminal, throw their arms around the guy's neck and tighten it if he fought back. If the bad guy was black, it'd just take a few minutes and he'd be dead. When they applied the same hold and pressure to whites, there was usually no long range effect. I mean it's kind of like boxing is rigged against whites by nature. While whites are generally stronger in the neck area than blacks, punches to that area aren't allowed. And, in the chin area, where whites are weaker than blacks, punches are allowed. In a society that isn't all white, whites are at a disadvantage in a boxing ring under the present rules. Now, in a street fight, put your money on a good rough and tumble white street fighter, who knows the truth of what I just said, because he'll usually win, provided he hasn't been neutered into not wanting to win against blacks for fear that this would constitute racism This is so, because if he's smart, he'll fight from his own strengths and use the other guy's natural weaknesses."

"Man, that sounds like bullshit," said Gil.

"No. I think it's true. Look, for about the past 40 or so years our government and others have had this agenda to minimize racial differences in people's minds in order to break down racial lines. I think what they're trying to do is create a Tan Everyman."

"Huh? Where do you come up with this stuff Alex?" asked Zack with an odd look on his face.

"I read a lot," I replied. "I guess I just connected up the dots. Anyway, here's what I think has been going on. The government, or parts of the government, or scientists, or whoever, have decided that if the races stay separate, that eventually we'll have a race war. So, to head it off, they've been trying to get us all to mix and mate so that we all have some genes of every other group and then we can't feel any allegiance to any particular race. It's like the melting pot, but instead of the old 19th Century melting pot which just had various Europeans thrown in to melt away various national differences—which were mostly artificial anyway—the new melting pot is including all the races so that what is melting is genotypes.

One problem in getting people to do this, is that if blacks and whites and yes, yellows, reds and browns all look at each other and notice many differences, then the people themselves may not mix and mate, but may segregate themselves. They may remain like with like. So, whoever is behind this mixing and mating has been engaged in a non-stop propaganda campaign to try to convince everyone that there are no racial differences that matter. They want everyone to think that all people are like, say, identical Bucks coming off the assembly line, and then almost as an afterthought some are painted one color and some another. In this view, nothing under the hood is different. So they try to tell everyone that all humans are almost genetically the same when the genes are checked. The problem with that argument is pointed out with the thing about chimps that we spoke about. Chimps are virtually identical to humans in their genes also, but the tiny 1.3% difference in genes between chimps and humans makes all the difference in the world.}

"So you're saying," said Zack, "that nature always works with tiny little differences and these tiny little differences result in major differences when expressed?"

"Right," I said.

"Maybe," said Gil, "it's like shooting a rifle. If you jiggle the rifle just a tiny bit as you hold it, the bullet will miss the target by a mile.

So, is the tiny jiggle a little thing or a big thing? It's a big thing in its result."

"Well, you shouldn't hate people because of skin color," said Zack.

"Yes, yes. That's it Zack," I said. "You see what you just did? You just repeated back one of the standard propaganda lines. Look at what you just said reflexively, after what we had said. You used the term "hate." We didn't talk about hate at all. We were talking about differences. You also said that the hate was because of 'skin color.' You see, your subconscious mind has bought into the propaganda and your subconscious brought up the concept of hate where it wasn't relevant at all. You know, skin color isn't like paint on a Buick. Skin color in people comes from the inside out. It's an outward manifestation of a whole host of differences that start right at the gene level.

The…call, them assimilationists, don't want you to know about all the differences. Now, it's not that they have to suppress all knowledge about differences, because the complex nature of our world kind of localizes this knowledge so people don't usually see all the differences. And, when they do see them, they fail to connect up the dots. Take basketball teams, for example. Most are all black or nearly so. Why? If you buy the propaganda, it's just a trick of fate or something like that. If you look at the real reasons, however, you'll see it's because blacks have a longer Achilles tendon and various other physical differences. Blacks can run faster, jump higher, and do a few other things better as a group than other groups. It's purely genetic. What about bone marrow transplants? You have to get them from someone of your own race."

"Well we can get blood transfusions from blacks," said Gil.

"Yes, we can. But, I'll bet you that in not too many years that will stop, as scientists discover many differences in the blood that they don't see now. But you know, there's another aspect to this assimilationists strategy. I suspect that those behind it are also trying to cut down on the black crime rate, by watering down black aggressive tendencies with white genes."

Zack looked at me for a minute as though he was thinking about all of this, and then said, "So what's wrong with that?"

"I didn't say that anything was wrong with that—at least not yet. And, besides I guess it depends on your world view. If you think that the way to evolve higher rather than devolve lower is to maximize the differences, then the more differences between the races the better. This would lead to separatism and segregation of some type. If, however, you think that the way to avoid conflicts is for everyone to be the same, then you'd be for assimilation."

"How's that?" asked Zack.

"Well evolution is about a trial and error process. Nature tries this, and then tries that, until something works. But there's more to this than that. Remember we were talking about how God, or nature, shuffles the cards to make different things including animals and plants and stars and planets and everything else in existence? Well, because the shuffle is done with the spiral—if you accept my theory—then all things will have to be logical and in keeping with the spiral. Now, think about it. We don't really have square planets or stars or square trees or square heads. Our universe is a round place. The sprial is a round force. It "wants" everything to be round and those things that aren't round are unnatural or are on their way to being round. If I'm right, we should probably be living in round houses or at least ones with rounded corners to be harmonious with nature. When we cut wood for our houses we take the natural cylindrical trees and plane them flat. Then we take this flat wood and build square houses. It's not natural and is counter to nature.

You know how we have business cycles and war cycles and the like? Well, cycles are just two dimensional representations of the spiral. Think of these various cycles as one of those kids toys made of flat wire in a flexible coil that walk down stairs. Imagine one lying sideways on your floor. It's tube. If you draw it on a piece of paper in two dimensions, you'll end up with just half of the tube. The other side of the tube is there and is as important as the part you see, only you don't see it. That's why predictions often fail. Those looking at the two dimensional graphs don't take into account the other side of the tube, and the forces that cause wars and business ups and downs are like oil running along the wires of the toy. When the oil is on the part that can be seen, predictions are accurate, but when it's in the back, the predictions can be off. Add to the confusion, the fact that it's hard to see the 'oil,' and you can see the difficulty predicting things. If, however, you lay out your graph with the backside of the tube showing as well as the front, you'd get a better record of predicting things."

Gil looked very bored about all this as we drove down the road, until we passed a Mexican market that had one of those pictures of the Virgin of Guadalupe painted on the outside wall of the market "Look at that," he said. "You see that? What does that look like? Never mind, I'll tell you what it looks like. It looks like a pussy. The Virgin is emerging from the cosmic pussy. Look, her head is where the clitoris would be, and her cloak is like pussy lips. It's as plain as the nose on your face. What do you think about that as an example of matter coming into existence? Maybe this works with that spiral or swastika. If you think of the swastika as having a central mouth as with a hurricane or tornado, then it's kind of like this pussy thing. Alex said, as above, so below, so why not as below so above? Maybe we can reason to God by looking at the small things and seeing if they are repeated in some fashion in a bigger sense. So, why can't birthing a baby be...not a metaphor nor a simile, but the way of all creation throughout all of existence, but just smaller and Earth bound? And, if you buy this idea, then maybe God really is a female and not a male."

"Man, I get the idea from listening to our conversation that we're three crazies tethered to the planet with a none too tight bungee cord," said Zack, after Gil had paused for a minute to catch his breath.

"Shit. Maybe that's just your legal training Zack," said Gil, "I've never known a lawyer who was creative in a far out sense. Lawyers are to imagination, what engineers are to quantum physics. Does that make sense? It may not be exactly parallel, but you get the meaning."

"Do you guys ever think about politics," I asked.

"Sure," said Zack. I used to be a Democrat, but now I'm a Republican.

"I'm sort of a libertarian with a small "l" said Gil.

"You know," I said, "when I was in college I was a member of SAF, for a while."

"What's that?" asked Gil.

"Student Americans for Freedom," it was founded by some big time conservatives, who wanted everyone to think that not all conservatives were old. We used to hang out at the college union on Saturday nights wearing suits and ties. I think it was just because we couldn't get dates. Man, cosmic pussy? There wasn't even any Earth pussy for us. We were mostly the nerds on campus, I guess, but our nerdiness was focused on politics. I got fed up with them after a while, because they seemed to slavishly worship a famous conservative and I saw too many of them listening to his every word with a glazed look on their faces. I sort of went toward libertarianism too, just like Gil; you know, with a small "l."

After a while I got tired of the libertarians too. It was too much of the same type that was in SAF. I figure I leaned more toward anarchism than libertarianism."

"You mean like bomb throwing?" asked Zack.

"No. You know that's largely a lie. Most anarchists aren't about throwing bombs, and many of the most intellectual ones aren't for eliminating all government as most people think they are. They just want the smallest possible government and they want it very close to the people."

"Hell, that's what libertarians want too," said Gil.

"Yeah, but here's how I distinguish between libertarians and anarchists. See what you think of this saying I made up. 'Libertarians giggle, anarchists laugh.'"

"I don't get it," said Zack.

"It means that there's a difference in style. Many libertarians are a lot like the SAFers. They look as thought their shoes are too tight or that their underwear itches or something. Anarchists, on the other hand, tend to look wilder and more unkempt or more like working people. I think that libertarians and anarchists have much in common. You know, most people in this country are really ignorant. Not just about politics but about everything. It seems that everyone has an opinion about things that they know nothing about. If you ask the average guy about anarchists, he'll probably tell you about bombs and about how they're communists. Of course, this is absurd. I mean if Bakunin or any of the other famous anarchists could hear this, they'd split their guts laughing. Most of them hated the communists. I think that the anarchists and the communists got mixed up in people's minds because many of them were in Russia and at about the same time, and most of them were running around with those big Russian bushy beards. Anarchists are against a strong central government. They want people to govern themselves right down at the neighborhood and village level, and they figure there's a lot more freedom that way than having some guys far away dictating rules and laws to the local people. Libertarians could buy much of what the anarchists say, but the libertarians are, in my opinion, much too restrained and timid."

"I've never figured out the Nazis," said Gil. "You know anything about them, Alex?"

"They were for socialism like the commies," I said, "but instead of having an international world view and agenda, they were for a national version, whereby the central government of Germany was for Germans only. The commies wanted to centralize and socialize the whole damn world."

"You know," said Zack, "I figure that our government system in this country really sucks. I'd rather have some sort of modified European system where the system didn't effectively shut out all but two major parties. After a while, the two major parties just look like each other and they don't have too much different to say. It just becomes a beauty contest with the most popular candidate winning. And he says about the same thing as the non-winning less popular candidate. I want a system where you have a communist party, a Nazi party, an anarchist party, a libertarian party. a cockroach party and all the other parties that anyone can think up and where if any of these small parties get enough votes, they're able to have some of their members take a seat in congress. With such a system, the extremes in the present two parties would have their own parties, and voters would be given a far greater choice of positions than they are now. The present too parties both pander to the middle, because that's where the most votes are. With many genuine parties, it would be more chaotic, but would also allow many more ideas to find a forum where people in greater numbers could consider them."

"Yeah, but that would lead to chaos," said Gil.

"So what?" replied Zack. "You know it's out of chaos that order comes. You know, I'm coming around to Alex's ideas on the spiral creating everything and of your idea of the cosmic pussy. We need a great shuffling and reshuffling of ideas and concepts and politicians. We don't need this static system we have today, where we eschew central planning as bad and then go ahead and do it anyway, but call it something else. You know, I remember reading somewhere about how scientists put different color dyes or paints or something into a big bucket and swirl it all around so that it's just a mess. After a while, the colors start separating out and make bands of color. It's a self-organizing, sorting out by spiral that is happening. We need this in human affairs. Let everything be swirled around. Let the great card player in the sky shuffle everything as it should be shuffled, and let the cosmic pussy birth star systems. You may ask where the male principle is in this cosmic pussy birth scenario. I reply, Immaculate Conception. As below, so above."

Now, we were all going off in a new intellectual direction. Meanwhile, the bus just kept moving down the road. "You know," I said, "maybe Zack's got something. Maybe men aren't needed. I mean, maybe there is no need for a male principle in creation. Yang and Yin? Why? Maybe there's just a Yang or is it Yin—whichever is the female principle. Maybe males are a mistake made by the cosmic pussy who tried to create drones or soldiers to take care of Her female children, but something went wrong and the drones revolted and took over from the females and said, "You ain't gonna be on top any more babe, assume the missionary position."

CHAPTER 7

*I*t was a little while later when something seemed to click in Zack. He got all wild eyed and excited. "Damn it," he said, "you know I know what I want to do. I think I've found a purpose. It think this cosmic pussy thing might have truth in it. Tornados, whirlpools, hurricanes, water in your sink, pussy. They have a lot in common. They all deliver something. You know, I was just thinking about the cornucopia—you know the Horn of Plenty—that the ancient Greeks or Romans, or whoever, believed would never be emptied? It just kept producing everything out of its mouth. But where did everything come from? There was the mouth. There was the spiraling body. Get that? The spiral again. Then at the end was just a point. A point. Get it? Just like Alex's story of creation starting with a point of light in an otherwise dark universe and from that point all came forth. Man, it's the same thing. The Horn of Plenty was about creation. Something came from…maybe nothing, but maybe from someplace else or maybe all things were gathered up and were transformed and then birthed. You know, we may call it the Cosmic Pussy, to be funny, but this isn't really about sex or even women. It's about God and creation and some of the ultimate questions. When we get back to San Francisco, I'm going to see if I can get some bucks together and buy some camera or video stuff. I figure there must be signs of the cosmic pussy everywhere. Maybe, I'll first go around recording those pictures on the side of Mexican restaurants and markets, and then I'll put them all together with water draining out of toilets and snail shells and stuff like that.

"Yeah, our friend, Zack, pussyologist," said Gil "Zack, you do us proud, man."

"Well, you can laugh at me, but think about the way a woman's body is put together. Her birth plumbing is a lot like the Horn of Plenty. Remember that as above so below and as below so above stuff? Well, maybe the way to find God is through pussy."

"Yeah. I like it," said Gil, "what a great religion."

I suddenly started thinking about evolution and all that again, and since my ideas seemed to be coalescing when I talked to these guys, I asked if they knew that Cro-Magnons and Neanderthals were on the planet at the same time.

"So what? asked Gil.

"Well, I read someplace that Cro-Magnon brains averaged about 1590cc, while modern European brains are in the 1500 cc range, and the Neanderthals had smaller brains than both of these groups. Could it be that the Cro-Magnons interbred with Neanderthals and devolved to modern man?"

"Why not?" said Zack.

I saw that they were interested, so I launched down this road of the mind with a lot of free association stuff. "You know what I said before about chimps and humans being alike, I read someplace that 98.7 percent of human DNA is exactly the same as chimpanzee DNA. This means that all the differences between humans and chimps is contained in only 1.3 percent of our DNA, or something like that. When we go to the zoo and look at the apes and the chimps, we probably think that they're pretty much the same except for size and a few other things. I wonder if chimps are looking back at us and saying, 'Let us out, brother. We're on your side. Why do you have us locked up in here with these wild animals—these apes?' You know, when I think of how close genetically we are to chimps and then I hear people say that we should overlook minor racial differences between the different human races, I wonder if it wouldn't be smarter to actually emphasize the differences. I mean, nature always has minor differences. I really believe, as we said before, that God is the big shuffler in the sky or something like that. His cards aren't even as complicated as a deck of cards that we use in card games, because he only has four different cards in his DNA deck. So He shuffles or plays solitaire with the four different cards made up of just four nucleotides whose names are usually shortened to the letters A,T,C,G. God just shuffles these four letters. That's his deck of cards for creating and changing life. Four card stud, or something. Well, not really four cards, because he has billions and billions of these cards but they all just have the four same letters. He picks them up, say, and lays them down as AATTCGGATCGCC, and whamo, he's just made a worm. Then he takes them up and lays them down as AATTCGGATCGCT, and maybe he's got a frog."

"Ill tell you what bothers me about all this," said Gil, "if we three goof offs riding around in a beat up bus can think all these things, then millions of others may also have thought the same things. So, we're just thinking that we're great thinkers, but we're not. We're just saying obvious things that all these millions of others have already thought."

"Well, you may be right," said Zack, "but, so what? Who cares if we're original or not original? We have as much right to be what we are and to say what we think as anyone else. And, if others have thought these thoughts, so what? Maybe it's just part of the collective unconscious or something. Or maybe we're something new. Maybe through some trick of fate, or maybe it was planned, we're some kind of three pod or something. Three electronic protoplasmic circuits that have never been put together in this way before, and because we are, maybe we're picking up stuff from the collective unconscious. Maybe the bus is like a radio case, and we're the transistors or tubes or whatever the hell is in radios these days, and with only one of us, you have nothing but dead parts. With two, you have the same thing, nothing. But, with the three of us sitting in this bus at this exact time on this exact trip, we have plugged into the collective unconscious or maybe we've actually plugged into God. You know how radio waves are all around us all the time, but how we don't hear them unless we have a properly working radio? Well, maybe God is around us all the time and we can't pick Him up unless we're properly working or unless we have the right fleshly equivalents of tubes and transistors. Maybe, the three of us together are a working radio, so to speak. I know that for some reason I'm enjoying the hell out of this little trip. I haven't been this up and positive for years. It's kind of as though a window shade went up. I feel good about myself. I feel comfortable. I feel energized. I know you guys probably feel the same, because I can sense it."

Gil was right of course, there was something about the three of us that made things work. I'd known Gil before and he was a good friend, but before we met Zack the energy wasn't there as it was now. It was sort of like how certain comedy teams, which are always just two guys, click, and others don't, but with us, we were a three man team. A Three-Pod as Zack had called it. So we continued down the road on our way back to San Francisco, virtually oblivious to our surroundings. This was a trip in the mind. The bus and the road were nothing except the things that kept us together and in touch with each other. It would be difficult to imagine three people sitting around a table for as long as we had been driving, just talking and talking. Surely, someone would have to leave or turn on the television or do something to break the spell. But this bus gave us freedom and movement, and we apparently needed that. I was dreading the end of the trip. At this time, I thought it might be great to be some kind of Lost Dutchman, forever sailing the roads of America, not to see anything, and not to get anywhere, because it was all just a wasteland of sameness working hard to shove everything under the Bell Curve and to conform all genes and religions and politics anyway.

No, it might be nice just to travel to hold the Three-Pod together. Driving and talking endlessly until the end of time. Trying to find meaning in a phenomenal world—a world of material things—when what we were really trying to find was in our minds all along. Or was it? Now, I was thinking of some people's beliefs about the soul being different from the physical body, and how this had led to all sorts of odd religious things.

The Christians think that the body is something evil and that it is to be overcome. I think they're wrong. I think the physical body is needed to have the soul or the spirit as surely as, say, a physical flower, like a rose, is needed to have the scent of that particular flower. In other words, the spirit, or soul, grows from the physical body. It is what the body makes it be, and it cannot exist without a body. It is generated by the body. Perhaps it is both here and there at the same time—I mean, maybe it's partly in this world with us and partly in the world with God. Maybe that's the link between us and God. And, if this is so, then why is our Three-Pod needed to accomplish this?

Why can't just one person make this link to God? Maybe that's why religious people, real religious people, real saints, and not the many phony saints who are named by some churches, are so rare on the Earth. Perhaps the Buddha really was the Buddha and perhaps he found a way to make the link. Perhaps we three have also found a way to make the link but it takes the three of us because individually we're not up to snuff. And, perhaps that is what this is all about. A rolling VW bus radio case temple of God with three transistors inside tuned into the infinite—receiving the God Waves and playing the tunes that we must play.

It is said that before God appears to someone, he makes them mad. Maybe, this isn't the way God wants it to happen, but he's unable to step or shift down his power adequately to touch humans without making them mad. Maybe to God, we're like snow flakes would be to a sentient fire. Every time the fire tried to touch a snowflake, he killed it because of his natural heat. Look at us. Three adults, not on drugs, not on alcohol. All reasonably bright and well educated despite our outside the mainstream life styles, driving around California in a VW bus as though we're some sort of latter day hippies. All the while we're traveling, we're babbling. And, what's more, we believe that our babbling is somehow important and that we've found the secrets of the Universe. Enlightenment in a VW. Well, Buddha found enlightenment under a friggin' tree, so why not in a VW?

CHAPTER 8

❁

*N*ow a new thought popped into my head. "Avatar," I shouted out.

"What?" said Zack.

"Avatar. Maybe one of us is an Avatar, you know, someone who is kind of a pre-God who comes down to the Earth in human form and touches everyone he meets with something special. Maybe one of is an Avatar. Maybe we're on the wrong track with this Three-Pod stuff. Are either of you two an Avatar?"

"Nope. Not me," said Zack.

"Me neither," said Gil. "How about you? You've been the one coming up with all these ideas. If any one of us is an Avatar, it must be you."

"Well," I replied, "I wonder if an Avatar knows he's an Avatar or whether he just forgets he's a God in human form. I sure don't feel like any Avatar. And, besides, does an Avatar descend into someone else's body that is already being used, or does he get born as a baby and grow to adulthood?"

"Man," said Zack, "there's that Cosmic Pussy again, birthing a God." He was serious and not mocking. He was really taken with this concept of the Cosmic Pussy.

"You know, Zack," I said, "you're going to have to clean up that designation a little if you're going to do a book that will sit on coffee tables. Maybe you should start thinking along the lines of calling it the Cosmic Vagina."

"Yeah. Maybe. But, then again, maybe not. I'm gonna keep it as the Cosmic Pussy for now, but you may be right in the long run."

"So anyway, "I continued, "maybe one of us is an Avatar and whichever one it is, just doesn't know it. It could be that the Avatar-hood stayed dormant until something happened and then a switch went on to activate the Avatar genes or cells or circuits or whatever. You know, I think it's going to rain."

"Rain? Don't be ridiculous. There isn't a cloud in the sky," said Gil. Just then, some clouds showed up and it started to rain, much to the amazement of Gil and Zack. You'd better believe that in context of the conversation that we were having that they were asking if I was the Avatar and such for quite a few miles. How did I know it was going to rain? I dunno. I've always had a sense about weather, but that hardly makes me an Avatar. Still, it was fun to be thought to be one for a few miles.

"I wonder if women need these kind of excuses to sit around and talk?"said Zack. You know, there's something kind of unmasculine about just saying, "Hey guys let's all sit around the table and talk tonight." It's too passive and feminine. I think men need physical activity while they're talking, or at least something beyond the mere act of talking. Men need excuses to talk. Some guys play cards or watch sports. I can't imagine guys who do that, ever talking about these things, though. Can you hear the conversation over the card table" 'Hit me Al. And, by the by, did you ever read Nietzsche?' Hell, you'd soon lose those friends."

"I read Nietzsche," said Gil, "but I didn't understand him at all. What the hell is Thus Spake Zarathustra supposed to be about, any-way? Do you know, Alex?"

"Of course he does," said Zack.

I wondered if I was starting to rub on these guys as being a know it all, but I decided to answer anyway. "Well, I know a little about that book," I said, "But maybe I'm wrong. Anyway, I figure Nietzsche was talking about the coming of the Ubermensch—the Overman—in English. This is often translated as the superman, but the term superman seems to have a somewhat different connotation in English, than in German, at least ever since the Superman comics and movies. I mean Nietzsche wasn't talking about some guy running around in tights and flying or anything like that. The Ubermensch was the next evolutionary step for mankind. The most telling line in the book, is where Nietzsche has Zarathustra say that Man is a rope over the abyss, or something like that. In other words, man is a bridge to the higher man. He is not the end of evolution. On one side of the abyss is lower man, and on the other is the higher man—well, wait a minute, not the higher man exactly, because the Ubermensch leaves the higher man behind. I think there's a lot of misconceptions about what the Ubermensch is supposed to be like. If I ask you, Gil, no you, Zack, what is the Superman supposed to be like, how would you answer?"

"I'd say that he was supposed to be strong, I guess," said Zack.

"How about you, Gil? What do you think he would be like?"

"Same as what Zack said, I guess."

"Good. Well, that may be true, but the strength of the Ubermensch as conceived by Nietzsche is more in the Ubermensch's, mind than in his muscles. Think about it. What does man have over the lower animals? I know, you've heard it's the opposable thumb. I think the real thing is our brains. That's the one thing that is really unique. If this is so, then it makes sense, at least to me, that man will evolve his brain. In other words, I don't think the Ubermensch will look much different than us. I think that he could walk among us and hardly anyone would notice him. I do think that his head will be a little larger and bulbous, sort of like a lightbulb, but that it won't be totally beyond the normal range of these things. Other than that, I think most of the changes will be inside where they're not seen. He'll just think better than us. Now, this is where I have some problems, because I'm not sure what 'think better' really means. I don't think it's just IQ points, but more like a combination of IQ, creative thinking and consciousness with a good deal of instincts that are fine tuned. He may also be able to process things he sees all around him and put them into new forms faster than the rest of us, and in doing so, he may have faster reaction times to various events. Maybe it'll be something like he can sense when a car is going to jump up on a curb, just because he got a quick glimpse of the car and there was something odd about it, that no one else notices. It's not that he has ESP. It's that his regular senses and his brain are more finely tuned. Hell, I suspect the Ubermensch is already walking among us. He may not even know that he is above the rest of us, and therein lies a danger for improving the species, because if he doesn't know that he is special he may just breed with someone who is far less than he is and thus lose his special genes. His children will devolve from what he is and not evolve as if he had mated with someone on his level. You know, the ancient Egyptians also believed in proper breeding, and the Pharaoh always married his own sister so the blood would remain pure and untainted. You see, they believed that the Pharaoh and his family were direct descendants of the Gods. Kind of what the Japanese believed about their Emperor and to a lesser degree what European royalty believed about their royals. It's kind of a Queen Bee psychology translated into human terms where all the commoners of a nation worship the Queen Bee and take great pride in her, because she's their mother."

"Did you say that the Pharaohs married their own sisters?" asked Gil. "What about birthing idiots like everyone thinks happens in the backwoods?"

"Actually, there's nothing intrinsically wrong with mating brothers and sisters and other very close relatives, and in fact, this usually improves the stock. What do you think animal breeders do all day long? People are just animals, you know. The same rules and laws put out there by nature apply to us no less than to horses. The problem with incest is that if the family has some bad genes, they are then sometimes combined and expressed in a baby. So, if a brother and a sister both have recessive genes for some disorder, and if they marry, the offspring will often carry the disorder. That's the story with the banjo player in Deliverance, I think. You got that straight?"

"Where the hell are we Gil?" asked Zack

"I think we're coming into San Rafael," said Gil. "You guys want to make a stop?" We both did, so we wheeled into a local burger joint, used the john and got some food. Then we filled up with gas. There wasn't anything we wanted to do in San Rafael, so we got back in the car and headed toward San Francisco again. We were only about fif-teen miles out now, and I was feeling anxious about getting there. It's kind of like you usually want to hurry up and get to where you're heading, but in this case I sort of wanted to slow down and not get there. Still, all three of us were giving a lot of thought to what we were going to do once we were back in the city. I told both Zack and Gil that they could probably stay at my girlfriend's place and besides there was about a 50/50 chance that she was off on a flight right now anyway. Pretty soon, we were going through Mill Valley and then Sausalito again, and we could see the fog up ahead over the Golden Gate Bridge. We could also hear the sound of the foghorns of the ships in San Francisco Bay. Man, I loved that sound almost as much as I love the sound of rain when it first begins to fall. "Aaaaaaaaooooooogggggggggggggggggaaaaaaa," came the sound from the wall of white fog below us as we crossed. It sent shivers up and down my spine to hear the sound and be in the wet fog. I was going to ask the other two what sounds they liked, but somehow the magic of our trip was already fading even before it was over, so we all just drove on in silence. I told Gil to head on up the Haight, and that's what he did. The fog was so thick that we had to drive at ten miles per hour in order to have any chance of being able to stop if we saw something ahead of us. Soon, we were in the Haight and we found a parking space and walked over to Carla's apartment building and went up to the second floor. I had a key, but I felt better if I knocked, so I did so, and pretty soon Carla answered the door. "Hi Alex. You don't have to knock you know. You live here too."

"Well, I didn't want to be presumptuous," I said. "Carla, this is Zack and this is Gil. These are friends of mine. Do you mind if they camp out here for a few days?" She said she didn't mind, so that was set. I took a shower, then Zack did the same and then Gil. I set them up in the kitchen. Zack was able to sleep under the kitchen table, and Gil had the little pantry off the kitchen. Carla and I had the bedroom. Carla was a good girl, but she did seem to take herself too seriously sometimes and she was incredibly jealous. I figure that must have been the result of being bottle fed or something, because I couldn't figure why she'd be jealous of me and other women. I love women, but hell, I'm pretty plain looking. I'm no great catch. Maybe because this jealousy thing was a new experience for me I was flattered. Still, when I say she was jealous, I mean she was really jealous. Sometimes when she'd go away on an overnight trip, she'd come back and check the towel closets to make sure there were no blond hairs on the towels. Any hairs had better be her shade of brown, or we had an argument. Whenever we had an argument, she'd go crazy. One time she tried to ram my motorcycle with her car. Well, no one is perfect and she was pretty attractive, so I considered myself lucky. I felt comfortable with her for the most part. Maybe that's part of my makeup—wanting to feel comfortable. I have to feel comfortable with someone or I don't even want to be around them. I guess that's one reason why I don't have too many friends. Carla's apartment was right on Haight Street, and it overlooked the panhandle so we could look out and see all sorts of weird happenings in the park. Not that we were peeping toms, but sometimes you just couldn't help it. Anyway, I guess the city government was pretty hip to the panhandle because they kept the bushes closely cropped lest they hide any nefarious sexual activity.

A few days later, Gil got a job as a ticket taker at an adult theater. It was one of those storefront things. He took tickets and sold dildos all at the same time and he also ran the projector. That's how I met the guy who owned the theater and a couple of others and some other stuff as well. He called himself Gino, and said he was Italian, but he had blond hair and spoke with an Irish accent. Hell, I didn't care. He could be anything he wanted, as far as I was concerned. I heard that on paper, Gino didn't own anything. All the records were in the name of some handy man who worked for him and who traveled to his theaters, doing maintenance work. Gino's business wasn't great thanks to the Internet, and because of all the competition in San Francisco, but he made a couple of bucks. So, I got to know Gino a little. He was older than the rest of us and always wore some of those expensive but tacky suits of all colors and textures, that made you think he had a lot of money but no taste.

Gino wanted to look like a gangster. People whispered Mafia, but I never really knew that for a fact, and maybe Gino just cultivated that image to help him deal with the rough characters he often had to deal with in his line of work. Gino gave a job to Zack in a janitorial business he owned. Zack said he was the only white guy working there, and he figured most, if not all, of the other janitors were illegal aliens. Zack figured that Gino was a good guy to know, because he had plenty of pictures of pussy lying around, and Zack was still planning on his Cosmic Pussy search. Zack was also able to buy some used video equipment, and before anyone knew it, Zack was actually filming porno films and selling them to Gino and others. Zack said they were easy to film but that there were some rules Gino had him follow, such as having a lot of closeups that would put a gynecologist to shame. Anyway, Zack learned a lot about the business this way, and got paid for it at the same time. Every once in a while, Gino would head down to Mexico and he would sometimes take this good looking chick named Wendy, who worked as a cashier at one of his theaters, with him. Wendy and I became friends, so she'd tell me about their stays in different resorts. She said that she had no idea how important Gino was until they went there and saw some very important people who owned hotels all acting very deferential to Gino and all going out of their ways to rush up to him as soon as he walked in the door. We figured that if he were a big Mafia guy, we probably would have read about him in the newspapers, but there was never a word. So we figured that maybe he wasn't such a big shot after all, or maybe we just didn't travel in the right circles and maybe the cops weren't on to him yet, or maybe he paid them off. Hell, your imagination would run wild with that sort of stuff.

One day, I was down at Gino's office and this guy from Jersey came in who really looked mob. He spoke to Gino for a few minutes and then Gino came over to me, and asked me to drive "Mr. Smith," over to one of Gino's theaters in Berkeley. Yeah, this guy was named Smith like Gino is an Irish name. Anyway, what the hell. So, Mr. Smith and I got into Gil's VW bus, still without the sunroof, and headed over to Berkeley across the Bay Bridge. Now, if you know anything about San Francisco, you know that it has two major bridges leading north. One is the Golden Gate Bridge, which isn't really golden but is painted red and looks sort of graceful. The other bridge is the ugly erector set looking Bay Bridge. It's just a sort of grey in color. That's the one we were on, now. Mr. Smith looked more like he usually rode around in big black limos with a couple of other guys all smoking cigars. He was definitely out of place in Gil's bus. He didn't say anything except to ask if I worked for Tony. I told him I was a friend. As we drove, my imagination started playing with me and it crossed my mind that Mr. Smith was a hit man who was going to whack me, for some unknown reason. So, as we drove, I kept my eyes on his hands to make sure he didn't go for a gun. Unfortunately, his hands were in his lap, so all the way over, I was looking at his lap.

"Youse gay, or something?" asked Mr. Smith.

"No. Why?" I asked.

"Youse keep looking at my crotch."

"Sorry. I've got a problem with the sun reflecting off the windshield." He accepted that explanation and we drove on in silence. I kept watching, but I was a little more careful.

When we got to the theater. Mr. Smith told me to double park because he wouldn't be long. He wasn't. He went in and a few minutes later came out with a couple of those boxes they use to carry movies in. We returned to San Francisco in silence, and I dropped him off in front of a hotel. I couldn't figure out if Gino wanted to humiliate this guy by sending him in Gil's bus or whether he wanted the guy to blend in with the college crowd or what. That was the last I ever saw of Mr. Smith. I can only figure that Tony had been showing a copy of a film that this guy or his friends controlled, and that Gino shouldn't have had the film in the first place, so the guy pulled it.

"Hell," Gino said, "there's nothing illegal about these films. The Supreme Court has already ruled on that. This is a First Amendment right. I don't do nothin' illegal. I don't sell drugs. I don't rob. I don't cheat on my taxes. I'm as clean as a whistle." If the cops ever got anything on Gino, I never heard about it. Zack kept making films for Gino and was able to put together a stash of a few thousand bucks over time. Then, one day, he showed up on Carla's doorstep.

"Hey, man, let's get Gil and let's go," said Zack.

"Huh?" I said.

"It's time for another trip. We're after the Cosmic Pussy. Remember?"

"Zack, I can't just drop everything. I'm still working at the newspaper and they'll fire me if I hung them up."

"I don't think so. You're about the only one down there who speaks English well enough to correct those ads. Just tell them you have to go away for a week on family business."

Zack was right. I was the only one who corrected ads whose first language was English. Man, the newspaper had made some big screwups because of the lack of English. There was a very large help wanted ad put in by one of those companies that was looking for cosmetic saleswomen. The headline read "Much Pubic Contact." in large bold type, instead of "Much Public Contact." I called my boss and told him I had to go out of town and he was understanding. "I also have to talk to Carla," I said.

"What's the matter, you pussy whipped?" asked Zack.

Well, after some more banter, I told Zack that if Gil was up for the trip, then I'd tell Carla and we'd do it no matter what she said. I called Gil at his room at the Poop. Gil had moved into the same room that dead Cookin' John used to have with his chickens and all, but John is six feet under now, so what the hell. Gil had taken over the restaurant from Gladys, when she decided she liked hooking better than handling food, but she'd fill in for him just about anytime he wanted. Gil was pretty good at the restaurant business and was running it about as good as Cookin' John had done. And, Gil was even banging the same chick that Cookin' John used to bang. It was kind of like Gil was Cookin' John's replacement in life. I mean it's sort of like John never left. Gil just sort of stepped into everything as though he was born to it. To my surprise, Gil said he was ready to roll right then and there and that we should come to the Poop. I left a note for Carla, telling her I'd be back in about a week, and Zack and I got on the rat bike and headed up the hill to Poop.

When we got there, I said to Zack, "Shit, people are going to thing we're later day hippies or something." As soon as I had said it, I was amazed that I had even formed the thought about caring about what other people thought. Apparently, the settled life with Carla had taken its toll on me, so it was probably good that this opportunity to take off came up to break the domestic trap.

"Don't worry about it. We look like businessmen and besides Gil's bus ain't one of them old flower power deals."

"Yeah, we look like businessmen alright. Three kooks riding around in a VW bus talking up a storm." I hadn't been up to Poop since the theater was being built in the basement. We pulled up out in front where the bus was parked, and I noted that the hole in the roof of the bus had been fixed. As we started to go in, Gil came out with dead Cookin' John's old lady, Alice, and was telling her that he'd be back soon. I figured that it must be true love or something, and she was a real looker, too. Then all of a sudden, she looked at Zack and me and asked if either of us would like a blow job for the road. So much for romance. She then asked if she could use the hog. I told her it was okay with me. We got in Gil's bus and drove off.

"Gil, did your old lady just ask us if we wanted blow jobs?" I asked.

"Yep."

"How do you feel about that?"

"Well, I'm glad you didn't say yes. I'm anxious to get this trip going."

So, we had a big laugh about that. Here I was figuring that Gil was all possessive of Alice and that they were a real number, but apparently their relationship was somewhat different than mine and Carla's. Man, Carla was a terror. If she caught me even looking at another woman, she'd blow a fuse. I always just figured that Carla expected me to also blow a fuse if she looked at another man. I don't know if I would have. Maybe jealousy is contagions or something. I did sometimes play at being jealous, to make her happy.

"Where we headed?" asked Zack.

"Where are we headed?" I asked, while looking at Zack. "You called this trip, Zack, remember?"

"Well, I sort of wanted it to be like the last time, but I don't necessarily think we have to go in the exact same direction, do you? I want to take photos of Cosmic Pussies along the way, so we need to head where there's a whole lot of Mexicans."

"They're all around us," I said.

"No. I mean, I want to see Mexicans in their own habitat," said Zack.

"I heard there's a whole country full of them to the south of us," said Gil.

"We don't have time for that this time," said Zack. "Maybe next time, though. Look, let's try to stay off the highways as much as possible, and let's not just feel that we have to get really far away. In fact, I'd like to cruise the Mission for a while to see if we can see any Cosmic Pussy. Is that alright with you guys?"

Gil and I agreed that it sounded like an alright plan, and so we left the Hill and headed down to the Mission District. We just cruised up and down the streets looking for those pictures of the Virgin on the walls. The first one we found was on the side of a little market. It was mostly all in greens and reds and was pretty crude. Zack told us to stand back and look at the picture and to imagine that it was a pussy. When we did so, it really did look like a pussy if you didn't focus on all the small details. The Virgin's head was the clitoris. The robes that were curled as though they were being blown in a wind looked like pussy lips. Zack got a bunch of pictures of it at different angles, and then took some video of it, in case he wanted to put on a lecture tour and show the videos. Gil and I got a big laugh out of that. We could imagine Zack putting ads in small town newspapers and tacking handbills up on light poles announcing "LECTURE TONIGHT ON THE COSMIC PUSSY: IT'S SIGNIFICANCE FOR MODERN MAN," or something similar. Still, we had to admit that at least Zack had found purpose in his life—perhaps it was a strange purpose, but who were we to judge?

We drove around for about fifteen minutes and we found another Cosmic Pussy and then another and then another. Soon, we were finding Cosmic Pussies all over the place, and we were starting to feel like Cosmic Gynecologists. Some of the Cosmic Pussies had other elements added to them that kind of masked what they really were, but if you once formed the thought "Cosmic Pussy" you could never look at another of these pictures and not see it.

As we were driving, Zack was telling us his ideas both for his book and for the slides or film he thought he'd use in his lecture series. "Here's how I see it coming together," he said. "The first page of the book, or the start of the film or slides, will be all black and then the next scene will have Alex's idea of creation—you know, a small pinpoint of light, but the pinpoint of light starts off as a circle, and morphs into an ellipse so that it looks like pussy lips, then the next picture shows light coming out of the pussy into our universe, you know, like it's being born. At that point, the Cosmic Pussy will turn sideways and look like a cornucopia that'll morph into a sprial galaxy. Then I'll go through various spirals such as the toilet thing and whatever else I can think of. Then I'll start showing pictures of the Cosmic Pussy as interpreted by these Mexican pictures. You know, I'm going to have to talk to some Mexicans about these pictures, because it's just too coincidental that these things would look like pussies and the subject of the pictures is a virgin. I mean, virgin is all about pussy, isn't it?"

So we drove on. This time we headed south with the idea of going to Daly City and points further down the coast. After all, we might get bored if we went the same way we went the last time. I told the other two that I kind of liked the idea of this Cosmic Pussy.

"You know," I said, "when people report ghosts or aliens suddenly appearing in their rooms at night, they often describe the air as shimmering in this same pussy shape and then the ghost or alien steps through or just appears in the opening. There must be some reason for that particular shape rather than say a circle. Maybe, it's just because we're linear beings and if we're going to step through something gracefully, the shape should be an ellipse rather than a circle. I remember when I was a kid I was amazed at the great diversity of life. Then I started reading and realized that most things just follow simple rules and are just modifications of other things. Take the potato for example. The thing we call the potato is just a modified root that the plant uses to store food. Or, look at a rose. The thorns are just modified leaves. It goes on and on like this. Things are just modifications of other things. When you think about he Cosmic Pussy, you have to also think about males and females on this planet. You know, they're not really that different. Did you know that we all start off as female and then we modify to become male? When you really study anatomy this is made plain. A clitoris modifies to become a dick,. Pussy lips modify to become balls. You know, I still think that women can get pregnant without men. All they need is something to activate the egg, and start it dividing. sperm does it in our normal reproduction, but I don't really think that sperm is necessary. I think men are God's way of speeding up evolution by creating more variety in the offspring of different species. I still think that God is trying to create a proper vessel for Himself, and that he's in everything but is limited in what He can do or what he can be by what he's inside of. Maybe it's like a car. If we drive a thirty year old car, we're limited to the thirty year old design. We can only go as fast as the old engine allows. If we want to go faster, we need to have a new car. Maybe God is trying to come up with that perfect car to carry Him around in and maybe that's why He's sent us on this trip so that we'll see the purpose. Think of God as the designer. He has to work within certain rules set, not by Himself, but by the physical characteristics of matter. All He can do is endlessly shuffle things in the hope that eventually something will be shuffled that will result in a higher consciousness creature which He can ride. Perhaps, that's what every single living thing in the whole universe is all about; just God's attempt to evolve his perfect vessel so that He can find fulfillment Himself. God must be very lonely and must want to experience things on a different level, and it is by bringing forth a flesh and blood creature that he can do this. When He's in a tree—He has the pluses and minuses of a tree. He can't walk or see or hear. He can only stand there and grow and experience the way a tree experiences. When he's in a butterfly, he can do no more than what a butterfly can do.

If you let your mind go and think along these lines, it all starts to make sense. You begin to realize that maybe God has given us clues everywhere to find Him, but we've just been too stupid for these millions of years. Maybe now we're starting to emerge from our sleep and maybe there are many people out there who are experiencing the same things we're experiencing."

"You mean legions of people looking for the Cosmic Pussy?" asked Zack.

"Well, maybe. You know how they say that when it's time to railroad, there'll be trains?"

CHAPTER 9

Zack figured that with his Cosmic Pussy work, he could, at the very least, get on some of those freaky TV shows, and that he'd get paid the going rate for such appearance; maybe $300 bucks or so, I guess. The thing with Zack, though, was that he was getting really serious about this Cosmic Pussy business. He would laugh with us and make fun of it, but you could tell that inside, he really was driven to see if he could keep finding more and more facts to support this hypothesis. Sure, Cosmic Pussy sounds like goof-offs in a locker room or something, but I was certain that Zack was more into the idea than some might think. Zack told us about this girl he met who also made porno films. He said she lived up on Russian Hill and turned out some pretty good product. As far as Zack knew, she was the only girl really making porno films as a producer and director. He promised to introduce her to Gil when we got back, just in case dead

Cookin' John's old lady decided to move on. Gil thought that was a pretty good idea.

So, we drove on, talking as we went. We had gotten pretty close to Half Moon Bay before we decided that we better try going north. So, we turned around and headed back toward the city. When we went through San Francisco, we didn't even stop, and just barreled right over the Golden Gate Bridge and headed up the coast as we had before. We decided to head to a little beach in Marin County which had an unofficial nude section on the other side of some rocks. We parked the bus, and walked down to the beach and passed the straights where they were all sitting out in their bathing suits. We climbed over the rocks and there we were. Maybe sixty people all nude, just hanging out and having fun.. We stripped off our clothes and edged over to where a couple of really pretty girls in their early twenties were lying on towels. Man, these two looked like they had just stepped out of Playboy—they were that good looking. We wanted to talk to them in the worst way, but we didn't want to make pests of ourselves or offend them, so we just put our towels down about eight feet from theirs, and sat there talking, all the while trying to burn the images of their bodies into our brains. We decided to throw a football we had brought with us for a while and thought that maybe that would draw their attention to us as wholesome sports types who weren't interested in them on a sexual level. Yeah. Right. Maybe they would think we were intellectuals and that we were shy and maybe that we liked them for their minds. Of course, they might think that we were gay, and just dismiss us out of hand. Maybe they were gay, I thought. Pretty soon, both of them sat up and I knew that they were watching us out of the corners of their eyes. Gil knew it too, and decided to get their attention by running and jumping into the cold Pacific. Now, Gil had spent much of his life in an area of the country where the ocean was too cold to swim in and where swimming wasn't done much, so he didn't have much understanding of the effect of cold water on the human male body. I tried to yell to him to not jump in the water, but he didn't listen. When he emerged, the cold water had done its job and Gil had shriveled up to the point that from a distance you might think he was a girl Anyway, the two girls had apparently been anticipating that, and they giggled to themselves. "Ahh. The silly mating rituals of the humans," I thought to myself.

Finally, Zack went over and introduced himself. After a few minutes of conversation he told the girls that he made porno films and would they like to be in one. Oh, no, I thought to myself, now we're going to hear some yelling. We'd better get ready to beat it. To my surprise, the girls said that they thought it might be fun, but they didn't; want to do anything too kinky. Zack asked them to define too kinky, and they said they wouldn't do anything with animals like those girls in Mexico. After I got over the shock of these two Earth angels agreeing to this, I started thinking that Zack was on to something. No wonder he didn't have a steady girlfriend, he didn't need one. His work was his pleasure. He got all the company he wanted and he got paid for doing it. Zack gave them his business card. Up until then, I didn't even know he had business cards, so I asked him for one. It read, Zack Norris, Film Producer, and gave his telephone number. Zack told the girls theat he'd be back in town in about a week or so and to give him a call and he'd set something up. The girls then said that they had to leave and did so. We spent a few more hours at the beach, and then jumped back in the bus and headed north again.

"You know," I said, "in Ireland there are people who are called Tinkers or Travelers. They're really gypsies but you're not supposed to call them that over there. Anyway, the Travelers travel the way we seem to travel. Maybe we're some sort of genetic Travelers. Have you guys heard about them? No? Well, let me tell you what I know. The Travelers are a legitimate sub-class of people in Ireland. They live in rickety old wagons and trucks and move constantly about. They'll stop in this town for a time and then move on to the next. The reason that they're also called Tinkerers is because one of the ways that they used to make money was to fix pots and pans. Now, they do automobile body work. They have no shops, they just set up beside the road and fan out over the village. If they see a car with dents, they approach the owner and offer to fix it on the spot. They work cheap, and because the Travelers always return, their work is usually pretty good, for the price. The thing about the Travelers is that their seemingly aimless wandering actually has a pattern to it. The various groups of Travelers have heir own routes. They'll go maybe fifty or sixty miles north and twenty miles east or west and then south fifty or sixty miles and then back over to where they started from. So they have these big circuits that they travel on over the course of a year or more, like planets orbiting a star. I wonder if this is some sort of leftover from the days of the Druids and if there isn't some deeper meaning to their life style and their circuits."

"You know I'm going to say this, even if it's obvious," said Zack. "Cosmic Pussy! They're drawing a Cosmic Pussy with their travels."

"Well, maybe," I said. "I don't know about that, and maybe someone should study them a little closer, but for the most part, they're a nuisance to the villagers. Have you ever heard of a Tinker's curse? You know, like when someone curses and someone else says that the curse is about as useless as a Tinker's curse. A Tinker's Curse is one that never comes true. It's an empty promise of bad things come that never come true. The Tinker ladies often show up on the doorsteps of villages, and sometimes in the dead of winter. With the Tinker ladies are usually several little children all too lightly dressed for the weather. The Tinker ladies then ask for money and food to give to their children. If the homeowner doesn't give them any, or if he gives them too little, the Tinker ladies curse the homeowner with the most horrendous curses you've ever heard. Things like the homeowner will die of cancer in days, or his dick will fall off, or his next child will be born without a brain or his wife will leave him for a goat. There's no end to the curses. Fortunately, they never come true, or if they do it's just a coincidence.

I wonder if the Tinkers are the direct descendants of an earlier people who lived in Ireland and if they aren't just acting on genetic memories. You know, I believe that there really are such things as genetic memories and similar things, even though most reputable scientists have discounted that as a theory. There was a Russian sci-

entist named Lysenko who taught that what we ⸱
inscribed on our genes and that our children woul⸱
things in some measure or other. I don't say that ev ⸱ ....g is so
inscribed, only that there are some things that are and that we don't
know exactly what triggers the mechanism in some cases and not in
others. It may have something to do with trauma or something. I
was thinking that you know how almost everyone is afraid of spiders? Well, why? Suppose that while we were living in caves, we were
prey to giant spiders who would eat many of us and drop on us from
trees and the like. Over the years, perhaps our genes started carrying
a picture and a fear of spiders long after spiders evolved to where
they're now just tiny things. Maybe we act out of the ancient message
in our genes. Maybe that's the way it is with the Tinkers. Maybe the
three of us have some of those Tinker, Traveler genes and that's why
we wander about like this. Maybe there's a lot of people like us. What
about those outlaw motorcycle gangs? They seem to have their own
traveling subculture.

If we think along these lines we have to eventually ask ourselves if
we truly have free will. I suspect that we do have free will within certain boundaries, and that if we try to exercise our free will beyond
these boundaries we'll be squashed like bugs. The only reason that
we think we have real free will is because we're not too bright. It's as
though we're all retarded and can be easily fooled and manipulated.
When you look at those we consider retarded, you see how easy it is
to control them. They're like little children. I once got a lesson in
relationships and people by observing a retarded couple on the
street. They were obviously retarded and both were mongoloid to a
lesser or greater degree. Anyway, the man did something that was
unlawful. It was something minor like throwing a gum wrapper on
to the ground. The female became very agitated and upset over this
trivial little thing all out of proportion to what he had done. She was
crying and acting as though the man had just hit her. He then made
a big show of comforting her and helping her through the trauma of

seeing him do this 'awful crime.' When I saw this, I started thinking about my relationship with Carla and wondered if some of the arguments we had, would be looked at by someone with a much higher IQ, as I was looking at the actions of the retarded couple. It kind of gave me a new perspective on myself and my relation to people and to everything in general. I decided that I was, henceforth, going to try to look at my arguments with Carla as though I had the higher IQ of the person I imagined looking at us. Maybe we can will our own evolution or maybe our own mutation."

"Man, I think going north got the juices flowing Gil," said Zack.

"Think about it. Maybe this makes sense and maybe it can be worked into the Cosmic Pussy theory." I said. This mention of the Cosmic Pussy got Zack's's attention and he started listening more closely.

"Here's how I figure this part of the big picture works," I said. "God, or nature, evolved us to the point where we had the types of brains that we now have. At that point, God, or nature—just call it God, for short—stopped pushing us along and said, "Now it's your turn. You have the brains, let's see you cause your own evolution by using the free will I have given you. If you are up to the task, you will select your mates wisely; overcoming the purely animal instinct to have sex, and you will have children who will be better than you, and thus advance your line along the path of evolution. If you are not ready, then you will mate willy nilly with people who don't share your blood, and your line won't evolve. If your children are lower than you, you will have started your line down the road of devolution that might lead to a final oblivion or lack of consciousness at some time in the future. Evolve, and you'll come to the light. Devolve, and you'll fall back to the dark."

"Why did you substitute light for evolution and dark for devolution?" asked Gil.

"Because it's like we were saying before, light requires energy to exist, but dark requires no energy. Dark is what is, when there is no energy. It is the great collapse. It took nothing to maintain the universe before light, but light requires incredible energy to just Be—to exist. This tells me that the way to Be is to expend energy and to struggle to the light. So anyway, God had us on a conveyor belt that was slowly moving forward. He didn't really know who would reach the end of the conveyor belt, but all creatures were on it. The end of the conveyor belt is the end of the relatively free ride on the conveyor belt because when it is reached, it suddenly reverses direction and pulls creatures back, unless they use their wills to leap off and continue on to more evolution under their own power. This end of evolution, is misnamed, because it's really just the end of automatic evolution. To go beyond, requires that we use our wills to find the right way. Humans have reached this stage. Now we must leap forward and will our evolution via our brains, or we will be pulled back down to nothingness. Oh, I forgot to mention that we can't just stay as we are now, this state where we seem to be stuck is not stable and we must make a move or we'll start going backwards. Not all of us will make it to the next level. In fact, millions and millions; make that billions and billions of us will never make it.

It could be that one of us sitting on this bus is the father of the next step for mankind, the Ubermensch—the son of the Cosmic Pussy. Perhaps, at some dim, future date some scientist will be digging in a field and discover Zack's skull, for example, and determine that this was the creature that started a great branching of the human species. "Lucy, I'm home," yells Zack as he kicks down the door of pre-Ubermensch humanity. All the modern humans in this dim future time are descended from Zack. Gil and I and all the rest of the billions of humans alive today were just dead ends who were replaced by the Zacks, who were the new models for a human like creature. Imagine. We're in the presence of the great Zack. And, maybe they'll find Gil's skull and mine next to Zack's and they'll say that we represented an earlier type—the true dead end on the human evolutionary tree. And, these future scientists may puzzle over why the great Zack's skull was found in the same place with two primitive ones. They may theorize that we were the slaves, or maybe, the pets, of the great Zack.

CHAPTER 10

*I*t was night when we got into Santa Rosa. We found a local bar and went in to see what we could see. Lucky us. There were two girls sitting at a table with no guys. I had the bartender send them over a round. The girls looked at us, then talked and giggled a little to each other and then motioned for us to come over and join them. They said that they lived in town and that they worked over at a nearby shopping center. They were roommates who shared a mobile home that their third room mate Nancy, who was at home, owned. The two girls at the table were Kara and Loren. They were in their late twenties or early thirties and seemed to be tired, the way people in small towns, who are resigned to their fates, seem to be tired. I suspect they had been the queens of the prom years earlier but, over time, the parties and the beaus just faded away. They weren't bad looking, but they sure weren't the lookers that Zack had rounded up back at the nude beach. It didn't matter. We sat around talking for hours. Zack then told them that he made porno films and asked if they'd like to be in one. Just as at the nude beach, I cringed. I was about ready to run for the door if the girls started screaming at us. Instead, they just laughed, and said that they'd think it over. We told them that we were just passing through, and after a while I guess they got comfortable with us and were convinced that we weren't serial killers, so they invited us to spend the night in their trailer.

The trailer park was an older one and some of the trailers had additions built on made out of corrugated metal and plastic. It wasn't what you'd call the Beverly Hills of trailer parks, but I'd seen worse. Their trailer was a pretty big one, and the girls each had their one bedrooms. As soon as we walked in the door, I was afraid that we'd be in one of those uncomfortable situations where no one would know how to bring up the subject of sleeping arrangements. This was partly answered when Nancy came out of kitchen and all three girls then went to talk privately for a few minutes. When they came back, Nancy took my hand and said to everyone else, "Goodnight," as she led me to her bedroom, which was the biggest of the three since she was the owner of the trailer. She had short dark hair and was about 5 feet tall, but she was thin. Thin, in my book, is always good. We immediately jumped into bed, and I promptly fell asleep. No kidding. The next day was Friday and Nancy had the day off, so when we woke up, we made up for my having fallen asleep the night before.

Later in the day it was time for us to go. Zack gave the girls his address and phone number in San Francisco and promised to put them in a film if they got down to the city. He told them that they should look at it as work, and that in addition to being paid, they could experiment with some sexual things that they might not otherwise dare to try. Man, that Zack had really found a niche. I figured that I might want to get involved in that line of work myself.

As we were leaving I felt lonely again, all of a sudden. Maybe this loneliness, or emptiness, or longing that I felt is what is meant by the word angst. What the hell were we? It really bothered me that I couldn't name what we were. This was the same thing that had been bothering me way back in New York. We were something...I mean our mode of living, behaving, doing, indicated that we were some sort of subculture of the normal culture, but we lacked a name. Were we nihilists? Were we anarchists? Were we travelers? Were we hippies? Were we Beatniks? None of the old labels seemed to fit, and I hated it because I had nothing to identify with. We were sort of like homeless people, but with homes. We were hobos with a car. We were bums with jobs. We were straights who were crooked. We weren't druggies. We weren't winos. We weren't suburbanites. We weren't urbanities. We were nothing. Yet we had to be something. I wanted the self-image legitimacy that can only be found if a thing is named, damn it!

It seemed that every generation had its people like us and each generation spawned a slightly different version. There were the American expatriates of the 20's and 30's. The beats of the 50's. The hippies of the '60's. We were none of these, because those times were gone. What the hell were we?

I could tell that others in society were trying to name people like us also. The PR types came up with Generation X, but this was a name that didn't really stick, besides it was used in tons of advertising campaigns and was just a little too manufactured to be really hip. It was the stuff of poseurs. It was the name that phonies used to describe themselves. No. We were different. We actually were sort of artsy. I wrote. Zack made films. Gil was a pretty good musician and played a half-dozen instruments. Gil, of course, was kind of our silent man. He was always there with us, but he was most usually the quiet one. As long as I'd known him, he'd been quiet. He never bragged even though he was a back up guy on some pretty big records, and had made pretty good money once.

We kept going north until we hit Healdsburg and then headed west and south. When we got to Guerneville, we stopped and had lunch at a fast food joint. We found several more Cosmic Pussies and Zack took photos and video of them. Then we headed back toward San Francisco. I figured that this would be our last short hop. The next time we headed out, I wanted to plan it a little more and go down to Mexico and see some of those donkey shows that I had heard about. I told the other two about this, and they pretty much agreed that we had milked this type of short trip about as much as we could. Zack was especially interested in Mexico because he was still in his chase for the Cosmic Pussy. Besides, he figured that he could make some porno films on a real shoestring down in Mexico. I asked him if he could speak Spanish, and he said that he knew a few words. I was already worrying that he'd get caught doing something illegal in Mexico and that they'd lock us all up and throw away the keys. As we were going down the road, Zack spotted a small bar that had one of those cosmic Pussy paintings on the side, so we pulled over and he took some photos and video of it. We then decided to go in and get a beer. Man, what a weird place. It was small, and dirty, and eclectic. The place served really strange combinations of beer and food. They had tiny tacos with some strange kind of meat along with pickled eggs and hot peppers. Actually, it all combined okay. Gil said that he was going to use the idea at Poop when we got back.

CHAPTER 11

"*U*bermensch" said Zack out of the blue. "That really interests me. Have you thought any more about that since our last trip?"

"Yeah, a little," I said. "I wondered what it would be like. I mean what physical characteristics would the Ubermensch have? Remember, I'm defining the term as the next evolutionary step for man. Not the final step, just the next one. I guess the Ubermensch will have a Ubermensch above him and then there'll be another above that one and then another and on and on. Then again, maybe that's not possible. There must be a limit to how far we can evolve. I'm assuming again that we humans are at the pinnacle of natural evolution on Earth, so we don't really know what the limits are. We've seen how other animals evolve and how they have all fallen short of where we are right now. At least, we're the only ones that really think. I know, I know, there are people running around saying that porpoises are as bright as us, but I think that's just silly, otherwise they would have taken more control over their environment. Is it reasonable to think that porpoises have philosophical thoughts and never try to pursue them in a physical sense by writing them down?

"Then again, what if porpoises really are so much smarter than us that they don't need writing or books because they all communicate with each other, and the ocean acts like the Internet so that what any of them knows is available to all of them if they simply tune in? What if porpoises somehow created humans to evolve to a point where humans could build things for porpoises, so porpoises could travel to other planets? You could go nuts with this kind of thinking. Anyway, I think that the Ubermensch will evolve and evolve and then have to transform into something else to keep evolving. Perhaps nature has already shown one way this can be done with butterflies and how they change from caterpillars into the final adult stage.

"There is something that troubles me with all this though. Once the adults of many species of animals reach the age when they can procreate, they, as individual animals, start dying as though a switch is thrown. Could it be that humans are the same way and that the reason we haven't evolved is that the internal 'die' switch is switched to on, so that we never reach an age when the next 'evolution' switch is thrown.

"Did I mention before that I think humans are supposed to live to about 1,500 years and that we're supposed to have regenerative powers? No? Well, I got that idea from the Bible where the generations just after Adam all started living shorter and shorter lives. I wondered why. Perhaps, it was because they were mating with the creatures native to this world who had shorter life spans and they picked up that and other genetic characteristics in their lines. You know the term Ichor? It was supposed to be the blood of the Gods—maybe the Gods were ancient aliens—and had various magical powers. Maybe the Ichor was watered down by mating with the ape creatures and humans are the result. Maybe the aliens were in short number as we discussed before, and their gene pool was swamped with the native ape creatures' genes. Maybe, this caused the ape creatures to evolve at the same time that it caused the aliens to devolve. They met in the middle and created a new species: And, on the sixth day, God created man."

"Man, I like that," said Zack. "You know how astronomers can tell us all sorts of things about far-a-way stars just by little movements or wobbles of other stars or by shifts in color bands, well, I'll bet if there were the equivalent of astronomers studying these things, we're talking about, that many seeming mysteries of man would be solved. I think the problem is that there really isn't some kind of scientific generalist who would be able to live long enough and be bright enough to pull various disciplines together to come up with the facts. Maybe also, since we're talking about genes and races and similar things, no respectable scientist would dare talk about it because the haters would attack him. Remember the big deal about IQ's and races? The scientist was just reporting that he discovered that different racial groups have different IQ levels and the creeps came out of the woodwork to smear him."

"Some of the theoretical physicists are coming close, to discovering the reality of existence," piped in Gil. "My sister is married to a physicist, so I thought it would be fun to talk to him about some way out stuff. Boy, was I wrong. He's as dry as an engineer or accountant. I asked him about some of the famous physicists that everyone has heard about, and he said that's not what most physicists do. Most just deal with common humdrum things. It's the theoretical physicists who run around talking the way we talk, and they're the guys who get all the glory, and maybe rightly so, but they work pretty much the way the three of us do, only they have the degrees and the science to take the idle speculation and prove it. We three can talk about these things, but if we had to prove or disprove any of our theories, we'd be hard pressed even to know where to begin."

"Maybe we're rebels," I said.

"What?" Zack always said something like that, but it was mostly rhetorical. He knew that when anyone of us just suddenly started with a non-sequitur that we were launching into a new subject or as was so often our case, we were just appending something new and that various things and ideas would branch off and then calve and do it again.

"I keep searching for what we are," I continued. "I don't think we have a word in English for what I'm trying to think of to call us. I once thought if this were Germany, we would call ourselves something like Neobohemianintellectualanarchistnihilistrebeltraveller-beatniks. That might work in German, the way they string words together like that, but there must be a better term, if I can only find it, in English."

"Why the big concern about a name?" asked Zack.

"Shit." I said. "Who knows? Maybe if I can come up with a good name then maybe a bunch of groupie women will all flock around also saying that they're the same thing."

"So you think that having a bunch of beautiful women around would put you at peace?" asked Zack. "Maybe you really should look into my esteemed line of work. You're trolling for the Cosmic Pussy too, but you just want to screw it."

"Ahhh, if it were that simple," I said. "When I was a kid, the dream I would have all the time was to build a raft and sail away to a deserted island someplace in the Pacific. I read everything I could find about islands, about rafts and about survival in the wilderness. I finally decided that what I should do is build a raft with one of those big tanks you find holding gasoline under the ground at gas stations, as the center of the raft. Then, my plan was to weld a 55 gallon drum into the bottom and one into the top, as doors into the big tank. That way, if the raft tipped over, it wouldn't matter, and I would be safe in the tank, and up was down and down was up. The island group I was planning of going to was the Marquesses in French Polynesia. Some of them are uninhabitable."

"You know," said Gil, "I'm not sure that we're much different from crazy homeless people. We seem to be rootless. We don't have real jobs or careers and we don't seem to have straight goals for our lives. We have educations, but I'll bet there are lots of homeless people who could say as much. It bothers me a little bit, because I really want a stable life. Not stable as others may define the term, but stable as it suits my personality. I'd actually like to have a wife and kids. I'm having fun now, but this isn't a life for the rest of my life. I want a home to go to each night. I want a job. I want some of the regular ordinary things." We had seen Gil in this kind of mood before. He was kind of morose and his mood was bringing us down too.

"It may sound pretty trite, but each one of us is going through this life for the first time and we're making it up as we go," I said. Some people have scripts given to them by their parents. The scripts tell the kids what they are to do in their lives. 'First, you'll go to this college, then you'll take up this profession.' Sometimes I wish my parents had done that with me. Instead, they just let me grow wild and find my own way. I'm with Gil on this a little bit. I don't know if my way is the right way. Maybe that's why I feel so lonely. I'm trying to find the right way, a way that isn't suffocating and straight, but which also gives me some sense of security and self-worth. I guess the best way to accomplish that would be to win a big lottery. Zack why don't you pray to the Cosmic Pussy and have it send us a winning lottery ticket?"

"That may not be a bad idea. You know how we keep saying, as above, so below and as below so above? Well, maybe what that's all about is that we're at the small end of some gigantic telescope—you know, where everything is small—and at the other end everything is the same, only much bigger. Never mind, I can't explain that. Let me try it this way, instead. In certain kinds of magic it is believed that something can represent something else. So if you act on some stand-in item, you can, according to this belief, cause changes in the other object that it represents. Voodoo does this with those little dolls that they stick pins into. Maybe what I have to do is talk to a real pussy—pray to a real pussy—and the message will be transmitted to the Cosmic Pussy."

"Try that and the chick will think you're a looney," said Gil.

"Well, maybe I can pray silently. I don't think I have to do any sort of ritual. I'll give it a try the next chance I get. Maybe those girls from the Beach would be good candidates to communicate through."

"What if it's only ugly ones that will work," I said.

"Man, don't even suggest that," said Zack, showing genuine disgust.

So that's the way it went. Always some banter back and forth that never really meant anything. Does anything mean anything? Maybe the word to describe us is existentialist, but I reject this because I don't want to follow what someone else set up. I want to have something new. I don't want to implement but to initiate. Still, like existentialists, our existence seems to precede our essence. We seem to be making up ourselves as we go along the road, and in our case, the road is meant literally. It's as though we're nothing unless we're on the road, but when we're on this road we feel alive. I think all three of us are in some sort of sync. I suppose that we could travel along in silence and still communicate, but that would have no purpose at all. I guess I'm looking for insights and for answers to questions I don't even know how to ask. If I were a true existentialist, I would think that the world is meaningless and absurd. I reject that, if not totally, then at least in part, because the world does have meaning. It has a meaning that I myself put to it for myself. A lot of what goes on is absurd, but not the type of absurdity thought of by the existentialists or maybe I got it all wrong. Anyway it doesn't matter.

If I'm making myself up as I go along, it is because I am willing myself to become what I want to become. I'm conscious of what I want to become and that's my problem because the means to obtain it are not known and this is what I'm making up. I am finding a way to evolve or mutate myself into the Ubermensch, or at least into a slight advance over what I am now. But, what is this higher man, this Ubermensch, really like? Is the Ubermensch a renaissance man who can do many things well? Is the Ubermensch even aware that he is the Ubermensch and does he feel superior to other men? And how exactly does one cause one's own evolution or mutation? Should one use chemicals, or electricity or something out of some science fiction movie? No. Those don't seem to be the right way at all, based on what we know about such things today. So, how do we bring this transformation, this evolution, this mutation? I decided that I must first hold certain basic definitions in my mind that were easy for me to remember. Evolution is a slow movement up the evolutionary scale and is usually done over millions of years. Devolution is a faster slide down the evolutionary scale. Mutation is a quick jump either up or down on the scale. What I was after, was a mutation to a higher state. Now, I was pretty certain that my outward physical form was pretty much set, and besides that could be changed as in cutting off an arm through surgery, but that wasn't a mutation, because if you cut your arm off, your children would still be born with two arms. I needed to change myself from the cells outward. The changes I sought, must be internal, and if such changes were made, then perhaps there would be an external manifestation. I figured that to accomplish these changes, I must use my mind itself, either directly or indirectly, to cause the physical cells to change. I must visualize what I must become and then act on it. I must hold a picture in my mind and let it act like a brace on a sapling that will cause the tree to grow in this or that direction. I must also remember that I must use the physical things of this world to trigger the internal changes. To this end, I would have to study the lives of highly evolved men throughout history to see what might have affected them. I must also use common sense to look to the things that I had intuited over these road trips. For the purposes of this mutation I assumed that there was a higher power of some kind and that it had brought mankind along to the point where our minds could ponder these things and where we might have to take over our future development or die out. Perhaps I was one of many millions who had been brought to this understanding, but maybe most of these millions had turned away thinking that such thoughts were symptomatic of madness. Maybe there were only a few humans who didn't turn away, and who continued on. Could it be that the Buddha was one of those people who mutated, but no one used that term and instead said that he had found enlightenment? Maybe, I was on to something and should pursue this.

"Do either of you guys know much about Buddha?" I asked.

"Yeah. I know a little," said Zack. "The guy was a prince or something and saw some homeless people and got sad. He then gave it all up and sat under a tree for a long time almost starving himself to death, and while in this state, he found enlightenment."

"That's about what I know, too," I said. "Do you think the essential thing in his enlightenment was the lack of food—the mortification of the flesh—or something like that?"

"I think it was a combination of things. I think that he really wanted to find enlightenment and that his mind subconsciously made him almost starve so that his body would release whatever hormones and chemicals that a body in that state releases and that these affected his mind and gave him a clarity that he lacked before."

"I was thinking along the same lines," I said. "You know, I think that's the key. You have to want something badly enough so that you first train your mind to seek it and once you've got that thought so firmly implanted in your mind, your mind will find a way. It will take over your body and make it do things that will cause the changes you want. This must get confusing because someone doing this must begin to wonder about who he or she really is. Am I my mind or am I my body? It's almost as though you have to step out of your mind to have your mind tell your mind what to do. Perhaps the answer lies in thinking of the mind as having many components as some psychiatrists do. Once again, we're held captive by our inadequate language. Mind must not be just one thing as we normally think of it, but several, or many different things. All of these have arisen from that mass of tissue called the brain. So, one part of the mind tells the other parts what to do. These other parts then engage the brain. The brain then starts things moving to create in flesh what the mind has told it to create. It opens certain ducts. It causes certain reactions. It changes the acidity of the stomach and the blood. It tries to get you, as a total creature, to act in certain ways that are needed before even further changes can be made. Maybe it will cause you to feel overheated all the time, in order to get you to move to a colder area of the planet. Maybe it will make you thirsty because it needs more liquids to change the cells. Maybe it will make you crave certain types of foods because it needs the chemicals in those foods to build a new you. All through this, you may not be aware of your brain working on these things that the mind told it to do, any more than you're now aware that the brain keeps you breathing. You don't have to say, breathe in, now breathe out. The brain does this for you automatically. Now, the problem at hand is to come up with a picture of the Ubermensch." I finally stopped talking to catch my breath.

"What are you talking about?" asked Gil. He was looking at me like I'd just jumped off a bridge or something."

"Oh, sorry. I guess the first part of my conversation was internal and you only heard the last part. I was saying to myself that maybe my purpose is to mutate or at least try to mutate to the Ubermensch state of being. I think I was resolving a lot of conflicts about this, but this has just led to some others. What I'm now trying to know is what the Ubermensch looks like in detail. I've decided that he must look much as we do. Well, maybe that sounds like a rationalization on my part, because I can't not look like I do in major ways. But, since I do look the way I look, I'd be at a dead end with this thing if the Ubermensch was, say, black or Asian. I don't think that's the case though, because this whole sort of Ubermensch thing was a white invention and I think it is one of the dormant programs in white genes. Or, and this leads to the same result, if I am, say, divinely inspired in this line of thought, then the divinity wouldn't want me to be a dead end. So, I can accept that there may be some subtle differences in appearance, but overall, I have to believe that the Ubermensch pretty much looks like us. If I can form a mental picture of the Ubermensch, and then hold this picture of such a being in my mind, and if I can somehow make myself look like the Ubermensch—take on the external differences—then I think I can get my mind working on creating the differences internally that led to the image being different. In other words, I want to method act the part of the Ubermensch. I want to play the character in real life and never be out of character. To do this, I've got to really get inside the Ubermensch. I've got to cut my hair like him, dress like him, eat like him, bathe like him, talk like him, use his facial mannerisms, move like him. I must wear the same clothes of the same fabric as he would wear so I can feel the texture of the clothes and the way they feel on my body. In other words, if I act the part, my mind may force my brain to make me him. I've got to be him in all ways to the smallest details. The big problem is I don't know anything about him. I don't know what he really looks like or what he eats or any of that stuff, because he doesn't yet exist as far as I know. This means that I, we, have to try to use our intuition to come up with the image that I can use. That is, if you'll help me.

"Geez," said Gil, "we've got the Frankenstein monster's brain here, asking us to help build his body so he can replace mankind with his kind."

"Sure, we'll help," said Zack. "mankind is pretty lousy as it is, so let's see if we can get you on the road to destroying us and replacing us with something better. I won't hold my breath though."

"You know," I said. "I wonder if the Ubermensch is really better than us. I mean, many people think that if we move higher, that we'll somehow be passive vegetarians running around flower dotted fields in togas. That might be completely wrong. It could be that the Ubermensch is a ruthless killer of all that we love. It could be that he looks at us the way we look at bugs and squashes us."

"You know," said Gil, "I think we need to go to the library when we get back to San Francisco and look up everything we can find on the Ubermensch. I'll bet the three of us can come up with a picture of this guy in just a few days at worst."

"I'll second that," I said.

"Resolved," said Gil.

We rode along in silence for a few miles, then I just had to speak. "I can't wait until we go to a library. I want to try to intuit this creature right here and now, because I want to start on the mental exercises before we even finish this trip. We'll just have to search our memory banks to come up with what we know and fill in the gaps that way." So that's what we did. We talked on and on about the Ubermensch—the Superman. We decided that since the Nazis were reported to want to create such a being, that the Ubermensch must look like a Nazi. that meant blond hair and blue eyes. I had the eyes, and we bought some blond dye at the first drugstore we came to. We then decided that he must also look Prussian, with a crewcut. We cut my hair with an old rusty pair of scissors we had in the bus.

Then Gil said that my walk was wrong. It had to be more militaristic. I had to look like Doc Savage, that old pulp fiction character from the '40's. A strong mind in a strong body. In fact, Doc Savage was simply an American version of the Ubermensch. He even looked German.

Zack then asked why that had to be the Ubermensch. Why, he wondered, couldn't the Ubermensch just be a highly intelligent short fat little man? I explained to him that by definition the Ubermensch was the next step for man—which is to say, a step up the ladder of evolution. Since we were working with common sense and intuition we decided that we needed to limit our universe of possible Ubermensch types and go with what little we knew, and try to build from there. With this in mind, we figured that since 90% of the world's people were non-white that the Ubermensch probably couldn't come from them, because then he wouldn't be rare. Besides, if we believed, as we had talked about before, that aliens came to Earth and created white people, then white people must be the next step. Even further, if we followed our own cosmogony about dark being the natural or at rest state of the universe, and if we added in our oft repeated saying "as above so below and as below so above," then with this logic, the Ubermensch had to be white. The same logic went for blond hair and blue eyes. We believed that these were some of the external characteristics of the Ubermensch. The "visible signs" as we came to call them. Then, when you add in the bit about sympathetic magic that we had talked about, it seemed that in some sense what we were doing was logical. It was method acting to become what you're trying to become or what you're imitating. If I could feel exactly like the Ubermensch, then maybe I could acquire the characteristics of the Ubermensch. Maybe by doing a good job of imitation I could fool my brain into releasing those hormones and other chemicals into my blood stream that would transform me into the Ubermensch.

What was more interesting to us than the physical things was trying to figure out what we thought the Ubermensch thought, and what actions followed his thinking. We reasoned that he must eat healthy food, that he probably didn't use drugs or smoke or do other things that would harm his body. We came to this conclusion from the belief that the Ubermensch was much as were our very distant ancestors who we believed were created by the aliens. In other words, the Ubermensch must have a life span of about 1,500 years, and tissue being what it is, smoking and drugs and other harmful things would tend to kill him off before his normal life span had run its course. Oh, that's the other part of this Ubermensch thing. We figured that since the Ubermensch to come was as we once were, or at least nearly so, and that since, in our view, he fell from grace or devolved, that we just might have those ancient genes lying dormant insides us just waiting to be triggered by some event external or internal. Among the things in the former category was the belief that

since our beards grow faster and thicker when a cold winter is coming that the body really can cause physical changes. So ultimately, if I
wanted to mutate I should live in the same geographic/climate area
as the ancient Ubermensch to fool my genes into pushing the right
buttons. Hell, this ruled out going to the South Seas and being pam-
pered by nutbrown island queens who, at least in my dreams, were
always naked. The climate was wrong. They were wrong. Such an
environment would never let the old genes express themselves, and if
they did, then mating with the naked nut brown island queens
would send the Ubermensch's genetic line in the wrong direction.
Damn, I'd have to live in the frigid north. I'd also have to have cattle,
as we figured the ancient Ubermensch must have. I remember having read that some of the longest living people in the United States,
on average, lived in New Hampshire. I've been to New Hampshire. I
could live there with no problem, but I wondered if that's really cold
enough. Why is living long important? Because, maybe the genes
that we're trying to have express themselves don't kick in until we
reach a certain age, and maybe that's why there aren't any Ubermenschen around now. Say the kick-in age is 200 years. Who the hell lives
that long? No one. So, we live short disease filled lives. Then, before
the Ubermensch genes get a chance to express themselves we die.

Somehow, I had the feeling that we were being led to our thoughts
and actions. Maybe that's what crazies also think, but I didn't think
this was like that. It did raise questions in my mind about the nature
of free will, and the nature of who we essentially are, though. Who
was I? Was I the physical body? Was I the brain? Was I the genes? Was
I the DNA in my body? Who was in the driver's seat of me? I couldn't
really answer my own questions. I could speculate, but that's all it
would be. In the end, I came to the conclusion that we are much like
ants and that our so called free will is really just like instinct. We
think we want to do something or that we can do something, but it's
not really us who are thinking this. It's something inside us that is
steering us by causing our brains to want certain things. I also

became convinced that the nothingness of our lives—the three of our lives—the lack of purpose, actually had a purpose of some type. It was while I was thinking along these lines that I thought of something that happened to me when I was about ten years old.

"Did I tell you guys about my UFO experience?" I asked.

"You talk so much, you may have," said Gil.

"I don't remember," said Zack, "hit me with it."

"Well, when I was about ten years old, I was standing at the edge of these woods not far from my home. It was a mildly overcast day, but it didn't look like it was going to rain. Then, as I was just standing there I could see clouds gather and get very inky black. They were also very low. I bet if I had been in a four story building that I could probably touch them. Anyway, all of a sudden, it started to rain. I then stepped further out into this little field next to the woods because I wanted to feel the rain. The rain drops were those big globs that you sometimes get. Just as I stepped out from under the tree, the clouds opened up above me but off to the side a little bit. It looked as though someone had punched an almost perfectly circular hole in the clouds. And then, as I looked up, a beam of light—sunlight, I guess—came through and hit me. Hit me? Well the light shined on me. Just as that happened, I heard this signing. It was sort of like classical music but different, because it was just voices with no instruments. Many voices. Man, I can't hum it for you, but it was beautiful. Then the hole in the clouds closed up, the singing stopped, and that was it."

"Did you see any UFOs or anything?" asked Zack.

"Nope. It was just as I told you. I call it my UFO experience because I don't have any other term for it. It's never happened again. Just that one time. In later years, I searched my memory to see if there were any of the other UFO trappings, such as lost time and the like, but I've never been able to remember anything else about the experience. I wonder today, though, if somehow I wasn't programmed at that moment the light hit me to be as I am today.

Maybe, aliens or God changed my brain so that I would be on this quest for the Ubermensch." The other two couldn't remember anything like that happening in their lives, so we didn't have one of those scenes where we looked at each other in some sort of mystical recognition and understanding. Life was just never as easy and clear cut as movies.

"Anyway," I said, "suppose aliens had been visiting the Earth and suppose they had created us. Maybe they now want to activate us, or direct us for whatever purpose they have. Maybe that's why we're wandering like this. It could be that they've done this to millions of others on the planet. Maybe there's three-pods out in VW busses all over the planet. Maybe it's important that the vehicles be VW's and maybe it's not. Do you know that Adolf Hitler helped design the VW Beetle?"

"He did?" asked Gil. "I never saw that mentioned in any VW ads."

"Vere are your papers," said Zack trying to imitate some movie Nazi. "You know, maybe that's it. It's something to do with VW's. Maybe, they've got some sort of computer chip implanted in these things to send out some sort of mind control radio waves or something to make us think and act in certain ways. Those devious and sneaky Nazis. That was their plan to conquer the earth all along. What an evil plot. Make these things cheap so that everyone could afford one, and then every time you go out for a drive you get a little more zombified and robot like. Hell, look at Alex. Before this trip, he had dark hair combed like your basic yuppie and now he's blond and looks like a Nazi. And, listen to me ranting on about the Cosmic Pussy. What kind of talk is that for a guy with a law degree? I should be out there in a three piece suit chasing ambulances." And so it went as we joked about all of these nutty things that we were thinking and talking about.

"You know," said Gil, "I once read that the Nazis went to Antarctica after the war and set up some secret cities under the ice. They had some kind of mystical fire and ice belief about the Universe and existence."

"Well, I wouldn't be surprised," I said, "with the stuff I'm thinking now, and with the little I know about the Nazis, it would make sense for them to head to someplace cold and where they could continue to evolve the Ubermensch without being observed. I wonder, though, how they could do such a thing. If they had factories, there must be some sort of pollution that has been given off and they'd be observed. Besides, the U.S., Russia, and a bunch of other countries have bases down there."

"Wait a minute," chimed in Zack, "don't dismiss this so easily. I did some reading on Antarctica. The place is about as big as the U.S. Do you think you'd be able to find a few thousand people in such a large area if they didn't want to be found?"

"Well, that's not a good example. In Antarctica they wouldn't have any cover except the ice and snow," I said, knowing what the retort would be.

"They're under the ice, man," said Zack. "The ice is two friggin' miles thick in places, and under the ice is land. Imagine the U.S. covered with snow and ice two miles thick. Everything would be covered. Mountains, rivers, valleys, you name it and it would be covered, but it would all still be there. Hell, suppose that the Nazis had really set their minds to somehow getting under the ice and had built tunnels and underground cities sometime in 1939 or so, and that they kept digging and perfecting all during the war. Suppose that this was a top secret and high priority project. Don't you think they could have gotten down under the ice? You know that the Nazis were ahead of us in most science. Hell, they had jet planes up and flying while we were still riding around in little prop things."

"Yeah, but we whipped them," said Gil with an uncharacteristic jingoistic sound in his voice.

"Sure we did," said Zack, "but you do know that Germany is only about the size of Texas, don't you? I mean, they're a tiny little country compared to the U.S. and they almost beat us. The point I'm making is that they just may be under the ice. And, you mentioned pollution? What about the hole in the atmosphere right above the friggin" south pole? Maybe that's a result of their pollution instead of being the result of everyone using cans of hair spray. Alex's talk about the Ubermensch needing a cold climate to evolve in, may just have some truth in it. White skin. Blond hair. Blue eyes. These are the features of people who evolve in the cold. White skin lets in more of the sun's rays in places that don't get much sunlight. Black skin keeps out the rays in places that get too much sun. Blue eyes are found in northern animals, even in wolves, but I don't know why. My theory is that there truly is a Lamarckism at work in genes."

"Huh?" said Gil.

"Remember, Lamarckism is the now discredited belief that acquired characteristics can be inherited," I said.

"Correct," said Zack. "So if you live in a cold environment you acquire certain characteristics to make life comfortable. These characteristics then make changes in your genes and your offspring will inherit them even if they themselves are born in a different climate. Eventually, they will lose these characteristics unless they return to the original environment. Of course, they don't do all this in one generation, at least I don't think so, but maybe some people can do this faster than others. Anyway, this goes right along with our whole talk about creating the Ubermensch. Say, if the Nazis were working on improving the race by acquiring the characteristics of the Ubermensch, then the South Pole is the place they would probably have to be, especially after the war. Of course, there are other places on the earth that might work, but remember, we're not just talking about hiding a couple of guys out in the snow someplace. We're talking about having a lot of people—enough to create an entire society and do all the functions that are needed in society and still have some quality of life. We're talking about thousands and thousands of people. Just for openers, say that the Nazis, over several years, took maybe 50,000 people to Antarctica. How many do you suppose they would have today, if they bred to their maximum potential? Say they took more women than men, because the men were needed for the war and because at that time, as now, they didn't have the technology to implant their embryos in cows, like we think the space ancestors, if they existed, might have done. Man, this whole thing just goes around and around, doesn't it? Anyway, let's just say they took 40,000 women and 10,000 men. You may know that in Nazi Germany, women were given medals for the number of children they bore. So, let's say that these women averaged seven children each, and that they had them in rapid fire order. Let's keep this simple and say that all of these children lived to adulthood. That would mean by about 1959 there would be around 280,000 new individuals born to the 40,000 original women who were of breeding age. By 1979 another generation would be born. Let's just say that the number of breeding females from the 1959 generation would only be half of the number of people born in the second generation, or 140,000 individuals. Further assume that each of these 140,000 women bore 7 children each. Now we have a new generation of 980,000 individuals that we need to add to those who are still alive from the prior generations. Of course, these are all rough numbers based on pure speculation, but it's possible. Also, count on all these people being mostly blond haired and blued eyed potential Ubermenschen. Now, also say that these new people living in Antarctica also had agents on the mainland. Aren't there a lot of ex-Germans living in Argentina, which is close to Antarctica?"

"Interesting," said Gil, "you know, I read the account of Betty and Barney Hill who claimed to have been abducted by aliens in New Hampshire, and they said the aliens looked like "Nazis." That was the word they used. Do you think our Ubermenschen from Antarctica are riding around in flying saucers?" "And what about the New Hampshire connection?" asked Zack. "Remember we were talking about New Hampshire before?"

"I don't know about this," I said. "It might be fun to speculate this way but I find it hard to believe that the Nazis had the technology to stay hidden beneath the ice for all this time."

"Well, said Zack, "remember they may have outside contacts. Maybe their technology was pretty much late 1930's when they started, but they must have constantly upgraded as the world changed. However, I just can't figure how they could afford to do all this on an ongoing basis without someone catching on. They must have had to sell something on the world market and I can't figure what that is, unless they've got gold, or diamonds, or some other similar things that can be easily sold. A couple of miles of ice is a pretty good screen for anything down below, and you know we're talking about a whole continent down there. Man, they could have a hundred million people under there and we wouldn't know it."

"Okay," I said, "so you guys want me to go to the South Pole to live out my fantasy of becoming the Ubermensch, is that right?"

"Well," said Gil, "that might be a little out of the question. New Hampshire will probably work okay."

CHAPTER 12

*W*e hit Mill Valley, and just kept on driving on toward San Francisco. We crossed the Golden Gate Bridge in a heavy fog. Naturally. We could hear the fog horns in the bay. Gil had to drive with his head out the window because the fog was so thick. We inched along. It was like being in a snow storm. Everything was eerily quiet and it was cool but warm at the same time. San Francisco, the air conditioned city as they called it. The city on hills. It was a great city, but probably not as great as the locals always wanted everyone to believe. Parts of the city reminded me of New England while other parts looked like Mexico. First there would be a clapboard house painted that deep red or gray that you'd find on similar houses in New England, and next door there would be a pastel stucco place like you might find in Mexico.

Zack and Gil dropped me off at Carla's. Even though I lived there and helped with the rent and the bills, I always thought of it as Carla's place. When I got out, I stood there for a moment and watched as the taillights of the VW bus disappeared into the night fog. It didn't take long in that kind of fog for the bus to fade, but the taillights left an odd red smear as the light diffused. Then, the red smear was also gone. I looked up to the apartment and saw lights on. I walked up the flight of stairs. I was apprehensive that I might find another man there and not know how I would handle that. I decided to ring the bell. Just a few minutes after I rang it, Carla opened the door.

"Where are your keys?" she asked sweetly. Too sweetly. This is how she would set me up for our knock down drag out arguments. She'd start off sugary sweet and lead me into an ever increasing barrage of questions, until she felt she had tripped me up. Then, she'd begin shouting and crying.

"I just thought it would be polite to ring the bell. You might have had company or something," I said.

"Who would I have for company? Do you mean a man? You know I only see one man at a time, and you're the one I'm seeing. You keep ringing the doorbell all the time, and I told you that I'm insulted when you do that."

"I didn't want to seem presumptuous…"

"You live here damn it. Don't you remember? We're supposed to be a couple. We are a couple aren't we? And where have you been? Why didn't you call? You know I worry. You show me no respect at all. You just come and go whenever you like. Do I treat you that way? I know why you rang the bell. You were either trying to show me that you're not committed, or you were trying to show yourself the same thing, or maybe it was both." And, so it went, as she gathered a head of steam. I just gave her polite answers and tried not to egg her on. She was my girlfriend, I guess. I mean, I liked her, but I hadn't really set my mind to having a long term relationship. I just sort of fell into this, and she kind of rushed me. She was attractive. In fact, she was one of those women who if you see them in clothes you might just turn away, because she was slender and had the body of a swimmer. But, when she took her clothes off, she was right out of the pages of a men's magazine, but with smaller boobs. No kidding. She was that attractive in the nude. And, I wasn't the only one who noticed it. Whenever we went to the nude beach, she was the star of the place, once her clothes were off. She had those small upturned breasts with upturned sort of bee stung looking nipples that were all pink, and her ass was perfectly proportioned from all angles. She was sort of short waisted and slightly swaybacked. She had a tiny dimple at the base of her spine where her back turned into ass. Maybe they just didn't make clothes to fit a girl who was so perfectly proportioned, because her clothes were mostly slightly baggy looking when she was dressed. So, she appealed to me physically, but her insane jealousy was something else. I don't use the word insane lightly either, because she would throw things and break down doors and try to hit me with her car. The funny thing about her rages was that if a third person happened on the scene, she could turn off the rage in an instant and look all innocent. It was like turning a light switch on or off. Bam. Instant light or instant darkness. That's probably what kept her from having a net thrown over her head, because few other people ever observed her rages. Of course, there is the possibility that I, by my very nature, just set her off and triggered her rages. Maybe it was kind of a cats and dogs thing, or maybe I was the match and she was the kerosene.

As time went on, Carla just got worse. She'd go on a business trip, and when she returned, she'd take every single towel out of the closet and check them for suspicious hairs. She would secretly mark the tires of my car to see if it had been moved, and if it appeared that the car had been moved, she'd ask if I had been out. If I said that I hadn't, she'd scream that she knew the car had been moved and she'd want to know why I had lied to her. She also had her friends secretly watch me and report to her on what I was doing. It was nuts. I finally sat her down and tried to explain to her that this was absurd. I wasn't particularly good looking. I didn't have any money. What in the world was she jealous about? I never in my life had girls chasing after me, and hell, it had even been hard for me to get a date before we were married. I told her that her jealously was misplaced. She said that she understood. She didn't. About a week later, we were in the supermarket and while I was selecting some onions, a girl came over and was picking up some onions at the same time. She said something like "There's no good ones here," or something similar. Then she walked away. Carla had apparently seen this, because she came over and asked if I knew the girl, to which I replied, honestly, that I didn't. Then I got the third degree about why had I smiled at the girl? "I wasn't smiling."

"What did you say to her?"

"Nothing."

"What did she say to you?"

"No good ones."

"Did you get her telephone number?"

"No."

"Did she get your telephone number?"

"No."

"Did you set up a date?"

"No."

"Do you plan on seeing her again?"

"No."

"Did you find her attractive?

"No," I lied about that one.

"Did you like her dress?"

"No," I lied about that too.

"Are you attracted to her type?"

"No," another lie.

"Have you ever seen her before?"

"No."

"Was she a regular shopper at the market?"

"I don't know."

"Where does she live?"

"I don't know."

"What does she do for work?"

"I don't know."

"Did you tell her that you're married?"

"No."

"Why not?

After all of this, Carla said that she didn't believe me and that she thought that I knew the girl and that we secretly met at the market and then went out into the parking lot and did what we wanted. Carla then wanted to know if I thought she was a fool?

"No."

"How could you run around on me this way?"

"I didn't."

"How did a blond hair get on one of our towels?"

"We wash in a community washing machine."

"The blond hair looked just like the hair on the girl at the onions, how could I explain that?" "I couldn't."

"Do you think you can run around while I'm on a flight?"

"No."

"What do you do with your time?"

"Work."

"What about when you're not working?"

"Visiting with friends."

"What friends?"

"Zack and Gil, mostly."

"And, what about Gil's girl friend?"

"What about her?"

"She has her eyes on every man that goes into Poop doesn't she?"

"Did you ever sleep with her?"

"No."

"Do you want to?"

"No."

"Did you ever ask her?"

"No."

"Did she ever ask you?"

"No."

"Didn't she ask me if I wanted a blow job? (uh oh, a trap. Carla had heard about what had happened). "She yelled something like that when we were leaving."

"Did you think she was serious?"

"I don't know."

"Would I like to take her up on it?"

"No."

"Why?"

"Because I'm married."

"What if you weren't married?"

"No."

"Why not?"

"Because she's Gil's girlfriend."

"What if she wasn't Gil's girlfriend?"

"She doesn't appeal to me."

"Do I appeal to you?"

"Yes."

"I don't have blond hair."

"I like your hair the color it is."

"Do you think my hair's mousey?"

"No."

"Why did you dye your hair blond if you don't like blonds?:

"Ubermensch."

"Huh?"

"Ubermensch. Superman. The next step for mankind."

"Huh?"

"It's a theory we're working on."

"Who's we?"

"Zack and Gil and me."

"Are you nuts?"

"Yeah. Probably."

So, that's the way it went. That's the way it always went. In a way I was flattered that she should be so jealous. I was unused to anyone caring about me and this was a new experience. Oh, I knew that it wasn't really me who she cared for and that this was just a neurotic thing that she must do with other men each in their turn. Still, she had a really great body, so I chose to put up with this silliness for her body.

CHAPTER 13

*A*bout a week later, I got a call from Zack who said that he was about to film something for Gino and he wanted to know if I'd like to help out with the lights and stuff. I told him that I would. I arrived at Zack's apartment right on schedule. Zack told me to act professional and not let on that I didn't normally do the lights, because that would make everyone nervous.

"All you have to do is move a light here and there when I tell you or move a cable if it's in the way. Be sure not to talk, because we'll be recording at the same time."

We went into the next room where Zack had his studio. It was just a large bedroom with the windows completely covered with aluminum foil to keep the light out. Zack immediately tacked up some beige bed sheets over the aluminum foil to give the kind of background he wanted. The only furniture in the room was a couch and a bed. Sitting on the couch were the two girls from the nude beach and the onion girl from the supermarket.

"Girls," said Zack, "this is my pal Alex. This is Tracy, "he said while indicating the one with short blond hair; "this is Linda," as he indicated the brunette "and this is Kim," who was the onion girl.

"Alex is going to help out with the lights, girls. The actor I have scheduled is Ted, he's done a lot of these films so he knows what to do. He should be here any minute." We engaged in some small talk for a few minutes and then finally it appeared that Ted was a no-show. "Well, all right, I'll have to be in the movie myself," said Zack. "Alex, let me show you how to work the camera. It's really very simple. The main thing is to just keep us in the center of the frame. We should fill the viewfinder. I'll walk you through this. We'll shoot in short sequences so you can learn your way. Just look through the viewfinder and don't jiggle the camera. Okay, Tracy, do you want to go first? Let me tell all of you how I do my films. They're very simple. The camera will open and find Tracy sitting on the couch. I'll be behind the camera and I'll ask you questions, and I'll tell you what to do. Just do what I tell you, and try to act natural. In this format, you should look at me when you talk, but ordinarily you wouldn't look at the camera. But we'll get into that a little later. Just talk to me in a normal tone of voice. The microphone is sensitive, so you don't have to speak louder than you would normally. All right, Tracy just sit there and get comfortable. Linda and Kim, come on back here, please. Okay, on three, we'll be rolling. One, two, three."

"Hi, what's your name?" asked Zack from behind the camera.

"Tracy," said Tracy with a smile as she sat on the couch looking at the camera.

"Have you been in a porno film before, Tracy?"

"No."

"Are you nervous?"

"A little."

"Well, you don't have to be. It's just very natural. You're a very beautiful girl, but I guess you've heard that before, haven't you?"

Tracy just smiled.

"Stand up Tracy and let's take a good look at you. You're tall, aren't you. How tall are you?"

"Five-eleven"

"Hmmm, hmmm," said Zack.

"Tracy, slip off your dress will you? That's it, just lift it over your head like you were at home. Beautiful. Look at that tan. You must go to the beach a lot."

"Yes," said Tracy who was standing there in a flower patterned sports bra and matching bikini panties.

"Can you take your bra off for us, please? Great. You look really great. How about your panties, just slip them off, will you? That's a girl. Wow! You're shaved. Now that's what I call a Bikini trim all right. Or is that a Brazilian? Do you know what a Brazilian is?"

"No," said Tracy.

"They pour hot wax all over...."Just then the telephone rang. I answered it and it was Carla, who said her car wouldn't start and she needed my help. I excused myself and left. Zack told me later that the filming went alright, and that he had whichever girl wasn't being filmed at the moment, work the camera.

CHAPTER 14

A few months later, I was getting all fidgety again, so I called Zack and asked if he was still searching for the Cosmic Pussy. He said that he was, so I proposed that we take a run down to Mexico to see what we could see. We agreed that if we could get Gil to go along, we'd leave the following week and plan to be gone for a couple of weeks, maybe a little less, maybe a little more. He wanted to know what I'd do about Carla. I didn't have any good answer, because I knew she'd just blow her stack. I was really fond of Carla, but her temper and her mannerisms were getting to me. I always felt that it as though she were playing characters from one of those 1960's movies. She seemed to expend most of her calories on saying things like "That's fun," about everything. "Carla, I'm going to the store," I'd say, and she would reply "Oh, that sounds like fun." "Carla, I'm going to the post-office." "Oh, that sounds like fun." I was starting to feel like I was in a beach party movie.

Finally, I told her that we were going on the trip. Her reaction was quick. "Oh no you're not. You're not going anyplace."

"Oh, yes I am," I said, "we've already decided."

"Well, if you leave this place, you'd better never come back."

"Well, if that's the way you want it, that's the way it'll be," I said.

I guess she didn't know that's how I always left places. One minute I could be here, and the next minute I'd be gone forever. It didn't much mater to me where I was. It was like electricity taking the path of least resistance. Carla was not the path of least resistance, right now.

So, I went in and packed most of my stuff in some boxes and put them in the garage. I called my boss and told him I had an emergency and I had to leave town for a while. I gave my keys to the apartment to Carla, and I rode off on the hog to meet Zack and Gil. I told them what had happened and that I needed a change of scenery anyway, but I would leave my hog at Poop while we went on our trip and when we got back, if Carla was still a no go, that I'd figure something else out at that time. We then packed what we needed in the VW bus and without any more fanfare, we set out south. We again decided to take Pacific Coast Highway, because PCH had the best views. We had brought our sleeping bags and the plan was to sleep outside as much as possible. At first we just barreled along, because we wanted to feel that we were going someplace and not just traveling in circles as we normally did in the past. This time, we had a goal to find more examples of the Cosmic Pussy. Zack had brought along some pretty good video equipment, and he figured that he could make some money on this trip by making some porno films if the situations presented themselves. Of course his main goal was to film every Mexican painting of the Virgin of Guadalupe that we could find. He apparently had decided that his Cosmic Pussy research would be better presented as a documentary type film than as a book, so that's what he was up to. He told us that he was also getting ideas for the voice over dialog from our conversations during our trips.

Down around Santa Cruz, we found our first Cosmic Pussy painting on the side of a bar. Zack filmed it, and then to my surprise, he got out of the bus and measured it and recorded it in a little book he as carrying. He explained that he had evolved this procedure from the early days and was now trying to be more scientific to see if all these paintings had common dimensions or other factors that might give clues about their genesis. Next, we hit another small town and found two more examples of the Cosmic Pussy. I was actually starting to enjoy this quest. The paintings were mostly all very crude. Other than the general features, they all appeared to be spontaneous products of local Mexicans. Many of them were painted in the Mexican national colors of red, white and green, with green predominating. Many others had all sorts of other colors. Up close, the drawings were crude in the facial features of the Madonna. From a short distance, however, they were all clearly vaginas to us and probably to anyone else who had once formed the thought. It was interesting symbolism. The virgin mother of Jesus emerging from the Cosmic Pussy of God, to have a virgin birth. And all this from a nation whose national food seemed to be a taco which also looks like a pussy. The cornucopia of the Universe, the Cosmic Pussy. Damn. The principle that brings something from nothing...a Cosmic Pussy. Could it all be so simple? Many of the scientists and philosophers of all times were all trying to find the Unified Field Theory—that one thing that would explain all that is—and there it was right before us forever; the Cosmic Pussy. No. They couldn't believe anything so simple. The secrets of the universe must be wrapped up in numerology or astrology or hidden dimensions or any of a number of arcane and esoteric things hidden from ordinary men and only capable of being seen by these learned alchemists of all ages. "The secrets of the universe are hidden away in secret caves under the Himalayas guarded by the Great Brotherhood of the big mumbo jumbo," says this expert over here. "Not so," says this other expert, "They are hidden in the pyramids of Egypt." "Not so," says yet another expert. "The secrets of the universe are at Stonehenge in England." And, thousands of poorly written books are pumped out on each of the various theories of the secrets of the universe. Even so, no one gets any closer to the real secrets. No one is able to answer the basic questions that mankind has always asked. Gods are created and discarded willy nilly over the centuries by races of men who have always sworn by their particular version of truth…ultimate truth. One can imagine cavemen having that mad religious gleam in their eyes as they tell other cavemen that the secret of the universe is found in a particular type of bison bone or that God is fire. Searching, always searching, for the big secrets, and never knowing that these secrets are contained in that smaller version of the Cosmic Pussy that is part of the body of that cave girl they just bonked over the head and dragged back to their cave.

Perhaps Zack was on to something. Maybe the secret of secrets really is contained in the vagina, but because of human modesty and attitudes toward sex and the human body, the secret has eluded humanity. Maybe, humans just didn't want to see what was right before them out of prudishness, or because it didn't jibe with their views of a male God. Maybe those enormous black holes in outer space are big female genitalia that suck in all that is within their reach and then from what has been sucked in, conceive something new and then birth it. Perhaps the universe is full of these Cosmic Pussies that just wander around sucking in entire star systems, tearing them apart and reconstituting them. I could imagine this being like giant tornados that would look like cornucopias from a great distance—huge horns of plenty, taking and spewing out new things without end. From nothing, comes nothing, but from something, can come something. When a woman conceives a child, the child has not been created out of nothing, but from something. So it must be with the Cosmic Pussy. Maybe it was true that some people had guessed at the nature of this Cosmic Pussy and had simply drawn it in different ways depending of their perspective or motives. Thus, some saw it from the end with the arms extended and drew it as a swastika. Others saw it from the side and drew a horn of plenty, or a wave pattern. Maybe there is an eternally pregnant and birthing universe.

Could it be that the Cosmic Pussy had to create males on the earth in order to get creation going? In the Cosmos, there was no male needed, but even when we think of the as above, so below expression, the big things seen through the telescope aren't exactly the same as the small things seen through the microscope, but the principles are the same.

Maybe the Cosmic Pussy has just a certain number of cookie molds into which she can pour living matter. Perhaps, for example, she has a mold that will create a certain kind of dinosaur—say, a Triceratops. When that certain creature died off and the world changed, the Cosmic Pussy still had the mold, but now the matter that she had available to make something was different. So she poured this different matter into the mold and what emerged was a Rhinoceroses. Then she designed a beetle that looks like a Triceratops. In went the raw material into the mold and out came a beetle. The beetle is thousands of times smaller than the dinosaur, but it looks like the dinosaur.

Then we have the hominids, including man. The mold is pretty much the same for all of us from the apes to man, but there are small differences, and isn't that what evolution is all about anyway, small differences?

"Hey, Alex," said Zack, "look at that cosmic Pussy over on that building." Zack was pointing to the side of what appeared to be an old closed down movie house made of red bricks. On one whole side wall, was a huge Cosmic Pussy painted with the Mexican flag colors of green, white and red. This painting was so big and so detailed that there was no doubt that this was a Cosmic Pussy. The artist hadn't tried to hide what it was, and must have consciously known what he was drawing. The Madonna was standing in the middle with her gown furled in the breeze so that the gown became the kind of inner pussy lips that are common in girls who have full facial lips. So above, so below, again. As usual, the Madonna's head was the clitoris. It's a wonder that someone with a blue nose hadn't had this painting draped or removed. Hell, if a bunch of little old ladies were sometimes offended by ancient Greek and Roman statues of nudes, this one would give them heart attacks. Maybe though, this was just such a common sight around here, that no one said anything or even really noticed it. Maybe it's kind of like when Catholics say, in prayer, 'Holy Mary, Mother of God, blessed by thy name and blessed be the fruit of they womb, Jesus.' Hell, they're saying womb. They're saying fruit. They're talking about the Cosmic Pussy, as a cornucopia giving fruit, and they don't even know it. I wonder how many good Catholics say their prayers and never really understand the words they're saying? Prayers have become dead formulaic things with no feeling and no meaning at all. And what about Catholic priests who, of course, aren't allowed to be married. Is this something to do with not violating the Cosmic Pussy—even the Cosmic Pussy when brought down to human size?

Zack was really taken with this particular rendition of the Cosmic Pussy and decided he wanted to find the artist. We asked at the stores in the neighborhood, but with no luck, and then we went into this little Mexican bar and asked the bartender if he knew who drew the painting on the side of the building. He said he did, but wanted to know if we were the police or from the government. He also wanted to know if there was some trouble about the painting. We told him that we weren't cops or from the government, and there was no trouble. We explained that we just liked the painting and thought it was very good so we'd like to congratulate the artist. The bartender then yelled in to the backroom, "Jose come here." Suddenly a little man who must have been at least 85 years old, and who was as skinny as a taquito, came out from the backroom with a mop in his hand. He was about five feet tall. He was dried up looking but he had an unflinching grin on his face. He was missing his front teeth, so his gums were always visible. It turns out the grin wasn't really a normal grin at all. The guy had that medical condition, whatever it's called, sardonicus or something similar and it makes those with the problem smile all the time. "Jose, these guys say they like your painting and want to talk to you, about it," said the bartender. Jose just kept smiling and nodding his head and didn't say anything, so Zack finally jumped in.

"Hi, Jose. My name is Zack. This is my friend Alex and this is Gil We were on our way down to Mexico and we saw your painting and wanted to meet whoever could paint that well."

Jose just kept on smiling. Zack looked at the bartender and asked if Jose could talk.

"Nope," came the reply. "But he can hear perfectly well. He just cleans up around here, from time to time, for food. Give him a few bucks and he'll probably draw something for you."

Zack gave Jose twenty bucks and asked him to join us for a sandwich and a beer. We ordered, and we all sat in this old greasy booth with torn red plastic seats in the dim bar light with the smell of stale beer in the air. We couldn't tell if Jose was mentally impaired in some way, or exactly what it was about him, but he seemed to be a little off. He just kept smiling and nodding. After trying to determine how he was able to draw so good, Zack asked if he had a model that he used when he painted it. Jose just kept grinning, because that's all he could do, and shook his head yes, and then wrote the name Lupe on a napkin. As he wrote the name he blessed himself. He then got up and left and motioned for us to follow him. We paid the tab and headed out the door. This reminded me of the movie Treasure Island where the good guys are being led someplace by crazy old Ben Gunn. Anyway, we walked down the street past all the little shops and closed up businesses and past the many second hand stores with signs in Spanish to a little house with a sign in the window that said in English, Fortune Telling. Jose blessed himself again as we got in front of the house and he motioned for us to go inside. We went in, and Jose stayed outside. As soon as we opened the door we were in a small reception room with tacky red velvet curtains covering all the windows and walls so that it had some sort of cheap but mystical feel to it. There was a counter with a bell. We rang the bell and a woman of about 55 years old came out to the front and asked what we wanted. We told her the truth, and that we had admired the painting, and that Jose had given us the name Lupe and sent us here.

"Are you from the police?" she asked.

"No," said Gil. "We're just three guys who live in San Francisco and we're on our way to Mexico."

"In fact," said Zack, apparently to allay her fear, "I make adult films for a living. Gil works in a restaurant and Alex works, for the guy I sell my films to. We're definitely not cops."

"Well, what is it you really want, and why are you so curious about Jose's painting?"

"Zack started getting into the Cosmic Pussy thing, and I figured we were about to be thrown out, but the woman suddenly started warming to the conversation, and she said, "I modeled for Jose for that painting about 30 years ago. I'm Lupe."

"When you say you modeled for the painting, do you mean that you're the Madonna or that the outside part that looks like a vagina is also yours?" asked Gil.

"I was both. I don't really know how much of that painting looks like me, but I was the inspiration," she said.

Zack could hardly contain himself. "Look, this may sound weird to you, but I'm making a documentary film on the subject of the Cosmic Pussy. Will you let me take a video of you?"

"You mean you want me to be in a porno film?"

"No," said Zack. "No sex. This is really a religious film."

"How much you paying," she asked.

"I'll give you fifty bucks. I can't afford any more than that. A quick fifty bucks and there'll be no sex or touching. I will need to have about an hour of your time though."

"Will those two guys be watching?" she asked.

"Well, I need them to help with the equipment. They're both pro-fessionals, and have helped me before. Is that a problem?"

"It'll probably be alright. Go get your equipment and come to the back door."

We went to where we had parked and drove the bus around to the back of her place. Lupe was holding the door open as we got out of the bus. We grabbed the equipment from the back of the bus and followed Lupe down a short hall with peeling paint, to her bedroom. The room was mostly bare. There was a small bed with a three foot wooden cross above it. Next to the bed was a small wooden table. On the table, were some unlit votary candles with pictures of the Virgin of Guadalupe on them. And there was an old oak veneer bureau over against one wall with the top drawer open and with a bra hanging out of it. The floor was bare wood that creaked when we walked on it. The only window in the room was covered with red curtains. After asking her permission, we tacked up a large black sheet over the window. Zack asked Lupe to strip and stand in front of the black sheet and to get as close to the standing pose in the painting, as possible. Lupe immediately took up the pose with absolutely no other direction from Zack, as though she did this every day. And, son of a gun, if she didn't look good. We hadn't planned it, but some light seeped in from around the black sheet sort of framing the whole thing like a big halo. Zack filmed for a while and then took some still photos. Then we took the sheet and laid it on the bed. Zack apologized to Lupe and told her that he needed some gynecological type shots. Lupe laid on the black sheet which we had draped over the bed. My eyes or my mind must have been playing tricks on me, because I swear it looked like light was again seeping out from behind the black sheet as it had when it was against the window even though the sheet was now on the bed with no light source. Lupe was a good looking woman, and she didn't look her age at all. Still, her stomach had lost some of that hard belly look of youth, but it wasn't flabby.

"Beautiful," said Zack. "Lupe are you Mexican?"

"Part Mexican, part white, and part Blackfoot Indian," was her reply.

There was nothing self-conscious about Lupe and even when Zack went in for closeups, she didn't mind. There was also nothing lecherous about it on Zack's part. He was acting like a professional scientist trying to analyze something. Lupe's vagina was the Cosmic Pussy made small. We filmed Lupe in every conceivable pose and took lots of still photos. When an hour was up, Zack told us to stop filming because that's what our agreement was with Lupe. We thanked her, and told her that if we came back through this way again, we'd stop and say hello. With that, we packed up our equipment and left.

As we started heading south again, Zack said that he found it interesting that this part Blackfoot woman had what he considered to be about the best version of what he thought the Cosmic Pussy should look like when reduced to human size.

"Maybe," Zack said, "we'll have to revise our idea of the Ubermensch. Perhaps he's supposed to look like an Indian and not a German Nazi. But, wait a minute, Lupe said that she was only part Blackfoot. Did she say something about the other half being Mexican? Remember, the French and the Irish and Germans were once down in Mexico in some numbers."

"So what do you want me to do now to be the Ubermensch? Should I dye my hair black? Get a tan? Try to look like an Indian?"

"Not so fast," said Zack, "we haven't figured this out yet so let's just keep going with you as a Nazi looking Ubermensch."

"So here we are," I said, "three characters from the Wizard of Oz all on the yellow brick road trying to find out what the hell this existence is all about. Over here we have a guy in hot pursuit of the Cosmic Pussy, which may or may not exist. Here, you have a guy trying to mutate or evolve himself into the Ubermensch. Then we have one lost soul in this bus to nowhere who seems to have no goals whatsoever. No something, to rid himself of the nothing. No target at which to aim. Gil, we need to find something to give you a sense of direction. There must be something nutty that you're interested in," I said.

Gil thought for a few minutes before speaking. "Well, maybe I'm the only sane one in this bus. Have you ever thought about that? Maybe you two guys are really crazy and have odd ideas. Maybe my role in this existence is to be the straight man. Maybe I'm a nut groupie of something. Perhaps, I'm the one who holds the bungee cords that are attached to your legs as you fly off the Earth into some never, never land. I actually enjoy all the conversation and these trips. I don't get along too well with straight people—no, no, I don't mean straight as in gay/not gay. I mean in the sense of people who just live normal lives. I know I look just like your average yuppie, but that's just an outward appearance. I think our trips, to me, are like fishing or hunting or golf trips for other people. You know, as I listen to us talk, I wonder if our differences aren't because we're brighter than most other people. Then I wonder if it's because we're dumber than other people. To tell you the truth, since you've been pushing this, I am interested in something and that's politics. Revolutionary politics. Maybe it's the revolutions themselves that I like, and the politics are secondary. Anyway, if I'm to play the game, and if I must define myself as best I can based upon what I find interesting to read about or think about, or fantasize about, then it would have to be revolutions. So I will be the wild eyed revolutionary in our unscripted meandering, at least and until something more interesting comes along. I therefore declare before the finder of the Cosmic Pussy and the Ubermensch aborning, that I will now act the part of the revolutionary."

"Bravo," said Zack. "Now we have rounded off our little band of merry men trying to find the Wizard. I don't know if we're exactly three dimensional and if we really fill in those gaps in each other's personalities as one might hope, but it'll have to do. Three loners, losers, in a bus traveling down the lonely road...."

"Wizard," I said. "Hmmm. That reminds me of a crazy guy I once heard in Boston. He was standing on a park bench talking to people. Skinny old guy with a white beard. If I were going to cast a movie, he'd be the wizard."

"The hairs on the back of my neck, just went up," said Gil. "You didn't hear that guy in the Common, by any chance, did you? And, was he rambling on about the destruction of America or something like that?"

"Yes," I said.

"You're not going to believe this, but I bought this bus from an old guy who used to spout off in the Common all the time. I wonder if it's the same guy?"

"I don't know. The guy I heard was weird. I remember when I was leaving he raised his hand and…"

"Gave you a three finger wave?" interrupted Gil.

"Same guy," I said. "Man this is really a coincidence, isn't it?" No one answered.

"So here, we are," said Zack, finally breaking the silence, "driving on through the blue mists of early night, looking all pale like some Edward Hopper meets Edvard Much painting. Three thin, ghost like strangers casting eerie shadows from the moonlight who can't get on or off the bus, because somehow they're both on and off the bus already. They're trapped, and they're all looking at each other with expressionless faces and all wondering if the others had the answers but knowing in their minds that the answers weren't to be had this or any other night. Still, the search must go on through all eternity. Maybe another night would yield up the cosmic answers. Maybe the next bus coming down the road would have the answers for the people watching it go by, and maybe the next lonely road would have the answers for the people on the bus."

"Well, that's a nice warm and comfy picture you have, Alex," said Gil.

"Tell us Commander Gil, of your revolution," I said in reply.

"Well, you know that we're oppressed in this country, don't you?" asked Gil, apparently to prime the pump of his revolutionary persona.

"Who's oppressed?" asked Zack. "You mean black people or what?"

"No. I'm glad you brought that up. The real oppressed people in the united States are white people. You see, whites are oppressed on one side by the ruling elites, who are mostly white like us—but they're alienated from their true selves—and on the other side by non-whites. It's a big squeeze. If we step a little out of line, the ruling elites—the white Uncle Toms—slap us with all sorts of bogey man names: "racist, bigots, prejudiced, insensitive." Meanwhile, these white Uncle Toms are busy gifting the non-whites with the fruits of our labor. When non-elite whites complain, they're told in subtle ways that they are defective, otherwise they too would be in the ruling elite class. So, the ruling elites who are mostly white themselves, preach to the non-elite whites about how they should live and act and react to other races in the country, and then these ruling class elites jump in their limos and head for their gated guarded communities before dusk. They don't want to be caught on the streets of post-American America where their non-white pets might mistake them for ordinary white people and rob, rape or murder them. It's a double standard, really. These elites control the press, the government, the religions, and you name it. They're the ones with the money, the power and the influence. They talk the talk but they don't walk the walk. While the kids of the non-elite whites go off to foreign wars, the kids of the elites go to Harvard and Yale instead. While the kids of the non-elite whites are giving up their places in college lines to non-whites, who take their place because of their ethnicity, the kids of the elites are getting into college through the back door. While the kids of the non-elite whites are losing their jobs as factories close down and move overseas, the kids of the elites are jumping in Daddy's private jet and flying over to visit Daddy's factories. I know that you've been raised to believe that we don't have classes in America, but this is a myth. We have less rigid classes than are found in Europe, but we still have classes. Sure, you can join the elite classes if you have enough money and if you conform to their world view. And, what is this world view? You probably thing it's conservative, but it's not. The world view of our present ruling class is what we might term pragmatic liberal. The underlying premise for most of their liberalism is what Alex was talking about on one of our other trips. They have a view of humanity as all being the same, and therefore if non-whites aren't fully represented in the higher echelons of various segments of society it's only because the defective non-elite whites kept them out.

"So, you have a tension in society that is maintained by the ruling elites—the White uncle Toms. They keep the tension on the non-elite whites by manipulating the non-whites. Should the non-elite whites get uppity, then the ruling elites play off the non-whites against them. It's a little like those water strider bugs that can walk across the top of the water because the surface tension of the water keeps them up. Those bugs are the elites. Down below, are the non-elite whites. Below them are the non-whites. The ruling class elites are known for their acts of noblesse oblige as they drive right over their fellow whites to gift the non-whites. Do you know that at the start of the black civil rights movement when that black woman—Rosa Parks—refused to give up her bus seat to a white man and was arrested, that most blacks were against her and considered her a nut case? As the years have passed, blacks have had their consciousness raised so that now virtually all blacks would say that had they been around back then, that they would have been on Rosa Parks' side.

"That's just like us looking back at, say, Copernicus and those other guys who said that the Earth rotated around the sun and not the other way around. Then they were tortured for saying that. Just about every intelligent person today would say that had we been alive back then we would have stood up for them. Sure we would have. Nonsense. Genius lies in being able to see what's real and what's false right while you're alive and not after its been sanitized for years. So it is with the oppression that white people are living under. Of course, it gets a little confusing for us, because we look at the elites and we see that they're white and they don't act like Snidely Whiplash and they sound reasonable, so we think that we're wrong and we internalize our feelings of wrongness and inferiority and we-our minds—never wanting to be wrong, make it so. It's like Alex trying to use his mind to become the Ubermensch, by getting rid of one template in his mind and replacing it with another so that his mind can make him into the new image. Most people have the wrong templates in their minds today and they're stuck with them until they can replace them with correct ones.

"The problem with replacing the internal picture is that the one you carry of yourself is often so subtle that you don't even know that's what is in you. If, for example, your parents told you that you were worthless or stupid when you were young, but then they apologized and said that they had just said what they had said in a weak or angry moment and didn't even really believe it or mean it themselves, but you did. You may already have internalized the bad view of yourself and your mind thereafter makes you be worthless or stupid, until you can exorcize this demon.

"So here we are in this country all living the myth of the 19th Century here in the 21st Century. We look out and we think to ourselves, this can't be right. We say that we have freedom, but what good is freedom if we don't dare go out on the streets for fear of being killed by some non-white criminals.?"

"Why does it have to be a non-white criminals?" asked Zack.

"Because, that's the way it is," said Gil. "Your chances of being attacked on our streets by a non-white are far greater than in being attacked by a white."

"Well that sounds racist," said Zack.

"Ahhh. You're showing the effects of the propaganda, my good man," said Gil. "For about forty years the feds and the social engineers have tried to convince you that to think in terms of races is bad. But think about it. Is it really? It's just demographics and it's just science. If all the little blue candies make you sick and all the red ones taste good, are you going to go on eating the little blue ones?"

"Yeah, but we're talking about people, not candy," said Zack.

"We're talking about basic principles," I answered. "We're talking about your personal safety. We're talking about survival. Besides, the term racist is misused to my way of thinking. It should mean that the person who is a racist notices that the races of man are different. They are in fact different, so what's the problem? You see, what's happened is that those who oppress us want to Mau Mau us with words to keep us in our place. They've put us in an intellectual prison ringed all around with the razor wire of name calling. If we try to move beyond the prison and think and speak about things that are beyond the current orthodoxy, they hurl those words at us: racist, bigot, insensitive, prejudiced, nazi, extremist, and on and on. This is how they keep us in our place once we start awakening to the true state of affairs. What the elites do, is identify those who are moving beyond the prison of the mind and they then try to isolate them from others by calling them names and demonizing them. And, once they're isolated and shunned by others, then they can be destroyed. Now, when I say it like this, you can see it clearly, but in actual fact, in practice, there are many other currents all flowing at the same time, so it is far more difficult to discern what is going on. There are other myths that tend to keep the people docile. The main one is that they can change things with their votes. In fact, the government only allows them to change what it wants them to change and if they go beyond what the government allows, the government overrules the vote. I know, you're thinking that you can make changes by voting in various elected officials, but in fact, behind all these elected officials is a monstrous bureaucracy—a gigantic machine that, if we were to portray it graphically, might look like something that might be built by Mary Shelley, Rube Goldberg, and Franz Kafka after an all night binge of kinky sex, booze and LSD. Sure, you can change the names on the doors of government, but the new people are just new cogs that are plugged into the same slots in the same machine. And, if the new cogs don't worked right, the machine either rejects them outright, or builds around them, and then in four years or so, the new non-fitting cogs are voted out of office as the machine seeks to protect itself, and keep itself as it was before.

This gigantic machine, this government behemoth, that puts its will on the people is out to protect itself, and you'd better believe that even the smallest cog in this machine is looking for that to happen as well. They want to keep the people docile and reasonably happy. They don't want the people to want true freedom, for true freedom, freedom to pursue individual and group destinies free of the intrusions of the machine, would mean the destruction of the machine."

"I don't get you," said Zack. "You sort of sound like a communist, but then you sound like a right-winger."

"That's like all three of us," said Gil. "We're all three not falling into pigeon holes very well are we? It's like Alex when he was talking about finding some name to define us and being frustrated in not being able to do so. I'm not for communism. It has a false view of man and therefore can't work as planned. I'm not for parlor conservatism, because it also has a false idea of man. Most of these political philosophies actually try to set forth their principles about man without really considering man. They posit all sorts of false ideas of the nature of us, and then build their philosophy around these false ideas. I think we have to start with genes. We have to view man not primarily as a philosophical creature, but as a genetic creature. Then we have to start defining or reducing man into separate groups, with the first cut based on genotype or race. I know that's not a popular thought these days, but it doesn't make it any less valid. Why would anyone consider a million years of evolution leading to a particular genotype less worthy than some person's notion that we are all the same and that there's no such thing as race? This recent idea to downplay the reality of race is as absurd as saying there are no different breeds of dogs. Why is the notion that we're all the same considered valid, even though we can see with our own eyes that we're not? Why is the idea that a million years of evolution is something that we should ignore? I say that genes are the most important things for all living things. I'll bet if you took a bunch of white people and isolated them on a desert island that they'd build a society and infrastructure that we would recognize as a white civilization—wait a minute, I bet if you took these white people when they were just little kids and somehow were able to make sure that they were fed and taken care of until they could fend for themselves, and if you could do this without tainting the experiment, that they would build a recognizable European culture—different only in that the climate and other factors would demand certain differences. After all, they couldn't be expected to build brick houses if the raw materials weren't there. I'll also bet if you did the same thing with all the other racial groups, that they too would build what they must build. We may all have a certain amount of free will, but there are limits to it. A certain type of ant will always build a certain type of nest, as will birds and so on. We are no less a part of nature than any of these other animals. Now, if we can accept that idea that race is important, then we are left to wonder what the hell America is all about. I mean, everybody is just jumbled together, and this is causing distortions in the big picture and it's leading to revolutionary pressures in our society. Those who have often ruminated about these things have always sort of figured that the revolutionary class would be the blacks, but history teaches us that most modern revolutions are actually led and fueled by the middle class whites.

"The revolution supreme, must be the French Revolution of 1789. I know you have pictures in your minds of peasants storming the Bastille and that sort of thing, but in fact that revolution was started and maintained by a very small group of middle class people. At various points in the revolution, the peasants did march, but by and large they weren't the sparkplug nor the fuel for the revolution. It takes an educated class—a class that knows that things can be better, to bring in revolution. I say that, because I think that America is now in a pre-revolutionary period. We're seeing all sorts of groups springing up all over the place and this is one of the things that happens in such a time. It is a time of increasing chaos and a time of great conflicts of ideas. Everyone, with some idea of how to improve things, seems to get a voice in such times as things are sorted out. Remember, we were talking about the swastika or the spiral sorting things out. Well, this is one of those periods. It was so in virtually all of the great revolutions of the past. Eventually, the people bubble up some leader who gives voice to most of the concerns of the people and who is strong enough to resist every little permutation of every little malcontent and at the same time keep these malcontents in the line of march until the perceived enemy is overcome. Then comes another time of difficulty, for once the big perceived enemy is overcome, a lot of the fringe groups now become disaffected with the leader of the revolution. This is so, because he can never implement all of their agenda and must compromise with those with different agendas. During this period, new leaders emerge to challenge the old leader and sometimes the old leader is destroyed.

"I think that the revolution that is coming to America is a white revolution. I think the targets of this revolution will be both the elite whites and the nonwhites.

"Something else to consider here is that in past revolutions—I mean those during the 1700's and around that time—the revolutionaries had just about as much opportunity to reach people's minds and hearts with small printed flyers and posters and other crude communications, as did the elites.. The elites had no great advantage in this area, as they have had over the past thirty or so years in America with their control of the big presses, the radio and televisions stations, so that elites in America have been able to control the information and to propagandize the people with what the elites wanted them to believe.

"The problem for the elites today, is that with the Internet and with fax machines and various other means of communication, including small newspapers, the people are able to communicate around the controlled media. Look at Waco and Ruby Ridge as examples. The feds were unable to keep the lid on these events. I also think that it's in the nature—genetic nature—of white people, to anger and act relatively slowly. That's what we're seen from both Waco and Ruby Ridge. The events happened and the people started a slow seething that increased and increased and then it seemed to die out, but I bet that a majority of the American people don't trust their government anymore.

"There's still a lot of those old WWII vets running around saluting flags and saying 'America, my country, right or wrong,' but there's a lot more middle class whites who remember Vietnam and many other lies of the government, who are pissed off and just aren't buying the company line with out some healthy scepticism.

"So, I know you're still wondering why I think this is going to be a black and white thing. The answer is that many middle class white people are fed up with the shuck and jive forced on them by the feds, while many blacks support the government these days…at least they support the big federal government and often don't support the local government. For whites, it's just the reverse with many more whites supporting local government and not supporting the feds.

"Go to any activist meeting these days, and you'll think you're in an all white country as almost all the people at these meetings are whites. If you ask them if they are excluding non-whites, they'll tell you that non-whites are welcome, and some of the most brainwashed will also tell you that 'some of my best friends….' Still, facts are facts. The revolution to come will be a white one, is my guess. It'll have economic and other factors as part of it, but mark my words, it's a white revolution we're heading for."

"Well, Gil, I suspect you've been thinking about this stuff for a while," said Zack. "How come you've been so quiet all this time?"

"I don't know, I guess I just didn't think you guys would be interested in this."

"I guess," said Zack, "we're interested in ideas of all types, and ones that we don't hear every day. Isn't this what we three are all about, to explore—and to make sense, at least to us, of a senseless universe?"

CHAPTER 15

We headed south and we were getting close to Big Sur, famous during the hippy days as a refuge for all sorts of strange types, but we hardly noticed. We were tourists of the mind rather that tourists of the external things. We were probably the least conscious travelers you'd ever want to meet. If you asked us where we'd been, we'd probably say 'down the road' or something like that. We were in this space ship of a VW bus, our lonely machine, our thinking machine. Our safe place where nothing was off base and where no idea was ridiculed and no one objected to anything any of us might say. This had to be true freedom. This had to be what the Ubermensch was like. His own morality. His own sense of right and wrong. Not bound by the chains of other people's sensitivities and philosophies. There was little self-consciousness among the three of us. We were friends in the real sense of the word. If any of us had said, to the outside world, the things we were saying among ourselves, we'd probably be locked up in the loony bin. But, here in this bus; just the three of us, there were no censors, no holding back about what we really felt and what we really believed.

"You know," said Zack, "I've been thinking about pussy and genes. I'll bet someone has a chart of some kind giving measurements of different pussies. Then again, maybe not. Do you suppose anyone ever thought that measuring pussies would be a scientific thing to do or do you think people over the centuries just considered this all a very dirty subject and something not fit to study? You know, in making my films, I've had the opportunity to see lots of pussies and although I never really thought about them in terms of genetics, there were very different characteristics. We talked about a couple of them, but now that I think of it, I'll bet that pussies may be a good indicator of race. For example, Lupe's pussy was a lot like certain Asian pussies I've seen, and that might indicate that Lupe and other Indians were descended from Asians. Now, that's not too earth shattering, I know, because science already says that, but I'll bet if we looked at representative samples of pussies from different populations, we'd be able to thereafter just look at a pussy and tell what group the person was from who had that pussy. Here's my preliminary and tentative pussy classification—subject to change of course.

White girls don't usually have a distinct pussy. It's just sort of an absence of a dick and balls. They have abundant hair and thin lips that are more like slits. They are also pink.

Japanese girls usually have a pronounced mons veneris and this seems to correlate, for some reason that I don't now, with thick ankles, and unattractive calves. They also have abundant hair, but their hair is usually straight and long as opposed to white girls whose hair is kind of kinky unless they're a certain type of Germanic blond and then the hair is often straight.

Cambodian and Thai girls have short waists and protuberant mons-venerises with sparse straight hair in a tuft that sticks out funny as though it were pasted on. Black girls usually have way too much hair and of course it's kinky. If you see a black girl who has sparse hair, she's usually a mixture of African and something else such as Asian or Indian. Also, most black girls have even less of a distinct pussy as far as the mons veneris goes, than do white girls, but they usually have much larger chits and bigger lips. Mexican girls vary, because most are part Indian and part European, and it depends on the percentages in the mix, I guess. Of course, some

Mexican girls are just pure Indian or pure European. I guess we have to focus on Mexican girls because it's Mexicans who paint these Cosmic Pussies all over the place, and also because we're on our way to Mexico."

So, we drove on, droning on, and only occasionally looking out the windows at the passing scenery. We weren't really interested in what was out there anyway, except as it related to those things we were each interested in and which might inspire us. We stopped in San Luis Obispo and tanked up. We also grabbed some food and changed drivers. Gil jumped in the back and promptly fell asleep. Zack got behind the wheel. I was riding shotgun. We took a detour through the city to see if we could see anything of interest. We found a couple of Cosmic Pussies, but they weren't anywhere near the quality of Lupe's. We took some stills and some video of them anyway. We got back on "1" and headed south. I thought about calling Carla, but figured she'd just be pissed off and would upset me, so I shelved that idea.

"You ever been to Los Angeles, Zack?" I asked.

"I was born there," he said.

"So you must know your way around?"

"Well, LA is a big place. Big but small. I had a friend once who described it as a hick town with borders fifty miles away from wherever you were. It's a place with no center. Man, it's not like San Francisco where you can get to most places on foot. LA in on a much larger scale. I was born in PV. Palos Verdes. I don't know too much about the rest of the place. I can find my way around, or at least I used to be able to get around without getting lost, but it's probably changed a lot."

"Well," I said, "the reason I asked is, maybe we can look around a little—maybe even spend a few days there if you and Gil don't mind."

"Nah. I don't mind."

We drove on through the night making pretty good speed. We flashed through Santa Barbara—mostly a college place—and we didn't want to get involved with apple cheek yuppies, so we kept going. Then we went through Ventura. We stopped again for gas and to take a leak in Oxnard, and then I took the wheel and we headed on. Dawn was breaking as we came to Malibu. "This is Malibu?" I asked. "Well the friggin' band should just keep playing. Man, I thought this was supposed to be some kind of fancy place. It's just a widening in PCH with the ocean and homes on one side and big falling down hills of dry gravel and rocks on the other side." We were out of Malibu almost before I knew we were in it. Next up, was Santa Monica. We drove around a little, looking at the shops and getting a feel for the place. The grassy areas near the beach were full of black homeless people and palm trees. Then we headed east up Santa Monica Blvd. towards Beverly Hills, and the rest of all that. Zack gave me the left/rights, and we ended up on Hollywood Blvd. It was morning so there wasn't the freak show I had expected. Zack said we might want to come back in the evening when the human creatures all come out. So, we went up and down Hollywood a couple of times, and noted that the asphalt glittered with bits of reflective material. We then drove down to Sunset and did the same thing. After San Francisco, I had a hard time with this place. It just all looked tacky. When we came to Alvarado we hung a right which sent us south again. It wasn't long before we felt that we were in another country. Hell, I thought, why bother going to Mexico? Mexico has come here. Where in the hell were all the California blonds I used to dream about while I was back in New York? I didn't see one blond, except a blond drag queen. About every few feet some Mexican looking guy would step out into the street a couple of paces and make some kind of hand signs. Zack said each hand sign meant something different that was illegal. Most of these guys were signing that they had false ID cards for sale. "See how they hold their hands with the index finger and thumb apart as though they're holding a driver's license or a green card between them? That's the ID sign," said Zack. "These guys over here," Zack said as he indicated some guys in a doorway, "are selling crack cocaine. Don't stare or they'll think you're narcs and they may be armed. This place is like the third world. You can get whatever you want on these streets. You can also get yourself killed real fast if you make a wrong move or are in the wrong place at the wrong time. This is the highest came rate area of LA."

We drove around MacArthur Park, threaded our way through some of the side streets, found another Cosmic Pussy, took photos, and then headed on down 7th Street to the down area of LA. As we drove, LA started looking more like what a city is supposed to look like. This could have been Boston, New York, San Francisco or any large older city anyplace in the country. The streets were dark even in sunlight, as the buildings blocked the sun. There was no vegetation to speak of. No palm trees. It was as though we had just left California and arrived in Pittsburgh.

We ended up on skid row. Here was the humanity. Here was life and death, and sometimes you couldn't tell one from the other. Here was the chaos. Here was reality. No pretensions. No allusions. Depressing? No. It was actually exhilarating. I wondered if many of these people would give up this life—the free life—for an overly manicured place in Beverly Hills. I doubted if they would feel comfortable in antiseptic surroundings. I thought again of the Tinkers of Ireland, and how they just felt more comfortable in their different lifestyle. I wonder if it wasn't the same with many of these people who slept in cardboard boxes on the sidewalk. They had no bills. They had no mortgages. They breathed the same air as the filthy rich even though these people were filthy poor. They could go to the same beaches as the rich. They could get around the city by bus or rail. They had food that was healthy and free. They had the constant company of many companions. It made me wonder if these people weren't better off in many ways than the guys who worked themselves into an early grave just so they could keep up appearances.

It was starting to get dark and we were pretty tired, so we headed away from skid row and ended up at this little plot of land where once there had been some sort of building. At least it had stairways leading up to it. It overlooked the Los Angeles Stock Exchange. There were bunches of cardboard box shelters and blue tarps covering people sleeping, and shopping carts full of what their owners' must have thought was worth saving. We parked the bus, grabbed our sleeping bags and walked over to where a bunch of homeless people were sitting around a fire."You folks mind if we sleep here tonight?" asked Gil.

"This here's a black camp," said one of the people huddled around the fire. "We don't want no honkies near us stinkin' up our camp." Sure enough, everyone there was black except the three of us. I guess we just hadn't noticed, and even if we had, we probably wouldn't have thought anything about it, since we were still pretty much aracial whites with low consciousness of the world, even though we might not have sounded that way to anyone who might have overheard our bus conversations. We were just three tired guys looking for a place to sleep. We decided to not get into any kind of row, so we got back in the bus.

As we were getting ready to drive off, one of the blacks approached the bus and reached over and tried to open the door. He apparently got a shock, because he immediately withdrew his hand.

We quickly drove off.

"What the hell just happened?" I asked.

"I think he got a static shock. The low life was probably wearing leather soled shoes and dragged his feet across the ground."

"Yeah, that's got to be it," I said.

We then looked for another place to sleep. We could have slept in the bus and we had before, but sometime we just wanted to have more room, and this was one of those times. In seemed that we drove for hours, but finally we came to a boarded up building on

Gage in an industrial area in the heart of blackest South Central, famous for riots and crime.

"You sure about this place, Zack?" asked Gil, a little wary after our encounter in the black homeless camp.

"Yeah. This should be alright. The place is boarded up and we're surrounded by industrial buildings, so we're probably alone here. I figure this general area is probably too dangerous or too far from free food for many homeless people to hang around in, so we'll be safe."

We slipped through an old alley gate that had a new looking chain holding it closed. I figured that if we could do this, then so could others. What if there were others in the building who didn't want us there? Well, I was so tired that I just deferred to Zack and his knowledge of LA. We found a broken window and crawled through. The place was some kind of old two story factory probably built in the '40's. It had junk strewn everywhere, apparently from a past tenant. We found a stairway and carefully went up. We didn't hear anyone or anything, so we figured we'd be safe. Just in case, we each armed ourselves with some heavy iron pipes that we found. The offices for the factory were all on the second floor. They were all wood paneled. A couple of them had old mattresses is them but they didn't look as though they have been used in some them. Maybe there had been some homeless people living here, and they were run off when someone came and put the new chain on the gate. Anyway, we found one large corner office that seemed to be defensible, just in case, and it had a window that we could use to escape through if we had to. There was a tree outside the window that I'm sure we could probably leap over to and then shimmy down in an emergency. For better or worse, this was it for the night. The office had its own restroom and two doors in and out. We rigged some boards to secure the doors from the inside and opened the window at the corner. I got in my sleeping bag, clutching my iron pipe, and promptly fell asleep. Fortunately, we didn't come under any kind of attack, and the next thing I knew I was waking up and it was morning. I woke the other two and we prepared to leave. Just then, we heard some noises from the other end of the factory. We took our pipes and sleeping bags and while watching each other's backs, we slowly and quietly moved down the stairs. As we came around a corner, I saw a couple of black homeless guys look up at us and then they ran for a broken window and jumped out. It looked as though they have been cooking something, so I went over to have a look. there on the floor was a dead dog that they had been cutting up and roasting over a fire. Just then, I saw one of them look back in through the window. So, I yelled to him, "Hey, we're leaving. We're not here about you. We're just like you. We're not the cops." We then left. Presumably the two guys reentered and finished their dog.

"You know," said Zack, "this is an area in transition. It used to be all black, but now the Mexicans are moving in and displacing the blacks. There's a lot of friction. Add to that, the fact that most of the markets are owned and run by Koreans and you've got trouble brewing. You know the Koreans are taking classes in black politeness or something, because ordinarily you don't see them shucking and jiving or smiling from ear to ear and slapping each other on the back, but take a look at that guy at that little store across the street." Sure enough, there was this small neighborhood market, and out front was a Korean shopkeeper with a Korean woman who may have been his wife, and they were talking to a couple of blacks men. The Koreans were being very un-Korean as they talked on in loud happy voices, grinning from ear to ear and doing a poor imitation of being black. It looked unnatural and painful, but apparently there had been some talk in the black community about how the Koreans had been dising blacks. So now the Koreans were being more black than blacks. I don't know if the blacks realized that they were being played to, but these two black guys didn't seem to mind. Maybe they thought the Koreans were honoring black culture, or something. I remember reading in the newspapers after the LA riots that although it was Korean stores that were attacked by blacks, the Koreans were calling for unity with blacks against a common enemy. Now, who do you suppose their common enemy was? White people. Of course they didn't come right out and say that, but that's clearly what they meant. They were talking about people of color uniting. And, just who are the only people of no color, as the term is used on the streets? Right. Is white a color? Not in post-American America. I wondered why so many white people just shrugged off these calls to unite against white people. I guess they are so propagandized that they're afraid of being called racists if they simply speak up and call these haters on their hatred against white people.

Anyway, we headed west on Gage, turned north on Fig, and then left, on Pico. This was the Pico Union District of LA. It was graffiti'd about as bad as anyplace I'd ever seen, so Zack figured we were in Cosmic Pussy land again, and we just kept weaving our way up and down the streets. We found three cosmic Pussies and we put them on film. We also passed three make shift shrines at various spots on the sidewalks in the neighborhood. These each consisted of several votary candles. The lit candles were in the bottoms of approximately nine inch tall straight frosted glass jars, especially made for this purpose. The jars were decorated with religious pictures, including the Cosmic Pussy. You could buy these in almost any store in heavily Mexican areas. There were also some flowers at each shrine; nothing fancy, just some flowers that looked as though they had been picked from a home garden. In one case, we saw a picture of a deceased gang member nailed to a telephone pole right above the shrine. The Mexicans would put these shrines out where a family member had been killed; usually in a drive by shooting.

As we were driving around, the bus bus started acting weird so we pulled into a garage to have it looked at. The white boss of the garage told his Mexican mechanic to drive the bus into the service bay. As soon as the Mexican touched the door handle, he pulled his hand away in pain and yelled, "Damn. I just got a shock."

The boss looked at us and asked if we had some kind of anti-theft system that shocked people. Gil told him that he didn't think he had anything like that. Then Gil went over and opened the door.

"See, no shock," he said.

The boss then went over and also touched the door handle and there was no shock, the owner got in and drove the bus into the service bay. "Maybe it doesn't like you," the boss said to the Mexican, with a laugh. "Take a look at the engine will you Jesus?" Gil opened the back and the Mexican mechanic opened the engine compartment door and looked inside with a flashlight. He looked around for a few minutes and then went over to his boss and spoke to him for a few minutes. The boss then followed him back and looked around inside the engine compartment. He then came over to where we were standing. "Which one of you owns the bus?" he asked.

"I do," said Gil.

"Did you do the work in the engine compartment?"

"No. What work?"

"You've got an aftermarket carburetor in there. I saw one of these a few years ago. You could actually run this bus on paint thinner, or maybe even moonshine if you wanted, by making a few adjustments to the carb." As he was saying this, his pet cat had walked up to the rear of the bus and was purring and rubbing itself against one of the tires. It then rolled over a couple of times and purred some more. "What the hell's wrong with the cat?" said the boss. "It's acting like a kitten." He shooed the cat away, and continued talking to us. "Oh, and someone has painted all kinds of symbols in the back of the engine compartment," said the boss.

"What kind of symbols?" asked Gil.

"Well, it's hard to tell because there's a lot of oily dirt in there, but Jesus blessed himself and said the Virgin was in there. I looked and there was a small painting that did look sort of like the Virgin of Guadalupe along with what looked like some spirals."

"Can I see them?" asked Zack.

Roaming the Wastelands   211

"Sure," said the boss. Gil and I went back to the engine compartment with them, and the boss shone his flashlight against the front
wall of the engine compartment and sure enough there were some
crude drawings against the far wall.

"I bought this from a crazy old guy who I think lived in it for a
while," said Gil. "What do you think causes some people to get
shocked when they touch the door handles?"

"I don't know," said the boss. "Maybe a prior owner tinkered with
the rest of the bus the way he did with the carburetor and did put in
some kind of anti-theft device, but then again, and this may sound a
little odd, it may be that your paint job is causing static electricity to
be picked up as you drive, and somehow stores it, so you're driving
around in what amounts to a big capacitor."

"What's a capacitor?" asked Gil.

"A way of storing up electrical energy, like a battery. This is just a
guess, but the rough paint surface may be doing something to the
electrical charge in the air passing over it as you drive and there may
be some other layers of paint or maybe even the metal of the bus that
is causing a sandwich of materials that is storing the electrical
charge."

"Well, why would it just shock certain people?" asked Gil.

"You've got me," said the boss. "Maybe it just has to do with
whether the people are wearing leather or rubber soled shoes or
something like that."

I looked at the boss's shoes and they were rubber soled, so maybe
that's why he didn't get a shock. Then I looked at Jesus's soles but his
were rubber also. I didn't say anything.

It turns out the problem with the bus engine was water in the gas
line and the mechanic soon had it fixed and we were on our way. As
we drove away, I started talking about what we had just heard. "You
know," I said, "both the boss and Jesus were wearing rubber soled
shoes, yet the boss didn't get shocked and Jesus did. Did you notice
something else different about the boss and Jesus?"

"Well, the boss was white and Jesus was mestizo," said Gil.

"Right," I said. "Could it be that genes somehow play a part in who gets shocked?"

"That doesn't make any sense to me," said Zack.

"Oh," I said. "Well, genes make a difference in who gets sunburned and who doesn't. Why can't they have something to do with shocks?"

"Interesting," said Gil. And that was the end of that conversation as we came upon another Cosmic Pussy on the side of a store and we got busy taking photos of it.

Then, as we were looking for some more Cosmic Pussies, Gil spotted a revolutionary bookstore and we stopped and went in and looked at the books for awhile, but we didn't buy anything. There were plenty of books on revolution, but Gil said he was already familiar with most of them and he didn't want to spend any more money than necessary. Anyway, once we were back in San Francisco, he knew some used bookstores where he could find most of these same books on the cheap, in case he wanted any. We got back on Pico and headed toward the ocean. We hung a left on Vermont and dropped down to Venice. Then we just cruised our way back to the Pacific. We spent the day cruising around Venice and Santa Monica looking for inspiration to prime our imaginations again. Some of the streets were wall to wall female hookers.

Zack was getting a lot of material for his lecture or book or whatever he was finally going to put together on the Cosmic Pussy thing. He figured that people would come just because of the name. If he had called this theory the Cornucopia of the Universe, it wouldn't pull anyone in, he figured, but with this pussy connection, it had a sex appeal even though Zack's concept was really pretty free of sex. Zack figured that maybe everything in the universe was like this Cosmic Pussy principle, and I reminded him that he was now often repeating back things that I had said before. I also told him that I didn't mind this, but that I thought he should be aware of where he was getting these things, lest he fantasize that God told him, or something like that. I had no pride of authorship in these various concepts, but perhaps this was a good example of how brainwashing works. It was almost as though Zack were hypnotized and then easily fell into a suggestible state every time we jumped in the bus. I'd say something or Gil would say something and then miles later, Zack would repeat it back, but usually with some minor changes, as though he had just thought of this or that thing all by himself.

It seemed that every time we got in the bus we somehow connected with the astral plane or tapped into the collective unconsciousness or plugged into the Cosmic Pussy, because the thoughts and ideas flowed like crazy and started to take on a life of their own. I wondered if we weren't just inhaling too much exhaust fumes. Or, maybe, the garage boss had been right in a way and the bus was picking up and storing static electricity and maybe we were being constantly bathed in some sort of electric field that was causing us to babble on constantly. I remembered reading about a guy who had a theory that when God talked to the ancient Hebrews He was really talking through a radio receiver and that the radio receiver was the tent and the Ark of the Covenant. If I remember right, he believed that the material of the tent; goat skins with fur attached, held static electricity from the hot dry desert winds blowing over the tent, and this electricity was used to power the Ark which was really a radio receiver getting signals from some space man, in orbit above the Earth, who told the Hebrews that he was God, in order to get them to do what he wanted them to do. I wondered then about different shapes of temples and religious objects and symbols and I wondered if it was possible that certain shapes or images, if made of certain materials, could act as receivers of God's thoughts. Maybe Hitler, who helped design VW's, had designed them in such a way that they were receiving some sort of cosmic rays or something, and the old guy who had owned the bus had just accidently done something to make the rays or whatever, stronger.

Maybe white people were part of the circuit of the bus and didn't get shocked or something like that but that non-white people would sometimes get a mild shock when they touched certain parts of the bus.

Whatever it was, it sure appeared that we had fallen into something. Man, as long as we could keep rolling, we were creative. I conjured up a picture of the three of us being strapped into a thinking machine with wires and electrodes attached all over our heads and to our hands and feet. And, this thinking machine was made to look like a VW to fool other people, but as we drove along, the VW generated thoughts the way it generated electricity for the battery. When it stopped, the battery would eventually wear down if you ran the lights and radio and everything. Maybe that's what we were, some sort of human radio receivers picking up energies of some kind, and it was these that were our genius, not us. We were just the tools being used by some Other.

"You know," I said, "I think that our destiny is to just keep rolling and that we have to figure a way to stay connected with the VW as much as possible."

"You mean more than we are now?" said Gil.

"Yes. I mean we were born for this day and age. This is the day of the drive-in everything. We can eat by going through the drive-up windows. Hell, there's not too much reason to leave the bus. We should probably even start sleeping in here more. Although we didn't directly say it, I think each of thought that this would have an effect on us. Sort of a controlled mutation environment on wheels. We were still all on our own individual quests. Zack was after the Cosmic Pussy and answers to existence. Gil was developing a revolutionary persona, and I was still thinking about the Ubermensch. It seemed, though, that we were hitting a dry spell of thought, and might need to try something new to get us thinking again. It might have been that with our lengthy open conversations we had just exhausted all the bits and pieces of various things we had been interested in over the years and now we'd run out of anything new to say. Years of living our separate lives in different locations with all the different experiences we had, were boiled down into our lengthy conversations. Now we were dry.

"I know what we need to do," I said. "We need to find a good used book store and each of us needs to buy one or two books on our interest, to renew ourselves. I know when I was a kid, I would always find inspiration at the library. I know that sounds kind of nerdy or something, but I spend hours and hours just looking through the stacks. I'd start with looking up something on rockets, and this would lead to gunpowder and the history of explosives, and then how to make it. This would lead to other things and to alchemy and to magic and on and on and on. I suppose if I could remember even a quarter of what I read when I was under 16, I'd be considered a genius today."

"You know," said Gil, "they say that we never forget anything, that it's always stored in our brains. I don't know if that's true or not, though. It seems to me that idea must be based on the brain being some sort of clay tablet or vault, I've read that some scientists now reject that notion and now favor the idea that memory is not inscribed or stored as much as it is constructed like some gossamer cotton candy or synapses in the brain. Did you know that they find geniuses have more copper and less zinc in their systems than other people?"

"Copper?" asked Zack. "Why copper?"

"Hell, if I know. They say that they do hair analysis of geniuses and they just find more copper and less zinc. Maybe it has something to do with electrical conductivity. Maybe those synapses work better with copper wires and maybe zinc slows them down."

"I wonder if those people who were all wearing copper bracelets a few years ago didn't have something?" I said. "Maybe if we just put some copper in our mouths, it'd get into our blood stream and help our brains?"

"Maybe it's toxic," said Zack. "Ill bet if we taped some pennies to our skin that our skin might absorb some copper."

So that's how we decided to tape ten pennies each to our bodies with duct tape. I taped five to my left side and five to my right. Gil taped five to his left leg and five to his right one. Zack taped all ten right down his spine. Certainly not an ideal experimental protocol, but at least we were trying. This turned out to be a dead end for us, and we each removed the pennies over the next few days.

We tried to find a big used bookstore to buy some books, and the girl at a fast food drive-thru window told us that there was a great one down the coast. We jumped on PCH and headed south again. As usual, we babbled on incessantly as we drove. Finally we got to a an urban area and found the store without too much difficulty. It was old and it was big and it was full of used books. I figure we could have spent a week in this place and still not see everything of interest to us. I asked for the books on philosophy, expecting to find a few shelves. The surly, butch, lesbian clerk then asked which philosophy. I said all of them. She directed me to an area of about seven aisles that had books on all sides from the floor to the ceiling. I finally settled on a dog eared copy of something on cosmic consciousness, which seemed to bridge philosophy, religion and the mystical. Gil found a book about old revolutionary pamphlets. Zack had a hard time deciding what to get and finally picked up a copy of an old Indian religious book. We headed back to the bus which we had parked out back behind the store. As we were walking down the alley, a black girl of about 20 with open sores on her face, asked us if we'd like a date. We thanked her and told her we had no money. We figured she must be in the late stages of AIDS; not that we would have agreed to anything even if we didn't think that. Street hookers didn't appeal to any of us. I got behind the wheel. Zack rode shotgun and Gil took up the seat right behind us. We decided not to spend the night in this place, so we headed south to one of the beach cities. It didn't take long to get there. We we found a health food store with a little secluded parking lot and a small wooded area around back where a bunch of homeless people were sleeping. We rightly figured that we'd be among like spirits in such a location. I went into the store, and as I was going down one of the aisles looking for some Vitamin B complex, a girl in a mini skirt about half way down the aisle in front of me, suddenly bent over to take a bottle from the bottom shelf. As she did so, I could plainly see that she wasn't wearing any panties. Something about her snatch looked familiar. No. It couldn't be. Nadine? I walked up to her and said, "Excuse me Miss. Did you once live in New York? She turned around and smiled. "Hi, Alex. Is this a small world or what?" I asked her what she was doing here, and she said she had moved out here a couple of months ago with a girlfriend who then left her, for a guy. She said that she worked in this health food store and lived down by the beach. I brought her up to date on what I'd been up to. I introduced her to Zack and Gil and she invited the three of us to spend the night at her place. We quickly agreed, got her address and said that we'd meet her there at 10 p.m. when she got off work. We took off and got a burger at a nearby greasy spoon and then went to the downtown area. The streets were crowded with surfer types. This place had the image of California that I had in my mind when I was back east. The only difference was that I thought all of California was going to be like this, not just a few square blocks. At the appointed time, we made our way over to where Nadine lived. It was an upstairs, one bedroom apartment next to an oil well with one of those praying mantis looking pumps going up and down constantly pumping oil into a nearby tank. She said that she got a good deal on this place because the sound of the well was constant, but that she didn't really mind.

Nadine's apartment was sparsely furnished. Sort of second hand store stuff.

"I've got New York tastes,"she said. "Alex did you ever go around and pick up discarded furniture in New York? Do you remember how the underground newspapers used to print the trash pick up times for the posh neighborhoods so people could get there before the trash trucks?"

"Sure. I got a couch and a couple of chairs up near Sutton Place one time," I said. Stacked against all the walls were paintings that Nadine had done. Most of there were junky commercial grade things. The sorts of things that you find in hotels to impress the folks from the country, or just to break up bare walls. They were collages and montages mostly with tissue paper stuck on the wet paint and with bits and pieces of shell and other beach stuff. She said that she sold a lot of these to tourists who were visiting the area because of the surfing reputation. She also had some nudes of women, that she had done. Beautiful women. One was a picture of a woman standing before a large window, completely nude and facing in. The view over her shoulder from the window was of a pier. "I really like this one," I said.

"Yes. It's one of my favorites too," she replied. "The girl is Donna. She works up at the Health Food store with me. She's absolutely beautiful, isn't she?" I could tell there was more than just a painter and a model in the way she said that, and I remembered how I thought I was going to go home with Nadine in New York, but lost out to a beautiful girl. I figured this was going to be a repeat. All four of us sat around the table drinking coffee and talking. We did most of the talking, telling Nadine about how we had been traveling around and how we had been experimenting with these different personas and ideas to see if we could make any sense out of our lives and the world. It was when Zack started telling her about the Cosmic Pussy that she lit up.

"You know," she said, "I've been thinking along those same lines for some time, but I've never been ballsy enough to ask any of my models to pose for a really close study. Do you have any photos you can show me of what you've seen?" Zack told her that we hadn't yet developed the still photos but that we had some raw unedited video footage that we could show her if she had a VCR. Of course she had a

VCR, she wasn't living out of a VW bus like us. So, Zack got the tapes and put one in. We fast forwarded through a lot of the extraneous stuff and then got to some of the Cosmic Pussy paintings. When we got to the large painting of Lupe on the side of the building. Nadine asked us to stop the tape. "That's absolutely gorgeous," she said, looking at the picture with a practiced artist's eye. "Do you mind if I make some sketches of this one?" Of course we didn't, so she took out her sketch pad and started drawing. We told her that we were also taken with this particular one and that we had interviewed the girl who had posed for it and had taken some tape of her also. Nadine wanted to see it, so we rolled the rest of the tape for her.

Zack then told Nadine about how pussies were so different on different women and asked her if she had noticed the same thing. She replied that she had. She thought like a man, it seemed. Of course, this bothered me a little because I guessed I wasn't going to get any loving from her. It was just about then that Nadine said "Zack and Gil you can sleep out here. Alex you can come with me, if you like."

If I like? I thought to myself. IF I LIKE? I calmly said "Okay."

So, we went into Nadine's bedroom and she just took off her clothes and got into bed and said, "Well, are you coming to bed or are you just going to stand there?"

She didn't have to ask twice. In the morning, I was the first one awake, as usual. I went out and walked around the downtown area and got a cup of coffee and read a newspaper. Then I had another cup of coffee and read another newspaper. I looked at the clock and it was still too early to wake the others, so I walked some more. I went out to the end of the pier and then went down and walked on the sand. The only other people out were the surfers in their black wetsuits. I couldn't see the fun of jumping in the ocean with a wet suit on. It was like riding a motorcycle with a helmet on your skull, I figured.

I liked the area. In a way, its beaches reminded me of the beaches in North Carolina which I passed through one time and which I always imagined that the beaches of California would be like; but never were. Still, it was relaxing to walk on the beach next to the ocean that I thought I was going to sail across on a raft when I was kid. Maybe I could still do that someday. Traveling on the roads of America was one thing, but it was restrictive compared to the ocean. After all, in the former, you had to stay on the roads that someone else had made so you were always going where someone else thought you should go. The ocean had no roads, and you went where you wanted to go. Maybe my personal longing was not to find comfort with other people, but to find meaning in going where others hadn't gone. "Geez," I thought, this sounds like that friggin' TV show about space. Some people believe that everything happens for a purpose. Thus, if you meet someone, there is a purpose in it. If you feel like you want to go here or there, there is a purpose. Perhaps, they're right. I know I decided on that beach walk to try not to fight my own inner instincts. I was going to use my mind to overcome my mind and let my mind hear all the signals that are around me all the time, even more than I had in the past. I was now going to follow hunches more religiously. If I had a feeling in my gut, I was going to listen to that feeling. To evolve to become more than human I was going to become less than human. I was going to listen to the animal instincts and become ever more one with the cosmos. One more resolution of the Ubermensch aborning. Did I really think I could evolve? Of course not. My form was set. I did believe, however, that my efforts to evolve could affect my DNA that would be passed on to my children.

I went back to Nadine's place and it was still too early, so I rousted the other two and I left a note for Nadine saying that it was great seeing her again, and we were on our way down to Mexico, but I'd stay in touch. We got back on PCH and headed south again. Soon, we were going through another beach city. I heard John Wayne used to live in this one. The last time I had heard his name was from the old guy in Boston. It looked like a rich place to live so that could have

been right. Anyway, we kept on going. When we got down to Laguna Beach, we pulled into a little pastry and coffee shop and went in and had a couple of coffees. Zack kind of liked this city because it was artsy. He said that he felt he could probably fit right in. I called Carla in San Francisco and the answering machine picked up. I left a message that I was all right and that we'd be coming back in the not too distant future, and I hoped that she'd still be there, but that I'd understand if she wasn't.

I also got a postcard of Laguna and sent that to her. Now at least she couldn't say that I never thought of anyone but myself, and that I didn't care for her. Then I thought maybe I should introduce her to Nadine. Maybe the problem with Carla was that she was a closet lesbian and didn't want to admit it and that's why she was so hard on men. Maybe she just didn't like the idea of men and wanted them to be more like women. That would be just the reverse of me with women. I loved the idea of women. Women were beautiful and sublime to me. I know that sounds corny, but it's true for me. There was a European actor who I once saw interviewed on TV with one of his mistresses and their young baby, and he was saying how he loved his wife and that she was at home in Italy while he was here with this particular Mistress. The interviewer didn't know what to say, but finally asked about his relationship with his wife and whether or not going off and having affairs and babies with different women put a strain on his marriage. The actor replied that his wife understood that he was a real ladies man and by this he didn't mean that women flocked to him, because he was so handsome or rich or famous, but that he loved women. All women. He was like a little boy in this regard, he said. The idea of women made his heart flutter.

Maybe I was a little like that. I did like the idea of woman. Sex? Sure, but there was more. It was something to do with aesthetics. Maybe men all carry one of those molds or templates in their heads that I thought of before and the mold is of some archetypical woman—a female ideal. Maybe the closer any woman is to the ideal, the more infatuated with her the man is. I started thinking that the term Cosmic Pussy might have too hard an edge on it. "Zack," I said, "maybe we should call the Cosmic Pussy the Cosmic Scallop. You know kind of like the bearded clam, but scallops have more of that, well, scalloped edge. What do you think?"

"Well, I'll consider it, but I'm used to the Cosmic Pussy," he said. "I know it'll turn off a lot of people when I go public with this, but it'll also appeal to a lot of people, because of its honesty. A scallop shell really does have the right image because a scallop has the right lip shape, but it's not really like a cornucopia. It grows something inside but the something it grows stays inside and is part of it. The Cosmic Pussy concept, on the other hand, has more of that idea that something is gathered up and something is created and is then spun out from the inside as a new thing in the Universe. Each child is like an entire star system expelled out of the Cosmic Pussy. You know, I've been thinking about this whole concept, and I just know that some people are going to say that if there's a female principle in the universe that there must be a male principle as well. I think that Yin and Yang opposites type of thinking is wrong and misses the mark. I think male and female are different but are manifestations of the same principle and the principle is really neither male nor female in its essential core. We interpret it that way, but that's just for convenience. The Cosmic Pussy is the furnace of the universe—a casting furnace. Everything that goes in it disintegrated and reformed, and then spit out as something new. When that something new eventually falls apart, it reenters the cosmic Pussy and is reshaped again and spit out once more."

"So, you mean like reincarnation?" asked Gil.

"No. The Cosmic Pussy is far too big to care about reincarnation of humans. We're just specks of dust to the Cosmic Pussy," said Zack.

"But, I thought you said that the Cosmic Pussy, or God, was trying to evolve a creature to carry its consciousness so that it would be fulfilled?" asked Gil

"Yeah, well we're all just guessing aren't we, so I'm just throwing out ideas that aren't fully formed and which may be wrong. I'm trying to prime the pump of our minds, and to do that you have to be open to thoughts no matter how silly they might seem. You know they say that geniuses are always childlike in their innocense and their sense of wonder. Maybe we're like that, but maybe it takes all three of us to equal one genius. I'm thinking of the three pod idea again."

We continued driving south through Orange County and into San Diego and we were getting anxious to see something different. As we rounded a corner we passed a large white building that looked sort of like a church.

"What's that place, asked Zack?"

"It looks like a Mormon Temple," said Gil.

"How do you know," I asked.

"That's how they build them. See, there's no cross on the steeple."

"What do you know about the Mormons?" asked Zack.

"They're an American born church," replied Gil. "Joseph Smith said he found some magic tablets that had the Book of Mormon written on them. They could only be read while he was wearing something special. Anyway, the Mormons used to believe in plural marriage—you know, the men could have a whole bunch of wives. Then the feds cracked down on them and the Mormons had a convenient revelation and dropped the plural marriage stuff. They also used to keep non-whites out of their priesthood, but public pressure mounted and they had another convenient revelation that let them in."

"I think it's screwy that various religions are changed after their founders die, because of government or social pressures," said Zack.

"Yeah, me too," said Gil, "but that seems to be the pattern. Most religions start off with particular views and beliefs that are supposed to be eternal, and then as years go by, they change to stay in fashion."

We drove on. Everything was the same. The U.S. had become culturally homogenized and was on its way to becoming religiously and racially homogenized as well. This fast food restaurant was the same as the next. There was little new to see. It was hard to retain a child-like sense of wonder when everything was already seen and known. Maybe Mexico would give us a different perspective.

CHAPTER 16

We rolled up to the border crossing point and were waved through by the guard. Once through the crossing point, we were in Mexico. The road ahead was obscured by a building and the road curved behind it. Once we got to the other side of the building we were suddenly and visibly in the Third World. The contrast between San Diego—even in this post-American America day of Third-Worldism in the U.S.—and Mexico, was easy to see. Maybe Mexico wasn't Third World at all but was Fourth World. Maybe America was now the Third World and this was even a step down. Suddenly, the roads were full of huge pot holes. Suddenly, there were shovel crews all over the place filling this or that huge pot hole in the road. Suddenly, everything was older, tackier and more thrown together as though there were no building codes of any type. As I looked around, I saw a police car, old and decrepit, and dirty, pull up to a curb and some small brown policemen with sweat stained shirts jumped out and grabbed a street vendor apparently for doing something or other wrong, that was not clear to me. They threw him into the back seat of the car as though he was a piece of rolled up carpet, and sped off. We went up and down the streets trying to get a sense of the place. This place was like something out of the movies. It was really decrepit. Then we started driving further out from this border area and suddenly the streets were wider and more modern. We got up into the hills that were all around Tijuana and saw some beautiful big houses under construction. Then we'd look down in to the small valleys below the houses and they were dotted with little shacks made of castoffs of wood, old garage doors, cardboard, corrugated metal and other odds and ends. These were real glorious shanty towns. They had small dirt roads and paths leading between the shanties, and there were kids out playing all over the place.

As we drove around, we suddenly came upon areas where brand new tilt-up concrete industrial buildings were going up that were every bit as good as any we had ever seen in the U.S. We went around a corner where there was a foundry of some type. Out back, between the foundry and a little shack of a house that must have been there before the foundry was built, there was a shallow pond about fifty feet in diameter. The pond extended from the back wall of the foundry to within a few feet of the house. In the middle of the pond, about fifteen feet from the house, was a big pile of slag of some type with smoke or steam rising from it. There was a metallic smell in the air. All around the island of slag there were about five or six little Mexican kids playing in the water. The water had an odd bluish green sheen on the surface that must have come from the foundry, and which must have had something to do with the casting process. I could imagine the kids thinking that they lived in a great place, because they had their own private pool, like the rich folks.

"Man, look at them" said Gil, "They're apparently trying to do what you've been trying to do, Alex—mutate."

"I wonder if we'll see any three-eyed kids around here?" asked Zack.

"Maybe some women with more than one Cosmic Pussy," was my lame contribution to the repartee.

As we drove around, we noted that Mexicans always seemed to dart into the street in front of cars without even looking. Zack said that it seemed to be a part of Mexican culture to tempt fate. These people were like snake handlers, he said. If they were good people, then God would not let them be hit. If they were bad, then it was just their time to go."I've noticed this with Mexicans and other mestizos who speak Spanish," said Zack, "they're really fatalistic. They are always tempting fate. It's like life lived as a bullfight. They trust in God and virgin. Say, take a look at that Cosmic Pussy on the side of that building over there."

We looked and saw a two story wooden building with a bunch of young women hanging around out front.

"I think that's a whore house," I said.

"What about AIDS?" asked Gil.

"It's the fatalism again, I said. "I guess they figure if it's their time, they'll go, and if it's not, they won't." We drove around Tijuana and its environs all day and all night, taking turns driving. By morning, we decided we had seen enough for this trip, but we thought maybe if we had more money next time we'd just keep driving south to South America. Zack had gotten about six more Cosmic Pussies on film, and that's all we had come here for anyway. Actually, I was getting antsy to get back up north to see Carla. As we were heading back toward the border, we saw groups of men around this little traffic circle all carrying auto body pick hammers and looking for business. "Man, it's like the Irish Tinkers," I said. "Maybe this is some sort of universal archetype. I bet if we went to Arabia, we'd find groups of men standing around just like this trying to take the dents out of cars. Whatever happened to the Earth of big farms and ranches and genteel men and ladies? We seem to have been transported to a planet that is way overcrowded. I remember reading about Calcutta when I was a kid. There were tales of people sleeping and living on the streets. Not just part of the time, but full time. Some of the people of Calcutta were born on the streets and lived out their whole lives there. Back when I was a kid I thought that was very strange. Now Calcutta has come here to the new world. The planet was getting so overcrowded, that something was going to have to break eventually to thin out the hordes. I don't think humans are evolving at all. I think they're devolving. What do you guys think?

"You may be right,"said Zack. "Hell, if evolution is a distilling process of some type, and if evolution is going on, then you'd think you'd see more people with rarer attributes, but look around you. We're the only people around here with blue eyes and non-black hair. That's pretty much the way it is up in Los Angels too. It sure does look like there's a leveling of human genotypes. Man, I'll bet that in a few years, we'll be as homogenous as Japan."

"Alex, didn't you say that white people are only 10% of the human population of the Earth?" asked Gil.

"Yeah, that's what I heard. When I first heard that, I was just a teenager and I thought that was ridiculous. After all, as I looked around in my home town, I only saw white people. I just figured that was the way the rest of the word was, with exceptions for some places like China and most of Africa. I figured there couldn't be many Chinese in the world because my family and I had to drive a couple of miles to get Chinese food. Boy, was I ever wrong.

You know, man is so arrogant. We think that we have free will, but we don't have all that much more free will than insects. The problem is that we can't see the long view of history. Our recorded history is only a few thousand years. That's nothing. You know there's a fly that is born that has no stomach. It is born in the morning and dies by night. That's it. One day is its life span. During the day, it breeds. It has no need for a stomach, because it doesn't have to eat. I was thinking; what if the fly did have a stomach, perhaps a vestigial organ, but that it still didn't eat? If these flies were intelligent, would they wonder why they had stomachs? Would they ask, 'Why do we have these organs for digesting food, when we don't have to eat to sustain ourselves during our lifetimes?" And if they found out why, would they, as a species, know cosmic despair? I also wonder if some of our vestigial organs be in the same category? Why do we have an appendix? Maybe, it was an organ that did something when we lived to be 1,500 years old as mentioned in the Bible? Maybe the darn thing doesn't even come into play until one reaches a thousand years old. Didn't we talk about my theory that we're supposed to live to be 1,500 or so years but because we've mated with the native creatures of this planet we've devolved and we're doomed to their shorter life spans and to being susceptible to their diseases?"

"Yeah, we talked about this before, but I still find it interesting," said Gil, sounding bored.

"Suppose," I said, "these flies with no stomachs were born on a rainy day and suppose that they could write. They'd write down that this planet was always rainy. If they were born on a sunny day, they'd write that it was always sunny. Maybe that's like us. We simply have not been recording history long enough to see the patterns and the cycles. Suppose we did live to be 1,500 years old? Then, we'd see a lot of changes and might be able to see the patterns of existence.

Here's what I think we should be like and what I think the Ubermensch will possess," I continued. "We should live to about 1,500 years. Some a little less, some a little longer. We should have the power to partially rejuvenate ourselves. I see this as like plateaus. We'll age for a couple of hundred years, and as we age, things will start wearing out. Say, our eyes start going bad. Then we'll hit a plateau and we'll partially rejuvenate our eyes so that while they won't be as perfect as they once were, they will at least be partially repaired. I don't accept the notion that we could ever live forever, at least not as we are now. Someday, we will probably be able to capture and store our personalities and implant them in something other than flesh that won't really be alive. I look at each of us as a totality. We are not just brain nor flesh nor any other single thing, but each of us is a combination of all the things that make us who we are.

"I think we should be free of most diseases and that our immune systems are of such a nature that they can fight off most germs on this planet. It think one of our main enemies for living long lives, is the sun of this planet. It think that we need to be in a cold, cloudy environment for our full development. I think that Christianity is one of the worst things to befall us…"

"What?" said Zack.

"I think that Christianity is one of the worst things to befall us," I repeated.

"Can you explain that," said Zack.

"Christianity is a religion that keeps us docile and from realizing our destiny. It preaches that we must be weak. It tells us to turn the other cheek. It is not a religion for free people. I don't think we'll be able to will our own evolution, which I now more than ever firmly believe we must do, if we keep practicing Christianity. It is a religion of decay for small minded people. We must get rid of it and we must systematically look at all other things in our lives that we have always just accepted and start getting rid of those things too."

"So, what do you want to replace it with?" asked Gil

"Why does it have to be replaced with anything?" I asked.

"Because we need to think that there's something bigger than us, otherwise life becomes futile and meaningless. We're born. We live. We die. I think we need to believe in more than this," replied Gil.

"Actually, I agree with you," I said. "The problem is that man has created religions for specific purposes. Some religions, hell, maybe all of them, were founded by neurotics who just wanted to force everyone else to live according to what the neurotics thought was right. Others were started as social systems; laws, really, to control people and make them act in certain ways that were socially responsible. No matter what the cause, all religions are some other peoples' ideas for everyone else. Why should their ideas be any more valid than yours or mine? Why can't we believe as we see fit and design our God—rather our concept of God—as we want? Ahhh. I know what you're thinking. You're thinking that what about the revealed religions where the religion was revealed by God, usually through some human messenger? Don't you think that's just a little too convenient? Anyone can say that God told them to found some particular religion. It's perfect. How do you argue with such a person? You can't use logic, because he can always say that God told him and that's that. It either must be believed or not. Accept it or don't. And, if you don't accept it, you'll be punished by God in some manner or other. Hell, we could found our own religion."

"That's it!" said Zack. I knew from his tone of voice what was coming next, and I knew that he'd be serious about it, so I just sat still. "We'll start a religion. We'll call it the Faith of the Cosmic Pussy or something like that. You know, it's no real problem. I know from my law, that we can start a non-profit corporation just like any other religion. Then we'll take vows of poverty and we won't have to pay taxes on our incomes. We'll just donate everything to the Church."

"We will?" asked Gil in an incredulous tone of voice that had an undercurrent of, 'Where in the hell did these nuts come from and what in the hell am I doing here with them?'"

"Seriously," said Zack. "Look, I haven't been joking all this time about the Cosmic Pussy. I really believe in the concept. I know the name makes it sound weird or pornographic, but get beyond that. I've been talking about a concept whereby God brings everything into existence through some sort of portal or cornucopia, and that the principle for this is found in vaginas. Listen, I'm not a complete whacko on this and I think this is valid. I even believe that you guys were sent to me to help me formulate these thoughts. I think we spoke of this before, so I won't bore you with everything, but imagine a black universe. It is pregnant with unseen matter—or proto-matter. For some reason, an intelligence starts among this matter. Maybe it's just the natural evolution of matter. Inanimate matter suddenly becomes aware that it is aware. It IS, and IT is an evolving intelligence and it doesn't need brain tissue. Maybe it's like light waves that can't be seen. Anyway, it is here and there and everywhere at once. As aeons go by, it evolves to ever higher levels of consciousness and wants to create our physical universe as we know it. It fools around with atoms or whatever, and causes light, visible light, to come into existence and this light comes through this portal, and the light sort of freezes and becomes all that we know in this universe. Now, why is that any nuttier than any other religion you've ever heard of?"

"Yeah," said Gil, "but, I'm not sure about that part about giving everything to the Church. The IRS won't stand for that will they?".

"They have to. They'll have to treat us exactly like any other church or religion. They can attempt to ascertain how serious we are about our beliefs, but they can never, never, never even attempt to show that our beliefs are ridiculous. Hell, we could worship cabbage in our back yard so long as we were sincere, and the IRS and the government would have to treat us just like Catholics, or Jews or you name it. You two may not believe in all of this yet, but I'm telling you that I'm as sincere as I've ever been. I've been having visions where I've been told what to do. Don't look at me as though I'm nuts. I'm serious."

"Sure you are Zack," said Gil

"No, Gil. Don't make fun of me. I'm very serious. I've been told by a being who appears out of the Cosmic Pussy that I am to the be founder of this religion," said Zack.

"When was that? asked Gil

"It's been happening for some time. Usually when I'm about to go to sleep, the air kind of shimmers in front of me and it parts in the shape of the Cosmic Pussy—it kind of opens up, and standing in the center is an Angel—I guess it's Angel. The whole thing looks sort of like those Mexican paintings of the Virgin of Guadalupe that we've been seeing, except the person in the middle is male. It's almost as though the being in the middle put his hands up and grabbed air in the middle of where he is standing with both hands and pushed it open the way you might stand behind a curtain that opens side to side on a stage and you just put your hands up and pushed both sides apart so you could come through.

The Angel or whatever it is, looks something like Alex's Ubermensch, I think. This Angel tells me that no one else can see or hear him, but that I have been chosen to bring the message to the world. And that I'm the link between man and the Angels and they in turn are my link with God. You know, I think this Angel has been here on the Earth before, but I don't think earlier generations described his entrance in quite this way."

"Oh, you mean the guys in the Old Testament didn't say that a Cosmic Pussy opened up on the mountain and gave them some stone plates with commandments on them? How odd," said Gil with a slight laugh. "I just can't figure that out."

"Well I'm telling you jokers that this is real. I don't know why I've been chosen and I don't know why you've been chosen to be my companions, but that's what's happened. I guess if we really thought about it, we wouldn't find this any more unusual than how the other religions were founded. Would God, looking for a messenger in this day and age to spread His truths, be looking for some guy wearing robes like in the Old Testament? That would be ridiculous. The people who carried God's word in the Old Testament, just wore the clothes that all people wore back then. Today, we seem to think that dressing that way is holy, or something. I think God has picked me."

"Why you? Said Gil "Why not some famous or rich person. Why not some big religious guy like the Pope or some big shot Rabbi or minister?"

"God doth work in mysterious way, my son." said Zack. "Not too many founders of the big religions were big shots in their own day. Maybe one has to be small to be selected. Also, maybe God puts out his message everywhere and only some listen enough to hear it inside."

"Look I can't believe that you're serious, Zack," said Gil. "Come on, level with us. It's just the three of us. You don't really believe that you've been receiving messages and that you're some sort of messenger of God, do you? If you say yes, I'm going to wonder about your sanity."

Zack was quiet for a few minutes. Then he looked at Gil and said, "Before I answer, let me tell you a little about the law again. As I said before, the government may not inquire into the validity of anyone's beliefs, but it may inquire into the sincerity. Suppose, someone from the government some day comes and asks you if I was just faking? You'd be able to say, "Yeah, he told me once that he's just faking."

So, with all of everything I've told you, let me say that I've never believed anything more in my entire life. I truly believe that I'm receiving messages. I know you're probably thinking that I'm schizophrenic, but in my defense I'll tell you that there is no schizophrenia in either my mother or my father's families as far as I know. I'm rational. I don't babble on any more than the two of you. I don't have strange fantasies. Well not too strange. I don't have an otherworldly mad gleam in my eyes. I don't hear voices—well, okay, I hear voices, but it's not as though I'm walking around the streets hearing voices and talking back to them. This is different. I also believe that you two were sent my way as a help in having me realize what I'm supposed to do in life."

"Well, what if the voice tell you to kill someone?" asked Gil with concern.

"It's not going to happen. Think back to what I just told you a few minutes ago."

"You mean about the government?"asked Gil. Zack said nothing. This left me thinking that maybe he was really making this all up, but that he didn't want to admit that outright to us, lest the government ever ask us about Zack and his religious beliefs. Then again, I wondered if maybe he really did hear voices and that he was trying to make us think that he was sane and that it was a put on. After a few minutes, Zack broke the silence and said, "You see, the earliest messages I received told me to hurt no one and that any other messages that counter these first ones are false ones and are not to be obeyed. I was also told that these earlier messages take precedence over later ones when there is a conflict of messages. This is because at the start or founding this religion, I guess I'm relatively naive or pure or something, but once I start spreading the messages, I'll be subject to pressures from outside that might modify the messages. I've also been told that the messages I'm receiving are similar to those that were received by other religious founders and prophets in the past, but that all other religions are now false."

"Well that's sure going to piss off a lot of people," I said.

"I'm only passing on what I've been told to pass on. I'll listen harder next time and maybe I'll hear something different. I look at this as though this Angel, or whatever he is, whispers in my ear and tells me to pass it on, like that old story about a joke at a party, and if I don't listen right, I pass on something that is different than it should be and the next one passes it on with even more differences and so on all around the room. Anyway, I've been told to write down what I'm told, and I guess that's pretty much what happened, with some variations, with many other religions. Most of these other religions, though, weren't for our people at all."

"What do you mean, 'our people'?" asked Gil.

"Why, white people, of course," said Zack.

"You mean that you're founding a racist religion?" I asked.

"I imagine haters will try to call it that, but I've just been told to spread this religion to white people only. I can only submit to the will of God."

"Man, you bet it's going to be controversial. You're just about saying that God only likes white people and I suppose by white people you don't mean Jews? I can't see this building into anything really big, here Zack. Could you maybe ask the Cosmic Pussy if you got the message right, on this one?" asked Gil

"I know it sounds strange, in this day, but maybe that's just one way to tell that I'm not making this all up," said Zack. "Hell, if I were making up something, I'd do it like all the phony preachers on TV and give the people what they want," said Zack. "I'm not a fool you know. I realize that I'll piss off Christians, Jews, Moslems, Blacks, Asians, many whites and on and on. But let me say it again, so you understand, I'm just telling you what I'm hearing and what I've been told to write."

"Look, I said, "maybe you've been influenced by all my Ubermensch talk or something. That was just chatter between friends. Sure I'd like to be able to really evolve or mutate, but I don't that's going to happen. I mean, I'm not insane or stupid. It's been fun, but I really do keep at least one foot firmly planted in reality. This stuff you're spouting, if you really believe it, sounds like you've gone off the deep end. Maybe you're just tired, Zack."

"Alex," said Zack, looking at me with suddenly very wise looking eyes, "you may think you're playing at this Ubermensch thing, and you may not truly believe it in your conscious mind. But have you considered that it's that attitude that's been keeping you from realizing this jump in evolution? You guys can play act all you want, and that's fine with me, but I'm not playing. I am receiving revelations. They're not just figments of my imagination. I'm not sleep deprived. I'm not under a lot of pressure. I haven't taken drugs. Give me the respect that I give to you two with your ideas. That's all I ask."

"Sure, Zack," I said "we didn't mean to make fun of you. It's just that this came on all of a sudden and we thought you were putting us on. I half expect you to suddenly start laughing at me for believing you now."

"No. I'm not going to laugh at you." said Zack. "Just remember that this is something I'm very serious and sincere about. I don't ever want the IRS to come to you guys and trick you into admitting that in your opinions, I'm not sincere in my religious beliefs. Do you understand?"

"Yeah, sure," said Gil. Now I was getting really confused. I didn't know whether this last statement was to tell us that he was joking and just wanted good cover when he declared his new religion to the

IRS or whether he was truly explaining what he believed. I guess we can never really know what others are thinking. I think that what started off as a lark for Zack with the hunt for the Cosmic Pussy somehow changed at some point into something really serious. Of course there is the possibility that he was led to this Cosmic Pussy thing and that it was never rally a lark, but he just didn't know it. I thought it might be interesting to see how his religion developed from this point on and to see what he actually wrote down when he claimed to be receiving revelations. Anyway, Gil and I noticed that Zack was forever writing in notebooks now. In fact all three of us had taken up this habit. I was writing about the Ubermensch and our travels. Gil was writing revolutionary tracts. Zack was writing revelations. For three purposeless guys, we had now seemed to develop some feverish purposes. I kept thinking that somehow this was all going to make sense and somehow there would be a roundness to this and that the three of us were needed for this roundness. Somehow, I thought this would eventually all tie together. Religion and the Ubermensch seemed to be working toward something, given the emphasis on white people in Zack's new religion, and in the fact that the Ubermensch was supposed to be white. But, I didn't see any real connection with Gil as a Revolutionary unless what this was about was Zack preaching the Ubermensch and Gill fighting for it, and me trying to be it. Then again, maybe Zack IS the messenger. I play the part of a priest and Gil is the protector of the faith. I don't know. I guess it could be jumbled up any way we wanted. Still, I kept getting doses of reality flitting through my mind. This is ridiculous, I kept thinking. These things we are talking about are larger than life, and we aren't larger than life people by any stretch of the imagination. We're three guys who are one step away from being homeless. We don't have any money. We don't have any fame. We don't have anything. Perhaps this is what it means to have feelings of grandeur. Do we actually think that the three of us are important in some cosmic sense? We're nothing. We're three losers. Three guys with no careers.

No real goals. No real prospects. Well, this line of thinking was leaving me pretty depressed, and I guess Gil could see it in my face.

"You're looking down, Alex," Gil said.

"Yeah. I suddenly felt down in the dumps. I just started feeling like a nothing. I'm powerless to change even my own life let alone the world."

"You know, Marx never had much money. While he was writing his revolutionary things, he was working off his kitchen table. That's the way it's been throughout history. The guys with all the money and fame during their own times are soon forgotten by history because they seem to do little. And, why should they even try? If they're rich and famous, what more do they want in their lives? It's the down and outers who are the changers of society. Sometimes, a person will start off in good circumstances and then leave them behind to pursue these same sorts of philosophical questions that we are pursuing. We're no different than all the great people who you read about who have changed the world. Don't ever think that you, or Zack, or me are nothings. We're on to something. I can feel it in my blood. I'm telling you Alex, if it were only one of us, then you might have reason for doubt, but look at us. We're three individuals who have each come up with a different purpose and destiny for ourselves and these three destinies are fairly unique, but they appear linked. Look at the way the three of us are. I don't suppose we're totally unique but I also don't think there are that many around like us. Three relatively intelligent people sort of cast adrift into the sea of life in ways that are certainly not ordinary. I mean, we're people who are wrong for the age we're living in. It's like that earlier thing of yours about trying to find a name for us so that we'd feel comfortable in being us. What are we? are we revolutionaries? Are we visionaries? Are we later day hippies? Later day beatniks? It seems to me that there may be some people like us in every generation, and in those generations where a name is thought of and which captures the popular mind then many more people gravitate to the movement and it becomes bigger just because it does have a name to rally around. It'd like us three to try to think of a common name that will link us together and to others of like minds. The name has to be big enough to include seemingly different types, yet inclusive enough so that we all know that we're part of this and not part of that. A religious name probably wouldn't work, because some of us aren't consciously religious. A revolutionary name might not work for the same reason. Same with a name having something to do with the Ubermensch. There must be something that all of us have in common. How about Seekers, maybe new Seekers?"

"How about Neo-bohemians? I said.

"It's kind of derivative, but until something else comes along, maybe that'll be a good name." said Zack. "Neo-bohemians. What do you think Gil?"

"It sounds all right to me," said Gil, "but I think it's kind of pretentious. How about "dregs."

"I don't know, that kind of includes everyone. I think we should call those of us who aren't just winos or crazies something like "Neo-Bohemians."

So that's what we settled on: We called ourselves Neo-Bohemians, for a time. Of course this was just a subspecies of dregs, in the way we figured things, but at least we had some purpose, and that's what made us different from some other dregs. Neo-Bohemians was broad enough to cover the three of us, and had a certain flavor that captured our life styles. It was also an honorable name. So now that was done. We set out to pursue our Neo-Bohemian destinies as each of us saw fit. Man, I kind of liked this. Neo-bohemian. This brought Nadine, Tracy, Linda, and just about everyone else who was part of our ever growing group of friends into the same orbit with us. You didn't have to join anything and there were no rules or membership cards or other restrictions. There were no hard and fast definitions of who was or wasn't a Neo-Bohemian. If you weren't part of the straight world and were some sort of artsy or philosophical type with some purpose, no matter how strange, you were probably a Neo-Bohemian. Our lives were a rejection of the straight world. We were people who, of our own wills, decided to take different paths than most of the people in society. Of course, many Neo-Bohemians were also probably partly nuts in one way or another. These were the rebels of society, but not just rebels against political things, although that was certainly part of it—these were rebels against he straight world; against other people's notion of what was right and what was wrong. These were people making their own morality, and living as they saw fit. They were beyond convention. They were often intellectual, but if Zack, Gil and I were any indication of how others felt, these were mostly white people who knew that were white. These rebels were enjoying their essential whiteness and, again, this is from the three of us weren't afraid to be white. At the same time, we were redefining what it meant to be white. Certainly, the three of us didn't want a world completely peopled by 1950's type whites. That paradigm of whiteness was what turned many of us off. We weren't about to toe the mark of what some stiffs in too tight shoes said was moral. Hell, we had every right to decide what was right and what was moral for ourselves. So, we had more than a little of the anarchist and libertarian in us, but there was more, because we had a lot of white self-determination in us as well. We believed that our destinies were linked to our genes. I wondered why this sounded so radical in this day? What was so wrong about saying that genes matter? I decided it was because of the propaganda that the elites had put on us for the past forty or so years.

"You know," I said, "I think it should really be "white Neo-Bohemians," because if it's just Neo-Bohemians, then non-whites will start saying they're also Neo-Bohemians, and we'll have lost our identity again." The others were silent, but I think they agreed.

Now I was thinking like the revolutionary and this was taking me in a new old direction again. "Gil?" I asked, "what do you know about elites?"

"Well the elites are the ones who control society. There are religious, political, social academic, business and press elites and probably more, but that's a starter. These are the people who are at the top and who wield more power than any one has a right to. In our country, these elites are mostly white, yet they turn up their noses at other whites and will drive right over them to help non-whites. These elites are the ones who are pushing all the mixing and mating in our society. These are the guys who will appear at rallies in the center of urban areas telling everyone that whites have to be more understanding and love non-whites. Then, before the sun goes down, these same elites jump in their limos and head back behind the walls of their gated communities. It's a form of noblesse oblige that they practice. They figure that if other whites haven't made it to the elite ranks like they have, then these other whites are somehow defective, and that the elites shouldn't be bothered with this rabble. The elites also seem to think that racial minorities, especially blacks, would all be rocket scientists had they not been kept back by the evil non-elite whites. You know, I'm relishing this revolutionary role, and I'll tell you, I think the next revolution is coming from whites and it'll have a large component involved with race as well as with other matters. I think there's a general revulsion growing among non-elite whites against all the discrimination they have faced these past thirty years. Talk about oppressed classes. In this day and age it's whites. I know that many whites won't understand this right now, but that's the way it is with all revolutions. At the beginning, consciousness hasn't been raised high enough so many of the oppressed actually identify with the oppressors and will attack their own people to defend the oppressors. In time, they start to wake up and realize that they had been in an almost hypnotic sleep like state. As they look around, they start to realize that in the past they didn't think that they were oppressed, because most of the oppressors were white just like them. There was an unspoken understanding on the part of the oppressed that they were just like the oppressors and all they had to do was just overcome their personal failings and work a little harder and then they too could take their rightful place among the elites. So, they day dreamed their lives away. They tried, they got tired, they died. The elites just keep being the elites. The elites would tell the non-elite whites that the latter had to send their kids off to various wars. Meanwhile, the kids of the elites went to Harvard and Yale instead. The elites told the non-elite whites that they had to give up their place in the job line to less qualified minorities. It went on and on. Still, white people had the notion that they had freedom. They were living in a fantasy of the 19th century. Freedom? Sure, so long as they did exactly what the masters in government told them to do. White people were reduced to the state of little children who were always watched over by their parents. "Why you can do whatever you want." was the refrain of the elites/parents. However, just try to do something that the elites/parents didn't like, and you'd see that your freedom was illusory.

The elites got the notion that all forms of man were exactly the same except for minor differences, so they figured that the melting pot had to be opened up and everyone would have to jump in. Few people questioned the premise, because they had been imprinted with the 'melting pot' scam ever since they were little kids. "Golly, hadn't we all come here and melted in during the 19th St century?" they seemed to say. What they failed to realize was that the 19th century melting pot was full of Europeans who blended their national cultures, not their genes. Hell, the non-Jewish white Europeans were all closely related genetically. What was the real difference between a Frenchman who lived on this side of the road in Europe and a German who lived on the other side? Not much genetically. Today, the elites want to throw in people who are not genetically closely related to create the Tan Everyman that we spoke of before.

Sometimes, false notions take on a life of their own and become something like perpetual motion machines. They just keep going on and on until finally the season changes after these notions have been shown to be incorrect. Then other notions take over. Today, with almost instantaneous media, false notions spread like wildfire and they often burn out just as fast, unless new fuel is thrown on them. I think what we're seeing in this country is a genocidal false notion about all people being the same. Then, those people who are more easily suggestible, and who have internalized this false notion, are committing their own genocide by jumping into the Neo-Melting Pot. I also think that we're in pre-revolutionary conditions. There is a quiet discontent everywhere among white people and many are saying that this isn't the country of their childhood. This is a country of unsafe streets and of rampant non-white crime aimed at whites. It's become a country where a few white elites sit at the top and lecture to non-elite whites that the latter must just be kinder and gentler and that they must turn the other cheek when they're attacked from one side by the non-whites and from the other side by the white elites.

Am I a revolutionary? You bet I am. I'm a revolutionary to give self-determination back to white people. You know, when one reads revolutionary literature—and most of it is from the left—one reads how the revolutionaries in mostly Latin American countries go up into the remote villages and teach the poor peasants that they are oppressed.

In America, instead of poor dumb peasants, we have dumb working whites who aren't aware of the oppression. They get a few crumbs from the tables of the elites, and figure that their lives are full. They have their TV sets. They have their VCR's. They have some creature comforts, so they just sit around like cattle waiting for the slaughter. They might wake up if they could see that the enemy is a cohesive system that is against them. If they connected up the dots of all the black crime against whites all across the nation, they might start taking up arms. What is actually happening is that the mainstream media tries to hide non-white crime while it emphasizes white crime in an apparent attempt to change perceptions so that people will think that fewer non-whites and more whites are responsible for crime than is really the case.

I think we spoke of this before, but one of the problem for the elites today is that they no longer have a monopoly over information. Today the world is more like the 1700's in access to the media than it is like the world only thirty years ago. In the 1700's the common people could as easily get their message out via hand bills as could the elites. This allowed the common people to counteract elite propaganda and to rouse the rabble to overthrow the elites. Then, with the advent of the modern media: big presses, radio, and TV, it was too expensive for the common people to get their message out, so they were just passive victims of all the propaganda that the elites could throw at them. It just wasn't a two way street. All the people could do was read, see, or listen to some elite interpretation of events. That day is over. Today, the common people have access to many small newspapers and small publishing houses, radio talk shows, and most importantly, the Internet. We're in a new information age and not that many people even fully realize what it really means yet. The common people are now writing letters and voicing their opinions on the radio and in small newspapers and over the Internet. Now the elites are unable to stop and manage the flow of information. This is having the effect of linking up individuals who had previously thought that they were all alone in their discontent about the government and the elites. Now they're communicating and they're meeting with each other. One thing is certain, if people get fed up enough with government, it's going to be easier for them to communicate their feelings to others as equals. There are no leaders. There are only communicators.

You'd better believe that all this is giving the elites fits, because they're used to not only controlling the information but controlling situations by identifying, demonizing, isolating and then destroying opposition. With the new organizational forms made possible by this new communication, the elites have a problem in fighting the opposition, because the opposition doesn't always have a traditional pyramid corporate structure. Thus, the elites can't simply knock out the leaders at the top, when there are no leaders at the top. There is a structure, but it's diffused and constantly in flux and changing. It's more the way, say the human brain works as a structure. There are nerve fibers and synapses all over the place. Where is the center of the brain? There is no center for all things. Damage this part and another portion often takes over.

So, I'll do my little revolutionary part by passing on information and by organizing as best I can and perhaps I will awaken some others to the big scam that is going on."

"Well, by emphasizing whites in this revolution, you'll be up against years of propaganda saying that race doesn't matter," said Zack.

"Yeah, but it's like you with the Cosmic Pussy religion. You too, are for whites only, and look at Alex. His Ubermensch is all about being white. All three of us will be called racists and worse by those who hate white people. Of course, many who call us names will be aracial white drones who will sneer at us as they march in lockstep to their extinction in the Neo-Melting Pot."

"I don't get it," I said. "Why is it wrong for three white guys to want to help white people through religion, revolution, and evolution? Who in the hell should we help, but our fellow white people? I think believing that white people should be generic or race neutral and that they should mate with people unlike them is an indication of the level of brainwashing white people have been subjected to. Whites have been demoralized like the American Indians. We've bought all the propaganda and believe that we have no right to be white or to relish our uniqueness in the world. We've been told that it is a wonderful thing to commit genocide on ourselves by mating with non-whites. This is absurd."

"Think about how many whites apologize about being white," said Zack. "You'll often hear a white starting to talk about race by saying 'Hey, I'm a honky...ha, ha, ha," or something similar to show that he's one with non-whites. In other words, these whites that do this are assuming the fuck-me position taken by various animals when they come across a perceived stronger or bolder member of their species. You see wolves, and other animals do this all the time. In people, it's really disgusting. But, it's a little different among whites than among other animals, because the whites who assume this position often don't really believe that non-whites are better. In fact, they often believe that non-whites are not as good as whites, and the submission shown by the white is part of that noblesse oblige racism I mentioned earlier. It's as though the whites are saying that they don't expect non-whites to really act as whites do, because, after all, the non-whites are defective and not up to white standards.

"However, here's where a lot of these aracial whites get it even more screwed up, because while they believe that non-whites aren't up to white standards, they believe that the reason they're not, is because of white racism—not because of genetic differences. These aracial whites believe that all people are really white people inside. Thus, believe some of these aracial whites, it's up to the whites to show the non-whites that whites love them—even with their birth defect of being born non-white—and that eventually, this white love aimed at the dark brothers and sisters will help release the inner white person."

"You know," said Zack, "in the Cosmic Pussy religion, we believe that the white gene pool is the property of all white people and that it must be kept pure. Those who mix and mate with non-whites aren't just screwing up their own genetic lines, they're pissing in the common gene pool that we all must drink from."

"Geeze, Zack," said Gil, "You just said 'in the Cosmic Pussy religion, WE believe...' who the hell is WE? And where did WE come from. You talk as though the Cosmic Pussy Religion were already a fait accompli. Aren't you just writing it now?"

"Well, it is completed," said Zack, "at least in my mind. WE is any-one who believes as I believe. From the sound of it, you two are believers in most of what has been revealed to me."

"I think," I said, "that we're going to have to deprogram whites before any of what any one of us says, will be accepted in even the most impolite company. You know that we're going to be called all kinds of names, don't you? Get ready for "racist, prejudiced, insensi-tive, Nazis, haters."

"You know," said Zack, "I don't really care if I'm called names. Maybe that's why I was selected—why we were selected. We're beyond caring. If we had been three guys in the normal work-a-day world, we probably wouldn't have been receptive to these revela-tions."

"WE again?" asked Gil.

"Well, I don't think it was an accident that I just happened to be on that road at the time you two came by, and I don't think it was an accident that you picked me up. I think we were meant to meet on that road. That means you're as much a part of the plan as I am. I may be the one actually receiving the revelations, but you two are needed. You're part of the recipe cooked up by the Cosmic Pussy."

"Hey, I just had an idea," I said. "let's use appropriate names for titles in the Cosmic Pussy Religion. Zack can be the chief Dildo, Gil can be Douche and I can be Trojan. The Douche will have the job of keeping the temple clean. The Trojan will be the protector of the faith. What do you think, Zack?"

"Are you serious?" asked Zack.

"Well, maybe not. I don't know. I was just going along with this Cosmic Pussy thing."

"You know, if we included blacks and other people in this religion we might have more members." said Gil.

"You don't get it Gil." said Zack. "I'm very serious about all this. I'm only telling you what has been revealed to me. I know a lot of it seems odd, but I'll bet other religions seemed very odd when they were first founded. This isn't something that I've thought up. This has just come in revelations. Hell, if I were going to invent a religion, I'd make it politically correct. I'm not stupid, you know. I didn't invent this."

Both Gil and I still weren't convinced of Zack's sincerity and we figured that because he was trained in the law that he had conjured up this religion as some kind of scam or maybe he did believe it but his revelations were things from the dark recesses of his mind. I had taken some psychology in college, and while I was by no means an expert on the human mind, I didn't see any of the things I might look for in someone who is seriously mentally unbalanced. I guess all three of us could fit a clinical definition of neurotic, but I saw no signs of psychosis in Zack. He didn't babble or laugh at inappropriate times. He didn't have extreme highs and lows in his moods. He didn't appear to have any fantasies—except for this religion thing, and we had been with him from the inception of this. Now, I know that schizophrenics are often extremely intelligent and that they can rationalize all their artificial constructs so that they make some sense and so that they are consistent with their four walls, even though there is a break from the outside reality, but Zack didn't exhibit any of the paranoia that often goes along with schizophrenia. It was just this thing about revelations. I thought I'd try to get more detail from him. "Zack, tell us again how these revelations come to you, will you."

"Sure, when I'm just about to go to sleep, or maybe I am asleep, the air in front of me starts to shimmer and then it parts like a Cosmic Pussy or like a shell standing on end opening. As soon as it's open, there's this Shining Being. He's a male with long blond hair, no facial hair. A slightly bulbous head and white gown. He tells me what to write down."

"You do know that Gil and I don't see anything at all, don't you?"

"I know, but that's the way it is. I'm just telling you what I see," said Zack.

"Well," and I chose my words carefully here, "how would you answer those who will say that you're just imagining it all?"

"I don't know how to answer that, except to say that this experience of mine is not totally unheard of in the annals of religious lore. It may be that this Cosmic Pussy and the Shining One I see have no objective reality and that they do exist in my mind, but it may also be that these images were sent or beamed into my mind," replied Zack. Hmm. I thought. He said beamed. Having thoughts beamed into one's mind by aliens or God or demons is a fairly common thing among schizophrenics. Zack could see me looking at him, and he apparently knew what I was thinking.

"No Alex, I'm not receiving thought control beams from my toilet or from little aliens living in our bus. Well, maybe it does have something to do with the static electricity in the bus or something like that, but I didn't mean it that way. I was just trying to say that whether what I'm writing has a subjective or an objective truth is not really important. I'll just keep doing the writing and I'll follow the instructions to form this religion and people can either believe it or not. My job is to write it down and to pass on the word. I can't make others believe, but I must at least expose them to it. I'll tell you this, I keep getting messages about an abomination of genes and a pollution of the blood. I know you're going to think that I've just picked up bits and pieces of our earlier conversations, and maybe that's true, but maybe I was supposed to pick up these pieces. I'll tell you why I say that. Some of the revelations are about the destruction of the earth by fire, a cleansing fire. Only those who are living in the ice will survive to start all over again. I'm also told that cannibalism will become common in a few years and that we're going to have some big wars. The population of the earth will be reduced to fewer than three million people."

"When is all this supposed to happen? asked Gil.

"I don't know. There's no time line that I know of. These images are just all a jumble, and I'm not even sure they're in the future. They may have been in the past.

"Here's something that should interest you, Alex," Zack continued, "the Shining One said that he is what the Ubermensch will look like. I think we had already pretty much figured that out though, hadn't we?" Still, it's just more confirmation that you're on the right track. The only difference is the hair style between your version and the Shining One. The Shining One said that his long hair was just the way he choose to wear it and most of the Ubermenschen actually had short hair like Alex."

"Okay," I said, "isn't this all just a little too convenient and don't all these pieces just seem to fit together too easily? I mean, your Angel just confirms what we've already been thinking. Zack, I don't really know if you're serious about all this, but my common sense tells me that you're just taking things from out here and weaving them together in some kind of whole. What do you think?"

"Well," said Zack, "I know I'm not crazy, because although I feel passionate about all this, I'm not obsessive about this stuff. It's more like I'm watching a movie and I'm just reporting what I see. They say that God works in mysterious ways. Maybe one of those mysterious ways is to somehow influence each one of us so that we'll prime the pump and come up with this religion. Maybe, Alex, you were directed to say the various things you've said about the Ubermensch and maybe I was directed to hear them and to internalize them and to regurgitate them in a slightly different fashion as a religion. I don't know. It's sort of like we're being manipulated and conditioned by the Cosmic Pussy or something. It's almost as though we're puppets and that we think we have free will, but that we're being pulled this way and that on little strings, for the purpose of some other will. I know that I'm just going to write what I've been told to write and I'm going to file for non-profit corporate status for this religion, just the same as the Catholics and everyone else. I may be the only one is the world who believes these things, and maybe it's because I'm nuts or have a chemical imbalance in my brain, or a brain tumor, but I'm going to do it anyway because this is my reality. Actually, I know that you two also believe, but you may not know you believe and you may not believe some of the frills, but in some part of you I know you believe the basics. After all, we've been together long enough now to know what the others are thinking.

"Here's what concerns me about all these revelations, Zack," said Gil. "What if you hear voices that tell you to kill people or bomb something? Will you obey?"

"Well in the first place," said Zack, "Im not hallucinating. What I receive as revelations don't come during normal waking hours. My revelations are like dreams to others, I guess. In the second place, I'm only told to write things down. I'm not to be someone who does much other than write things down and pass them around. In the third place, if I heard voices telling me to do any harm to myself or others, then I' d seriously think I'm mentally ill. Believe me, I have a very sharp grasp on reality. Look, what if I tell you two something and you swear to never tell anyone else? Do you swear?" We both agreed to say nothing. "Well these revelations may be less than I'm making them out to be. It might just be that I've thought these things and decided to put them in the form of revelations so that they couldn't be challenged. I mean if they're from a higher source they either must be accepted or not. It's a matter of faith."

"So, you're saying that you're not having revelations, and this is all phony?" asked Gil

"I didn't say that," said Zack. "I just don't want you two to think I've lost my mind. I'm as rational as the day we met."

Well, with that latest ambiguity, our minds were put to rest a little. After all, at least Zack was mentally flexible enough to say what he had just said instead of being a complete whacko who would start breaking things if he were questioned about his revelations. Still, what Zack had said could be taken in a couple of different ways. I chose to take it to mean that he was sane. I know that crazy people are often going to claim sanity, but except for this religion thing, Zack was even saner than Gil or me, in my opinion. So, we drove on and on and on. Three ghosts looking out the windows of the VW van but seeing nothing, and not caring where we were. We were just being and existing in our own little self-contained world that somehow needed to keep on moving to generate what we were trying to find. Maybe it was like the motion of the van or the tires generating something that got into our minds. Maybe this was the automobile version of the old clakety clak of train wheels on the tracks and that it created something that eventually hypnotized us. Maybe the van moving was like some sort of electrical generator that generated electricity when it moved. Whatever it was, I was convinced that our creativity was somehow related to the constant movement. Whenever we had tried to sit around a table and talk, the conversations were sterile and predictable. We talked about all the same sort of things that anyone else would talk about. But when we were on the road this way, the thoughts just came crashing over us faster than we could really grasp them. I kept feeling that I was missing something that would hold all of this together. Nazis under the ice. Volkswagens. Ubermenschen. Cosmic Pussy. Revolutionaries. Swastikas. White people. UFO's. Did any of this absurd free association mean anything in an objective sense? The way we traveled, we didn't even really need windows except to see drawings of Zack's Cosmic Pussy and to get food from the drive through windows of the fast food places. It was as though we were some sort of space travelers hurtling through space and through all time. We didn't need windows on the space ship, because nothing outside mattered to us and there was nothing to do even if we saw something with our eyes that would harm us. If we could see it with our human range of vision it was probably already too close to do anything about it, so we relied on our instruments and our lives were lived inside the walls of the spaceship. Maybe this was how moles or worms lived under ground.

They didn't need eyes because there was nothing to see. They could smell or otherwise sense things with other sensory organs far better than they could with eyes, which, after all, required light to see things. We were the three eyeless beings traveling down the road as though the road were a worm hole. There was no light that could deliver the correct pictures through our eyes to our brains, because the light we needed was not even in the visible spectrum. Maybe that's what this was all about. We had been sent on this and our other trips so that we would learn to see with our inner sense rather than our eyes. Maybe we were being forced to rely on vestigial senses beyond the usual five senses to move to higher states of consciousness. Maybe we were being evolved or put into a state or condition where we would evolve ourselves without even knowing it. Maybe we were being prepared for something. Then again, and this seemed far more likely, this was all about nothing. We were must three bums going no place, no time, no how. Maybe we were just, as I had thought before, like lab rats being sent through a maze to see if we could figure our way to the reward. And, what was the reward? In our case it probably wasn't a piece of cheese, but maybe it was higher consciousness or enlightenment. Enlightenment? No sitting around under a tree chanting OM for us. What if mystics got it all wrong and that meditation was the wrong way. What if no one in history could really find enlightenment unless they drove down the road in a VW bus going at least 45 miles per hour on certain routes and roads? What if no one in history had done these things exactly as we were now doing them, and that because we stumbled into this method we were being enlightened. It was like the monkeys in a room with type-writers and all eternity who eventually wrote the works of Shakespeare.

"Do you think we're bums?" I asked neither one in particular.

"Bums?" It depends how you define the term," said Zack with his lawyer trained mind.

"Well, I mean hobos," I answered. "People without meaning. People who just drift through life. Yeah. I'd say we're bums or hobos, just the same as everyone else on this planet. Look, everyone is drifting through life. Some think that the little meaningless things they do are important...extremely important, but usually they're not. What's the difference, really, between some hard driving executive shuffling papers on his desk all day long and some schizophrenic frantically searching the gutters for some imaginary magical paper that doesn't exist? They're both engaged in meaningless tasks but they're both engaged in tasks that have meaning for them. What would be the difference if the three of us were billionaires and this bus were a Rolls Royce? Would we live any longer? Would we eat any better? What would be the difference? There would be subtle shadings of difference, but nothing that really matters. At least not in the cosmic sense. I think we need to take a longer view of history. You know those bumper stickers that say "The one who dies with the most toys wins"? I've always thought those were absurd, but they also spoke to the state of mind of those who would even bother to put those things on their bumpers. It's as though the purpose of life is to amass great quantities of things—toys, and that this somehow makes you a winner at the time you die. What an absurdity. There must be a higher purpose in living than that, and even if the higher purpose isn't something that is imposed on us from a god, then it must be a purpose that we ourselves come up with, but it must be a purpose that involves the essence of our beings, like evolving. Maybe we're here to evolve. We've talked about that before and we keep coming back to it. Suppose our lives are as meaningless as the lives of worms. We're born to eat and breed and die. Period. This would mean that there's no purpose for us, although there may still be a higher purpose that is being worked out by the Cosmic Pussy. But, suppose we worms have evolved brains and that we have decided that we will invent our own purpose and that we will then take over from God or from nature. What purpose would we come up with? Would it be to amass wealth? That's no purpose. If we were to cogitate a purpose it might be that we were going to wrest control of our destiny and our fate from nature and will our own evolution—that we would attempt to move higher, and by higher we must mean to improve our brains, but not just the normal intellectual parts of our brains; we would want to improve our consciousness. We would want to be more conscious so that we could be even more conscious and even more conscious than that."

"You know," I said, "you've just taken your Cosmic Pussy religion into the territory of the Ubermensch."

"He's also walking into the territory of the revolutionary," said Gil. "Hell, let's just have a revolution to overthrow all that now passes for human civilization and replace it with the Cosmic Pussy religion which will have as one of its goals the creation of a race of Ubermenschen and then we'll all just move to the South Pole and live happily ever after under the ice."

"You know," I said, "the more I hear us talk, the more convinced I am that we three really are people out of time. We were born too late or too early and we're kind of in a limbo. We're not exactly like others around us, are we? We're sort of like those artists and writers who went to France way back when, and formed an American expatriate society within the larger French society. They were like us, only they had something to gravitate to. We have nothing. Oh, I forgot, we're neo-bohemians or whatever it is we call ourselves. Somehow all of this doesn't always give me comfort, because I guess I just need to belong to something. I've always been different but I think that may be because the things that I could see that I could join, didn't appeal to me. They were always too restrictive or too uninteresting for my tastes. Now, if this neo-bohemian thing catches on, and if people start hanging around in coffee shops once again, and start doing things that aren't just part of the larger culture, and if these people are into art without being poseurs, then maybe it'll be a home for me."

"You know," said Gil, "maybe neo-bohemian isn't a big enough term. How about rightwinganarchisthihilistzenexistentaialistinte llectualneoboehmianreveolutionaries."

"That's sure catchy," said Zack. "It's one of those terms that will just be on every lip. If you're serious, maybe you can work with the letters and come up with something a little more manageable."

"Does anyone know where we are?" asked Gil who was sitting in the back.

"Yeah, we're back in San Diego," I said. We're heading back north. As we drove, we could see cars pulling over to the side of the freeway to pick up illegal aliens who had gotten around the border check point on foot. Why even have a border, I thought, if it's that porous? I had heard talk that the Mexicans wanted to take back the south-western states of the U.S. and rename them Aztlan and that they were going to do this by simply inundating us with their walking invaders. What a great way to invade a country. Don't send armies, that would just give the Americans a cohesive enemy against which to rally the people. Instead, just slip in millions and millions of high breeding men, women, and children and when you have enough political power from the sheer weight of your numbers, make the states more and more Mexican. That's what seemed to be happening. One of the loopholes in the U.S. Constitution was that the children of illegals who were born on American soil were Americans. Then, because the children needed care, their illegal parents stayed to take care of them. This was helping turn the U.S. into a Third World nation. Perhaps what we needed was to have a vast new migration from Europe to this side of the Atlantic and then we could send all these European immigrants down to Mexico to take it over in our own walking invasion. Hell, we'd done this before with this country so why not again? Maybe Gil was right about this revolutionary stuff. The U.S. government was way out of touch with average people. It didn't help us. It didn't protect us. It just attacked us and told us what to do. When we said that we wanted to pursue our own visions of life as we saw fit, it told us that we had to think and act the way the government wanted.

"Propaganda," I said.

"What?" asked Zack.

"Propaganda is the way this country and maybe the whole world is run today. In the old days, the elites could just crack the whip or kill a few thousand people to have their views of the world and of man prevail, but today it's done with propaganda. It's no less evil though. People are manipulated by the elites who control most of the mass media. The propaganda is often subtle and it's not all planned out. It's just a general attitude that the elites put out and which is picked up and spread. Look at recent movies. Almost every action film now has a black star and a white star. Is that the way most people actually live and associate? Of course not. Most people stay with their own kind. They're just more comfortable around people like themselves."

Suddenly, Zack started reciting a poem:

> The Stranger within my gate,
> He may be true or kind,
> But he does not talk my talk-
> I cannot feel his mind.
> I see the face and the eyes and the mouth,
> But not the soul behind.
>
> The men of my own stock,
> They may do ill or well,
> But they tell the lies I am wonted to,
> They are used to the lies I tell;
> And we do not need interpreters
> When we go to buy and sell.
>
> The Stranger within my gates,
> He may be evil or good,
> But I cannot tell what powers control-
> What reasons sway his mood;

Nor when the Gods of his far-off land
Shall repossess his blood.

The men of my own stock,
Bitter bad they may be,
But, at least, they hear the things I hear,
And see the things I see;
And whatever I think of them and their likes
They think of the likes of me.

This was my father's belief
And this is also mine:
Let the corn be all one sheaf-
And the grapes be all one vine,
Ere our children's teeth are set on edge
By bitter bread and wine.

"You took the words right out of my mouth," said Gil, "what the hell is that?"

"The Stranger, by Rudyard Kipling," said Zack. "I memorized it years ago for a class in college. I got in trouble for reciting it, because it wasn't considered PC. I wonder how Rudyard would feel today? At the time he wrote this poem he was in India and he was writing all kinds of stuff about a land that was certainly far different from England, at that time. Today, he wouldn't have to go to India. He'd only have to go to London. You know, maybe we're supposed to save the white race. Perhaps that's what all this weird stuff we've been talking about for so long is all about. Maybe America is now so far gone that it's going to take a complete overturning of all that society has become in the last 60 or so years. You know it just pisses me off to think that screwball politicians are ruining our country with half-baked ideas about the nature of man. We're white people, damn it, and what the hell is wrong with that? Who said it? Alex, I think. Whites are only 10% of this friggin' planet's human population, and non-whites figure there's too many of us and are trying to extermi-nate us. In this country, we grew up thinking that we were some kind of majority on the planet because for so many years we were living in separate white communities. Now we're seeing what our ignorance has caused. Now, we're facing extinction. First we're killed in the streets and in our homes by non-whites. Then we're encouraged to mate with them so we're killing ourselves in our bedrooms by that most horrible weapon of mass destruction—sex."

"Wait a minute," said Gil. "now it's all starting to make sense. Hell, we've been on this quest for the Cosmic Pussy, and Zack has just called sex a weapon of mass destruction. It's a friggin' sign. the Cosmic Pussy is trying to tell us that women are the gatekeepers and the protectors of our blood. The Cosmic Pussy chooses when to open and when to close. It has created all of this, and it has placed itself in women to act just as it acts in all of creation. It is the controller of our destinies. The Cosmic Pussy is under attack right here on earth. Maybe we're supposed to protect it." We drove on in silence for awhile and then Zack said that he was very tired and asked if I could take over the wheel. I did so.

CHAPTER 17

$\mathcal{A}$fter a couple of hours, Zack woke up and told us of his newest revelations. He said that in the new society we were supposed to create (and this in itself was something new) all women of child bearing age were to either be pregnant or nursing. He said that the way to protect the sacred eggs (another new term) was to make sure that the Cosmic Pussy could not make use of any sperm that found its way in simply because it was already pregnant through purpose. So women were to select their mates wisely by looking for the sacred signs (Was this a new term too? I was losing track.) that were revealed in the appearance of the Shining Ones. The women were to try to birth the Ubermensch (Well, what the hell about me? I was already born.), and that by carefully selecting mates and by proper diet and other controls including living in a cold climate, that the babies born would start moving up the evolutionary ladder.

I was starting to question the wisdom of the possibility of being able to birth the Ubermensch through selective breeding like this. This was eugenics for a new day, and the old eugenics hadn't worked that well, it would seem. Maybe by always trying to birth the best babies, people would just be too picky and would always find possible mates too imperfect. Maybe the answer was to breed like cockroaches; go for sheer numbers instead of just a few of high quality. And who the hell were we to determine what high quality really was anyway? Then again, if horse and dog breeders could breed their animals for certain traits that the breeders had determined were quality traits, why couldn't we do the same thing with people? It was up to us, to determine what we felt was needed to breed better. What we really needed was a remote piece of land where we could move all the people who believed as we did, and where we could build a whole new society. A new nation. A new culture. We'd eventually be able to breed a whole new species of people. Where could we find such a place? Then I started thinking about the South Pole again. Man, it made perfect sense that if the Nazis were thinking like I'm thinking, that they would have built bases under the ice. I couldn't figure out how that would be possible, though. Could a large group of people possibly stay hidden beneath the ice for all these years with all the modern snooping devices such as satellites and sensitive cameras and instruments? Hell, you couldn't hide a modern civilization without leaving some trace or other. When a modern civilization makes things, it gives off heat, and the heat can be seen by satellites. But then I came back to the hole in the Ozone layer above the South Pole again. Could that be an indicator that an industrial civilization was living beneath the ice and that was who was destroying the ozone and not just a bunch of old ladies using too much hair spray?

If it was Nazis below the ice, they would have had to have started that back in the late '30's. Did they have the technology back then to do this? Then I remembered reading something about how Nazi doctors had done experiments on people by using extreme cold. Weren't those experiments something to do with conditioning for cold weather? Maybe they were trying to invent some sort of natural anti-freeze in the blood? Then I also remembered reading about some guy in Germany who had a theory about fire and ice, and that it was these two things, in his view, that created everything, or something like that. His particular emphasis was apparently mostly on the ice part of this theory, and there was something mystical about the ice. Man, I'll bet the Nazis really did set up something below the ice.

The only thing I couldn't figure out is how many people they would have down there. To get enough people to build a new master race, they must have had to do some computations and come up with some sort of ideal number. My guess was that it had to be in the thousands, but maybe they figured less. How would they have gotten many people, down there? Probably submarines, and subs couldn't hold that many people. Surely, some word of this would have leaked out into the world. Suppose that just a few high ranking people were in on this secret and suppose that it was mostly women and children who were taken down there—pregnant women. Yes, that made sense, and the Germans were very logical. If you're going to transport someone and you needed at least a certain number in the new colony, make sure that every woman you transported was pregnant before she boarded the sub. That way she took up the room of one, but was actually two, and if the child she was carrying was from a man not destined to be under the ice, the gene pool would be kept a little more diverse. You wouldn't need too many men, because one man could impregnate, theoretically, thousands if not millions of girls. You just needed to make sure that the few men you selected were of the very best breeding quality. Maybe the ratio would be something like one man for every fifty women or something like that. Female babies would be ready to breed when they reached early teens. So, let's see, just for the heck of it. Say you brought fifty pregnant women and one man to the south pole. The women were in different stages of pregnancy and none of them were pregnant by the one man who went with them, in order to not have too many of the same genes in the population. Some of the women might start having children within weeks or arrival, and all would be delivered of their babies within 8 months. Those who birthed first, could be made pregnant again within a few months. With these fifty-one original people, you could theoretically—and this doesn't count twins or still births or other such things—double your population in one year and from then on it would grow even faster. This assumes that they were working on the same basis as Zack guessed they might; every woman pregnant or nursing all the time until menopause. It would be like chickens laying eggs and the population would grow at an incredible rate. Also, there would actually be far more than just fifty women to start with as certainly more and more subs would slip under the ice and drop off new shipments of pregnant women on some sort of regular schedule, until the end of the war.

What about problems with inbreeding? That shouldn't be a problem so long as all the people were genetically fit. It's like that thing we were talking about how the Pharaohs always married their sisters. It wasn't the close relationship that caused the problem, it was the possession of some defective genes that were dormant unless they were matched up with the same defective genes from the other partner. That was the real problem with marrying close relatives. Besides, there would be new people arriving all the time. What about food and energy and natural resources? They would have it all if they were down below the ice on the land that's there. Remember, Antarctica is an actual continent covered with ice. And as far as being detected, hell the ice was two miles thick in many places so they'd be hidden on a continent about the size of America covered with ice. Who in the world could ever find them? Imagine a race of people cut off from the outside world, living in ice tunnels and building a new civilization that would one day emerge, and conquer the world? Could it be that this is what the Nazis were always planning on doing? Could it be that their various military excursions were just diversionary tactics to take the world's eyes off their real mission? What about Betty and Barney Hill who claimed to have been abducted by aliens in New Hampshire? They described the aliens as looking like Nazis. Could the Nazis be operating flying saucer bases from the South Pole? Man, I could go and on with this kid of thinking. Suppose you were trying to hide out and create the Ubermensch, what would you do? If it were me, I'd make sure that I got under the ice just as quickly as possible, and I'd have special boring machines to tunnel through the ice and the dirt down below. Maybe the machines would be a combination of heat and giant drill bit. If engineered correctly the things would slice through the ice like a hot knife through butter. I'll bet they actually found some caves beneath the ice on the surface of Antarctica, so that most of them don't actually live in ice caves but in cities built underground in dirt of Antarctica. That makes more sense. From underground they could bore outward and mine precious minerals…perhaps diamonds. There were supposed to be a lot of ex-Nazis living in Argentina. Isn't that convenient? The closest land to the South Pole and it gets overrun by Nazis. Why would they pick Argentina? Could they have tunnels under the ocean between the south pole and Argentina? Hell, they've had since the 1930's to plan and build such things. Wasn't it also the Nazis who believed in a hollow Earth? Maybe they found the entrance to the middle of the Earth under the ice. If that's the case, there could be millions of them living in the Earth's core. So, here I am up here trying to evolve or mutate or other wise transform myself into some sort of over-man, and maybe the friggin' Nazis have already done that. This brought me back to thinking about how we all seemed to have these thoughts when we were driving around in our VW, but when we weren't in the damn thing, we didn't have all these thoughts.

Maybe we really were receiving thought waves via the VW but maybe they weren't originating from the Cosmic Pussy as Zack thought nor from some dead revolutionary leader (did I mention that yet?) as Gil thought, but from the Nazis. How could that be? We received these thoughts while we were in the VW. Maybe many VW's are rigged to receive thought control waves? It was more likely that someone had put drugs in my coffee of that I was losing my mind. Still, while I realized that such thoughts are probably the sorts of things that schizophrenics might have, these thoughts weren't controlling me. They just sort of floated into my mind like any other thoughts. They were wild speculations. Nothing more. I still had complete control of myself. They say that great geniuses are always child like and that everything is always new and exciting to them and that they discover new things by asking childish questions of everything and by questioning the basic premises of all things. Maybe that's what we were doing. I suppose that if we were somehow validated that I'd feel better about thinking along all these strange lines, maybe that's why I had always been looking for some umbrella term to describe the way I was. If I had only gone to more college and majored in physics, I could get away with being odd and just pretend that Like Einstein I was just thinking much higher thoughts than everyone else. Since I didn't have those credentials, I was stuck with just being odd.

We drove on. First if was day, then it was night, then it was day. We were like the Flying Dutchman, forever doomed to sail on through the world and never finding a port.

"You know," said Gil, "I've been receiving messages too. It think I mentioned that to you Alex, but Zack you probably didn't hear it. I'm receiving messages from some dead revolutionary who fought with Che Guevara and who was with Bakunin in Russia."

"That's not possible. Those people lived years apart," said Zack.

"That may be true," replied Gil, "I think somehow I'm getting messages from some sort of universal revolutionary—some spirit who inhabited different ages and different bodies. Have you ever heard of something like that in ghost lore before? Well, whatever this is, it is coming to me out of a fog just as I go to sleep. I don't see any face, just mist, but here's something interesting. The mist or fog appears in the air sort of like the Cosmic Pussy."

"Ill tell you what I think is going on," I said. "I think that we're all three the victims of something like mass hysteria. I'll, bet we've been breathing in too many fumes from the engine or something like that. Of course it just may be that we three became friends because like birds that flock together we're three neurotics whose neuroses make us appealing as friends to each other. We're kindred spirits and we don't make fun of each other as would straights. I'll bet that we're feeding each other's psyches and that we're then reacting to the bits and pieces of stuff that we hear but in ways that we can personally relate to."

"You know what I want to do?" asked Zack, "I just want to get a tatoo of the Cosmic Pussy. I'll bet I can find a good tatoo artist who can copy that Cosmic Pussy painting of Lupe. Maybe you two should get tattooed also. Gil can some revolutionary thing or other. Maybe a red flag—isn't that the color of revolution? Alex can get some sort of swastika."

So, as with so many of the ideas that popped into our heads, once the idea was out and floating around, it became an obsession with us to find a way to fulfill it. Now, we were looking for Cosmic Pussies and tatoo parlors. Finally, we found a tatoo parlor in a run down area of L.A., a city that we have been driving around in for some time without even really knowing it. We went in. The guy was covered with tatoos himself, including ones all over his bald head and face. We figured this guy was a professional. We told him that we were in a hurry and that we wanted three tatoos. We showed him the photo of Lupe's Cosmic Pussy painting and asked if he could copy it on Zack's chest. He said that he could, but if we wanted a rush job, all three of our tatoos would have to be in blue ink, instead of in colors. We agreed. Then as the tatoo artist was getting Zack ready, Gil and I checked the tatoo artist's stock designs to find something we liked. As we were doing that, the artist drew the Cosmic Pussy on Zack's back with a marker. The tatoo was going to be about ten inches tall. After doing a pretty good drawing free hand, the guy grabbed the needles and did the outline of the picture over the marker lines he had drawn. He worked for about an hour and it was finished. Zack's back was pretty messy looking but the artist said it would heal just fine. He gave Zack some instructions on how to avoid getting infected and then it was Gil's turn. Gil wanted the tatoo on his right biceps and he had picked out a picture of a military assault rifle that originally had the slogan "Black Power" written above it. Gil had the artist do the assault rifle, but had him change the slogan to "Endless Revolution." When that was finished, I had a rounded swastika put on my right biceps. It was more like a spiral galaxy than the Nazi swastika and I had fire springing from the arms and clouds surrounding the whole thing that looked a little like the Cosmic Pussy.

After the hours in the Tatoo parlor, we headed out to get a bite to eat at a local fast food joint in the downtown area. For some reason we just liked this chaotic downtown rather than the prim Beverly Hills area, maybe it was the chaos and the naturalness of the place teeming with life that we liked. It was like Koala bears in Australia that would die if they didn't get the leaves from a certain species of Eucalyptus tree. Hell, how finicky can a creature be? No overly pristine and sanitized areas of the rich for us. Down here, there was life and death. It was the way life really was in the world for all creatures. We were people as cockroaches. We found a way to live and to do what living things do. We bred and we struggled. We survived and we weren't picky about how we survived. We needed money and we found a way to get it. I thought of how some people had these plagues in their offices or homes that showed magnificent bald eagles in flight. It was clear that the people who owned these plaques identified with bald eagles. Now, I liked watching these great birds and even hawks in flight as much an anyone else, but the friggin' things are dying out while the cockroaches are surviving. Maybe the U.S. should have the cockroach as it's national animal instead of the Bald eagle.

No wonder the world wasn't full of Koala bears. I was still thinking of birds and evolution and it occurred to me that maybe evolution moved along by what made a creature happy and comfortable. For birds, this must mean some aspect of flight, since most birds are truly engineered to fly. However, I wondered why some birds do better in water, and why some don't fly at all. This brought me back to niches in nature. If there is a niche, then some life seemed to find a way to fill it. But even more than that, not just some life, but usually representatives from the various orders of life would find a way to fill it and prosper. You'd have an insect, a mammal, a reptile, a bird and so on all staking out a particular little territory if the space were large enough. and you'd have a whole little miniature symbiotic system in, say, a backyard. The family dog would run around the place pissing on everything to claim it as his, and to warn off other dogs. The family cat would do the same thing for catdom. I wondered if bugs also marked out their territory this way.

We found a side street that looked safe. At least it had no gang graffiti, and we parked the bus and got some sleep. This was our base of operations for the next few days. Then we tired of this and hit the road again and headed back toward San Francisco. We wanted to get back but we also wanted to take as many side roads as possible so long as they were going in a generally northerly direction. Zack was looking for more examples of the Cosmic Pussy. Gil was looking for places to start a guerilla war. I was just doing what I had always done; being lonely and looking for something that I couldn't find because I didn't know what it was. Could it be that I was just born lonely and wanted to go back to the womb? Nah. It was more like I was from a different planet and I had been put here as a kid and I still remembered the other planet on some level but I had been made to forget it in my conscious mind. There was always something that made me feel that no matter where I was, I wasn't at home. I was always trying to find my way home, to a home that I couldn't remember but which somehow was a place where everything was warm and comfortable like those pictures in kids' books where the rabbits or mice or whatever lived in cozy tree stump homes with windows and crooked chimneys. This world was so different from that, at least in my mind, that I seemed to be caught in an Edward Hopper painting. All light was steely blue and cold and cast cold long shadows that were long and thin, against a bleak grey background. The people were thin and pale as though dead. There was no warmth. Maybe I was thinking in the wrong direction with this Ubermensch stuff. The thought of the

South Pole or any other cold place wasn't all that attractive to me. I liked the look of those paintings by Gauguin in the south seas. Beautiful nut brown women with bare breasts showing, always looking happy and with lush foliage and bright colors. That was attractive to me. Ubermensch? Did I want to be above those island scenes? Maybe what I really wanted was to be the Untermensch. Sometimes the thought of just lying around in a hammock in the south seas sounded very good to me. Maybe that's why we hadn't evolved as a species very much. There was always the call of some south seas island that appealed more than the intellectual bare boned thoughts of evolving via the cold. If you're comfortable, why even bother to evolve? Life was very short and why should we try to be the next step for man, when others were hanging out in the south seas and chasing all the pretty girls, who didn't want to escape, around the islands. Then I naturally started thinking about Christian morality that said we were supposed to deny the flesh. I didn't buy that. At least not for the reasons that Christianity gave. I always believed that we found ourselves through the flesh. Maybe the rules in Christianity, which after all, was just a new version of Judaism—call it uncircumcised Judaism—were really very ancient rules to help man evolve, written down, not in logical arguments about why something was good or bad, but with threats of eternal damnation if you did or didn't do certain things. Suppose those ancient aliens I thought about, had landed in the Middle East and that certain of the aliens, against their own laws had started screwing the ape creatures and that the children born of these matings were part alien and part ape creature so that as generations passed, they became more attractive to the aliens and the mating continued and the leaders of the aliens knew that this would kill off the aliens in time. Maybe the aliens—assuming that they lived to be 1500 years old or so took a longer view of history and they then pulled back out of these lands leaving offspring that now lived for 30 or 40 years as was the rule back then, and after a very short time the aliens were forgotten except as gods. The aliens who were still aliens and who hadn't blended with humans would probably try to steer the people on the planet by playing on their fears and hopes. The aliens would be the gods talking from the clouds. Where had the aliens actually gone? Maybe to the tops of mountains. Mt. Olympus, the home of the Greek gods was probably a good location. Now, when I was a kid and I thought of mountain tops, I always pictured them as being pointy things, and they often are, from a distance, but up close, there is often plenty of flat level ground. The ancient aliens could have easily built entire cities up on the mountains and they could just as easily have kept the man creatures from down below from getting up there. At best, there would have only been crude trails that could have been easily booby trapped or otherwise guarded against the humans.

As we were driving down the road, we came upon a girl, with a backpack, hitchhiking. She had scraggly brown hair and looked dirty, she was pretty skinny and looked to be about 25 years old. We stopped and offered her a ride. It was immediately clear from her manner and what she was saying that she had mental problems. "You guys aren't rapists or murderers are you?" she said in kind of mumbling disjointed voice. Zack, who was driving, looked at Gil and me and we all just shook our heads that it wasn't such a good idea to give her a ride. Zack, said, "Sorry. I don't think we have enough room. Good luck." As we were driving away, she was shouting and giving us the finger. "Man, said Zack, that's all we need is to give a ride to some whacko. Who knows what she'd claim after we gave her the ride. Hell, she might run into the first police station and start screaming that we kidnaped her. I like to help people out, but this is a dangerous world these days." So we rode on. I was thinking about how Zack had told us a lot about his Cosmic Pussy quest and I had talked a lot about the Ubermensch—or had I just thought to myself a lot about it? Well, anyway, Gil was the only one who hadn't fleshed out this revolutionary part that he was playing, and I wondered if maybe we had just sort of forced that persona on him. When I asked him, Gil said that we hadn't, but that he was still digesting it all. He said that he'd actually been interested in revolutions and revolutionaries since he was a kid, but that he was most interested in not the actual fighting, and battles, but the literature of revolutions. If he were a revolutionary he figured that he's be a pamphleteer or writer of revolutionary tracts, to motivate those with more action types of personalities to do what they would do.

"Actually, said Gil, "I'd like to take a little of all the things we've talked about and wrap them up in some kind of grand new political/religious philosophy. That's what really needs to precede any revolution. It's not enough to just rail against the oppressors; you also have to have some plan, some shining ideas so that while you're teaching about the oppression, you're also offering something new to replace it. That's what the communists normally do. They have a vision of the world where the people aren't exploited, and they offer this vision at the same time that they're attacking the old order. The problem is that their vision hasn't worked out too well in practice. It sounds good in theory, but it apparently fails to take into account the real nature of man. I think it's back to that stuff that Alex was talking about how people aren't all the same and if you think they are, that you'll always be wrong as you try to put new philosophies into practice. The so called lumpen proletariat isn't so lumpen. It's a bunch of individuals who have been leveled economically, but not in genes, abilities, or desires. Some will struggle harder than others and the reason they're struggling is to amass power or wealth—often not just for those things, but the struggle to get these things gives them purpose and a feeling of comfort. That's what makes them feel good about themselves each day. It is these individuals who pull the lumpen proletariat forward into better lives for all. If you deny these strugglers their struggle, and level them with all others then not much happens. That's one of the problems with communism. One of the other problems is that it tries to plan everything too closely. You know, the five year plans and that sort of stuff. It just doesn't work. I'm for having government as close to the people as possible so the people can govern themselves. However, I kind of like the talk of evolving a people, and I wonder if the masses would see that as a desirable goal. I also think that we might be able to will our evolution. What could be a higher goal for a people than to see everyone improve generation after generation? Of course this would require some sort of central control until the propaganda, convincing people that this is desirable, took hold and then, hopefully, it would just keep on going as people realized that as the population got more intelligent that there were practical benefits such as fewer violent street crimes and less social dysfunction, while the quality of life of everyone was going up. Evolution truly must be a distilling process where you start with a vast amount of raw material and then you distill it to remove the impurities so that the end distilled product is only a fraction of the original mass. The problem is how do you do that with people.? I think we need to scientifically determine what really does constitute a step forward before we do anything. What would we gain if we bred a group of super geniuses who had so few muscles that they had to sit around like a pile of mud, or who didn't have the strength and vigor to reproduce. What if we bred super geniuses who were also strong, but who died by age 15? What would we have gained? There has to be a balance. Have you ever seen some of those amateur weight lifters who have worked too much on their upper bodies and not on their legs? I've seen a couple. They have these little chicken legs and great big puffed up chests and shoulders. They've forgotten to go for a balanced appearance."

"Steroids," said Zack.

"What?" I asked.

"Those guys who look like that, often have been using steroids and that's why they have those chicken legs.

"Okay. Well, Gil's point is still the same. They are unbalanced, and that needs to be avoided. If I had a billion dollars, I'd probably go buy some remote land somewhere and populate it with people from the cities who meet certain criteria. You know all those runaway girls we hear about in the press all the time? I'd set up shelters in the big cities where I'd have experts inspect them for quality and if they wanted, they could then come to the farm and work where they would be loved and where they could help breed the new people. To make this work, I'd need more of a religious philosophy and maybe that was where Zack comes in. I'll bet if Zack tried real hard that he'd have a revelation along these lines and then he could write it down in his book about his religion as something from God." Zack didn't say anything but just kept driving. After about an hour he asked me to spell him at the wheel and he crawled in the back and went to sleep. When he woke up a couple of hours later he told us that he'd just had a new revelation. The Shining One had appeared and told him to write that believers were to set up remote breeding places where the faithful would go and have children in a pure environment. He had also been told that he was to send missionaries into likely parts of the world to find converts and if the converts were worthy that they would be invited to stay on these breeding farms for as long as they wanted. If the converts were girls and had babies that they couldn't or wouldn't care for then the farm would take care of the kids as children of the Cosmic Pussy.

I figured it was great having a founder of a religion right here with us, because revelations supporting our various positions were never more than a nap away. And, who could say that these revelations were less real than the revelations supposedly received by Moses or Muhammad or a score of others? Zack was a prophet for this new age of ennui. Zack was as much a product of our time and place as was Moses of his, Jesus of his, Muhammad of his, Gautama of his, Zoroaster of his, and on and on and on. All addressed certain things that they saw in their societies that they felt were wrong. They all overturned other religions then current. Only time—much more time than we would have on Earth—would tell if Zack's religion would do the same.

It seemed that we were making our own morality and living moral lives as we saw fit. I liked that, because that was one of the indications of the Ubermensch if I had understood Nietzsche correctly. We were above the rules and mores of other lesser men. Why should we have to live the kinds of lives that some other guys thought was the correct way to live? Why should we accept their rules? Why shouldn't they accept our rules. We had as much right to make rules as anyone else. If Zack said that we were to marry hundreds of women, instead of just one, why couldn't that be the law? Why must we passively accept what some other guy thought was prim and proper for the running of our lives? That was the key. Our lives. These were our lives and we didn't really know what would happen once we die, but we did know without a doubt that at the very least we had only one go round. Why shouldn't we make that certain one go-round what we wanted it to be instead of what someone else wanted it to be? Let those who would tell us how to live, live the way they wanted, and we would live the way we wanted. so long as we didn't harm anyone else, it was just none of their business. I told all these things to Zack and suggested that it would be great if his religion encompassed such things to give our life styles a legitimacy—a something bigger that we could point to—and say that we were living as our God dictated we live.

Sometime later, Zack had another revelation and apparently God did want us to be able to marry hundreds of women and to mate freely with as many women as possible. It was, explained Zack, God's way of populating the earth with our kind of believers. "Does God have anything we shouldn't do," I asked. According to Zack, God wanted us to perfect ourselves and our lines. We were to try to have children who were better than us. At the same time we were supposed to try to mutate ourselves. It was that old Lamarckism again. If we could improve in this life then our children who would receive our genes would be a little further ahead.

"You know," said Zack. "Women are born with all the eggs that they'll ever have in life. I believe that number of eggs is around 200,000. So, in theory, each woman could have 200,000 children if the eggs were harvested. Men constantly produce sperm throughout their lives, so maybe that's why the Cosmic Pussy is important to us. Women are the protectors of a treasure trove of eggs of our people, that must be protected. I've received a revelation that because men constantly produce sperm that they are the engines of change in the species and that the sperm changes and modifies over the years to be able to help babies born from the eggs adapt to environmental changes. If the man went through some good changes, then the sperm might be improved and this would help the children born be better."

I started thinking back to the time at the nude beach where Gil or Zack, I couldn't remember which, jumped in to the cold Pacific to impress the girls and came out looking like he had a cocktail frank and two olives as cold made his scrotum retract up to the body to maintain a certain temperature. That's the way men's bodies worked. In hot weather their testicles moved further away from the body and in the cold they moved closer. The sperm, it seemed, needed to be within a certain temperature range…or…what? What would happen if they were too cold? Could that be the key to the mutation to the Ubermensch? Cold? Is that why our imaginary Nazis; at least I think they were imaginary, had this thing for the ice? Is that why I had intuited that I had to be in a cold climate in order to evolve? It was seeming more and more clear to me that the prime external ingredient to evolving was cold. But was it any cold? What about moist cold as opposed to dry cold? Was it better to have continuous cold or better to have rapid cold and then rapid heat. Too much cold must not be good, but what was the optimum temperature? And was it the scrotum that was really what needed to be cold or perhaps it was other parts of the body including the brain that would release hormones and make the changes. Maybe there was even more to this.

Maybe one needed a certain diet along with the cold and the proper genes, and maybe even the right belief was what was needed to mutate. I then thought about the Eskimos who lived in the cold most of their lives. They didn't seem very evolved, I thought. I must still be missing something. Wait a minute. Eskimos weren't really evolved for the cold at all, they just adapted to it. They had darkish skin and dark eyes and dark hair. That wasn't a creature that was evolved for the cold at all. The Eskimos were more like south seas people. They were just trapped in a cold environment that they had not evolved to live in. White people with pale white skin, blue eyes and blond hair were adapted to the cold or was it that they were adapted to low sunlight or maybe both? There were many questions I had about all this, but I had to assume that since I was a white person, I was of the right type to evolve to the Ubermensch—because if I wasn't, then why in the hell would I want to even try it? It seemed that our three paths, religion, evolution and revolution were converging, and integrating into a cohesive whole, although it was still a little too early to say that definitely. Still, the three of us did seem to be on the same track in the same train even if we were in different boxcars. We were rushing headlong down the track to a destination we couldn't yet see; but as we moved on we were getting stronger and stronger and more and more firm in our resolve. Our resolve for what?

Zack told us again that he was writing down all his revelations and that they were in chapters and each had a chapter title to identify them instead of just numbers for chapters. Some of the revelations were a single page, some were several pages. The revelations seemed to come as answers to specific needs or questions rather than as just general revelations. Zack said that's why he had revelations about things we were talking about just after we talked about them rather than them being this phony buttressing of the things that were important to us. "Nothing happens in a vacuum," Zack said. So, Gil and I were as confused as ever about Zack and his revelations. One minute we figured they were phony, and the next we figured they were real, or at least real to Zack. I don't know if I could buy into some angel coming in a Cosmic Pussy only to Zack while he slept. Of course, I had heard of visions of the Virgin Mary that Catholics had claimed to have had, and those sounded similar to what Zack was claiming to experience.

They say that a prophet is without honor in his own land. In our case, maybe Zack was without honor in his own van. What had people who had been around ancient prophets and messengers thought? I know that people tried to kill Muhammad and thought him mad. Something similar had happened with Jesus and with Moses and thousands more whose names aren't even remembered, because their religions failed. Maybe all these guys had the madness of God. Maybe none of them did. Maybe some of them did and some of them didn't. who knows? Maybe no religious leader ever seems bigger than life when he is sitting right next to you in a van or on a donkey or a horse. I guess if Zack stayed true to this religious "calling" for enough years that Gil and I would eventually come around and believe in him or at least believe that he wasn't putting us all on.

Gil and I figured that it wouldn't hurt anything to become believers in Zack's religion. After all, every time we thought of something neat to put into the faith, Zack would have a convenient revelation and there it would be. I thought religion was supposed to be about denying yourself things, but Zack's religion wasn't like that, as far as we could tell from the things that Zack had said. Gil and I hadn't actually seen any of the revelations, that Zack was writing down in those spiral notebooks. Thank God for these spiral notebooks. Zack was using some for his religion. Gil was using some for revolutionary things and I was using some for both the Ubermensch and for recording our travels. Recording our travels? Sounded like a travelogue but I was writing down very little about the external trip we were on. It was nothing. This was the age of TV, there wasn't too much out there that everyone wouldn't already know about. I suppose I could try to be cute and clever and notice little things like a spider on the window or the way the sun set over the ocean, but for now at least, that wasn't of much interest to me. Out there was out there for everyone to see. In here was something else again. In here was the whole universe and maybe a whole new way of life.

To the world, we were probably just three losers. We certainly weren't in tune with the work-a-day world all around us. Perhaps we were missing something in not living a straight life, but I mostly didn't think about that.

As we were going down the road, we were suddenly passed by an old pickup truck with a Harley in the back and two scruffy looking guys driving the truck. Gil wondered aloud where they were going.

"Don't you know?" asked Zack.

"No, how would I know?"

"Those are a couple of those outlaw bikers. The hog must have broken down so they're on the way up the road to get it fixed, I guess, so they can rejoin the rest."

"What do you mean the rest?" asked Gil

"Hold on," said Zack. "There do you hear it?"

As we listened, we did hear a sort of buzzing that seemed to be getting louder by the second. Suddenly it turned into a roaring. We looked out the back window and there behind us way off in the distance we could see the entire roadway full of motorcycles all coming our way. In a few more minutes they were all around us, and then they sped on down the road.

There must have been a couple hundred of them, and Zack was right, they were all wearing outlaw biker rockers on their jackets. This made me think that the three of us weren't as far out of society as I had first thought. Those guys on the bikes had been around on the outside for years. They really had their own sub-culture and their own laws and rules. Maybe they were the Ubermenschen. No. They couldn't be the next evolutionary step for mankind. I was looking for more of a Renaissance man for my Ubermensch. I mean shouldn't the next step forward for man be better looking, stronger, brighter than most other people? If he was to be a step forward, he must have something better than other people, otherwise he wouldn't, by definition, be a step forward.

I started thinking about hybrid vigor; the phenomena that occurs when you mate two different types of whatever. The offspring often exhibit what is called hybrid vigor which is to say that they are often stronger or bigger or brighter than the parents. Now, on the surface this would indicate that the different races should mate. What happens in nature, however, is that subsequent generations fall back to a mean which is often not as good as either of the means of the grandparents. Still, if we breed all white guys like some of these European countries, are we going to have a bunch of pale white sissies running around the place? I've seen movies from some European countries and the men all look like skinny women. Somehow that can't be what the Ubermensch is meant to be. Wasn't Nietzsche trying to birth the blond beast? What does that mean? Was his ideal some sort of Viking looking person with bulging muscles but with the brain of a genius? Can you have both? aren't we up against certain weight, size, capacity limits the way an engineer is when he designs, say, an airplane? I mean, he could make the thing strong and impervious to bullets, but then it wouldn't fly because it would be too heavy, or he could make is super fast and sleek, but then you couldn't put people inside. Maybe that's what the Cosmic Pussy is up against with people and why She or nature is constantly experimenting with new forms to try to find some way around the natural physical limitations. Perhaps, if you give a man very quick reactions you also have to hardwire more of his brain to circuits to the eyes and muscles at the cost of hardwiring circuits to the higher brain functions. Maybe, it's sort of like the Cosmic Engineer had only so much calcium or other raw materials and He could put proportionately more in the brain or in the muscles or other body parts, but to do so He must rob from other body parts. Maybe if he took all that he needed for the brain to make a super genius he'd have to sacrifice bone or muscle and he'd end up with a marshmallow man. Nature doesn't seem to waste much, so there must be some reason that man is the way man is, I mean having the shape we do instead of the shape of a starfish of a slug. Why would we have our brains in our heads instead of our chests? The answer is pretty simple. Common sense tells us that it's in our head because that's where our main sensory organs are. Our eyes connect directly up to our brains, so there's no need to waste extra wiring to bring visual images from eyes, say, on our stomachs or toes, way up to our heads. One had to wonder, though, was the brain designed to help the body or was the body designed to be the carrier for the brain? I suspect that the brain was to help the body, and that it just evolved so that it became the master of the body instead of the other way around. And, the body exists to carry the genes which may be the ultimate puppet masters of every species and which try to replicate themselves to dominate all other genes.

CHAPTER 18

"You know," said Gil, after what seemed like hours of silence, "I think we represent something new in revolutionaries. We're middle class, I guess, and there's not much new in that because most revolutions were really started and maintained by the middle class. I know you have pictures of people swarming up from the sewers of Paris during the French Revolution of 1789, and that probably did happen, but it was at a later part of the revolution that had already been just about won by the middle class. The way I think we're different is that we're awakening to a country that is racially divided though certain elites are trying to hold it together by playing the non-whites off against the middle class whites while trying to differentiate themselves in the minds of the non-whites. This shell game has been going on for about forty or so years, and maybe we're among the first whites to catch on to what the elites are doing. While most whites are probably looking at the elites and wishing that they could be just like them, we're saying to hell with them. To hell with all conventional things except the conventional things that we ourselves decide are conventional. Most whites are decadent and dispirited and they're dying off.

"Can't you feel it? I can feel revolution in the air. I actually like conflict and struggle. I think I can see a partition of the U.S. coming in the not too distant future. The battle seems to be between the genocidal mixer/maters and those who believe that the races should be separate. I'm in the later category like you two. I guess we each have our own reasons. Zack's is religious. Alex's is evolutionary and mine is revolutionary. There's just another sign that our lines are converging as we were talking about before. The three of us together, what we used to call the Three Pod...remember that, those miles ago? We three seem to have a fully rounded philosophy between us. The only thing I haven't heard us talk about is the economics of the things. You know Marx and Engels and those guys were heavy into the economics of their systems. Other revolutionary theorists have also been into the economic angle, but most of that stuff just bores me. Still, to be fully rounded, really fully rounded, we'll have to think about an economic system to replace what we have now. Capitalism has problems. The rich are just getting richer and the poor are getting poorer. A new system has to keep the incentives for the rich to keep building new businesses but it has to help the workers as well. You know, I think we need to have more of nationalism, but not the old jingoistic nationalism; we need a true racial nationalism. We need a nation that is ours and ours alone. If we screw it up, that's our problem, but if we build something big, that's our gravy. We shouldn't have to carry people unlike ourselves in our nation and we shouldn't be forced into considering some non-white who happens to live across the street from us and who works in the same factory and waters his lawn the same way, as our brother. Genetically, we have nothing in common. What is real is from the genes. All the other commonalities are just window dressing. Fluff. Transitory little nothings. We need a racial state that is protected by a religious ideology that keeps it that way on the command of the Cosmic Pussy. In this racial state, we need to have a grand national purpose: breeding the Ubermensch."

Just then, Zack started to have a fit. This was very troubling since he was the driver. I managed to grab the wheel and ease the van over to the side of the road. Zack just sat there with his eyes open and his mouth pulled back in a grimace while shaking all over. Suddenly he came out of it and started talking. "Hitler didn't die," he yelled.

"What?" said Gil and I at about the same minute.

"Hitler didn't die," Zack repeated. "He left the bunker through a back entrance wearing a disguise as a farmer. He had cut off his mustache. His guards, who were also disguised as farmers, took him to Bremerhaven where he was put on a sub that had been waiting for him. The sub sailed to the South Pole. Don't you see it? We've all been receiving thoughts about these various things. Hitler lived under the ice. It was the cold and the protection of the ice blocking out the sun and some other things that kept him alive into very old age. I had a vision of this, but it got blurry. I think his people are beneath the ice and they're boring under the Earth. They take the long view of history and these past sixty odd years are as nothing to them. They believe that they will inherit the Earth and they're getting into position to do just that. They started the AIDS epidemic to kill off all non-whites and homosexuals. Don't you think it's interesting that those two groups are the primary victims of the disease and those two groups were also the primary enemies of Hitler—if you consider Jews as non-whites? Hitler wanted a behavior and racial specific disease and AIDS, while not perfect, was pretty close. The virus dies in the cold, so the people below the ice don't have anything to worry about."

"AIDS dies in the cold?" asked Gil, "that's the first I've heard of that."

"It's from my revelation," said Zack. The virus is easily killed by the cold. The doctors haven't caught on to this simple fact yet, but if they had better record keeping they'd find that AIDS is biggest in the summertime and in places where there is warmth year round. It's really a monkey disease that Hitler's people extracted while they were in Africa. They had been holding back on releasing the disease because they wanted to develop a vaccination. When they could never come up with a vaccination...wait a minute...they don't need a vaccination. That's why they've released the virus now. None of the people below the ice will get AIDS even if the virus gets through the cold, because they're all immune." Their genes protect them.

"Man, that's some revelation," I said. "Zack you're getting weirder and weirder. I've never heard any of this stuff before. Now, why in the world would the Cosmic Pussy tell you all this?"

"I don't know, things are just popping into my head. Aren't you guys experiencing the same thing even a little? I know you are, you've both babbled on about things that you didn't know anything about before we started taking these trips."

"Man," said Gil, "We're turning into three Edgar Cayces."

I figured there was little harm in trying to puzzle things like AIDS out, but the way Zack was talking it was almost as thought he had just read something in the newspaper—perhaps a newspaper of the future. Cold? I guess we'd just have to wait and see if that was found to be an effective way kill the virus or whether this was just Zack using his imagination. Anyway, I suppose if it's cold enough the cold will kill anything, so perhaps this wasn't much of a revelation after all. Nazis below the ice? Hitler still alive, or still alive long after we thought he was dead? I was starring to get a headache from all the craziness of the three of us.

"Did you ever think," I said, "that we three might just be mental patients locked away in a mental ward and that we're just imagining all of this? Even better, how about I'm the mental patient and I'm all alone and you two and this bus are all figments of my imagination. Maybe I'm just sitting in a chair in some semi-vegetative state dreaming all of this. I can almost step outside of myself and look back. There I am, in a robe sitting in a chair babbling incessantly. I have to babble incessantly because I'm talking for three characters. I don't even like to think like this, because how can we know if it's true or not?"

"Do either of you know where we are?" asked Gil.

"You're driving Gil and you don't know where we are?" I said.

"I've been driving in this fog for hours. I can't see anything, but somehow what I do make out looks a little familiar."

"Did you just hear that foghorn?" asked Zack. "I think we're back in San Francisco."

There was something surreal about our trips. We never seemed to see anything. Every other place was always pretty much the same at this place. We were definitely not your average tourists or sightseers. Maybe I was too close to all of this to figure it out. "Gil, stop for a minute. I'm going to get out and stand beside the road. You drive off and then turn around and drive past me slowly. I want to experience us from the outside." I got out and stood by a street light that was all eerie in the fog and this was a really thick San Francisco fog that was almost a white rain. Gil and Zack drove off. As they did so I swear I heard an electrical crackling sound the way you sometimes hear from high power eclectic lines, and I also swear that the bus seemed to have a greenish glow all around it. Then, the tail lights got fuzzy and disappeared into the fog almost immediately. The bus turned around and came back. Again, I thought I could see the slight green-ish glow and the headlights diffused in the fog, and I could hear the crackling sound again. The bus came up beside me and I could see Zack looking out with no expression on his face. He looked blue as though he were dead. He didn't smile. Then the bus was gone, again. They then turned around and came back and picked me up. "Man," I said, "you guys looked really weird, and the bus had a green glow. How'd I look?"

"You looked pale and blue and like death," said Zack.

"Yeah, like a zombie or something," said Gil.

"That's how you guys looked to me too," I said. "The bus looked like it was moving in slow motion. It was like something from a movie."

"So, I guess we're back in San Francisco," said Zack. "Now what?"

"Well I guess I'd better go see if Carla is still around." I said.

They dropped me off at Carla's place. I just could never really think of it as my place. I rang the doorbell and she let me in. Instead of yelling at me she said, "I've been transferred to Los Angeles. Do you want to move down there with me?"

"And leave San Francisco?" I asked.

"Well, the city's changing anyway. I don't think it's as much fun as it used to be. It's up to you though. Maybe we could get a place down in Santa Monica. Maybe even buy a house. I'd like to have a little house and stop moving from apartment to apartment, wouldn't you?"

Actually, it did sound pretty good. I was just afraid of losing any more of my freedom. First, I'm tied down to Carla, next I'll be tied down to a house. Then children. It's not what I was trying to do with my life. But then again, what the hell was I trying to do with my life anyway? Drive around with two freaks in a VW bus until we all died of old age? No. I was a writer or an actor. Maybe I was a writer/actor or an actor/writer. Could I make any money at either of those two things. I didn't know. Maybe Los Angeles would be better for this sort of stuff. That's where the movies were being made, so it couldn't hurt to be near all that. So that's what we did. We threw our stuff, including the Harley in a big rental truck and headed south. I drove the truck and Carla followed in her car.

LOS ANGELES

CHAPTER 1

I nstead of Santa Monica, we found a place to live in the same beach city where I had spent the night with Nadine. I thought it wise not to mention to Carla that I'd spend a little time here with Nadine not too long ago. I didn't even know if we'd ever run into Nadine again, anyway.

I had some head shots made up and sent them off to all the agents in Hollywood. I got one call from an agent. I went up to the see the guy. He had an office in an old building at Hollywood and Vine that had the look and feel of something from the 40's. The agent looked like something out of a '30's potboiler. He was a skinny little guy with pasty looking skin, nervous tics, and dirty looking blond hair. He was wearing a wrinkled cheap white shirt. His name was Vic. I t looked like Vic lived in his office. I half expected him to pull a fresh shirt out of a desk drawer. Anyway, Vic signed me up. After that, he would call me and send me on appointments. Somehow Vic's idea of my type and my idea of my type were different. I went on this one call and the trailer was full of black guys. No kidding. I was the only white actor there to read the lines. I was called in and given a side to read in front of a video camera and a couple of casting guys.

"Okay, read the part of JB," said one of the casting guys.

I read from the script. "Let me ax you this Bubba, you grab somethin' when that store done burned?" The casting guy said thanks and that I had given him a great reading. He'd be in touch. I never heard from him again, of course.

Vic then sent me on a call where I had to read for a part in a movie about some vegetable from outer space. The reading was in some guy's garage up in one of those neighborhoods that the liberal elites like to tell working whites they are supposed to love. I was supposed to play a Mexican truck driver and the lines sounded like something the Cisco Kid's pal would say. I didn't get that part either. Somehow my blue eyes and, still dyed, blond hair weren't what the director had in mind. Man, this screwball PC crap was getting weird. The people making the films knew damn well what they wanted a character to look and sound like, but because everyone was afraid of being un-PC, they had to waste everyone's time by interviewing midgets for the roles of giants and whites for the roles of blacks and blacks for the roles of Asians. It was idiocy. Since I didn't have anything better to do, I just kept going on all these goofy calls whenever Vic called. This went on for a few months and during that time my relationship with Carla was getting very sour. I just knew this was going to happen. Our personalities were just too different. She had a smarmy manipulative way about her, and she seemed to expend most of her calories subconsciously trying to do imitations of starlets from Beach Party movies from the '60's. If I heard her say "Oh, that's fun," about one more thing, I was going to explode. I just wasn't a character out of one of those surfer movies. I finally just got on the Harley and headed back to San Francisco. Screw this living with Carla stuff. I took a room at Poop and went back to work taking tickets at Gino's porno theater. When I wasn't working, I was writing and I was still pursuing acting. I got some small parts in some local commercials, but I was more a writer than an actor. My new strategy was to write a screenplay and hopefully sell it, and me, to someone who would produce the damn thing. If I could do that, I'd get paid as a writer and as an actor.

CHAPTER 2

Z ack was starting to get a large following. He'd do weekly readings from his revelations at the little stage at Poop. Every time he'd give a reading, more people would show up. This was good for Poop's business, so Talkin' Bob encouraged it.

Zack would sit up on a big chair in the middle of the stage and tell the drunks, outlaw bikers, hookers, porno stars, queers, transvestites and other flotsam and jetsam the truth according to Zack.

The Cosmic Pussy Religion had evolved a little since I last saw Zack. Now, it almost worshiped women. Maybe that's the wrong term, but it became kind of the way the Virgin Mary is to Latin Catholics. The idea of "woman" was given great importance, and the vagina thing was sort of just assumed without being emphasized so much. Man was to honor her and protect her from outside forces. It was sort of like the way bees were organized. But in the Cosmic Pussy Religion all the women were supposed to be Queens or Princesses and the men were Kings, breeders, soldiers and workers. What Zack had started as a religion in which a man would have many wives, had been changed somewhat so that a man would first name a Queen who was in charge of the Princesses and in keeping the hive orderly. The Queen selected which of the Princesses should sleep with the King each night and this was based on who needed to be pregnant. From time to time, certain of the Princesses would split off and start new hives with other men. Zack had bought some land on the way up to the nude beach that had an old farm house and some barns on it. That was the main colony. I went up to visit and the place was packed with people all doing a variety of things. It looked a little like one of those old hippy communes, but here the people all wore the same kind of plain, somber, loose fitting, grey pajama outfits. They were all wearing some sort of grey skull caps that went to just above their ears. Everyone appeared to be happy, but they didn't have that old hippy neurotic glow around their happiness that spoke more to smoking too much weed than anything profound. Zack was working right along with everyone else in a garden where they were growing food for the group. All the women were pregnant or were nursing. That was just like the earlier revelation that Zack had passed on. The men were all close shaved and all had their hair dyed blond. They looked military. Even the women had their hair dyed blond and cut short in military style.

I guess Zack had taken some of his thoughts and mixed them up with mine and with Gil's to fashion this religion, because there were pieces of all three of us here. Gil's revolutionary thoughts, my evolutionary thoughts and Zack's own religious thoughts combined to make something that apparently, judging from all the people around here, was appealing to many people. I wondered how he'd fare if the national press got wind of all this and started printing things about how this was a group of fascists or racists or whatever smear would sell the most newspapers. I brought this up with Zack and he said that he would actually welcome that and that he had revelations about it that had already been incorporated into the faith. He thought that it might actually bring more people into the religion.

Zack said that he sent people out into the streets each day to sell copies of the religion's newspaper and copies of his Cosmic Messages, which was, he said, the equivalent of the Koran, the Bible and other religious books. He gave me a copy and said that I should read and study it and that I'd find all the answers that I'd been looking for all my life.

"Come on Zack," I said, "this is Alex. I was with you when you wrote most of this stuff. You don't really expect me to believe this do you?" I was trying to get him to admit some petit fraud or scam.

"Alex, you never really understood," he said. "This is real. I'm not faking or pretending. I believe this with all my heart. Do yourself a favor Alex and read and study the book and if you have a pure heart and an open mind, you may find that you're awakening from a life-long sleep. You know this religion isn't about Zack. It's not about me at all. I may be the one who received the messages, but I'm just the instrument. I'm not perfect or special. I'm like the typewriter being typed on by God. These people don't worship me or think I'm a God or anything like that. All I am is a messenger. Nothing more and nothing less. God speaks to our people through me. It's a simple as that. I"m like the speakers on a radio. The messages come in through my essence and they go out through my mouth or my typewriter." I took the copy of the Cosmic Messages that he had given me and promised that I'd at least glance through it when I had time. I left, saying that I'd come back soon.

Cosmic Messages was divided up into 315 verses, or chapters, that all stood alone, so you could pick the book up and start at just about any page that fell open. Some of the verses were less than a page in length and some were many pages long. There was no preface. I started with Verse 1 called "The First." "Awaken and look upon me for I am sent by the Lord of all the Universes to speak so that you may write down what must be written and so that you may then spread what you have written to all who have the Sacred Essence. You are not insane, O, Messenger, you are looking upon the air shimmering in front of you and it parts from top to bottom and therein am I, who am sent. I am called Angel by some and Shining One by others. Write as you are commanded." That was the end of The First. Clearly it was an introduction as to what this book was all about. The

Cosmic Messages was a book full of practical advice and commands. I thumbed through it and stopped at a verse entitled The Cow Born. This was pretty much what I had once told Zack while we were driving around about how I wondered if we were here from another planet and that we were carried around in cows. I thumbed on again and there was a verse called The Ice. This one told of people living beneath the ice. A few more pages and there was the Three Travelers. It seemed that virtually everything in Cosmic Messages had something to do with Zack, Gil and me from when we drove around in the VW bus. There was a small verse entitled Catnip Tea, that caught my eye, but there wasn't much to it other than that it was said to be good for people, and some things about how those with certain genes got more benefits from the tea than others. I couldn't find any revelations that started before we met up with Zack. There were, however, verses that appear to have been written once Zack founded this religion. Among these, was one called Protectors of the Messenger. This was all about the believers taking steps to protect the Messenger; not because he was holy but because he was the only direct contact they had with the Shining One who in turn was the contact with God. Zack taught that each and every believer was always in contact with God, but that through some quirk of fate, Zack could see and hear the Shining One so he was the instrument of the Lord. I was reassured when I read in a chapter called The Messenger, that Zack claimed no powers of any kind and not even the power to intervene with God for any of the believers. In fact, in that chapter, it was stated that the Messenger was to be the servant of all believers and that it was not his function to give orders or to tell people what to do. For that purpose, there were to be others who would take up leadership roles. Zack seemed to view himself and the book as one. It was the written version and he was the living spoken version. His job was to spread the message to all who had the Potential.. They would then have to find their own way or be further influenced by others in the religion who had been selected to teach and instruct.

Apparently, Zack didn't really want to be a cult figure and certainly didn't want people to personally follow him. It was stated in the Cosmic Messages that to follow the Messenger would be like following a typewriter because the Messenger was no more important than a typewriter.

There were chapters on how to dress and cut your hair, and what to eat, how to pray. How to position yourself toward non-believers. How to work in the world. How to purify. How to evolve. How to mutate. When to fight. How to handle persecution. What to look for in a mate. How to raise children. It went on and on. It covered all areas of life in great detail so that believers could always know what was expect of them at all times and in all circumstances. In "The Light" I read:

"All was dark. The Sacred Coil was not seen. There was darkness and nothing else but darkness for darkness is what exists when nothing else exists in our universe. Darkness takes no energy and no effort to be, for it is that which is not. It is, without effort. Light takes energy and effort to be and when the energy and the effort cease, the light is extinguished. This is so throughout the Universe in all things large and small. God is in the light and wants the light to prevail over the dark, for God was the bringer of the light to the worlds of man. All the things of the world that are light are yours and are holy. Man is to evolve toward the light and away from the dark and this is why there are fewer white people than dark people, for the latter were the first creatures on this planet and the former were the more recent development. Light grows from and feeds on the dark. Dark is collapse and total dark is total collapse.

"Evil ones come to the lands of the people of the light and they teach falsely that the light ones, the white ones, are to lie with the dark ones for in this way will they show that they love man. Do not be deceived, O you faithful! It is not man you are to love, but God. God demands more light. The Sacred Coil is within, and it is without. God commands you to avoid the dark in all things. Seek out all things that are of the light."

"Sacred Coil?" I wondered about that. It seemed to be another new term introduced by Zack and maybe it had something to do with DNA or the way the bus seemed to collect and distribute some sort of energy that may have been electrical in nature. It also reminded me of the little antennas on the roof of the bus. The Cosmic Messages went on in that vein and then there would be a chapter on wearing cotton clothes only, of about the Essence which seemed to be similar to soul mixed up with genes or blood and consciousness as well as being a spark of God within. Fire was used in many of the ceremonies of the religion as was ice. There was a great need for ritual and actual purity of all things, and for these purposes there were pages on using salt and vinegar, alcohol, fire, bleach and water to purify. There were pages on healing. There were also verses on the proper form of government for believers. Apparently, Zack believed that religion was all encompassing. I was wondering how Zack could cover for the problems that hadn't yet come up since this book was already out in a bound version. Then I saw the Verse "Changes" in which God, through the Shining One, said that so long as his Human messenger lived, there could be additional revelations added to the book. It was also stated that the Messenger was imperfect and the he could make mistakes. That was apparently one of those fudge statements that Zack, who was a lawyer, put in so that he could make later chapters that would contradict the earlier ones. A little ambivalence was, it seemed, both a lawyer's and a messenger's stock in trade.

It seemed that what Zack was doing was fashioning a tribal religion for one people only, and that he realized that, given the assimilationist spirit of the age, he'd have trouble converting vast numbers of white people, to this religion so the growth was really expected to be from births of those who he was able to convert. Once the few were converted, they became breeding stock for the next generation of believers. It was to be one big family, all related by genes, beliefs

and customs. In a way, this harkened back to the way nations originally formed out of tribes, but Zack's plan was to prevent the nation
he was forming from being invaded by others. Nation? Yes. It seemed
clear that Zack was making a religion and a nation, and a new people. He was also purifying the genes by inbreeding within one racial
group.

As I was starting to think that Zack had set this whole thing up to
get rich, I read a verse that said the Messenger and the true believers
were to live simple lives with few possessions. There was more talk
about clothes and how they were to be made of cotton and were to
be washed after each wearing and before entering the temple The
idea in clothes was that they were to be plain and clean and one was
not to wear anything that could not be worn for doing manual labor.
So, even if one were an executive, his clothes must be plain and of
cotton. One could, apparently, wear a suit coat, but it too must be
cotton and it must be roomy and one must be able to do manual
labor while wearing it. Useless items of clothing such as neckties
were not to be worn. It appears that nothing was done for pure deco-
ration. Comfort was the most important thing in clothes. Household
furnishings were minimal and consisted of beds, couches, plain
chairs those sorts of things. Modern appliances were no problem and
believers could have TV's, radios, computers, refrigerators and all the
rest of it, but they were not to make their houses places of personal
vanity. It seems that Zack was trying to make all believers equal in
status, by preventing ostentatious displays. Life was not to be lived to
amass great personal wealth, but to further the faith in the short run
and to improve their lines in both the short and long run. A person
was considered holy and wealthy partly based on how many children
he or she had. The relationship of believers to the outside world was
a delicate one. Outside laws were to be followed when they didn't
conflict with the Cosmic Laws as contained in the Cosmic Messages.
Religious leaders weren't appointed by anyone, and Zack wasn't anything like a Pope. Religious leaders bubbled up from the believers,

and one of the goals was for these leaders to learn while living at this place and then to travel out to other areas of the country and the world and to form colonies with Temples. They would be successful or unsuccessful depending on their own abilities to gather others around them. This was all written in the Cosmic Messages. The religious leaders or teachers were to leave when they felt called to do so. They could take some other believers with them if they all so chose. They would travel to some other city or town, and set up a Temple. The Temple was to be much like this one, which is to say, it would be a center for religious and social activities of the believers. The believers then would try to buy up property in the immediate area to be close to the Temple. Other believers would open stores to service the needs of the believers. In this regard, it was written that believers should eat food that had been grown and processed only by other believers whenever this was possible. This was part of the extensive purity laws that Zack had received. Food that had even so much as been touched by non-believers must be made pure through an extensive washing ritual which was such a pain in the neck that it encouraged believers to just deal with other believers. This caused some believers to become farmers where they farmed according to the Cosmic Messages. Others made clothes. Others handled the food. Since believers believed in taking care of their own, they developed their own security forces. What Zack was developing, was an entire small nation that would exist within the borders of other nations, and which might eventually gobble up these nations from within and transform them into what Zack had set forth. It would do this by births of many new believers and by conversions. Zack's religion was complete unto itself. It fulfilled all the functions of a nation. If believers were attacked by outsiders, the outsiders would be dealt with very harshly by secret warriors sent by the believers. In this regard, they believed in harsher punishments than even the old eye for an eye routine from the Old Testament. Their rationale was that if someone intentionally harmed a believer and if this person was a non-believer then that person had to have expended extra energy to cause whatever harm he did, and he would therefore reap extra energy back in the form of punishment.

All the crimes against believers were listed, and many took account of race in the punishment. If a non-white raped a believer, the punishment was death. If a non-believer white, raped a believer then the punishment might be death or it might be something lesser. These punishments had to do with the defilement of the Cosmic Pussy, and the eggs that the religion believed were the property of the religion and must not be defiled. Property crimes were treated with considerably lesser punishments, but any crimes that harmed the Essence—that caused a lessening of the purity or number of believers received the harshest punishments. Judges were to be religious leaders who were well versed in the Cosmic Messages. Zack envisioned setting up small courts in the local neighborhoods that would handle most small disputes. It also seemed that most of the "officials" in this faith would sit on prayer mats in front of people they would be talking to, judging, or meeting with. I sort of liked that, because it was a break with the ways of the west where those in positions above others would begin to lord it over others even when they didn't mean to because of sitting behind big desks or sitting above everyone on a dais. Zack had it set up so that everyone was equal in clothes, in life styles, and in most of those things that make up any society. I was starting to wonder if he had given up on capitalism as an economic system when I came upon a verse that addressed this and which made it clear that capitalism was still valid but it had to be a form of capitalism that recognized the fact that one didn't become wealthy in a vacuum. If one made a lot of money, that person had to thank his genes and the gene pool in general and also had to thank the society that he lived in for making this possible. This being the case, he owed more to the gene pool and to the society than those who weren't as well off. To the former, he owed many, many children. If he was a billionaire, then he could afford to have hundreds of children, and he should do this, so long as he did not carry any genetic defect that could be detected. It seemed that most of Zack's messages, as far as they related to man, started with the genes and his messages were gene specific; his religion wasn't for all mankind because not all mankind would be in contact with God. This was made clear in the verse called THE ESSENCE. This mysterious Essence that Zack always referred to was, as I already mentioned, a little like a soul but it was more. It was also, apparently, a little like parts of a radio that would allow the person to receive God Waves that came from the Cosmic Pussy. Actually, that wasn't quite right. It appeared that Zack had refined his system. The Cosmic Pussy was hardly ever mentioned, now. This had been transformed into what he called the Vortex. God was the force behind the Vortex and from the Vortex came all of existence. According to the Cosmic Messages, God put Essence only into white people and it was coexistent with but not the same as white skin. White skin, blue eyes, blond hair and long heads, certain bone structures and a few other things Zack called the External Sacred Signs. One must try to evolve one's line toward acquiring more and more of the External Sacred Signs in this faith. These external signs were an indication of the purity of the individual, but they were not the only signs for there were also internal signs and these were things that had to be observed by the way a person was. Was he smart? That's a sign. Was he noble?

That's a sign. Was he this or that or the other? Those were signs. It seems that Zack had found a way to incorporate all his theology into flesh so that one had to exist in order for the other to also exist. In other words, one could believe all the things that Zack taught, but if one didn't have the Essence, then it did no more good, than a radio without the right parts did in picking up radio waves.

Man, so here we had a religion that grew out of the travel of three guys who didn't know where they were going in life. I kept reading the Messages, and they seemed to answer all things, if you just freely interpreted them. Got a dispute with your neighbor over a dog? The answer was in the Cosmic Messages. A love one has died? Turn to the messages. How do you raise children? The messages told you. Someone has wronged you? Seek the answer about what to do in the messages.

I wondered if people in other religious that were founded long ago, and that now were respected, felt as I did about such things when they were this close. I mean, Zack? A guy we picked up while he was hitchhiking, as a great religious leader? Well, Jesus was a carpenter. Muhammad sold carpets. There was really nothing so weird about Zack's religion and Zack after all. Both Jesus and Muhammad, to name just two religious leaders, brought new religions into being that were different than other religions then in existence, and which swept away these other religions to one degree or another. In a verse called THE OVERMAN, Zack got into all the Ubermensch stuff that I had been working on for so long. Zack, or the Shining One, or God, or the Cosmic Pussy, or whoever, said that man's purpose was to transform to higher states and that he would never be fully complete until he meshed completely with God. To close with God, man must constantly improve. Zack likened this to climbing stairs with landings every so often. Man, according to Zack, was on one of those landings now. He needed to find his way to the stairs going up. There were many choices. Some of the stairways led to dead ends and some actually wound around and led down. Up was to higher consciousness and light. Down was to lower consciousness and dark. Zack claimed that it was only through this religion that man could find his way up. The most controversial part of Zack's teachings involved race and ethnicity, because he taught that only white people could find their way up. Zack swore that this was a direct revelation and wasn't a product of some anti-white hatred on his part. "Look he said, in every age, religious leaders come along and question the current orthodoxy and are controversial and turn the whole world upside down. Jesus did that. Muhammad did that. Moses did that. The things that they overturned in their day made them controversial back then, and if they had taught what I now teach, there would have been very little controversy then as would be the case if I taught now what they taught then. If I threw the money changers out of the temple as Jesus did, do you suppose that would be controversial today? Of course not. The revelations that I've been given about race are controversial today, because the opposite view is considered to be a sacred cow. I can't simply walk away from what I've been told to teach because it's controversial. I can't bury the truth because it hurts feelings or questions what everyone is taught today. All I can do is be the instrument to write down and spread these truths. There's no hatred in any of the things that I've been told to write, only love and honesty. If some think they are preaching hate, then let them look into their own hearts for what must really be there. There is no hatred in my heart nor in this religion. Read the verse called "RAC-ISM" and Alex and you may understand."

I did read that verse, and in it Zack explained that the word racism only meant to believers that they noticed that the races of man were different genetically from each other. The term was distinguished from "race hatred" which is how the term "racism" was usually, incorrectly, used. Zack and his religion didn't run from the terms racist and racism; they simply defined them the way they meant them. The verse went on to explain that there were three basic things needed to close with God. The first, you had to be born with and this was called Right Blood, or as I already mentioned, Essence.. The second was called Right Belief, which was further defined as the belief in this religion and in Zack as the messenger. Right Belief also activated the Right Blood or turned on the lights of the Essence. Next came Right Action which was all that one did in life. It meant acting in accordance with the teachings. With these three things, according to the religion, man could evolve toward God. If you lacked any one of them you were inert and couldn't benefit from the religion. If you read the Cosmic Messages and didn't really internalize what was taught and have it change you on a sub-cellular level then you might as well have read a romance novel. So, too, if you lacked the Right Blood. Without the Right Blood you could have Right Belief and you could have Right Action, but nothing would happen. The verse talked about the radio again. If it lacked the right tubes, all the beliefs in the world that it could pick up radio waves wouldn't help and all the turning of switches on the radio (Right Action) wouldn't make it work. I wondered if Zack was aware that most radios don't have tubes anymore, but if you analogize tubes to circuit boards, the point was the same. Still, I wondered if this religion really caught on if in some distant future day people would wonder what the hell radio tubes were?

"Zack, you know that this emphasis on genes, blood and race is what's going to cause controversy so why can't you change it just a little to make the religion open to everyone?" I had asked this before in a slightly different way, but I wanted to see if Zack was really serious about what he said were revelations.

"Alex, I told you before, these are real revelations. I haven't made up any of this stuff. I know that a lot of the verses sound like things we discussed or experienced while we were on trips, and they are, but that doesn't make them any less valid. Maybe that's the way God works with us. He just infuses general thoughts into our brains and then later, for whatever reason, they became more concrete with those who pass them on to others. Look, if I wanted to make up a phony religion I could do it and I would do it with all the namby pamby stuff that wouldn't offend anyone. I know, that given the temper of the times we're living in, that this emphasis on race and genes is going to cause all sorts of problems for us, but again, that's out of my hands. I only write down what I'm told to write down. Perhaps, it's precisely because of the temper of the times that these revelations have come at this time. Back when people were largely confined to specific geographic areas because of poor transportation, people could breed true and move evolution along. But now, it's like one of us said before, the world is moving toward a great leveling of the populations and instead of having distinct types we're moving toward a Tan Everyman—a creature with some genes of every other group. Not white, not black, not red, not brown, not yellow but a combination of them all. Maybe this is not what God wants and that's why I've been called on to pass on these revelations. Look, it's clear to me that this mixing and mating is not what God wants and that may be why we were first led to all this via the Cosmic Pussy concept. It's all about breeding correctly and to the maximum. I'll tell you this. I'm not pleased with being chosen for this because I was never even particularly religious. This isn't something that I sought out, and it's not anything that I can even make any money from. I will tell you, though, that I'm happy most of the time in being able to do something that appears to be worthwhile. I don't like being called names, and that part of it doesn't make me happy. I'm still enough in this world that I'm hurt when the newspapers print stories about this religion and me and smear us. You do know that some of the newspapers have printed stories about us, don't you? One of the San Francisco papers did a feature article calling us the Nazi Religion. A tabloid printed something saying that we worshiped Hitler and that we believe Hitler was living beneath the ice with six million Jewish slaves. All those pieces did was gin up awareness about us. And while it hurt us a little at the same time it gave us millions of dollars of free publicity and we got a lot of new converts. Come with me, I want to show you something." We went over to a barn and went in. Inside, there were about thirty people, both men and women, sitting on mats on the ground and in front of them on a slightly raised perch, so he could be seen and heard, was a guy with a beard. As he sat there cross legged, he was lecturing those in front of him.

"Those people are getting ready to leave here and go out in the world and start their own colonies. This will always be the Mother Colony and the others will be daughter colonies, but they won't receive any order or commands from us. They'll use the same holy books that we use for their guidance and they'll receive bulk copies of our newspaper to sell to raise money and get new members in their areas. That guy over there with the tatoo is going to Atlanta. he's already rented a storefront that will serve as his residence and as his Temple. He'll try to bring in as many people to the truth as possible Some of those he converts may want to come here, for more instruction, or they may not. That's up to them. In time, some of those he brings in will move out and start their own Temples and colonies.

"I don't see how you can maintain any orthodoxy that way," I said. "What's to keep some of these people from saying that they've found a better way and that your way is lousy and then split off from you? Also, what's to keep some of them from renouncing the racist teachings as false and saying that they were brainwashed? You do know that many people who are drawn to new religions or cults are very neurotic and are looking for authority figures and structure, but that some then turn against the new religions or cults and become the biggest enemies of the religions or cults. don't you?"

"There isn't anything we can do about that," said Zack. "We know it'll happen. We also know that those who hate us have probably sent in phony converts to do just those things and to try to neutralize and destroy this religion. We also know that many religious converts to this faith as well as to all others are people who are looking for psychological father and mother figures and other such things and that some of these will eventually be disillusioned and leave while calling us names. The only thing we can do is teach the truth as we receive it, and to emphasize that our holy books are supreme and must not be deviated from. I can't even change anything that has been written. I can have later revelations that change things, but once I've written down a revelation, it stays written. Also, if you read the Cosmic Messages, you know that I am the only Messenger. There will be no more after me, so this should make sure than no phonies come along to change this religion. You know, Alex, I really believe that God will destroy this planet if we do not succeed with this faith. You know we don't accept the Bible or any other religion's books as holy, but we do look at them, and most of them are guides for some people at some time. One of my revelations says that what happened in Sodom and Gomorrah really did happen but that all the modern talk about people of those cities having sex with animals was really about people having sex with non-whites who God considers to be lower animals. When the two Angels—who we would call Shining Ones—were sent into those cities to find a righteous man, they were actually trying to find whites who still followed God's laws about miscegenation. They weren't trying to find a man who prayed a lot, as you may have learned in Sunday School. The Bible is full of things like that. Do you want to hear a few more?

I nodded.

"Okay, well even the story of Adam and Even and their children shows that Adam and Eve weren't the first hominids on the planet, they were just the first white people. Look at Cain and Able. Look at all the stories in the Bible and especially in the Old Testament and what you'll see is the story of our people coming to this planet and how they interacted with the native hominids—the ape creatures—and how the ape creatures became more, and how our people became less by their mixing and mating. Original sin was these whites mating with the ape creatures. This religion that has been revealed to me can reverse that process and start us back on our God given destiny. Is it hard for some people to believe these things when they have been subjected to years of propaganda about how we're all just one big happy humanity? You bet. Some of our revelations talk about the persecution that believers will have to endure and how many will fall by the wayside and choose not to struggle against the overwhelming odds of a world gone mad. One of the reasons that we like to have our people live around each other is to give each other strength in moments of weakness when all about them there are people who are calling them names and saying that we are evil. We are the paragons of virtue and goodness on this planet. We are here to save mankind from destruction and to do God's work. You know, I've often thought about this religion in terms of movies. You know how you'll sometimes see a movie and all the people in the movie believe one thing and there is one hero who believes something else? Of course, the movie maker has been heavy handed to make sure that the audience, each and every one of the people watching, feels sympathy with the hero, and just knows that had they been in the real world version of the movie that they would have stood with the hero. They would have known the truth. In the real world, however, they would have more than likely sided with all the people who were against the hero. That's just the way it always is. Look at Galileo. He was pretty much alone in defending Copernicus's theory that the Earth rotated around the sun and not the other way around. Most of the people of that time sided with the church and persecuted poor Galileo. It's no different now. This religion is challenging the current orthodoxy and is saying things that are far different than the company line. In a world where race is being de-emphasized and some are saying that the concept of race is false, we're saying that not only is race important, but that it is the most important factor relating to people. In a world that encourages racial mixing, we say that racial separation is God's law. When we say these things, we are called haters and told that we are divisive. Yet, we have no hate at all. We just want to pursue our religion as we see fit, free from the intrusions of outsiders. We believe that this is our right—our right as human beings—in any country in the world. We don't get our freedoms from government, but from God. We are as we are, and there is nothing else required to have a right to be as we are. We think, so we have a right to think. Our existence is proof that we should exist."

"Yeah. But you know that the elites in our society are going to come down hard on you, and they control the law," I said.

"Well, that may be, but any laws that they make for any religions must be enforced equally for ours. They can't make laws that only impact us or those laws will be overturned. If we want to erect giant swastikas in a town square, then we have as much right to that as Christians have a right to erect crosses and Jews to erect Menorahs. If they are told theat they can't erect these religious symbols, then we also will not be allowed to do so. In other words, the government can't treat us any differently than any other religions. If hate filled individuals try to persecute us and shut us up, the laws that protect every other religion will protect us too. We're going to be a force for change in society, Alex, you can count on it. We're going to defeat evil, stop genocide, and do the work of God. We're here to stay. You know, I've been reading more and more about other religions, because I believe that it's important to understand them and their histories so that we can understand what will happen to us. You know how respectable the Mormons are today? Well, they were just as controversial in their early days as we are now.

The problem with the regular Mormons though, is that they compromised their principles to avoid further persecution. They used to believe in having multiple wives just as we do, but the feds cracked down on them, so the Mormons had a convenient new revelation that changed that. They also used to believe that only white males could hold certain church positions, but they caved in on that one too. In our religion it's not possible to cave in on such things. What is written will not be changed—that is, the important things won't be changed. Some of the revelations, however, are about minor things that I may have heard wrong and they can be changed. These are usually little toss away things that are only mentioned once as part of something else. The major revelations which are the subjects of the verses are never to be changed even if every single member of the faith is persecuted and killed for their beliefs. These are God's laws, and they stand for all time because God stands for all time. We believe that God is also evolving, but His evolution is different and would never cause Him to give revelations that counter the earlier ones. You know, the Shining One said that God moves in a different sense of time than we do, and that in some regards, the Shining One is like a step-down transformer passing on to us what God thinks. I think that's the Essence of this religion. It is what God thinks and wants. It is less about worshiping God as God, and more about worshiping what God thinks and wants And it is put into a language that we can understand. In this regard, I'm the interpreter of these things. The Shining One talks to me, but it's more like thoughts coming into my mind in blocks rather than a word at a time. My mind apparently turns these blocks of thoughts into individual English words. At least that's what I think is happening, but I could be wrong."

Zack continued, "This religion is far different than any other religion that I know of. It teaches that believers are to be honest and kind and not harm living things unless needed for food or safety. It teaches that believers aren't to be belligerent and aggressive, but that they are to try to understand those who might mean them harm. There's not much new in that, because many religions preach that, but in this religion, once the believer is convinced that a non-believer or group of non-believers means harm to the Essence—either the individual Essence carried by the individual believer or the group Essence, the believer is to do all in his or her power to destroy the hater. Furthermore, a believer doesn't have to wait to be attacked by a hater before acting. If the believer is convinced that a hater will harm the Essence when given the chance, then the believer may make a preemptive strike to prevent any harm to the Essence. You see, it's like I told you before, this religion is partly about having our people survive on this planet of the apes. There is danger all around us. Most of our people; our genetic people, are blind and stupid to the danger of mixing and mating. They've actually taken this great danger and turned it into a positive in their mind. "Oh, yes, we're so modern and we're so unbiased that we're jumping in the sack with people of all races and we're having little non-white children left and right," seems to be what they're saying. What they are doing is pissing into our gene pool from which we must all drink and claiming that they have a right to do so because it's their piss. They are causing the devolution of our people. We could show them this in scientific terms, but they wouldn't believe it, because they're bigoted haters masquerading as compassionate souls. I would ask you, if a person is compassionate toward germs that will kill a person, is that person really compassionate?

Now, with this religion, we don't have to try to justify our beliefs. What we believe is from God and no one can argue with God. All argument must end with what the Creator has said. Those who hate us; and you'd better believe that all non-whites have a genetic or instinctive hate for whites, will try to trot out their own scientific facts to prove that we should hop into bed together, but they cannot argue against God. God said it. End of argument. Period. Look at the children of whites and non-whites. They always look non-white, because they are non-white. It's easy to be non-white, you just have to stop trying to be white. It's the old thing that you said once, Alex, that light takes energy and dark takes no energy. To be white requires struggle and light. Now, when we talk about non-whites being harmful to us, we often mean this in the way that some creature, by its very existence and through no conscious effort, is harmful to other creatures. It's like germs, as I just said. Germs don't really want to harm us. It's just that their life form and ours are at odds. It's genetic. God hasn't made a universe in which the sheep lie down with the lions. He's made a universe where everything struggles to dominate—to be the king of the mountain. That's the way it is with whites and non-whites."

"Well, I know a lot of people feel as you do Zack, but I can't see how this religion of yours will ever catch on. It flies right in the face of what most people have been taught in this country over the past forty or so years and it lends itself to being called all sorts of names. It's almost as though this religion had a sign on it saying 'persecute us.'"

"Alex, we're planning on moving further away from people so that we can practice our religion with no intrusions," said Zack. We're buying a bunch of land up in Montana as a starter, and if that doesn't work, we'll move even further out. If we breed as we're supposed to, we should be able to be the dominant force in Montana politics in a few years and then we'll be able to put our laws into effect. It's just a matter of numbers. If each of our women has ten children each, and that's what has been revealed as a number to shoot for, and if more and more people come to us from our various colonies, we'll start taking over Montana a town at a time. Then we'll take over Wyoming and so on. Let there be a few wars and diseases like AIDS to decimate the non-believer population, and with us largely protected from these things, because of our beliefs, our diffusion to different places, our isolation, and with our much higher than normal birthrate and we're going to prevail. Remember how you said how you thought our people used cows to carry fetuses? we're looking into that as well. We know that without large numbers of believers we'll be easy targets for the haters, but once we get the numbers, we'll call the shots and our people will be protected from the bigots. Our religion is about our people. Our blood, or genes, which we call Essence, is our link to God. You know these things already from your reading, but you still seem skeptical. Alex this is for real. We're not fooling around with this. We believe this. Gil is with us. I guess you know that. Gil's main function is to see that we're protected, and he does a very good job at it. I don't tell him what to do, but I will tell you that people who have attacked us verbally or physically don't usually do it again. Gil believes in this religion as much as I do, and I trust him with everything. Do you remember Nancy, Kara and Loren? They're with us now."

"You mean the girls from the mobile home?" I asked.

"Yep. They moved the mobile home down here. They're not around just now, because they've gone up to Montana to help get the farm up there ready for most of us to move there. We'll keep this place as long as it keeps drawing people from San Francisco, but if it becomes a burden, we'll sell it."

"Zack, I was wondering about Tracy and Linda, you know from the nude beach, have you talked to them?" I asked.

"No. But why don't you invite them down. They seemed to like you especially. They'd be good breeding stock."

"Breeding stock?" I said, "I don't know if they'd like to be talked about that way."

"We all call ourselves breeding stock. I'm breeding stock. You're breeding stock. We're all breeding stock. There's no insult in this. We're God's breeding stock to help Him carry out His plan. Even the Bible said be fruitful and multiply. That's all that we're doing, but we're also being a little selective in our choices. We take the long view of history and we know that if we follow the revelations, that eventually we'll prevail. We believe that we'll be the inheritors of this world. I know it seems far fetched right now, but we believe that we can out-breed all other peoples and that we can survive many major diseases and other catastrophes that are coming. These things will wipe out a large part of humanity, but we'll keep on breeding like cockroaches. Remember how we used to talk about those bumper stickers that said that the one who dies with the most toys wins? Well, we'll be dancing on the graves of those who thought that way. I plan on having at least a hundred children myself; more if God wills it. There'll be lots of different mothers, but all my kids will have my last name along with the mother's last name just to avoid any potential problems later on with people too closely related carrying genetic problems and having children together. You really should join us Alex, you were really instrumental in starting all of this. It was you who made the decision to pick me up on that road. You know the play, "Waiting for Godot" where the guy just stands at the crossroads waiting for Godot. And Godot is supposed to be God, but Godot never shows up? Well, maybe life does imitate art. Maybe I was waiting beside that road for God and you and Gil showed up and brought me to Him. The fact that you're not conscious of being directed to do that is irrelevant. I believe that you were sent on your travels so that our paths would intersect and I believe that you still have a major role to play."

"So, you're saying that I should join you and believe in the Cosmic Pussy who talks to you at night about Nazis beneath the South Pole?. Yeah. That sure sounds, sane." Zack looked a little hurt when I had finished, so I quickly jumped back in, "I'm just kidding Zack. But it does sound weird if we put it in those terms. You've got to admit it."

"I know," he said. "But, if you put any religion in those kinds of terms, they'll sound weird. How about Christianity with all the talk of blood and drinking blood that looks like water and eating flesh like the Catholics do? They're all weird, and I think our religion is actually less weird than all the others. The important thing about our religion is that it's from god and not from man. Our religion is God's religion for man.

CHAPTER 3

I went back to San Francisco for a bout a week and then I felt com-
pelled to take Zack up on his thought of inviting Tracy and Linda
from the nude beach down to his place. I gave them a call and told
them about Zack. They said that they'd read something about him in
the newspaper but didn't make the connection that he was one of the
guys with me. They didn't associate porno making Zack with the
religious Zack. They said that they'd like to visit just to see us, and
wanted to know if they could just drop in whenever they got a
chance. I told them that would be fine and that I was sure Zack
would remember them.

About three weeks later, I got a call from Zack saying that Tracy
and Linda had just shown up and that I should come over. I went.
They were just as beautiful as ever, and I started thinking of breeding
stock. Zack was as persuasive as in the past and you could have
knocked me over with a feather when these two beautiful girls agreed
to join the religion. They said that they'd probably not move to the
farm, but they'd like to study the religion for a while and maybe visit
every so often. Zack told them that would be fine and that they
would be good breeders and would bring some beauty to the gene
pool. I just about fell over when they weren't insulted by this. They
said that they weren't ready to have children just yet, but they'd be
thinking about it. I noticed that there were a lot more people at the

farm than the last time I'd been there, and there were a lot of old school busses all painted black with images of the spiral and the Cosmic Pussy, which had now been completely transformed from the Mexican version to one with a Shining One in the center. Each bus also had the slogan "God is truth."

Ever being the one to want to dot the I's and cross the t's and to have things named, and defined, I asked Zack if he'd ever named the church. He told me that it wasn't a church. It was a religion. A church is a Christian concept and this wasn't Christian. "We call the religion "Evolvism,"for lack of a better term," he said. "We may change that later on; I don't know, but it'll work for now."

"What's with all the busses?" I asked.

"Most of us are leaving for Montana. Some will stay behind to build up another group and then eventually they'll move up with us too and we plan to keep doing that. We'll recruit wherever we can find our people living in fear in the cities or being repressed by the government or otherwise not living up to their potential. we'll recruit and we'll save them one by one."

"And what if they want to leave the ranch?" I asked.

"No problem, Alex. I think you've got the wrong idea about all this. We're not a cult and we don't force anyone to do anything. Everyone is free to come or go as they desire. Sure, we have peer group pressure that we'll bring to bear on those who are straying, but there's no compulsion or force. I'm going up to the ranch. We're going to leave on Wednesday. Here's a map of where it is. If you decide to come up later on, just come. Bring some women if you can…Evolvists need women!"

So, I left the farm and went back to San Francisco. A few months later I got a postcard from Zack saying that everything was going great and that I should really come up and visit or stay with them for as long as I wanted, or forever. He also asked me to go by the farm and make sure everything was okay.

I went to the farm and the place was full of people again. I gave my name to a guy standing at the front gate, who I took to be some sort of sentry or guard, and I was surprised when he said "You're one of the Messenger's companions aren't you?" I wasn't sure what he meant, so I just stared dumbly. "You're Alex and you're a companion just like Gil, right?

Now, I got it."Yes. I'm a companion. You know, I've been away. How many companions does the Messenger have?"

"Two, of course," was the reply. "Just you and Gil are considered Companions because you were with the Messenger in the early days and traveled with him. We've read about you in the Book of Traditions." Man, this was really getting weird. Now, there was a second book. First there was the Cosmic Messages and now his new one. Also, this supposed non-cult was starting to look just like a cult ; a personality cult with Zack as some sort of man god and Gil and me as being close to it.

"I hope the book doesn't speak of Gil and me with any kind of reverence or anything like that." I said.

"Oh no. It's nothing like that. Zack is the Messenger so we sometimes call him that, but we're all equal here. I'm sorry if I put you off with the way I asked if you were one of the Companions. I guess it must have sounded like something out of a movie. Zack doesn't have any pretenses for himself and he says that you and Gil don't either. He also says that none of you are holy as people on the outside might ever think of that term. In fact, the only reason that you're called Companions is that it's an easy way to refer to you. You can imagine that there's a lot of interest in How Zack came to receive these messages and you two are part of those early days."

"Are you getting ready to go up to Montana?" I asked, because I didn't have anything else to say.

"Nope. Baja." was his reply.

"Baja? Isn't that going in the wrong direction?"

"Zack says he's had a new revelation and that we're supposed to take over Baja and make it an independent nation just for us. It's to be a place where we won't be persecuted."

Well that was certainly a new piece of news. What the hell happened to the ice and all that, I wondered? Baja. Hell, that place was a desert. It was hot. It had sand. It had cactus. It had Mexicans. And, what about this business about taking it over?

"Did you hear that directly from Zack?" I asked.

"Right from his mouth. Gil is in charge of the operation down there but will coordinate with people up here." I wondered if these people had all lost their minds. What had started off as a lark with three guys riding around in a friggin' VW bus and simply free associating bunches of different ideas had now led to a new religion and an invasion of Mexico. How in the hell they thought that this little rag tag band could invade Mexico, was beyond me. Someone was going to get hurt. This was absolutely nuts. Did they expect the Mexican government to just stand by while this took place?

"Let me see if I understand this," I said. "You're planning a military invasion of Mexico?" I was unable to disguise the incredulity in my voice.

"Military invasion?" came the reply. "Sorry, I didn't mean to give you that impression. We're just going to move down there. We're a genetic invasion of Mexico. Zack figures that we've been receiving illegal immigrants from Mexico for years, so we'll just turn the tables on them and start wetbacking south." Well, that was interesting. It would be fun to see if Zack could get enough people heading south to ever transform the place. He'd need millions of people, and I was pretty sure that he didn't have anywhere enough people. In fact, I guessed he only had a few hundred members of his religion at best.

"Here's a map of where Zack is setting up camp," said the guard. I looked at it and it was a photocopy of a portion of a regular road map like you might buy at a gas station and it was marked up with directions. I put it in my pocket.

CHAPTER 4

$\boldsymbol{I}$ t wasn't too long after that conversation I had at the Farm that I started seeing more and more hawkers on street corners selling Zack's newspapers. There were banner headlines saying things such as, "God wants Baja to be a separate nation," and, "Take back Baja—it's your country." Soon, the big daily newspapers started writing stories about this.

All of this talk about Baja must have gotten into my subconscious, because one night I had really vivid dream about it all that seemed like a movie. In my dream I could see Zack recruiting people from Europe and Canada to help in his invasion. He was not wrapping this movement totally in his religious views, but it was evident that he was also recruiting for Evolvism at the same time. Soon, all the TV news shows were doing big stories on this twist on illegal immigration. It was actually sort of laughable as the tables were turned on Mexico. The Mexicans were coming up here and the white folks were going down there. The people motivated by Zack were mostly rough-it types who didn't mind sleeping out in the desert. They didn't require much to live on, and they sure didn't get much. There were attacks by Mexican Bandidos, who were often really just disguised Mexican police, but Zack's reverse osmosis illegals started fighting back. Baja was starting to look like the old west in the U.S.

all over again in Mexico. The Mexican government appealed to Washington to stop the influx of illegals, but to no avail. This was probably because they had been sending their nationals north for so many years, and Washington thought this was fair. It also seemed that this movement had caught the fancy of many Americans as well as many Europeans who were now flocking to Baja. As with prior "invasions" of genetic Europeans, the ones who flocked to Baja were mostly the misfits of their old countries and those who had some type of attention deficit disorder that caused them to always roam. It helped bring in more people after Zack, through anonymous sources, let it be known that they had discovered a vast field of gold. Of course, this was a lie. Suddenly there were thousands of Poles, Russians, Irish, and Germans, as well as many from other European nations moving to Baja. It was like the old American European melting pot, but on speed, due to modern mass transportation. In my dream I just bemusedly sat back and watched as Zack manipulated public opinion. At least in my dream, Zack was proving himself to be a genius at propaganda. Every newspaper and magazine in the country was running daily and weekly stories about this Baja affair. The stories were all slanted to the particular audience who bought these publications. The supermarket tabloids had the usual space alien stuff. The weekly news magazines ran stories about the geography and natural resources. There were dozens of stories giving various justifications for the invasion. Some were based on moral principles—"We're going to save the people down there from poverty." Others were based on legal and historic precedents. Some were based on religion. Some on international law. Zack had even released documents that he claimed proved that Baja was always an independent state and not a part of Mexico nor of the U.S. and that it was the property of Irish, French and German immigrants who lived there a couple of hundred years before and that Zack and his people were the natural heirs to the land.

Then, again in my dream, I could see newspaper headlines about atrocities against the believers by the Mexicans. There were photos of little American kids with their throats slashed, by Mexican soldiers. I could see that Zack had simply faked most of the photos, using his knowledge of cameras. The photos caused an immense uproar in the U. S. and citizens were demanding that American immigrants be protected. The U.S. finally send a military force down to Baja to protect US. citizens and this set off a real firestorm in Mexico, as might be expected.

Soon, the U.S. and Mexico were waging an undeclared war. It didn't take long before Mexico was defeated, but the U.N. got into the picture and demanded that the U.S. not annex Baja as part of the U.S. because this would be seen by the nations of the world as a new imperialism. So, a compromise was worked out between the U.S. and Mexico whereby the U.S. would pay Mexico for all of Baja and would also give Mexico billions in additional foreign aid. In return, Mexico would give up any claims it had to Baja. Baja would then become an independent nation.

The U.S. wanted something in return, so it wanted the new country to be loyal to the U.S. To accomplish this, and to still have some color of legitimacy, Congress held hearings with the leaders of those who had invaded Baja. This meant Zack.

So, Zack appeared before a joint meeting of a new ad hoc Baja Committee set up by and consisting of 20 members selected by the House of Representatives and the Senate.

"Could you please state your name for the record, sir?" said the Senator.

"Zack."

"State your last name please," said the senator.

"I just use Zack," said Zack.

"Now, Mr. Zack, we understand that you have many of your followers living in Baja, and that you believe that the U.S. should install you as the head of a new government of what will become an independent nation until such time as democratic elections can be held? Is that a fair summary of what we're about here, today?"

"That's a very good summary, Senator. It is our land. We shed our blood in Baja and we're going to continue living there. We'll also defend our land. The Mexicans have no claim to this land other than that they said it was theirs, but as you know, our people were there early in Mexico's history and also before recorded history according to revelations from God, so we were first."

"Well, Mr. Zack, as you know, the U.S. has a very strong constitutional bias against theocracies, and it sounds as though you want to establish such a theocracy. Can you comment on that please?"

"Thank you Senator. Actually, we want to set up a government where all people can be free and where they can worship or not worship as they please with no interference from government. As you are aware, Senator, I am an American citizen and most of the people in Baja now are American citizens. We would attempt to have dual citizenship if that is possible, and we would model our government on well established U. S. principles."

And, that's pretty much the way the session went. One Congressman from Utah asked Zack a little more about his claims on the land.

"I was first led to this land by images of the Virgin of Guadalupe, and then I was shown ancient writings on stone tablets," replied Zack. "I was able to read these tablets which told of our coming to Baja many thousands of years ago. Over the centuries, we left to join with our people in another area of the world, but it was our intention to return. We have now returned in much the same way one will leave a house on vacation and then return to it. Baja is our house."

"Let's assume, for the sake of argument, that you can make some legitimate claim to Baja because of something from the past. Why should we help you? Our treaty with Mexico and our payment for the land should make it U.S. property," said another Senator.

"Well, Senator, I mean you no disrespect, but the fact is that Baja is our land. It is to be our refuge from the attacks of those who want to carry out genocide on our people. We will live in Baja and we will make the desert bloom."

As usual, the government hearings were a bunch of bull presided over by a gang of pompous flatulent elites who wanted the people back home to see them on TV and suck it all up. Baja became a separate nation and the temporary government was set up by Zack. Zack was no fool and he played it a little the way Israel had played it before the state of Israel was founded. As with the Jews, Zack always claimed that God gave his people Baja for all time and for him not to take it would be to disobey God. His proof was sketchy at best and relied on faith, but like most people trying to assert their right to something, Zack's proof gave him the color of authority so long as he held to the public belief that it was correct. Zack set up a defense force—commanded by Gil—of course. He set up all the institutions of government and a complete society wide infrastructure normally found in any civilized nation. When this was done, the U.S. gave foreign aid to the new nation of Baja—and thus to Zack and his religion.

Everything in my dream was now moving so fast that it had a surreal effect. It was as though time was suddenly compressed so that events—major events on the world stage were now being controlled by a weird latter day hippy named Zack. I couldn't believe that the Zack who Gil and I had given a ride to just a few years ago was now in charge of a nation. Yet he was, at least in my dream vision.

It was clear, though, that Zack wasn't pleased with the relatively slow population growth of his believers, even though they were popping out babies like an assembly line. To speed up the population growth, he set up a kind of reverse income tax whereby there were financial rewards for those having the most babies and financial debits against those who didn't have as many. Zack taught that the greatest good anyone could do for this new society was to have children.

Accordingly, the society owed a debt to the people who had the most children. Zack also stepped up his recruiting in Europe and sought out people for the gene pool who had the types of characteristics he most needed. He was looking for blond, blue eyed breeders with strong bodies and minds. When he compromised on anything, it was usually on the hair color and the strong minds. So he did take in a lot of people with dark hair—many from Ireland. But, Zack insisted that if they had dark hair they must have blue, grey or hazel eyes. There was just too much variation among white people to be a stickler and dictate some sort of clone appearance. Money soon became a problem for the new nation, as there wasn't any industry to speak of. Zack did what he could to encourage new industries to move to the area and he promised that he would be able to supply cheap white labor. Although the big corporations tried to pretend they hadn't heard the white part lest they be accused of being racist, they were attracted to this, because they knew that they'd be getting intelligent skilled workers who wouldn't have too much social dysfunction. The cheap part of the labor was a serious inducement. As time went on, the government was starting to take on the religious overtones of the Evolvists. This was seen as a good thing. In Evolvism, alcohol, drugs, tobacco, in fact anything that could be ingested that would harm the Essence was forbidden.

About a week after my dream, I packed a back pack, and as the fog was coming in, I headed south to Baja on my old hog. Now that I had made up my mind, it was though I was possessed. I rode and rode and rode, getting off the main road only long enough to go through drive-ins to get food and coffee, and coffee and coffee and more coffee. The trip seemed to go slow because I was so fired up to get to Baja. I was planning on riding straight through, but when I got down to the beach city I decided to see if Nadine might like to come with me. To my surprise, she said that she was ready for a change. At this time, she had two room mates so it was no big deal for her to just tell them that she'd be back, but that they should pay all the rent in case she didn't show up. She told them they could keep or sell whatever she left behind—clothes, and stuff like that mostly, also some of her paintings, that she didn't like much anyway. So, she packed a couple of bags, grabbed a few other things and I helped her load them into her old Ford. She then followed me as we headed south.

After a couple of miles I had to stop to take a leak, so I pulled over by some bushes.

Nadine pulled up behind me and yelled out the window, "You know, you're supposed to drink your urine."

"Oh?" I figured she was pulling my leg.

"No. Really. It's good for you. You just recycle all the vitamins that are now concentrated in the urine."

"Hmm. Do you want to drink my urine?" I asked.

"No. You're supposed to drink your own. I drink mine all the time, and I have tons of energy. Mine is bright yellow because of all the B vitamins and other things I take every day. It really has no odor. I usually put it in the refrigerator to chill it."

I told her that I'd have to work up to doing that, but that maybe after I saw her doing that several times, I might consider it. She asked if I wanted to have kids, and I told her that I did. She said that she was feeling as though her biological clock was running too fast and that she'd like to have some as soon as possible. This made me a little squeamish, because I was afraid that she thought that she and I were going to be a permanent couple.

"You know," I said, Zack and his people don't really believe in monogamous relationships. Their ideal is to produce the most quality children in the shortest period of time. You remember Zack had all that Cosmic Pussy stuff, right? Well, he doesn't talk about that so much anymore, but it's still a big part of his belief system. He expects women to choose proper men, because a woman is tied up for nine months and her choice had better be a good one. The women with Zack also don't expect the men to be there all the time or to only have sex with them and the men don't expect the women to only have sex with them either. Zack is trying to rebuild society without the jealousy and other things that have kept the population down. All the children are the children of all believers. The Evolvists make a stab at identifying the children by giving them a man's last name along with the mother's last name. But all that is really certain is the mother. Because of this, the society is more matriarchal than we are used to in the west. A woman is the protector of the eggs of the people and she is also the protector of the children. A man protects from external threats and provides food. I know it sounds a little like Zack and his people are hunter gatherers but it's more complex than that. There's a real interesting relationship developing between the Evolvists and the rest of the world.

If this were a hundred years ago, Zack and his followers would be facing some angry locals just as the Mormons had in their early days, but because we're living in a PC age, anyone who tries to demonize the Evolvists often gets the tables turned pretty quickly and they give up. When people shout that the Evolvists are an evil cult, Zack shouts back that these people are religious bigots trying to destroy a religion that they don't agree with. With his own little newspaper, and with friends and co-religionists Zack has cultivated in the big newspapers, he's always been able to head off the haters before they could build up popular sentiment against the Evolvists that might lead to actions against the religion. Before we knew it, we were in San Diego and still barreling south. We got to the border, and instead of seeing Zack's people manning the border, as I had thought would be the case because of my dream, there were the regular Mexican border guards. We drove right through Tijuana and kept heading south, staying as close to the ocean as possible. We followed the directions from the map and then, about a hundred miles south of Tijuana, we came to a large cactus with a spray painted bright orange spiral on it just as indicated on the map. As indicated on the map, we took the rutted gravel road that was right next to the cactus and headed west.

The road was so faint that had Zack not painted the cactus, I'm sure we never would have seen the road, which wasn't more than a couple of tire tracks leading over some small hills covered with cactus. As I rode along, with Nadine in the car behind me I reflected on what Zack was up to.

The Evolvists wanted to build an almost bohemian culture but only for white people

They believed that God commanded them to remain only around white people. Zack believed that just the presence of non-whites would tend to block the God waves that were picked up by the Essence. By living all by themselves down here in Baja or even up in Montana, or any other place that was completely white, the Evolvists would put many miles between themselves and non-white genes. Zack sometimes said that it was a little like looking at the stars. You could see them much better if you were away from the light pollution of the urban area. So it was with Essence and God Waves. You could tune in to God much better out here away from the pollution of other people's genes. I wondered how the Evolvists planned to keep their areas exclusively whites in a world that wanted everyone to be brow. Things in this universe were never easy. There were always conflicts and struggle, and that was the way things were here in Baja also. Of course, Zack loved the struggle. He said that to be truly happy, we must understand that this existence is always one of struggle and that if we tried to deny the struggle or hide from it, then we would never be happy, but if we cherished the struggle like standing in the face of the storm and if we were defiant and not meek and mild that we would be one with the storm and the struggle and that we would be embraced by God. "All is struggle," was one of the precepts of Evolvism and this was so much so that Strugglers was another name for believers. They were a hard lot and not to be confused with the hippies of an earlier day, as some people seemed to think. These Evolvists asked no quarter and gave none. In a sense, they were a warrior people evolving to ever greater warrior status. Ancient Greece had its Spartans, modern America had its Evolvists.

The Evolvists were the misfits of modern society. Zack and his religion were like a magnet for them and they started flocking here from all over the white world. It was a white thing, and this continued to rub many people who believed in homogenizing mankind the wrong way. Zack answered them by saying that those who verbally attacked his religion were haters and bigots who wanted to force their ideas of the way the world should be on everyone else. "Why," Zack would ask rhetorically, "should those who believed in Evolvism have any less right to put forth their ideas than the haters and bigots who were attacking the Evolvists? What made the haters and bigots think that their ideas and notions were better than those of the Evolvists?" When Zack stated it this way, it made sense to a lot of people and clearly Zack was wining the public relations battle. And, in modern society the public relations battle was THE major battle.

CHAPTER 5

$\mathcal{N}$adine and I finally arrived at Zack's camp, or Colony, as he called it, as the sun went down. It was a bunch of ramshackle tents, converted school busses, and various kinds of shacks, covering the hills all around the beach. It looked like some sort of third world squatter city, or maybe like a hippie commune from the old days. It wasn't nearly as busy as I had thought it would be from my dream. On the top of a hill overlooking everything was the main temple of the Evolvists. It was as ramshackle as everything else. Essentially is was a great big building made out of a pastiche of wood, corrugated metal, plastic and other assorted things laid out in the form of the Evolvist's swastika. The center hub was the holiest spot, that only Zack could enter. Around the building, was a fence with warning signs telling everyone that only believers could enter this sacred ground. There were groups of men walking around on the grounds who were wearing long black cloaks. They looked something like monks, but the cloaks were all of cotton, which was the sacred fabric of the religion. These were the Guardians of the Faith. They had been accused in the main stream press of carrying out attacks on those who had attacked the faith, but Zack denied the charges. The Guardians lived apart from other members of the faith in special monastery type buildings. Although they seemed to have the trappings of various other monks in other religions, these trappings could be deceiving, because the Guardians were not celibate and they were expected to father children as part of their religious duty. It was said that many people applied to be Guardians, but that every single one had to be hand picked by those close to Zack. And, before they were allowed to enter the Order of the Guardians of the Faith, they had to be personally approved by Zack. The Guardians were told that they were selected because they had desirable genetic traits that the Evolvists wanted to encourage and that because of these desirable traits or characteristics, they were expected to father as many children as possible but that they were not to become involved in the ordinary affairs of the world and they were to never consider themselves as better than other believers. In fact, the Guardians must be the most serving of all believers. Their absolute obedience and vows of silence to the outside world could not be compromised. Even giving the appearance of telling the outside world about the secrets of the Guardians was punishable. It was the responsibility of each Guardian to be strong in the face of all challenges, and to do what was asked without question. It was rumored that when the Guardians were sent into the outside world to carry out vengeance against enemies of the faith that they would often travel in disguise. The only sign of recognition was a special tatoo that each one had on his upper right arm and a special ring that they all wore. The ring had a representation of the Sacred Coil in the form of a double helix of DNA.

In Zack's belief system, the Evolvists came from the white gene pool but the act of their Right Belief and Right Action raised them beyond the normal people who shared the same genes. The goal of the Evolvists was to be a separate people and to be able to look at all the rest of humanity as an older, earlier, defective version that should be allowed to die off as they were replaced by the hew humanity. The Evolvists were the Ubermenschen of the next evolutionary step for mankind. With this in mind, the Evolvists had developed their own ethics and morals and these were different from the lumpen grey mass of mankind that didn't believe. To the Evolvists, killing those who didn't believe and who were harmful to the Evolvists or through whom the Evolvists could gain some advantage or funds for the work was no worse than killing a chicken for a meal. Of course, a lot of this wasn't known except to the Guardians and a few others. Zack looked at humanity as being within concentric circles. The greatest mass was all the non-whites who inhabited the large outer circle. Next came the 10% of the world's population that was white. The next circle had those of that 10% that had the desirable characteristics. The next circle was of those who had become believers. Then there were even smaller circles. Zack looked at the circles as being semi-permeable membranes except for the one between all the non-whites and whites, which was not permeable. But the other membranes would allow whites to trickle in and keep working their way through the various circles to the center and in the absolute center was God. Now, this gets a little confusing, because while God was seen to be in the center, God was also seen to be outside looking at all the circles and also to be in all the circles. Was God inside the non-whites? The answer from Zack was that He was, because God was within everything. However, God was restricted by what he was in. God in a rock had the characteristics of a rock.

God, in the belief system of the Evolvists was always struggling. This idea of theirs that God was not complete, was contrary to the teachings of most other religions and it led to all sorts of differences in the way the Evolvists looked at all of existence. For example, since God wasn't finished, it meant that God was also evolving and struggling, but it also meant that God must have had a beginning. Since God was evolving, this meant that He was changing and in changing, He might be fallible. This emphasis on the struggle was extremely important to the Evolvists and it was considered one of the basic principles of existence. Zack had incorporated much of what he, Gil, and I had discussed in the past into his religion and it kept popping up in different places. The Evolvists believed that one could not really know the nature of God. In this respect they were somewhat like the Hindus who had thousands of aspects of the ultimate God Brahma. In fact, parts of the Evolvists' studies involved reading the old books from other religions. The Code of Manu was particularly important to the Evolvists because it set forth the Caste system used in India. What Zack pointed out, was that the Hindu word for Caste meant 'color' and the castes which we, in the U.S., were always taught as being determined almost completely based on occupation were actually based on the skin color of the people. The Brahmins were the whitest people and the outcastes were the blackest. The Code of Manu gave the smallest details of the relationships between the castes.

While many in the outside world often just dismissed the ancient books as being the product of bigots from an earlier age who simply didn't have the modern knowledge of races, Zack and his people said that the ancient books contained the truth in many respects, and the modern world was wrong. If the word "racism" hadn't been already taken on various connotations in the world it might also serve as one of the names of Evolvism, although since Evolvism was bigger than any racism confined to the Earth, it really wouldn't be as all encompassing as it should be. Cosmic Racism? Maybe. But it was more and it didn't have anything to do with racial hatred, but with the evolution of light from dark. In a way they had kind of a Zen way of looking at their version of Enlightenment…Awakening. Maybe you just had to get it, and logic and sophisticated arguments would not help you get it if you didn't have the capacity to understand. Then of course to have this capacity you had to have the Essence and even if you were non-white but said that you got it you couldn't really get it. You could only intellectualize about getting it, and getting it wasn't an intellectual thing but something that came from within. I think I got it, because much of what Zack spoke and wrote I knew before he did. He seems to have refined it and written most of it down, but it was from our conversations.

I think that if one wanted to attack Evolvism he would have to do it with fear and lies and hope to brainwash people against it, because it really made sense if you thought about it and used various analogies, metaphors and similes to try to understand. Essence was like radio tubes. Essence was also called blood and genes, but was actually more. It was also like soul but was more. Essence was the core of white people, you had to be born with it. God could be received by the Essence like radio waved could be received by a properly working radio with the right tubes. But, the radio had to be turned on, and this was the Right Action part of the three basic things one needed. These three basic things, as I read before, were Right Blood (proper genes); Right Belief (this faith); Right Action (those things that flowed naturally from the other two.). With these three things one could close with God and one could begin to mutate or evolve. 'Why was it that only white people had Essence?' was something that people often asked. The answer was simple, and was another question. How come only white people have white skin? I mean the logic of the religion was there, even thought logic wasn't needed to understand.

If God wasn't finished, then what would keep him from withdrawing his grace from whites and giving it to non-whites? He couldn't do it. God was the ultimate cause, but it would be like a person starting a forest fire. He started it but he couldn't control it. Once started, it acted in accordance with its nature. It was a little like that with existence according to the Evolvists. God brought the fire and was the fire but was outside and inside all at the same time. Zack also spoke of God being complete in every tiny bit of everything. I think that was from our conversation about holograms being complete even if you smashed them apart. I guess if one wanted to compare Evolvism with all other religions and philosophies there would be lots of similarities, but I guess that could be said of all religions.

God wasn't seen as love in Evolvism, but as a vibrant attacking force that didn't come into existence with a whimper but with gusto. This was not exactly a war God, but not exactly a mealy mouthed whining puke of a God either. God was, and He was, because he made Himself Be. This was the God of Evolvism, a God that demanded to be more and who wouldn't hesitate to destroy galaxies, if he could do so, to get his way. This was a bold God of life and chaos. God did not turn the other cheek, but attacked, attacked, attacked. God was the consciousness, the intelligence and the personality of the universe. This was not a God that sought to coexist with anyone or anything else. This was a God on His way to being more. As above, so below, and the way God was, according to the Evolvists was the way they were to be. The Evolvists were the in-your-face-you-fucking-slimeball-scumbag-religion, if you didn't respect them. These weren't a bunch of mewling Milquetoasts. They didn't apologize for who or what they were or for what they believed in.

Important to the Evolvists was their Ideal Person. This was a Ubermensch; a man above, though the concept included women as well. The Ideal Person was one who worked with his hands at finger-nail dirtying jobs but who was also a philosopher or intellectual. The Ideal Person wasn't some sissy sitting around in the living room thinking up things, but rather a person with dirt on his or her hands who was experiencing the world from the bottom on up and who was living life to its fullest. The Ideal Person to the Evolvists was what we might call something of a middle class person, if we didn't define that term solely in terms of finances. This person wasn't in the middle between the rich and the poor necessarily, but in the middle between the white elites and the non-white underclass. The Ideal Person was not coarse, and could easily fit in at the fancy diners of the wealthiest, but he could also fit in down at the corner greasy spoon. I wondered what Nietzsche would think about such a Ubermensch. I also wondered what the Nazis would think of this one above man who didn't mind dirt and sweaty work. The Ideal Person wasn't one to manipulate others and who would easily lie and steal just to become wealthy. On the other hand, this Ideal Person would lie and steal to fulfill his destiny which was spiritual. The morals of the Ideal Person were what he and his fellows in the faith had determined, not things that had been imposed by others. This of course, had to be a source of conflict, because there would be those hyper-individualistic types who wouldn't accept any outside authority, but there was the beauty of the religion, because the highest authority was the Cosmic Messages, and all who believed, had to honor those. Any laws which were in conflict with the messages was ruled to be an illegal law and one which would not be followed. Zack liked to tell his followers that every single believer was equal to every other believer before God, but that those believers who put more into the faith, would naturally rise to positions of respect before all the believers. Zack said that he wouldn't appoint anyone to high positions, so no one should suck up to him for favors. It was the believers themselves who had to bubble up their leaders and remove them if they lost confidence in these leaders. The leaders were needed to do those things that needed to be done, but they couldn't command anyone to do anything. They could only point out what the Cosmic Messages said about various things, and they could ask certain believers to do or not do things. At least that's the way Evolvism was in theory. In practice, it started becoming more codified as the numbers of believers grew. There simply had to be law and order and a proper administration for the common good. Again, this was all covered by the Cosmic Messages, and if it wasn't, then Zack would have a revelation and it would be covered.

CHAPTER 6

❀

Nadine took to the life like this had been her life long destiny. Within a month, she was pregnant as were all the women believers who weren't nursing. Talk about kids. This place was literally crawling with kids. They were everyplace. There were also hundreds of cows wandering freely through the colony. Think of an old dusty western town from a movie where you have packs of dogs running all over the streets on all fours. Now fast forward to this place, and instead of dogs running around on all fours, substitute kids and cows. Kids crawling. Kids waddling. Kids running. Kids jumping. Kids. Kids, Kids. Cows, cows, cows. It was evident that Zack really was serious about repopulating the world with his believers and that he wasn't just talking big. That's how to picture this colony of Evolvists. A dusty ramshackle 'town' composed of tents, shacks and assorted busses and other vehicles, absolutely bursting at the seams with white life. I remember seeing pictures of the Okies in the Dust bowl days, and this reminded me of that. I don't say that with any kind of ill will, because I actually loved this place. It was a place full of life. There was nothing sterile or mannered about this place or the people. This was vigorous, vibrant life. It was like a pile of garbage full of maggots...life, glorious, fighting, struggling, life. Zack had more revelations concerning having children and these confirmed that the way to move higher was to have the greatest number of children. The best house in the community was to be built for the woman who had the most children. If all the women had about the same number of children then the houses would be roughly equal. The women were the Queen Bees of this society and all the men and barren women had to do what they could to help these women.

When I thought about it, I couldn't remember any other human societies that I had ever heard about that was exactly like this. In many societies, the women were thought to be unclean during their periods and were kept apart from everyone else, and in most others the women were treated like second class citizens. Even in those societies where women were given respect, it wasn't anything like the Evolvist way of treating women. I said it before and maybe that was really what they were doing—they were treating their women as Queen Bees whose main function was to have as many of the eggs that God had given them, as women, bear viable offspring. The Evolvists actually wanted every single egg carried by every single Evolvist female to develop into a child, and they were working hard to make that a reality. The scientific aspects involved in all this breeding were handled by a special Order of priests. Much of their work was involved in keeping good records on what kind of babies were being born, and doing all the measurements on them to see if any progress was being made in evolution. This same Order would prevent carriers of clearly defective genes from passing on these genes. They didn't wield this power of prevention too much, figuring that great numbers of babies were required and that they couldn't be too picky so long as the babies had the outward Sacred Signs, and most notably white skin and white facial features.

I learned that Zack hadn't abandoned the old thinking about the ice and that he was actually planning on setting up a colony at Antarctica when he had enough volunteers. As with all the colonies of the Evolvists, the Antarctic one was to be a breeding colony. One of the main things that was watched with any new colony was how many children were born who were healthy and who lived to have children of their own—at least that's what was planned. So, if the colony at Antarctica didn't produce as many health living children as a colony in Baja or in Canada or any other place, then Antarctica was not considered a proper place to maintain a colony. That was really the key as to which lands the Evolvists believed that they had a Divine Right to take and own. They asked: 'Is this land conducive to the greatest number of healthy births and population growth of Evolvists, or was it not?' Those places where the Evolvists multiplied the slowest were unholy and not fit for Evolvist habitation.

The thing with the Evolvists was that they were true believers and they had a zeal coupled with a no-nonsense approach to getting converts that was something to behold. These weren't drug addled little teeny boppers running away from home and finding a surrogate parent in Zack. Many of these people were military veterans and middle aged people. Sure there were plenty of teens and younger too, but the point is that this movement of Zack's had captured the popular imagination. I constantly wondered at that, because Evolvism was clearly 'racist' as the term was often used by the larger society. I mean it excluded all but whites of European ancestry who weren't Jewish. This meant that it allowed in only those that Hitler would have called Aryans. I guess one thing that Evolvism showed was that you could believe in racism and not be an ignorant hater, and that you could still choose to be with your own people no matter how you defined "your people." These Evolvists simply chose to check out of the larger society and follow their own lights and to hell with the rest of the people who the Evolvists believed weren't conscious enough to see that the Evolvists were right.

"How can we not be right?" asked Zack of his beliefs. "We're trying to save our people from extinction. What could be righter than that? Should we spend our time, money, and energies on saving some snail from extinction while we, as a people, are dying off? Does it matter that the rest of the world may not see things as we see them? You know the Bell Curve and how everything can be quantified and will lay out in the shape of a bell Curve? Well, most things will cluster in the middle of the curve—the upper broad part of the bell. Out on either end will be those either below the average or above the average. Well, we Evolvists are way above the average on the Bell Curve for consciousness. We're way over on the far leg. Should we not notice that we notice? Should we pretend not to understand what we understand? Should we put our blinders on so that we'll fit in with the rest of society which has gone mad and is hell bent on destroying itself? You may remember how people used to say that humanity would kill itself off with nuclear weapons, and how people were building bomb shelters and planning on how to survive. Yet today they really are facing destruction by mixing and mating. They will cease to be as distinct genetic types and will blend into some lumpen mass. Is this the way to find God? Is this the way to evolve? Is this the highest destiny of mankind, to collapse down the evolutionary ladder into a pile of manure? Isn't evolution to move higher? aren't we moving higher when we are more like the light? Isn't God in the light? Each one of us has to know in his heart, in his brain, and in his Essence, that even if alone, our beliefs are correct, and they are correct because they are not the product of man. Zack is nothing. I'm like the pen in your pocket that you use to make notes. I'm like the stylus that writes in clay. I'm like your typewriter or computer word processing program. I'm absolutely nothing. It's probably a good thing that I am such a nothing, because I wouldn't want you to follow me. I'm probably at least as imperfect as anyone of you and maybe more so. Maybe that's why I was selected to be the one to write down the messages—so my personality wouldn't get in the way of the messages. It's funny, really, when those who hate us want to attack us, they often attack me personally and point out all my failings. I don't even argue back, because most of what they say is true. I did drink. I did smoke. I was, and still am, outside the norm of straight society. So what? You all know that. It's no secret. The real question is whether or not what I'm passing on to you is real or could it be that I'm doing this for some personal monetary gain? You all know how I live. I live here with you and I live no better than any one of you. I have no special privileges. I command no one. I work in the fields just like each one of you. I dress like you. I eat what you eat. No, my friends, I'm not gaining anything personally from this, except that I believe I'm doing God's work and if God want to reward me in any way, then that's all right with me, but don't count on that happening. My work is my reward as your work is your reward. We'll all move toward God together through our individual and combined efforts. If I move higher, then so too will every one of you whose belief is as strong as mine and whose actions are as devoted as mine. If you live with pure blood and pure motives and follow this path, you or someone in your line will move higher. We will save our people from extinction, you and I. As the world plunges into a new darkness of humanity, we will be the beings of light. As white people get tricked into giving up their sacred essence by mating and mixing with the others, we alone, will remain pure, but more, we will become even purer as time goes on and as we breed away defects built in to our lines over the centuries. We will become even whiter as the years pass, and this is the way to God. And no matter what the others throw at us, no matter how much they persecute us, God will be on our side, for we alone, of all man forms are His people. Never doubt it for a minute. God will provide."

Zack now had things going on many different burners all at once. At the heart of his organization were the local Temples that he had first started. I could see the wisdom in having them. They were more along the lines of Islamic Mosques or Jewish Synagogues than Christian Churches that took orders from one central religious organization. The local Temples were the centers of the Evolvist activities and anyone could start such a local Temple who was a believer. Each Temple had to draw its moral and financial support from the local Evolvists not from any central organization. However, each local Temple had to send ten percent of its contributions back to Zack's central organization, in order to get approved copies of the Cosmic Messages and receive Zack's newsletter. Everyone who belonged to a local Temple had some job or other within the Temple. Evolvism wasn't a spectator religion. Each person had to do for himself what was needed to be in tune with God. There was no priest who would intercede for an individual believer. Those in positions of power in the local Temple were more like teachers or guides, and they could not deviate from the Cosmic Messages without being thrown out by the other believers. The local Temples served as courts, social gathering places, relief centers, and whatever else that was needed. They were the focus of the Evolvist community. They were like the hub on a wheel and the spokes and outer rim were all the believers. The ideal of the Evolvists was to move into a community and slowly take over the whole community one house and street at a time without generating any publicity that would drive up prices. Once they had a large enough population, the area would be called a Colony.

I saw Zack fairly often, although I was camped way out on the other side of the Colony from where he was living. Zack was sharing his place with at least a dozen women and apparently they were all having sex with Zack. Zack told me that every one of them was pregnant, and that he'd need to take in some more women soon so he wouldn't be wasting his seed on women who had already received. He said that he was preparing a message to be sent out to the Colonies and the Temples, to send more women down here to Baja.

Sure enough, more women soon arrived and Zack was living with another fifteen women who I assume also became pregnant. I was starting to wonder if all the children in this place were Zack's, or whether any of the other men ever impregnated any women.

"Of course other men are getting women pregnant, Alex," Zack said, when I asked him about this. You know, you've probably got pretty good genes, how about diving into the gene pool with the rest of us? You've been here long enough to know that our mating rituals are pretty open and that we don't encourage possessiveness. The goal of every Evolvist is to birth better people than we are ourselves, and our way to do that is to birth as many people from our select gene pool as possible. Sure we're hit and miss like the larger society, but we're a damn sight less hit and miss because Evolvists all have to be non-Jewish white European descended people to begin with, and this keeps other races out of our gene pool where they would pollute the pool and stop the evolution. Oh, I'm sure that some other genes may sneak through either because the person in the colony may have grandparents or great grandparents or even a parent who wasn't of the Essence, but in time, such non complying genes will wash out as we add more and more of the genes of the Essence. You know, I've received revelations that explain why we need to keep other races out of our areas. One reason, is that their presence tends to block the God waves that we receive. The other is that people are always shedding bits of DNA. It's in microscopic bits of dander and dry skin and in pieces of hair. In fact, we're always in a soup of DNA whenever we're around other people. God wants the soup that believers are in to be comprised only of white DNA."

I told Zack of my dream about Baja becoming a country, and he nodded as though he thought that would be a good idea. He told me that the Evolvists hadn't had much trouble with the Mexican government, and the local Mexicans pretty much left them alone because he posted his property with traditional paintings of the Virgin of Guadalupe. "The Cosmic Pussy watches over us, man," said Zack.

"Man," I said, "your religion just gets more and more un-PC as time goes on. You know that people are saying that you're just trying to do what the Nazis wanted to do."

"Yeah. But, this isn't my religion. None of this is from me. It's all from God. Do we believe God, who is un-PC or do we believe man to be PC. For us, there is no choice. We believe God and we trust in Him. We do what He wants. Also, what we're doing is pretty much what every conscious society has wanted to do in one way or another once they gave some thought to these things. After all, why should humans, who are supposed to be the most intelligent animals on this planet, mate in a haphazard fashion while these same humans go to great lengths and expense to develop various breeds of farm animals and pets? Why should animals improve their breeds, while man is the victim of mindless prejudices and bigotry against breeding the best to be even better? We both know the answer to that. Some people have the notion that it would be unkind to tell some people that they were inferior in the traits that these other people wanted to breed for, and that there would be all sorts of cries of racism and the like. Well, we Evolvists have simply given the big cosmic finger to all haters who want to keep us mired in the muck. We say that God has told us to mate only with our own people and that if other people don't like it, then they should discuss it with God. We Evolvists will always follow the literal words and commands of God. There can be compromise. There can be no softening of our positions. Our laws regarding these things are set in stone. They cannot be changed. They will not be changed. You know, Alex, I've received revelations that who ever tries to modify, de-emphasize or change our laws is to be cast out and that in future ages believers are to look to what we do now as their models. Never are they to be less than us. If we have an average ten children per woman, then believers in future ages cannot have any less. If we demand purity of genes and if we determine that to find this we must first look to the Outer Sacred Signs of white skin, blues eyes, blond hair, and particular body type and all the other things that we look for, then believers in a future age may not change them.

I know as you look around you'll see lots of people with brown hair and green, grey or hazel eyes. These things are considered lesser signs than the white skin which is an absolute and which is coexistent with Essence. The hair and eye color will be changed through proper mating. Every Evolvist wants to be replaced by his children who are purer than he or she is. We try to improve our lines in every way, and I suspect that in a few generations, you'll find that most

Evolvists are blond, and blue eyed because we have been commanded to breed for these things.

While we are attempting to raise our birth rate so that we are the most fertile people on Earth, we are also encouraging other peoples to lower their birthrates. With a few more wars and diseases, the non-white population of the earth should be cut way back, and then our higher birth rates and the natural pressures of a burgeoning population will cause our people to go through a non-ending expansion that will eclipse anything that ever happened in our past. We'll be a steamroller rolling right over this planet with our kind. Eventually, this planet will be transformed into a planet with all white people. The non-white peoples are the earlier models and even many white people are earlier models. They are all now obsolete with the advent of the Evolvists. We are the new model, and we're even trying to build a better replacement for ourselves, and those that replace us will no doubt also work on building a better replacement for themselves. We don't have any illusions that we are the best or that we are the end of evolution. We see ourselves as a bridge between the others and the new man. We're like Nietzsche's Ubermensch that you tried to become. If our children are all smarter, stronger and better than us and if they just bulldoze us into a ditch because we're then the old models we'll consider it a success in what we have been commanded to do by God. Does this sound cruel to you? Well, nature is cruel and it really is a survival of the fittest universe. We want our genotypes to survive and improve.

We're all subject to the external forces that shape evolution. The real difference between Evolvists and the others is that we're taking a conscious hand in our own evolution. We believe in Willed Evolution and Willed Mutation. We're not just going to wait a million years for nature to stumble around to try this and then that. We're taking over from blind nature and we're going to make our lines what we believe they are supposed to be. How do we know what is the right path of evolution? God told us. God sent the Shining Ones to serve as ideals for us to study and copy in all ways. We are to become the image of the Shining Ones. You should already know all about this Alex, because when you cut your hair and dyed it blond, you were following what we believe is a good way to do this trans-forming that we are attempting. It's like we said before about method acting where the actor does everything that his character would do, right down to wearing the same kind of socks and using the same toothpaste. You see, our minds take in messages constantly from everything around us. This being the case, we want to control and send the right messages at all times to our believers. Who's to say that some famous man wasn't set upon his course of action in life by some small thing in his environment or some combination of small things? Maybe it was the smell of a fiower or the feeling of the wind when it ruffled his shirt when that shirt was made of a certain fabric or when it fit him in a certain way. The point is that our minds take in everything, and we want to control everything to our ends, if pos-sible. It's like our discussions about the cold and cloudy places being better for white people We still believe that. Baja isn't the end all of our journey on this planet, but it was a convenient stop. If I'd had my druthers, Baja would be cold and cloudy instead of hot and sunny, but it's just one of those things that God led us here. We still have Montana, and we've got an active colony started up in Alaska now. We're constantly looking at how each colony is developing. If Alaska proves to be going in the right direction faster than, say, Baja, then we'll all move to Alaska or Canada or other cold places. If it doesn't, then we won't.

The revelations tell us that we have free will within certain geneti-cally determined parameters and that we are to use our free will to find our way on the path to God. The revelations are guidelines and they are law in the things that they address, but some of them leave room for us to find our way. It's this way with which lands are to be ours by divine right. We're excited, Alex, that we have found our purpose as individuals and as a people. We have real purpose. Each day, when I get out of bed, I can hardly wait to begin the Lord's work all over again. Do we get upset that we're often called names by those who don't understand or who simply hate us? Sure, sometimes it may get to some of us, but mostly we just bounce right back. We know that all of existence is struggle and we also know that struggle is not just physical struggle but mental struggle as well, especially with humans, because the big difference we have over other animals is our brain. This being the case it is not strength of tooth or claw that is most important to us, but strength of mind. We also know that living is about overcoming obstacles. If those who don't understand, or if those who hate us, throw obstacles in our path, we'll still keep struggling. You see, we don't believe that there was ever some wonderful golden age in the past, nor will there be one in the future. What will last will be the struggle. In knowing that, we accept the struggle for what it is and we're happy with it. You know that we prefer to pray in the outdoors, no mater what the weather and that we don't wear any special clothes to protect us from the weather, other than those things that would maintain health. One of the reasons for that is we stand in the face of the storm which is symbolic of the struggle and we meet it head on. If we had a hurricane down here, you'd find that all the believers would be out in the open, feeling and experiencing it. They wouldn't be foolish enough to stand where they could be harmed by the ocean or flying debris, but they would stand in the face of the storm and feel its full fury over their skin."

CHAPTER 7

I learned much about the Evolvists during my stay in Baja. There was a reason for everything they did. They kept a fire going in their temples to signify the first light of God. They wore various versions of the Spiral which they considered to be representative of the Cosmic Pussy or of the active creating destroying aspect of God. They openly displayed the Evolvist's version of the swastika, which was similar to the tatoo I got so long ago. Long ago? It wasn't that long ago, but somehow it seemed like a million years ago.

I asked Zack about Colonies in Germany and whether they openly displayed the swastika there, since the German government had outlawed the showing of swastikas in the country. He said that they did have a colony and that they did display the swastika. They took a lot of heat from the repressive government, but when it was pointed out to the government that this particular swastika used by the Evolvists was a religious symbol, not unlike the Christian cross or the Jewish Star of David or Menorah, the government relented, but tried to have the Evolvists conform to a very precise version of the Swastika that could not be confused as a Nazi swastika. The Evolvists refused to do so on the ground that this was interfering in their religion. Again, the government gave in. I suspect that had the Evolvists not had so many members around the world when all this happened that the German government wouldn't have given in to them, but they were now afraid that the Evolvists would create an international stink about being denied their religious freedom under the 'Neo-Nazi government of Germany which once oppressed Jews and was now oppressing Evolvists.' In both cases, the German government was using the same rationale. The only thing that had changed was their victims. Now, Jews were protected and white people were victimized, if they dared to BE white.

Did the Evolvists mind the problems they were having with the German government? Of course not. The Evolvists loved turmoil and chaos and struggle. One of Zack's messages was about how the Evolvists were to be like a raging river while other religions were like stagnant ponds. He also often said that Evolvism was like a wild forest compared to other religions' mowed lawns or overly maintained flower gardens. Chaos? They were the religion of chaos. But chaos to the Evolvists was good. It had no bad or evil connotation to it as seemed to be the case with the word to many other people. Sartre said that man had no values external to himself and that man chooses his values and makes himself. The Evolvists recognized no man made values outside of their own values. Their own values they attributed to God. Some people believe that the Universe is without purpose, and that the whole of creation was just ridiculous. To the Evolvists there was a purpose and the purpose was to evolve. The great sorting out done by the Sprial was the means. It was to bring order out of chaos and then to return to chaos again and to reshuffle and do it again. It was a great cycle that would be repeated over and over again. The Evolvists believe that if the Universe appears to have no purpose it is just because our human perspective is too limited. It's like the old story of the three blind men and the elephant, except in the Evolvists view you need to shrink the three blind men to the size of atoms and then ask them to describe an elephant. On that scale, they probably wouldn't even be able to distinguish the atoms of the elephant from other atoms nearby. It'd be like being a point among many points in a pointillist's painting. You don't know where anything stops or anything else begins. That's the way humans must of necessity view the cosmos and God. And, from that perspective, they, we, can't really know much about either. We just can't understand something that is so far beyond us. Science fails us. Our senses fail us. Our reason fails us. The only thing that we can rely on is our belief. Here, we enter the world of the theoretical physicists and the mystics, because now we leave the phenomenal world and enter the world of those who deal in abstractions and what ifs. This is a world peopled by adult children with intellects so far beyond the normal that these people seem childlike to the rest of humanity. And the rest of humanity laughs at these science/mystical/philosophers and giggles at their silly ideas, but in the end it is these intellectual who lead mankind forward as their silly ideas are taken over by the more practical engineers who turn the abstractions into metal and plastic and dials and gauges.

If we are to look upon the face of God, what shall we see? Shall we know it as the face of God? Will it have a nose, eyes, ears? The answer is that the face of God has always been before us. It is the cosmic version of the swastika. It is the spinning far-a-way galaxies as they go through their own birth, life, and death cycles. They start as a pinpoint of light. The light moves and spins on its axis. Arms are seen on the sides of the spinning center. This is the cosmic swastika. This is the engine of creation. This is the face of God. This is the cornucopia. This is the Cosmic Pussy. This is the cosmic dance. This is the great shuffler. This is the will-o-the-wisp. It has been there in our skies since before we had skies. It has been in every storm that has ever existed. It has been in every bowl of water that is drained from the bottom. It has been the whirlwind. It has been the vortex. It has been the water spout. It has been the hurricane. It has been the tornado. It has been the intertwined strands of DNA. It has been in the way trees grow. It has been in our consciousness since we existed and it has popped up in our art without people realizing where it came from. Dorothy in the Wizard of Oz was carried away by the Spiral.

When she took the Yellow Brick Road it was a spiral. When Gil, Zack and I traveled in the bus, we were following a spiral. The truth has always been right there before us in all things, yet few have ever sensed its presence. When told that it is the swastika that is the truth, men in this day run from the thought. And, in running, they run away from God, yet they never know this. They run from God and they run toward all that is of decay and devolution. They accept man and man's truths as the truth, because these things sound good for man. Man? Man is nothing if he is not struggling to be more. Man? Do not listen to man. Listen to God. God is within you if you have the right blood, the right belief and the right action. That's what Evolvism is all about.

The Evolvists were that loud banging on the door at nidnight that woke you up and saved you from a fire that was about to destroy you. You didn't want to wake up and you were lost in your dreams that all was well in the world, but the banging was so loud that finally, you couldn't deny it. No, the Evolvists weren't that polite little tapping at noon to bring you to the door where you could be handed a religious flyer. When you heard the banging and opened your door at midnight, you didn't find some little zephyr mildly blowing down the street. You found a screaming, howling, wild storm. When you opened your door you didn't find a pinched faced missionary standing there, telling you NO. You found a lusty person of the flesh who told you YES! The Evolvists were that sledge hammer smashing down walls, and not some little ball peen hammer tapping its way through. Does this mean that the Evolvists missed the little things and that they were mindless brutes bent on destruction? No. It was their ideal to have a strong mind in a strong body. The wielder of the sledge hammer in Evolvism would be a genius with a muscle man's body, and the sledgehammer would be used with intelligence and force. The Evolvists were an active people, but they also had their quiet contemplative moments. Zack said that there was something in Evolvism for everyone and that both the bookish and those who never read, would find things to satisfy them in Evolvism. Believers weren't forced into any modes of behavior that seemed unnatural to them, although they were directed in the way of Evolvism as they would have been if they had been in any other religion. The Evolvists sought to have a true feeling of community where everyone was a brother or sister to everyone else and where people would be fair with each other and not seek to gain any advantage over others. This required honesty and this was much prized in the Evolvist colonies. There was little pretense among the believers and they were open with each others. There was very little verbal sparring to gain a superior position over those one was talking to. Because everyone dressed alike and lived alike, there was no false pride among the believes and they truly were all equal.

Evolvism blew down the doors of convention and demanded: Live! Do not deny your flesh. Do not deny your senses. Do not deny life. Be fruitful and multiply!

Some of the stories about the Evolvists in the tabloid newspapers focused on the sex angle and said that the "cult" was all about free sex. Interestingly, this actually helped recruitment. Zack said that he didn't care what initial motivation brought people to the faith so long as they became believers once they were there for awhile. The sex thing wasn't really that big a deal inside the religion, because it was like going to a nude beach. It was just natural and available, so it has none of the smarmy connotations found in the outside world. Snide and sneaky little sex jokes just weren't funny in the colonies, because there was nothing dirty about sex to the Evolvists.

Every day, more and more people would arrive and they were all welcome if they were of the Essence. The colony just kept expanding like some sort of amorphous single celled creature as it absorbed more people. Many people also left. Among these were a lot of the fortune hunters who never did find any gold, but a lot of them decided to stay. There were lots of runaways from the north, who, for whatever reason, left their homes and instead of going to the big cities and turning to drugs and prostitution, just came to the colony instead. Part of the appeal was the fact that the Evolvists would take care of any children left on their doorsteps who were white, so the young mothers were free to just drop their children off at the colony and leave. No one ever put any pressure on them to stay or to return, but they were welcome to come back if and when they were ever ready. This children were considered children of the whole colony, and as with all the children, they were the greatest treasure of the colony and the religion.

In many ways, the Evolvists had a tribal sort of existence. I often looked at the way they treated each other and how they related to everything in nature, and it was a little like looking at an Indian tribe. They were a whole little society all to themselves. They produced their own food, and they had started making things to sell to the outside world. In this, they followed in the traditions of some other religious "cults," throughout history. They made furniture. They made clothes. They made blankets. They made a wide variety of small religious art objects. They also made small home "temples" that were basically wooden boxes about one foot deep; one foot wide and two feet tall with double doors on the front that opened out. When opened, the home temples displayed an Evolvist swastika that was carved into the back wall. In front of this was a shelf with a small votive candle with a variation of the Cosmic Pussy. Below that, was another shelf with Zack's Cosmic Messages. The idea was to allow people to have their own temples right in their own homes. The Evolvists also started selling fish and the meat of various animals that they raised along with vegetables and fruits. All things sold by the Evolvists were guaranteed to be pure according to the Evolvists purity laws. They continually added new ventures to support their work, and it was hard to keep up with them. This was no lazy group of people lying around hoping that food would find them. In keeping with their ideas of struggle, they struggled all the time to improve and be better both as individuals and as a people. A people? Yes.

They had started seeing themselves as a distinct people and this led to even more interesting results as they moved into political activism.

Zack would say that although they shared a common blood with other whites, the Evolvist's right belief and right actions had caused the transformation of their blood so that they were now a distinct people and they were on the way to increasing that distinction and would eventually, at some future date, probably not even be able to mate and produce offspring with other whites who had been left behind while the Evolvists continued to evolve.

Gil and I weren't supposed to have any special favors because of our Companionship roles, but what happened in practice was that many girls were attracted to us because we were Zack's Companions. Needless to say, Gil and I were soon fathering babies all over the place. I kept worrying that this whole new society that Zack had set up was going to collapse and that we would be brought before regular courts and be made to pay for the upbringing of a couple of hundred kids whose mothers claimed that we were the fathers. It was a recurring nightmare, and I talked to Zack about it. He assured me that the Evolvists were a people unto themselves and that we lived under our own laws and were accountable only to our own. I still wondered, however, what would happen if some of the girls who had come here—especially the neurotic ones—went back to straight society and falsely claimed that they had been held as sex slaves against their wills and forced to have babies for the cult. This sort of thing was not unheard of in the world of religions, and even Zack had to admit that many of the early people who had been attracted to the faith were not as sane as he would have liked. Neurotics of various types were always attracted to religious cults; and the literature was full of stories of them then being deprogrammed and turning against their former friends in the cult. To try to head off the inevitable, Zack had all new arrivals sign a statement that they had come of their own free will and that they were free to leave at any time without notice and that no one would try to keep them or intimidate them in any whatsoever. Zack and I both knew that this statement could and would still be argued against by any loony who might wish to leave and who was deprogrammed by some other loony in one of the main line Christian churches who always seemed only too eager to believe in sexual abuse, satanic worship, and dark rites. This said more about the mental faculties of these who believed in all of these things than in the fact of what they believed. In the past, similar loonies were able to harm many people of various religions. Joseph Smith and the early Mormons come to mind. One big difference between the Evolvists and many earlier religious people who always seemed to want to turn the other cheek was that the Evolvists would fight back. The Evolvists believed that it wasn't enough to exact an eye for an eye when someone wronged you on purpose. After all, you were just minding your own business and this other person had to go out of his or her way to harm you. This other person had to expend energy and disturb you. This being the case, this other person should not be let off with an eye for an eye, but should pay to the tenth power, if that could be determined. If an outsider harmed or planned to harm an Evolvist, the Evolvist could harm him ten times as much and the Evolvist could then confiscate all the worldly possessions of the outsider. These possessions were to compensate the Evolvist for his wrong and any excess would be distributed to any other Evolvists who might have aided the wronged Evolvist in getting revenge. Anything left over would go to the religion itself, because in wronging one Evolvist every Evolvist was also wronged. Although this may sound harsh, what happened was that once the Evolvist laws were generally know, few people would willingly harm any Evolvist. Oh, one other thing, vengeance was considered a sacred duty of Evolvists. This made them relentless in hunting down any wrongdoers.

CHAPTER 8

The sun was just breaking in Baja, and it was that time of day between night and day, a time when little zephyrs would rise up, and for a few brief minutes gently awaken you before dissipating before the heat of the rising sun. The colony was coming to life, and people were leaving their various cabins, tents and other accommodations to do the Lord's Work. It was going to be a hot day, and it was already far muggier than was normal, due to a tropical depression a couple hundred miles to the south. I could smell the ocean, and this was something that one didn't often experience on the Pacific. Now, the Atlantic was a different story, and it had a distinct smell and it had seasons of smells and tides of smells and days of smells. The Atlantic was an ocean that you could smell. The Pacific just sat there like a vast swimming pool, without the odor of life and death and change, as though nothing ever dies or rots in it. No decay, equals no smell. But today, I could smell it. It was a weaker version of the Atlantic, but it was still noticeable. I figured that the tropical depression was going to turn into a hurricane. I looked for signs. The land birds weren't flying, indicating that we were in fact in a tropical depression. The sea birds were flying away from the ocean, indicating that they were fleeing a storm. The clouds were high and spotty. The ocean was unusually calm. I was hoping for a storm. The real problem I had with Baja was that It was never very stormy. It was almost always hot and sunny. I yearned for a cool, cloudy, rainy place, for a change. Maybe I'd move up to the colony in Alaska. I knew Zack wouldn't mind, because he needed more people-more breeders-up there. The problem Zack had was that even though he did everything possible to discourage a personality cult around him, people just wanted to flock to be near him. He understood it and knew that this was just a natural thing, because he was the one who had founded this religion and he was the one who still received revelations, but he wanted the colonies to grow and expand and not just have one very big colony. Money was always tight with the Evolvists, but money wasn't really needed for the type of existence they had set for themselves. They lived off the land and the sea, and they traded and sold things with believers and non-believers. New believers would often give most, if not all, of their worldly goods to the community, but this wasn't mandated. Zack wanted to make one of the prime money raising sources also the means of propagating the faith, so he increased the production of the Cosmic Messages and the Evolvist's newspaper which was sold on street corners all over the world. The hawkers would keep a small percentage of the money they received for selling the newspaper, some would go for the local Temple and some would go to Baja. They also set up a website where they put out their message and offered things for sale. I said the money was tight, well what I meant to say was that money was tight for individuals in the faith on a day to day basis, but in fact the Evolvists had some very large bank accounts and were investing in land and stocks and other investments that they considered prudent. As the faith grew, many experts from all walks of life had joined the Evolvists, so there was no shortage of good financial, legal, medical, engineering, and you name it, brainpower among the believers.

It was interesting watching this develop, because here was a group that was trying to collectively will their evolution or mutation as a group. They were self defining themselves and they were demanding self-determination for their group. It would be a little like a bunch of baseball fans suddenly getting together and saying that they are a people and that they were a legitimate sub-group that had to be treated as any other sub-group or minority in the larger society.

One of Zack's strengths was the ability to delegate various duties to people and to bring out the best in the people he had delegated to. Zack was kind of an umbrella under which all the rest of the believers sought shelter. I never heard Zack yell or raise his voice in anger at any believers. Perhaps, this was made possible by Gil who was the strong second man in the religion. Gil was the one who coordinated all the dirty work and rough stuff. If someone needed to be disciplined, it was Gil who would take care of the job.

About noon, the storm hit. It was too weak to be a hurricane, but the winds gusted strong and blew sand all over the place. When the full brunt of the storm hit, Zack went up to the top of a small hill followed by hundreds of believers and they stood there facing the storm.

Zack was yelling, "Is that the best you can do? Is that the storm? Do you call that a wind?" over and over. It wasn't that he was insulting God, but rather that he was reveling in the storm and asking for more. He was telling the Cosmic Pussy that he wanted more. He was struggling. It was part of the whole struggle belief he had. All of the believers were soaked to the skin before the storm ended. Then they walked down from the hill, where the now emerging sun quickly dried them off.

Zack had created quite a society here. There was no crime to speak of. People could and did walk around the Colony at all hours of day and night without fear. Zack explained that this was the normal way of white people in all white societies and that most of the crime in the outside world was caused by non-whites.

One thing that really bothered Zack was how to ensure that he was breeding for the right qualities. He didn't want a bunch of geniuses who were too weak to take care of themselves, and he didn't want a bunch of muscle bound lugs who couldn't think. Until some better method of ensuring that the Colony evolved instead of devolved, he pretty much let nature take its course but he did instruct the women that the choice was largely theirs because once they were pregnant they had to carry a baby to full term and once the baby was born they had to be mostly responsible for it so long as they chose this path. This being the case, it was up to the women to select their mating partners with intelligence. They couldn't just go for the best looking men, although that was always an acceptable means of selection as the Evolvists didn't want to create a new race of uglies. Both men and women were encouraged and were given the right to ask questions of their prospective mating partners about their own parents. "At what age did your parents die? What did they die of? Are your parents proportional in their height and weight? Is there any cancer or other disease in your family? Is there any heart disease, diabetes, mental illness? The questions went on and on, and Zack had even prepared a questionnaire that he required all the men and women to fill out and make available to prospective mates. Naturally, this system led to some guys becoming studs who were in big demand, and others having trouble getting laid—at least to a non-impregnated female. Once the woman was pregnant she could select less qualified men to sleep with her, since they wouldn't be producing any children of their recreational unions.

From the look of the babies born in the Colony, who all appeared to be happy and healthy, this simple system worked pretty well. Of course, there were those that Zack had appointed to study eugenics and the genetics of the people, and their advice was often sought by believers and especially by female believers.

It's a good thing that Zack liked women, because he was in big demand, since many women flocked to have a baby with him. Because the demand on Zack was so great, he established a rule that he would spend one night with each woman who wanted and she should try to pick a night when she could conceive. After that one night, the woman would spend other nights with other men, so it was never all that certain that any one child was Zack's or some other guy's. The beauty of the Evolvists belief system was that it didn't really matter who the father was. The kids were the kids of all.

CHAPTER 9

*I*n addition to the revelations, Zack would give little talks or lectures. He claimed no divine authorship of these, and let everyone
know that these things were from himself and that while he might
believe these things or live in ceratin ways, that this was just a personal choice and was not binding on anyone else. What actually happened, though, was that many people wrote down every word Zack
uttered, and every action that he took, and these were printed up in
small books published by the Evolvists at their printing plant.

I probably knew Zack better than anyone here except for Gil, but
maybe my insight into the human condition or psychology was more
sensitive than Gil's, because I came to believe more and more that
Zack was like a sponge and that he just absorbed things around him
and that he actually believed that they came from God or in the case
of his talks and lectures, were the product of his own mind. It was
like anything that caught his fancy was soon spread to everyone in
the religion.

This especially came home to me when I spoke to Nadine and she
said that she had spent the night with Zack and about two weeks
later, Zack was giving a talk about the healthful properties of drinking your own urine. I asked Zack if he had learned that from Nadine
and he said that he was constantly learning things from everyone

and everything. He felt that part of his mission was to absorb wisdom from all sources. I was happy with his reply for two reasons. The first was that he was aware that he was absorbing things and, second, he didn't lie about it. This gave me a lot more faith in Zack than I'd ever had before. It was just something about his honesty in these little thing that impressed, and the fact that he didn't try to take credit for the thing about urine. It's odd, but this one little conversation made me want to learn even more about Evolvism and to take it more seriously than I had before. I came across a quote from Zack in one of those little books about his day to day activities that I especially liked. Zack said "Never claim great intelligence or virtue, because if you do this, you will always be challenged both by yourself and by others to prove it, and thereafter you will waste a lot of energy trying to live up to the self-definition. It is better to claim no special intelligence or virtue, because then you can be free to be yourself." This sounded a little squishy and passive, but I kept learning Evolvism was multi-layered and was by no means the cartoonish representation of a religion that was often presented to the general public by the popular press. As I got into Evolvism more and more, it became plain to me that everything, right down to the smallest details had been thought out as much as a Japanese Tea ceremony. The clothing that the Evolvists wore, for example, was made from cotton that was now grown by Evolvists in Arizona. To remain pure, it was never handled by anyone except Evolvists. This was one of the rules of the Evolvists for having a clean product or food—it had to be handled only by Evolvists at all stages. They believed that because all people and animals constantly shed bits of dry skin, hair, and other things that contain their DNA that these tiny pieces of DNA would pollute things used by the Evolvists and were also the cause of much sickness. So, the cotton was grown by Evolvists. It was picked by Evolvists. It was turned into cloth by Evolvists. It was transported by Evolvists. It was made into clothes by Evolvists. It was worn by Evolvists. Now, all of these same Evolvists who were busy with

Evolvist clothing needs, also made other non-pure clothes for the general public and this was a source of funds for the Colony.

It was the same with the food. There didn't seem to be any food prohibitions, and the Evolvists ate beef, even though they considered cattle to be the carriers of the seeds of the Ancients. The main thing was that everything used in the production of anything for the Evolvists was supposed to be made by the Evolvists themselves. Naturally, there were items that they did not yet produce which they obtained from the outside world, but these items had to be purified before they could be used to produce anything for the Evolvists. When they bought machines, for example, they had special people who would purify them in accordance with Evolvist law. This usually involved a prayer and also the washing down of the item with a solution of bleach and water or some other disinfectant.

As time went on, certain rules and laws were hardened, but none were ever softened as far as I could tell. Whereas before, members would voluntarily tatoo the Evolvist swastika, spiral, or coil on their bodies, now all members of the religion were to receive such a tatoo, usually on the upper right arm, but in other places in special circumstances such as with a person who might not have a right arm or a person who might already have some other tatoo in that spot.

Zack was unable to set up a shoe manufacturing plant, so he bought one that had been producing the type of shoe favored by the Evolvists. This was a sturdy, black, work half-boot with a steel toe.

As far as those Evolvists who worked in the outside world, they were still expected to wear Evolvist clothing. This meant they could not wear wool or synthetic fabrics, but must wear cotton. Leather was also approved. The Evolvist clothing manufacturers came out with a line of suits made entirely of cotton. These, like all Evolvist clothing, were loose and extremely comfortable. They also fulfilled the other Evolvist rule that any clothing you wear must be of a type that you can do hard physical labor while wearing it. The ideal here was that the Evolvists were all workers and must be able to work at any dirty job at any time. This meant that they couldn't have fancy clothes to wear to the office and another set of clothes for physical work. They had to be one and the same. The Evolvists also covered their heads, both men and women, with a kind of skull cap that covered the whole head down to about the ears. The most devout wore the skull cap all the time while others would wear them just for religious observances. Usually, it was made of stretchy fabric that fit any size head and kind of looked like a filled in spider web.

The Evolvists were definitely evolving as a group. The question remained, however, whether or not all their efforts were having any effect on the genes, which was what they were really after. Maybe they were nuts to think that they could breed better or cause their own evolution, Scientists usually went through hundreds of generations for short lived fruit flies in order to study mutations. What chance did the Evolvists have when human generations were so slow in changing? Even though the Evolvists had rid themselves of Judeo/Christian conventions regarding sex and marriage so that the proper age for sex was when the girl had her first period, and even though this did speed up the number of babies and shortened the generations, I couldn't see how the Evolvists would succeed. I brought this up with Zack and he gave me answers that anyone would have predicted: "God makes it possible. We're humans and have greater brain power than other animals so we can use our brains to force changes in our bodies."

I was wondering if the Evolvists were on the right track with this exclusively white business. I wondered if maybe it wouldn't be wiser to take, say, beautiful smart and strong people of all races and blend them together to create a new person rather than taking all white people even if they were fat, ugly, loud and rude. Maybe we should just throw them out and bring in the attractive non-white ones. Just as soon as I thought that, I realized that was wrong. The Evolvists couldn't do that. They were stuck in this little that they believe was commanded by God. They were trapped into doing what they believe God wants and they can't change that. It's funny that the people on the outside keep writing stories about the Evolvists having all these wild sex orgies, and yet the Evolvists were just mating in accordance with what God wanted them to do. Still, I wondered. Would it be better to try to build a smart and strong blended race; a Tan Everyman? I mean there were millions of stupid, ugly and weak white people Why in the world should they be considered proper breeding material by the Evolvists instead of people of other races who did seem to have more desirable characteristics.

"I've thought a lot about that too, Alex," said Zack, when I asked him about it. "You're completely right. Man, there are some horrible white specimens and some great non-white specimens, and believe me I've been tempted to seek a revelation getting rid of the exclusively white thing, but then I realized that maybe God is testing us to see if we will truly believe his revelations and resist the temptation of mating with more attractive or intelligent people who aren't white.

"You know, Orthodox Jews are supposed to have sex through a hole in a sheet. Maybe they were faced with the same dilemma as us and that was their response to it. Still, we do have many pretty women here, and if God's plan works as we think we understand it, we should be breeding even more such women as times goes on. We're certainly trying to improve our lines in our genetic pool."

As I looked around, I saw white trailer trash. I saw people who I wouldn't be interested in spending five minutes with. I saw people who were disgusting. But, I also saw some beautiful people and most of the children were beautiful. I guess the parents who are now ugly, must also have been beautiful as kids, so I was afraid that the result of the Evolvist breeding would be that as this generation grew up like some of their ugly parents and mated and had kids ugliness would be passed on. Zack assured me that those whose job it was to encourage the best to mate the most, also encouraged the less desirable to mate the least and that they were watching each and every life in the Colony. This gave me a really creepy feeling and certainly wasn't my idea of true freedom—being watched over all the time.

"Zack, that sounds horrible," I said. "Who wants to live their lives being watched over constantly?"

"Maybe I just stated it wrong," said Zack. "That's not what I meant. I meant that people were watched over in the sense that the breeding was being watched over, not every thing everyone did all the time. It's more as though we are all concerned about breeding up, so we, as a society, simply encourage people in the right direction."

Zack said that it was important to increase the numbers of believers with not as much regard for the quality of the stock and that later on, when the numbers of believers had swelled, that a new stage would unfold as things became more selective. "You know," Zack said, "we're not just trying to breed white flesh, but to improve the stock. This takes time, and it takes vast numbers of people. We must never let ourselves become a special few. We must be a teeming new life, like maggots on garbage."

"Nice picture, that," I said jokingly.

"Well, that may not sound too nice, but that's what we want to have. We want to have this whole planet teem with our life form, and when we're numbering in the hundreds of millions and the population pressures are so great that we can't stand it, we'll start having great waves of expansion as we did in the dim past. Our tribe will move out to the rest of the world. You know," said Zack, "we have some serious defects as a people that we need to correct. I'm thinking specifically of false altruism and false compassion. So many of our people, and I don't just mean our believers, but whites in general, seem to be like cat ladies. They'll drive right over needy people to help get a cat out of a tree. Listen to this situation: Suppose a believer were walking down the street and saw a house on fire that was occupied by black or other non-white children. Should the believer risk getting burned to run in and save them? Ordinary society would say that he should. We, however, say that he shouldn't, because the destiny of non-whites is not his concern, and what would be the good if he saved a non-white who grew up to murder a believer? The believer who helped save them would be guilty. Now, don't think that we are a cruel people…well, actually we are cruel by outside standards, but we believe that our duty is to our own people and not to others. We may be a little fatalistic here, but we believe that God creates and God destroys. We should not interfere when God does these things with other people, but when He does anything to harm our people, then we must override God and help our flesh. Yes, we obey God, but He has given us brains and the revelations to know what is right and wrong. Now, it would be different if God gave us a revelation saying that we should not even help our own people, but He hasn't. God asks us to make distinctions between what happens to our own people and what happens to other people. We are to protect our own and never bother with the others. This outrages some others who want all man forms to consider them-selves all one people with only minor cosmetic differences, but this is our way."

I stayed at the Colony for eight months and then decided it was time to move on—before any of my kids, if any, were born.

I asked if I could use the VW bus, and Zack gave me a funny look and then had me follow him. He took me into the holiest of holies of the temple. The very hub of the swastika. That no one but Zack was supposed to enter. In the middle of the room, sat the VW bus."You know," said Zack, the radio on the bus works now."

"You got it fixed?" I asked.

"Nope," said Zack. "The only time it doesn't work is when you and Gil and I are in the bus. Any other three people and there's no problem. Somehow, it took the three of us to complete the circuit. One of us alone and it doesn't work, but with the three of us, the bus was like the Ark of the Covenant and we were driving around in it getting messages from…God, I guess. Anyway, I'd like to keep it here, but I'll give you one of the other VW busses that I bought for the Colony. None of the others work the way this one does. I figure, whoever had this before Gil, really did do something strange with the odd bumpy paint job and the drawings in the engine compartment. It sounds a little like Voodoo, but I think it really is some kind of receiver, or consciousness expander."

We left the Temple, and Zack did get me another bus. It looked identical to the one in the Temple, and was even painted the same copper penny color. I touched it, but the surface felt different.

"We tried to duplicate the first bus," said Zack, "but no matter how we tried, we could never get it just right."

The first Colony I visited was in a run down area of Los Angeles that we had seen before. It was an old loft down by skid row. I introduced myself to the people living there—about ten of them, it seemed, and noted that they were all wearing the same clothes as the folks down in Baja. They said that they spend a lot of their time handing out flyers and meeting with people who might be interested in knowing more about Evolvism. They also said that they often had to fight with haters and bigots who would attack them for their beliefs. Given the nature of the population in Los Angeles—a majority were non-white—this wasn't surprising. Los Angeles was looking more and more like a Third World city. Go to the downtown areas of the city and you'd be hard pressed to find any white people. This Colony was certainly much smaller than one might expect for something called a Colony. It was more like a flophouse. I saw four young babies with the Evolvists. Because word about the two Companions of Zack had spread, apparently throughout the colonies, I was treated with the utmost respect and everyone was open with me, as far as I could tell. All ten adults said that they'd like to move on to Baja or Alaska but felt an obligation to wait until their numbers here had risen to a level where they wouldn't be missed. They were apparently trying to do a one for one replacement. As each member brought in a new member, the sponsoring member would then leave the Colony and go to another Colony or set out to try to establish a brand new Colony. They figured that the optimum size of this Colony in this one loft was probably no more than twenty adults with whatever number of children they could breed. I thought that would make them like sardines, but it was their Colony and their choice. They were also talking about getting a farmhouse out in Riverside County to the east of Los Angeles as part of this Colony. Then they could keep the city Colony to attract runaways and lost souls and send them to the country if that was their desire. Although It seemed to me that this would then constitute two separate colonies, they felt that it would be necessary to consider them as just one Colony to avoid having the Los Angeles Colony just shut down as everyone might want to move to the more desirable Riverside location. As a single Colony, they felt that they could control the flow of people better. As with all the colonies, this one had a leader who saw to the details of the organization. He was informally "voted" in by all the other believers in the Colony and would serve as long as they wanted him or for as long as he wanted to be the leader. Under him, he had two sub-leaders, and one Guardian. The Guardian was actually sent by Gil to help the Colony protect itself against anyone who would harm them and to keep Gil informed of things relating to the Colony. The Guardians were usually, as was this one, a tough looking ex-military guy. This and other Gurdians were usually called "Bob" by the believers. I was pretty certain that few, if any of the Guardians were really named Bob, but that was just one of the security devices used by Gil to protect everyone. I knew from my conversations with Gil that all the "Bobs" had different identities when they went about their work. If a Bob had to disappear because the outside authorities wanted to talk to him about something or other, Bob could take a powder and no one would know anything about him to put the authorities on his trail. The Guardians in the colonies didn't need any orders to do what they did. They were like a guild and acted according to their secret instructions from Gil, apparently. If someone attacked a believer while the believer was handing out flyers, for example, and this believer then told all the other believers about the attack in their nightly open meetings (always attended by the Guardians) and the person attacked was able to identify the attackers, the attackers would apparently be visited by Bob. If the believer who was attacked could not identify the attacker so that he could be found, then the next time a believer handed out flyers in that location, Bob would be nearby, usually in disguise. It was rumored that one time a believer was handing out leaflets in Chicago after previously being attacked by a black street gang, and three members of the gang came back to attack the believer again. Then, again according to the rumor, the single Guardian, who was disguised with a beard and laying in a doorway pretending to be a wino, took out a .44 Magnum and killed all three of the gang members on the spot. The Guardian then left the scene. The believer who was handing out the flyers also left but was stopped by the police a couple of blocks away and questioned. He told the police that he didn't see much but that some guy, he thought he was black, just walked up and shot these three guys. He figured it was some sort of gang rivalry. Shortly after that, the New York Bob left for other parts to be replaced by a new Bob. I wondered if the Bob here in LA was maybe that old New York Bob, but I never asked and I knew he'd never tell me anyway. Naturally, there were stories in the press about the mysterious murders and attacks on those who had attacked the Evolvists, but there were also rumors among the believers that after a few newspaper reporters, who had written stories considered by the Evolvists to be attacks on the faith, turned up missing, there were fewer and fewer such stories. My guess was that the rumors weren't true, and were just rumors, because the Evolvists really didn't seem that organized to me to be able to do such things. I also believed that the Guardians were just volunteer security guards to help prevent haters and bigots from harming believers.

One believer told me though that the Evolvists believe in individual responsibility and they held those outside the religion who attacked the religion, personally responsible for such attacks, even if the person were some how able to hide behind a burecratic anonymity. Because Gil wanted the Guardians to continue even if something should happen to him, he had set up a Guardian Council consisting of seven people who were not known to anyone but Zack and Gil. They remained anonymous even to each other by wearing hoods that covered their faces, when they met together. If any of the seven consistently—which is to say three times in one month—voted against the actions that the rest of the seven had approved, then this person would be replaced on the council. Votes were done with black and white marbles. Black was "no" or "guilty." White was "yes" or "not-guilty."

Another arm of the Evolvists was the Public Information officers. These people tried to kill off negative stories that they got wind of while pushing positive ones. They used all the modern techniques including press releases, immediate telephone contact to the media in response to negative stories, TV and radio appearances by positive spokes people and all the rest. These activities of these folks was public knowledge, but as with many things in Evolvism there was also a hidden side to their activities and in the case of the Public Information officers the hidden side was the gathering of intelligence on "enemies" and the writing and distribution of demonizing stories about those who opposed the Evolvists.

Then as the religion grew, there were Finance, Education, and other departments whose head executives all reported directly to Zack. Evolvism was becoming a very big undertaking. One of the things that Zack insisted on was that every believer be given some religious job to do, and that every believer be given plenty of opportunity to work in several jobs to find which ones suited him or her best. Zack didn't want any calcified structure that saw itself as separate from other believers. He even took pains to keep the most secret of the workers the Guardians from going off on their own tangents. The Guardians were only to protect believers from non believers;

never from other believers. As between believer and believer, such matters and conflicts were handled by the Evolvist's own police and courts.

Another thing that Zack was very adamant about was the establishing of many groups with cross-memberships and purposes so that there was a great degree of overlapping and competition between the groups on various issues. In a sense, the Evolvists had set up their own government, but they had also set up training for believers in organizing and mobilizing for the purposes of the religion. It was like a giant spider web with so many connections that to unravel it all would be almost impossible. Maybe synapses in the brain would be a better metaphor because as soon as one small group would fade out of existence, another would spring up with the same members or the same members plus or minus a few, with the missing ones going to other groups. There was a true revolutionary ferment brewing in the religion that was given structure and held to the right path by the tenets of the religion. It was a mob with a purpose.

Naturally, it was difficult to keep the religion from being infiltrated by those who hated the Evolvists, but Zack always told all believers to uphold the law and if the Evolvists own law hadn't occupied the field, as for example with traffic tickets, then the outside law was to apply. He also told the Evolvists that they must not be caught up in illegal activity and that if any other believer tried to get them involved in something shady, that they were to report this to the Evolvist Police. Often, Zack said that the government and others who didn't like the Evolvists would infiltrate agents provocateurs into movements like this one only to talk weak minded individuals into criminal activity so that they could be arrested or turned against the organization and made into moles to keep on spying.

"The enemies of God are everywhere," said Zack, "do not be tricked and do not be fooled. We are doing God's work and we must follow His word as revealed to us. If you cannot honestly do God's work, then you must leave our colonies, and if you are a true believer but can't follow our ways then you should select a solitary way to contemplate what is in your Essence."

CHAPTER 10

I left the LA Colony and headed up the familiar road to San Francisco. About an hour out of LA, I came across a girl hitchhiking. She was skinny and she was about twenty years old, with long blond dirty looking hair. She was wearing shorts that looked something like lederhosen and she had on rugged looking hiking boots and had a backpack at her feet. "Where are you headed?" I asked,

"San Francisco, then Alaska," was her reply. Afraid of getting trapped by a hitchhiker who might be nuts or boorish or who might smell bad, I said that I could take her part way, perhaps as far as San Francisco. She accepted the offer and we took off. She said that her name was Jane. She said that she was a college student but had run out of money and had dropped out to see a little of the country. I asked if she was afraid about hitchhiking and she said that she was as careful as she could be in accepting rides. She didn't take a ride in any car that looked like it had automatic locks on all the doors or was missing the lock release on the inside of the passenger's door, that could be operated by the driver. She wouldn't accept rides with more than one man in the car. She wouldn't take rides from anyone who wasn't white. She also tried to size up the driver by looking at him, the way he was dressed, his mannerisms and the like. Generally, someone with a new vehicle seemed safer because they probably had more money invested in the car and had more to lose if they did anything wrong. She avoided extreme cowboy looking types.

"There's a certain look that I avoid," she said "I call it the extra Y chromosome look."

"What?" I asked.

"Well, you know that women have two X chromosomes and that men normally have one X and one Y chromosome?"

"Yeah," I said.

"Okay, the guys with the double Y chromosome have the normal X and Y, but they then have an extra Y. This makes them super males, and I don't mean this in a good way. They have overly aggressive personalities. They have too high a sex drive and they're often getting into trouble with the law because they make up their own laws and rules as they go and they won't bend to authority. It's their way or no way and they'll fight to make it their way. Now, if this sounds like they do this through some conscious thought process, I'm giving you the wrong impression. These guys aren't usually particularly bright or anything like that."

"So, they're not Ubermenschen in the Nietzsche sense?" I asked, wondering if she'd even have the faintest idea of what I was talking about.

"Exactly," she said, "how do you know about that?"

"Oh, I read a lot, I guess," I said, how about you?"

"I've been reading up on Evolvism, and they talk a lot about that sort of stuff in that religion. Have you ever heard about them?" she asked.

"A little. Are you an Evolvist?" I asked, noting that she wasn't wearing the Evolvist garb.

"No. But I want to visit them for a while and that's why I'm headed north. I hear there's a bunch of them in San Francisco and also up in Alaska and I want to go to both of those places."

"What were you saying about the Y chromosomes?" I said, trying to get her back on that subject.

"Oh yeah. I got sidetracked there," she said "well, the men with the extra Y chromosome also have a certain look about them. Their facial bones seem to be too angular, and their skin is usually pulled tight over the bones. They often have sunken cheeks and acne. I've never seen one who was fat, so I reason that maybe the extra Y chromosome helps produce an overabundance of testosterone that probably keeps them thin."

"Huh? How did you jump to that conclusion from what you just said," I asked.

"Well, it's just common sense really. Look, when you castrate men, they often get chubby and pasty looking—sort of like dough. I figure then, if you go the other way and have too much testosterone that you'll be more sculpted, and will be as different from the norm on that side of the scale as the eunuchs are on their side."

"You know," I said, "you've started me thinking about this whole Ubermensch thing. I've spent some time wondering what the Ubermensch would be like, and maybe you've hit the nail on the head...accept for the fact that you don't think the extra Y guys are too bright. Suppose that they're actually very smart, really smart...geniuses? And suppose that they had all the other traits you've mentioned..."

"You'd have super predators-human hunters—killers with no conscience," she jumped in. "You know these extra Y types also often have many tatoos and that's another sight I look for. do you have any tatoos?"

"Yeah. I've got one on my arm," I said.

"Can I see it?" she asked.

"Later, when I'm not driving."

"Do you have any other tatoos?" she continued.

"Nope. Just the one. I don't think I have an extra Y chromosome, if that's what you're getting at. Do I have the facial features of someone with an extra Y"

"No. Not really, but I'm just an amateur at this and I'm just guessing about this stuff. What the hell do I know?"

"So why do you want to joint the Evolvists," I asked.

"I was a philosophy major and that sort of thing interests me. Religion is just philosophy with God added in, and with a strong often irrational need to believe by the faithful. That's really what distinguishes it from philosophy. You know, if I had a philosophy and if I wanted people to respect it and not just bury it on the back of a bookshelf, I'd turn my philosophy into a religion. I'd just say that God or Angels had given me this philosophy." She finished and was silent. It was odd how much this young girl seemed to know about things relating to Zack and the Evolvists and I now started to wonder if the Feds hadn't planted her on this road hoping that I'd give her a ride. Was she some sort of infiltrator, I wondered. I decided to probe her.

"How long were you standing out there before I came along?" I asked.

"Not long. I just got out of another car, when you came up," she said. "Why?"

There was something about the way she asked why, that made me think that she was on to me, so instead of just asking her a whole bunch of questions and alienating her, I figured I'd just stay on my toes and watch for any signs of her being out to set me up in some way. So I answered, "No reason. I've done a lot of hitchhiking and I was just curious." Maybe I was just being paranoid, but then again, I was aware of how the government with all the tax money of all the people of this country at its disposal could be devious and could spend money on all sorts of little plots and agents provocateurs. If she was an agent of the Feds I'd probably be a pretty good target, being one of the Companions of Zack. They could figure that I must know all sorts of things. Maybe they were trying to get something on some of the Guardians or were trying to prove that the Evolvists were some sort of criminal enterprise. I guessed by best bet was just to be myself and not try to impress her with things that I knew about the Evolvists—or things that I might pretend to know but didn't really know. Up close she was actually much prettier than I had first thought and her hair wasn't that dirty. It was dirty the way girls say their hair is dirty, meaning it hasn't been washed for a couple of days and is slightly oily; not the way men say theirs is dirty. What the hell was this thought process, a battle between my feminine and my masculine sides about dirty hair?

We rode on in silence for a little while, and then I decided to talk about the Evolvists to see how much she knew. "What do you think about that Cosmic Pussy stuff?"

"Oh, you mean, the concept of God or the creative part of God being like a vagina?" she asked.

"Yeah."

"I like that idea. I know it gets snickers when it's called the Cosmic Pussy, but I think the concept is solid. I mean why not have creation be like that if you're God? A woman's reproductive system in a metaphor for creation, I think. In a way, it also makes men respect women more and treat them as equals. I think humankind puts too much emphasis on duality; the old Yin/yang, male/female type of thinking. I bet you don't really have a duality or opposites in the universe but different aspects of the same thing. I mean if we think of hot and cold, for example, we're thinking of opposites, but if we say that we're thinking of temperatures then we might see hot and cold as gradations of the same thing—'temperature'—rather than as opposites. Night and day are just gradations of time as experienced on a planet that rotates around a star. Besides, they're not absolutes. You don't have absolute day and then have absolute night. You have a period of time when the sun gives us the most light and you have a period of time when it gives us less light. They are really the same things, and to think of things in terms of opposites leads us to some false thinking about reality, and leads us to a bipolar view of the cosmos and all that is in it even when we don't consciously have such a view. We think of good and bad, for example, not often thinking that these are relative terms and are not opposites, but in thinking in terms of opposites we go to war and, of course we are always the good side and the other side is always the bad. Good/bad, bad/good, we are brought up thinking in dualities, but the universe is much different than opposites. We need to get beyond these culturally defined concepts so that we can truly understand," she finished. I didn't say anything, and I was getting a little weary of everyone I came in contact with, pontificating and intellectualizing as though they were the only ones who had ever thought of any of these things and as though their thoughts were just so important. Still, Jane had a way of speaking with a little whisper of a voice that you would most often find in certain Asian women. It was a voice like a little butterfly and the little laugh that went with it was just as pleasant. "Oh, good grief!" I thought. I can't believe I even thought in those terms." She also said things in a very light way without really emphasizing or punching out any particular points and this was nice. I contrasted her in my mind with, say, a big brassy cowgirl who would be shouting these positions and laughing out loud. Maybe, I wound have put her out of the bus a long time ago if she had been like that. "You know," I said." I swing from an existentialist view of reality where there is no purpose to anything and we are all living in an absurd universe, to a kind of transcendentalism where I'm trying to understand reality by looking inward to intuit what's out there—and this, of course, subsumes that there is something out there. I find the Hindu thinking that all is just illusion to be absurd all by itself. You can go nuts when you start thinking about all this and looking at different philosophies and religions, because each one seems to make sense when you're studying it, but then you move on and study another and then that one makes sense and you forget about the first one. You know, and I was telling someone else this, if I invented or thought up a philosophy I'd probably make it into a religion and instead of the tenets of the philosophy coming from me, I'd say that they came from God."

"You mean like Evolvism?" she asked. After she said this, it made me think of her as being a plant or mole, even more than I did before. Perhaps she was trying to get me to admit that at least I think Evolvism is a product of Zack's imagination or that Zack, Gil and I conspired to invent Evolvism.

"No. I don't think Evolvism was the product of a man. At least they claim that it is revealed by...what...Angels? Shining Ones?" I replied, acting half dumb.

"Well," she said, "I'm a realist or skeptic, I guess. I think all religions were invented by man and I think all the founders of the various religions probably did what you just suggested. They invented a philosophy, and then to give it credibility they claimed that it came from God."

"So, you don't believe in any religion or God?" I asked.

"No. Actually, I think I'm probably an Evolvist or an evolving Evolvist. I don't really care if the religion came from God or from Zack, who is the founder of the religion, I'm more concerned with the tenets of the religion and whether they seem to make sense to me. What I've read and heard about Evolvism makes me think that they do make sense to me. So if the Evolvists believe that they must say that the philosophy came from God to have some people believe in it and live their lives in accordance with their rules, who cares? It gives many people something bigger than themselves to believe in and gives them comfort in times of need to know that there is a purpose. I imagine there are cynics like me in all religions and I can further imagine that some of those cynics are the most devout in those religions. Anyway, I want to be around some of those Evolvists to immerse myself in their way of life and thinking to see how it feels to live it and not just read about it."

"Why didn't you just go down to Baja?" I asked.

"I don't like the heat," she said. "Besides, I read that the Evolvists believe that the cold is needed to help them evolve. I think with that idea it's kind of weird how so many of them ended up down in Baja, but apparently that was a path that was open to them and they took it as interim step. I mean, their faith is called Evolvism, and it too is apparently evolving and mutating to take advantage of changes in the political and social environment that they find themselves in. I've always wondered though if they believe in evolving, and if they believe that God is evolving also how they can come out with any sort of bedrock beliefs. I mean, what's to keep them from saying that God has now revealed that they're supposed to do just the opposite of what they've been doing all along? In some other religions, God is seen as unchangeable and it makes more sense to invent Him that way if you want your philosophy to remain unchanged."

"I think," I said, "that the Evolvists don't mean that God is evolving as you use the term. I think that they mean that God is becoming more, more God, more conscious. Maybe I know a little more about the Evolvists than I thought, but it seems to me that their view of God is different from most other religions. God, to the Evolvists, is in man, but He's also outside man, and He is man, but He's more than man. He is part of history, yet He's outside of History. It think that the Evolvists consider all other views of God as too confining and they even consider their own views too confining. But they have to have some views so they can at least try to grasp the concepts that they believe God reveals to them. Ultimately, Evolvism is a religion, and as such, you must at some point reach a place where you say that's what it is. Either believe it or don't. In other words, Evolvism, like every single other religion ever invented, will not hold up under our limited logic. It's too complex."

"I don't think I can agree with you that it's too complex," she said. Zack says that everything is simple, it's only the explanation that is complex."

"I like that," I said. Of course I did, I think that I used that before Zack and Zack heard me say it, but I didn't tell Jane that. Of course I wasn't really sure that I had said it first. It sometimes seemed as though Zack, Gil, and I were one consciousness with three bodies.

We drove on in silence. After a while, I let Jane take the wheel and I crawled in the back and slept. When I woke up, we were in South San Francisco, and closing fast on the city. "Do you know where the Colony is?" I asked.

"Some place on one of those hills," she said. "I forget the name, funny sounding. If I heard it again I'd know it."

"Russian Hill" I asked.

"No."

"Nob Hill?"

"No."

"Near the Bay?"

"That sounds like it. Do you know how to get there?"

"Sure."

So we headed for the Hill to find the Evolvist Colony. I already knew where it was, at least I think I did. I gave her the left/rights to Poop. When we got there we saw the Evolvist Flag, a black background with a white Evolvist version of the swastka. We parked and walked in. Wouldn't you know it, Alice was there and she saw me right away.

"Is Gil with you, Alex?" she yelled.

"Nope. Not this time." I replied.

"What about Zack? she asked.

"Same." When I said this I saw Jane looking surprised, but biting her tongue.

"Is this place all about Evolvism?" I asked.

"Yeah. said Alice. "We've all converted and the Evolvist religion now owns this place. Zack hasn't been around in a long time. I guess he's busy down south. You seen him lately?" "I saw him just before I started the trip up here. Alice, this is my friend Jane. Jane wants to know about Evolvism. Do you think we can stay here for awhile?" "Of course you can stay here. Hell, you're one of the Zack's Companions and Zack has told everyone that anyplace you or Gil show up, you are to be treated as though you're Zack. We've only got one room empty, can you two share?"

I looked at Jane and she nodded yes. "Yeah, I guess so," I said, trying to act cool and indifferent.

When we were alone, Jane asked why I hadn't told her about me. I told her that I was just sort of along for the ride and all this talk of Companions was kind of weird to me. "It sounds almost Biblical," I said. "Every time I hear the term Companions I picture Gil and me with long flowing beards and kind eyes, wearing Biblical looking robes while, carrying staffs and acting pious. That's not at like it was. Even if we were to translate the old Biblical costumes into modern dress, it still gives a false idea. I mean we weren't just following Zack around waiting for him to say wise things. We were three guys riding around first in a VW Bus. It's nutty. If people are already starting to think of Gil and me as 'THE COMPANIONS," what the hell's it going to be like in a few years when we're dead? Can you imagine the movie of this? There's Zack looking like Jesus and there's Gil and me looking like two of his disciples all working for God. Damn. For Christ's sake, Zack is a porno film maker. Gil is…I don't know, Gil is just Gil, and I'm next to nothing. This whole thing has gotten really weird. I feel like I'm on a carnival slide or something and it just keeps moving me along—maybe a conveyor belt is a better analogy. Anyway, I don't know diddly about Evolvism. I spent time with Zack before Evolvism and I've spent time with him down in Baja, and he's my friend, but I'm sure not worthy of being a COMPANION. Sure, I was with him so I was his companion, the way you were my companion on this trip, but there's nothing holy or sacred about me at all, and it seems strange that some people are buying this companion stuff. Maybe Zack wants to be some sort of religious leader, but I don't.

Even Zack has tried to stop others from thinking of him or us as some sort of special people. I'm not surprised that people would flock around Zack, though, because I think he really believes that he is receiving revelations from someplace. At first I thought he was faking, but as time went on, I became more and more convinced of his sincerity. This doesn't mean that he really, objectively, is receiving revelations, but only that he believes he is. It may be that Zack is just suffering from a mental disease, or that he has a brain tumor."

The Evolvists had built a temple in the basement of the Poop down where there was going to be a theater. One wall had been painted with a cosmic pussy on it and in front of it there was an eternal flame, that they kept going all the time—as you would guess from the name. The rest of the basement was just open floor, which the Evolvists had covered with polished wood. They prayed in the Muslim fashion, by kneeling on the floor and often bending forward to touch the forehead to the floor. Some used prayer mats with Evolvist scenes and others just used the bare floor. I figured that this was a tradition that was still evolving, because I hadn't seen this form of praying in Baja, or Los Angeles. The Evolvists here were also completely vegetarian and this too was different from Baja and Los Angeles. They, like all Evolvist colonies apparently had a "Bob" or a Guardian, but he was away on business at this time. The leader of the Temple was a guy named Rick. He looked like an ex-biker and was covered with tatoos. He seemed to be a pretty nice guy, if just a little too intense, but he was always polite to me.

We only stayed in San Francisco for a couple of days and then decided to head north once again. As we started out, I wondered if I'd ever get to Alaska. Zack and Gil and I had headed north a couple of times but never got very far. We headed up the same roads and highways that Zack and Gil and I had been on so many times before, and I was starting to feel like the Flying Dutchman cursed to follow the same general aimless path throughout eternity and never being able to get to shore. Just always sailing on and on and on.

"You know," said Jane, "I wonder if we really can use our wills to help our bodies mutate or evolve. I mean, it's a nice thought but it might be just a little too dippy. If we have a broken a, we can't will it to fix itself.. What makes us think that we can will our transformation?"

"Zack says that by following Evolvism closely, one can use the Will, with a capital "W" to make such changes. I had a long talk with Zack about this, and it all makes sense the way he explained it, but I'm not so sure I can do it justice. Anyway, it all comes back to the trio of Right Blood, Right Belief, Right Actions. Right Blood is what makes it all possible or gives us the potential to make it all possible. The other two have never before existed, according to Zack, but they came into existence with the advent of Evolvism. Right Blood as you know from your reading is another term for Essence. Essence is something that only our people possess..."

"I don't get that exactly," she said as she interrupted me.

"Well only our people have white skin and have other genetic characteristics that are unique to us. If we can believe that we have such different characteristics—and we must believe that, because we can see them—they're a fact and beyond argument, then we should be able to believe that there are also characteristics that we can't see. That's what Zack is talking about with the hidden or inner signs as he calls them. We possess them just because w were born with them, but they're dormant and must be awakened and developed.. These things have been dormant for the most part, with a few exceptions throughout history. Sometimes, someone or another has sort of stumbled on them or had experiences with them that are often called the supernatural.

ESP and all that stuff seems to have something to do with the Essence, but Zack was never too clear about that. I asked Zack one time where the Essence was located in the body and he said that it was in every cell. I asked where in the cell it was located, and he said that it was dispersed throughout the DNA. You know that verse in the Cosmic Messages called, THE ONION, where a man peels an onion to try to find the essence of the onion and only finds more and more onion right through the whole thing? That's the way it is with our Essence and also with God, apparently."

"You know, sometimes I wonder about what is right and what is wrong and whether Evolvist ethics are correct or not. Do you ever wonder about things like that?" she asked.

"Sure, But I think I came to our…what is now called Evolvist views, on that before Zack. To think about it, you have to think about various other religions and the societies in which they exist. You know how you said that you thought that all religions were man made? Well, I agree with you and I even think that Zack would too. Now if we accept this as true; that religions are made by man and if we understand that most of our laws, our so-called non-religions or civil laws, are actually from religions then we can see that our laws and our mores and ethics are religiously based. So, why should we just accept the religious laws of some other religions? Why should we Evolvists honor the religious laws of religions that we don't believe in nor accept as true religions? These other religions often say that a woman must be 18 years old before marrying or bearing children. This is absurd, and against nature. Nature, and God is nature, says that a woman may have children when her body can produce children. That's the correct time, not some arbitrary time set by man. Even the laws on inheritance and food preparation and the like, right down to the smallest detail are ultimately from some religion or other. Why should we Evolvists accept those as valid?

I think we Evolvists; and I'm thinking of myself more and more as an Evolvist, have our own system and that it is complete and logical within itself and that we don't need outsiders telling us what do to, how to think, how to act or how to live. The others' society is full of crime and social problems. The Evolvist society has none of the outsider problems. The others' society is trying to incorporate all the races of man into some lumpen proletariat Tan Everyman, and failing at every turn. We Evolvists say to hell with that. We're happy with our own blood people, thank you, and if you don't like it, then screw you. It really pisses me off when I think that some of these intellectual boobs in the outside world think that they can impose their views and attitudes on me. What makes them think that their ideas of right and wrong, and of how to live, and what to believe, are right and mine are wrong? And wrong by whose standards? I reject their standards. I reject their mix and mate world view. I reject them. They are as low as worms in my view, and they are to be despised and spit upon. They are fecal matter and disgusting bigots who claim that they are against bigotry but who push their own variety of bigotry."

"Hmmm, said Jane. "Something seems to have struck a nerve with you. You know you sounded a little like Nietzsche's 'Thus Spoke Zarathustra' then. I mean, your contempt for ordinary men reminded me of that book."

"Thank you," I said. "I'll take that as a compliment. You know, I've drifted my whole life. I don't know why. It was just something in me that made me drift on. I wasn't ever very happy in the drifting, but I did like being free of any restraints. Maybe I have the gene for Attention Deficit Disorder, or something. Have you ever heard about the Irish Tinkers?

"No."

"Well, Zack and Gil and I talked about them and we thought that maybe they had a gene that caused them to constantly travel. One of the other names for Tinkers is Travelers. It's against the law in Ireland to call them Gypsies, now. They were once thought to just aimlessly travel around Ireland, but in recent years it was found that they more or less traveled in circular routs that would take them a year or so to complete. They just always traveled the same roads doing the work of tinkers and what not to earn money. Any time the government tried to settle them, the Tinkers would pretty much destroy their apartments because they really did prefer the life on the road. Sort of reminds me of the America Indians. Put them in jail and they often died, or is that just a myth? I don't know, but I think that the Evolvists who now live more like the Indians or the Tinkers then settled people are probably feeling the same freedoms as those other peoples. When you look at old photos of the old west you see white men and women all wearing uncomfortable looking "civilized clothes," while the Indians all look so natural and comfortable. It's as though whites are afraid to let themselves go and this is reflected in their clothes, which bind and restrict the body as well as hide it. I wonder if this is a genetic trait or whether it's just something that has grown up in various white societies over the years? You can't tell by looking at the Evolvists whether the way they dress is natural or not because they're new and they're consciously trying to be different from the rest of society. Give them a couple of hundred years and then look and see how they dress and act. I wonder if they'll revert to standard white fare or whether they'll always remain different? I'll bet in a thousand years, the Evolvists may be the last white people left on the Earth as they're about the only ones who have a strong and unchangeable prohibition against mixing and mating. The revelations are set in concretes about never changing those laws that prevent Evolvists from mating outside the blood. The punishment for that is death. Perhaps, this is our modern version of having faith even though we're thrown to the lions. You know, when the Christians were thrown to the lions, most of society was against the Christians. They were looked on as a few nut cases, and malcontents, much as the others now look at the Evolvists.

"It takes real strength to believe what you know is right when all around you believe differently," she said.

"Man that's the truth," I continued. "Whenever we see movies of heroes from earlier days, the scripts are written in such a way that the audience can identify with the hero and we all "know" that even though all the other people in the film are against the hero, that "we" would be on his side. Of course, the reality is that we would more than likely be with all the other people calling the hero names and attacking him. When you're actually living history before it is history, you have to be very special to not get caught up in the mood and the hysteria of the moment. Most of us would go along with the crowd and we would be part of the lunch mob. I'm beginning to think that Zack, Gil and I were thrown together by God to help each other and to brings this faith into being. Had Zack been given a ride by some businessman that day so long ago, he probably would have just gotten out at his top and disappeared into the woodwork of humanity. But, because Gil and I were the ones who gave him the ride, Zack's awakening, or enlightenment, or madness, took place.

I wonder if the Evolvists came under a really concerted attack by the haters on the outside—I mean a full on propaganda attack to demonize them—how many of the Evolvists would remain strong and true and how many would just drift away to calmer waters? What about you, Jane?"

"I don't know," she said. "I like to think about Evolvism, but I'm not a true believer yet. I guess I'd have to have that level of belief before I could answer your question, and I don't really know how to get to that level other than just talking to you and visiting the colonies to see what seems right to me."

We went to sleep that night in a room up on the third floor. At about midnight, I could hear the rain falling and I was feeling very uncomfortable about being inside. It wasn't claustrophobia exactly, but a stuffiness that just always existed inside buildings. I got up and got dressed. I looked over to where Jane was sleeping soundly, and I suddenly felt very lonely again. Alone in all the universe. Alone with people. Alone with God, if there was a God. I went downstairs and got in the old VW bus and started driving. I could hear the fog horns out on San Francisco Bay, as I headed the bus south. Baja was calling me home to my new country where my people lived—the misfits of a new nation—a new Europe, that was being built in the image of the European descended people who took and held the land, the way the United States had once been built by these people, before it lost its way and became part of the Third World. I wanted to be part of something that was young and growing and which was full of life and had purpose. I wanted out of the decaying wasteland that had painted itself into a philosophical corner and now could not save itself. I wanted to be away from the genocide and the extinction that was daily happening in the United States. I wanted to be away from dying white people who cared more about material things than in having children. The brown people often called white people, the old people. In too many cases, it was true. Too many white people were old and decrepit and afraid of life even when they were young. They were dried up husks. I wanted to be among living, expanding, unafraid white people who didn't apologize for being who and what they are. I wanted to be among people who lusted for life and who felt their highest and best calling in life was to have children, and who were valued for having these children. I wanted to be where I could reject the artificial unity and conformity of genes, religion, nations, and thoughts that the assimilationists wanted to force on all people. I wanted to be away from the decaying white people who were so far gone that they couldn't even see their own extinction looming. I wanted to face the challenges of surviving as an individual and as part of a distinct people that was emerging, like white maggots crawling out of the dead carcass of the white race. I wanted to be part of something that screamed at the cosmos, 'Is that the best you can do?" I wanted to be part of a new species aborning. I wanted to be part of life. The Cosmic Pussy was calling me, and it was saying, 'Holiness is not in the denial of the flesh, but in its exultation.'

Let the old people stumble through life seeking their deaths while starting at shadows and imagining that they are being guided by a prissy God that they themselves invented in their own death seeking, life denying image that they needed to give credence to their death philosophy and their denial of their own flesh and sexuality. What incredible arrogance for such people to deny life, when the cosmos itself was a validation of life. Over the centuries, the dying white people reinforced their death beliefs with a belief in a mythical God who they believed actually cared for them, when in reality they had no greater purpose than to be sentient fertilizer for the planet, unless they demanded more and made it so all by themselves. I wondered if such people thought they could simply approach existence with moist, doe eyes and think that all would be provided them. Did they think that life was about lying under a fruit tree, and fruit would fall into their mouths, and nothing more was required? Did people think that they could invent life denying religions, philosophies and moralities and that somehow they would survive because they were meek? Did people think they could live by denying life and all its turmoil? Did people want nothing more but to stop struggling and lay down and close their eyes in the dung heap of history and become one with the dung heap and cease to be different?

There is no beginning, and there is no end in the cosmos or on Earth. There is only change and the natural conflict and struggle that exists whenever there is more than one thing in existence. BEING is a constant struggle against NON-BEING, and the struggle is played out in ant hills and in the cities of man. Life demands to be heard and screams out that it will claw its way to the top of the heap. Those who lack the vital force of healthy life are dead inside and they shall become extinct as individuals and as a people. Let them go the way of the Dodo, they are committing their own genocide.

Besides, I had to go to Baja. I had a dream.

0-595-22811-9

Printed in the United States
41327LVS00006B/10